ATLANTA MONSTER

WAYNE WILLIAMS AND THE ATLANTA CHILD
MURDERS: TWO JOHN JORDAN MYSTERY
NOVELS

MICHAEL LISTER

PULPWOOD PRESS

ISBN-13: 978-1-947606-06-7

Pulpwood Press

P.O. Box 35038

Panama City, FL 32412

HOW TO READ THE JOHN JORDAN BLOOD SERIES

The Blood Series

This *New York Times* bestselling and award-winning series features a conflicted detective—a cop with ties to Atlanta who also works as a prison chaplain in Florida. He's a man of mercy and justice, compassion, open-mindedness. He's also a smart, relentless detective.

The John Jordan mystery series is character-driven and realistic—thoughtful mystery thrillers involving the hero's journey of a good man trying to be even better, as he helps others along the way.

Like John Jordan, the author, Michael Lister, was a prison chaplain with the state of Florida before leaving to write full-time.

If you're new to the John Jordan series, you can begin with any book, but we recommend one of these 3: *Power in the Blood, Innocent Blood,* or *Blood Oath.*

Power in the Blood, the first fiction the author ever wrote, was published over 20 years ago, and though it's recommended, the books in the John Jordan series don't have to be read in order.

All the books in the series are novels—mystery, thrillers,

whodunits—except for the 3rd book in the series, *Flesh and Blood*, which is a collection of short stories featuring temporal and metaphysical mysteries. If you don't care for short stories, feel free to skip *Flesh and Blood* and continue with the fourth novel *The Body and the Blood.*

If you decided to skip the short stories and continue on with the novels, we recommend that you read the short story "A Taint in the Blood" in the book *Flesh and Blood* to find out what happened to Laura Matthers from *Power in the Blood.*

The 7th book in the series, *Innocent Blood*, is a prequel going back to John's very first investigation. Though the 7th in the series, it can be read 1st or 7th since it's a prequel.

The 10th book in the series, *Blood Cries,* is the second in the "Atlanta Years" series within a series following the 7th book *Innocent Blood.* It can be read 2nd or 10th.

The 17th book in the seres, *Blood Stone*, is the 3rd book in the "Atlanta Years" series within the series following the 10th book *Blood Cries.* It can be read 3rd or 17th.

John Jordan is an ex-cop in books 1-10, but once again carries a gun and a badge beginning with book 11, *Blood Oath.*

All of the John Jordan novels are available in high quality hardback, paperback, ebook, and audio editions.

Interspersed throughout the "Blood" books there are other related books that are part of the John Jordan universe. These books are extremely important to the series and provide essential backstory for characters, connections, and locations of series regulars. Most of all they answer the questions most readers want to know. They include *Double Exposure, Burnt Offerings, Separation Anxiety, Thunder Beach,* and *A Certain Retribution.* These are "Blood Series" books without being John Jordan Mysteries.

We hope you will enjoy all the books in the John Jordan series and eagerly await each new entry.

Be sure to join Michael Lister's Readers' Group for news, updates, and special deals on the John Jordan series.

INNOCENT BLOOD

A JOHN JORDAN MYSTERY

INTRODUCTION BY MICHAEL CONNELLY

by Michael Connelly

The reading of a novel is a mysterious and sacred thing. A solely internal process, it relies totally on one's empathy, the ability to connect with another being – the story's protagonist. To me it's like thumbing a ride and getting into a car with a stranger behind the wheel. Except this driver doesn't ask where you're headed because you are going wherever he goes. So you head off and over time you get to know the driver. You can't help it. You learn all about him as he drives. You pick up little stories, little moments of character. And yet he won't tell you where he's taking you. But that's okay because not knowing the destination is the key to a good ride. And if you are lucky the conversation and the scenery along the way is equally as interesting as the final destination.

It is a massive investment of time and creative energy to read a novel. You have to build characters in your imagination, even if they're villains and you don't like them. You create landscapes and emotions. It's all very risky. Because the emotions are real even if the story isn't. A sacred bond develops between the reader and the stranger behind the wheel.

All of that is why you are in for a great ride with this book and why the following pages hold such a treat. If you are like me you've already invested heavily in the driver of this car. I had been in the car with John Jordan before on several journeys. I had picked up the vibe of his past. Something dark and damaging. They say the past informs the present. Well, this man's present seemed to be overwhelmed at times by the past. It hung out there just off the edges of each page.

Now, with this novel, Michael Lister brings the past across the margins and onto the page. Now you get to know things. Now you get to understand. It's a bold move by an author. The man with a mysterious past is a tried and true literary archetype. It worked with John Jordan for many years. Why mess with a good thing? Well, maybe because as a creator Lister wants to push things in from the margins and examine them and not rely on familiar archetypes. It's risky but the pay off can be high. It is here in Innocent Blood. Lister gives a unique edition to the John Jordan story. Another great ride with a very assured driver behind the wheel.

-- Michael Connelly

1

In 1980 I came face to face with the Atlanta Child Murderer.

I was twelve years old. The same age as many of his victims.

This singular experience not only forever changed me, but actually altered the course of my life.

But long before this seminal visit to the city of Atlanta as a child, long before this encounter with evil, I was obsessed with the monster who was littering the woods of the metro area with the broken bodies of little black boys.

It had begun on July 21, 1979, when Edward Hope Smith went missing.

He was last seen leaving the Greenbriar Skating Rink on Stone Street, parting ways with his girlfriend at the intersection.

His body was discovered seven days later in a wooded area in a ravine just off Niskey Lake Road by a woman looking for cans. He had been shot with a .22 in the upper back. The area, surrounded by loblolly pines, white oaks, an occasional dogwood, and creeping kudzu vines, was a popular spot for people to dump their trash.

It was said that by the time his body was discovered, a vine from a nearby tree had already wrapped itself around the boy's lifeless neck.

My obsession had continued through the disappearance and death of Timothy Hill, a thirteen-year-old boy and friend of an earlier victim, Jo-Jo Bell. Timothy went missing on March 13, 1981, and was last seen in the area of Lawson Street and Sells Avenue. His body was found seventeen days later on March 30th––the same day Ronald Reagan was shot by John Hinckley, Jr.––by a boater in the Chattahoochee River near Cochran Road. His partially submerged body was some twenty-five feet from the bank. The cause of death was determined to be asphyxia by suffocation.

There were other victims, of course, but they weren't children and I wasn't nearly as obsessed with them.

Children disappearing, dying, being discarded––some seventeen so far––held my developing mind hostage, seized my attention, captured my preteen imagination like nothing before ever had. And it was only partially because of the cruel and capricious nature of the killings, the fragility and vulnerability of childhood, and the fact that my dad, the sheriff of the small Florida Panhandle town where we lived, had a friend on the task force that was so ineffectually working the case. It was mostly because of how each and every little boy looked like and reminded me of my best friend in all the world, Merrill Monroe.

My fateful confrontation with the killer took place during the final weekend in November 1980, surrounded by gaudy gold Christmas decorations and to the soundtrack of traditional Christmas carols played through cheap speakers, the thin, electronic noises of video games, the wooden pop of pinball machines, and the desultory sounds of the city Sherman had burned to the ground.

Our parents had brought us to Atlanta, on what would be our final family vacation, to stay in the Omni hotel, to ice skate and shop, to play in the arcade and ride the gigantic escalator to the carnival in the clouds, to experience the spectacle of a hotel that could hold more people than lived in our entire little town.

While Nancy, Jake, and I skated and played, Mom drank and Christmas shopped, and Dad watched TV in the room when he wasn't meeting with his friend on the task force.

The Omni fit its name—*all* or *of all things*—for the mammoth structure seemed to my twelve-year-old self to contain all things. Whether shooting up several stories in seconds in the elevator or riding the enormous escalator to the fair or looking out the window of our room at the tiny figures ice skating below, the hotel held so very many larger-than-life and unexpected attractions, and yet retained an open and airy quality of hushed tones and lost sounds into which it seemed everything else in the world could easily fit.

Outside the hotel, fear and palpable racial tensions pulsed through the city. Inside, everyone whose job it was to cater to our comfort tried to pretend there *was* no world outside this one, but an uneasy anxiety coiled beneath the surface betrayed them— not unlike the one I sensed just behind the strained civility displayed by my parents.

It was during the afternoon of our second day that I saw him, the monster dressed like a man. And not just any man, a soft, slightly effeminate, light-skinned black man in a long-sleeved, large-collared silk shirt with thick wire-framed glasses and a big afro—only part of which was visible beneath a Braves baseball cap.

Nancy was teaching Jake to ice skate in the large round rink right in the center of the hotel. I was in the video game arcade trying to beat my best score on Space Invaders.

I had just failed to prevent the invasion when he walked in carrying a handful of flyers.

Unhurriedly and unapologetically he scoped out the arcade.

After identifying his marks, he began approaching black kids by themselves, handing each one a flyer, asking them if they wanted to be a star.

The flyers read: CAN YOU?? Sing or Play an Instrument * If YOU Are Between "11-21" (male or female) And Would Like to Become A Professional Entertainer, "YOU" Can Apply for POSITIONS with Professional Recording Acts No experience is Necessary, Training is Provided. All Interviews Private & FREE!! *

There was something off about the man, some seeming contradiction between his arrogance and neediness, something loose and lascivious in the way he moved and looked at the kids around the arcade.

When he approached a short, scrawny kid of about ten years old in a blue turtleneck playing a KISS pinball machine, the kid shook his head without looking at him.

"Look at me, little brother," he said.

Continuing to play the game with intense concentration, he shook his head again without taking his eyes off the ball.

The creepy man then laid the flyer on the glass top of the pinball machine, blocking the boy's view and causing him to lose the turn.

"You heard of the Jackson Five, ain't ya? You could be like little Michael."

That stood out to me because I had just seen Michael Jackson in a silver-and-black sequined suit, backlit by a shimmering green light, performing *Rock with You* in the room before I came down, and he wasn't little anymore.

The boy abandoned his game and walked away with his head down.

When the dull-eyed, doughy young man followed, I stepped away from Space Invaders and in front of him.

"He said he's not interested," I said.

"Whoa, little man," he said, holding the hand without the flyers up in a placating gesture. "I'm just trying to help the youth of our city reach their potential."

I didn't say anything, just stood there.

On the same day all this happened, little LaMarcus Williams was murdered less than fifteen miles away from where we were standing at that moment. It would happen just six hours later in a place that would come to hold great significance for me, but it would be a full six years before I knew anything about it––when it became the first murder investigation I ever conducted.

"What's your name, boy?" he asked.

He had been leaning back considering me, eyeing me up and down, a bemused expression on his wrinkled black face.

I didn't respond, just held his gaze.

"Where you from?" he asked. "Ain't here, is it?"

Anger flashed in his face when I still refused to respond.

"Just 'cause I prefer chocolate don't mean I couldn't go for some vanilla," he said.

I still didn't respond, just stood there, every muscle in my undeveloped body tense. I wanted to look around, to see if there were any adults close by who might help, but I didn't want to break eye contact with him.

"I can make you talk little man," he said. "Make you do other things too."

My pounding heart was pumping adrenaline through me and I could feel myself beginning to shake.

He stepped toward me.

Just before I took a step back, there was a flash of movement behind me.

"What's going on here?" a security guard asked.

He had just come up behind us, a pale, thin, older white man in a too-big hotel security uniform.

"Nothin'. I's just leavin'. Little man here misunderstood my intentions. That's all. It's cool."

With that he turned and slowly swaggered away, down the game aisle and out the door.

If I had known then what I found out later––that the latest

victim, Patrick "Pat Man" Rogers, had told Mary Harper that a man wanted to record his songs right before he went missing, I might have been even more suspicious, might have said something to someone about the soft man with the handful of flyers harassing kids in the arcade of the Omni hotel, and I might have actually saved the several victims still to come.

But I didn't know and I didn't act and it has haunted me ever since the moment when––seven months later, on June 21, 1981–– Wayne Williams was arrested, and the satan who had laid siege to South Atlanta and frightened a nation finally had an all too human face.

2

During the seven months leading up to the arrest, unaware I had actually met the man the manhunt was for, I feverishly followed every step of the investigation––all the media coverage, every report of a missing child, every discovery of another dead body.

Dad fed me what information his friend on the task force was feeding him, and I ate it like a crazed starved thing.

All through the Christmas season, I observed and obsessed, studied and stewed, but no children disappeared and no other bodies were discovered in December.

The holiday break ended and I returned to school.

Then Lubie Geter went missing on January 3rd.

He was last seen at the Stewart-Lakewood Shopping Center selling Zep Gel car deodorizers outside the Big Star Food Store. He was wearing a purple coat, a green shirt, blue jeans, and brown loafers.

From the moment I heard he was missing until his body was discovered on February 5th, I vividly imagined the horrors he was subjected to and then pictured his lifeless brown body decaying in the woods of Decatur every time I closed my eyes.

While Geter's family and the nation waited for news of his fate, a friend of his, Terry Pue, disappeared on January 22nd. When I heard this I lost even the tiny broken fragment of hope I had that Lubie might still be alive.

Terry Pue was last seen spending the night in a fast food restaurant on Memorial Drive and trading bottles for money at a nearby shopping center.

The next day, his body was found off Sigman Road in Rockdale County. He had abrasions on his elbows and bruises on his head and died of asphyxiation by ligature strangulation.

On February 5th, Lubie Geter's body was found by a dog off Vandiver Road. He was wearing only his white jockey shorts. His Levi's blue jeans and brown belt were found a short distance away inside a brown paper bag three feet deep in a creek. He died of asphyxiation by manual strangulation and his body had been mutilated by animals.

During this time, I was living an uneventful small-town life. School. Basketball. Birthday parties. Sleepovers. Chores. TV. All the while preoccupied by Atlanta, the slaughter of the susceptible, the woeful wails of the inconsolable, the citywide search for a seemingly supernatural serial killer.

Mom and Dad argued about how much he should share with me about the case. Mom and Dad argued about everything.

The world kept spinning and Atlanta's children kept disappearing. And dying. Two in February. Two more in March.

So much death. So much decay. So much despair.

And then it stopped. Or seemed to.

On May 22nd at three o'clock in the morning, Wayne Williams was pulled over by an Atlanta police patrol car and a second unmarked car with federal agents in it. This was after his 1970 Chevrolet station wagon was spotted turning around and driving back across the James Jackson Parkway/South Cobb Drive bridge immediately following an officer staked-out beneath the bridge hearing a loud splash in the water of the Chattahoochee River.

Later that same day, Williams was questioned by FBI agents at his parents' home where he lived.

Two days later, on May 24th, the naked body of Nathaniel Cater was found floating downriver just a few miles from the bridge.

On June 3rd, Wayne Williams was questioned again by FBI agents at their headquarters about discrepancies in his statements. He was also administered a polygraph examination that showed he was being deceptive. Later that same day, his home and vehicle were searched.

On June 4th, Williams called a press conference, addressing what was happening and answering questions from the media.

When I saw him on TV, I told my family about what had happened in the Omni arcade back in November.

"Are you sure?" Mom had asked.

Dad nodded his certainty and support. "You realize," he said, "you may have very well saved that little boy's life—him or another kid he could've picked up there that day."

I hadn't thought of that.

"Do I need to give a statement?" I asked Dad.

"I don't want him involved," Mom said.

"I'm already involved."

"I doubt it'll be necessary," Dad said, "but I'll call Frank and ask him."

Late that night I found my dad dozing in front of the TV and gave him a handwritten statement I had worked all evening on.

"I'll get it to the task force," he said.

I nodded and turned to walk out of the room.

"Proud of you," he said, squinting at the sheet of notebook paper I had just given him.

On June 21st, Wayne Williams was arrested.

That evening I was reading in my room when Nancy's best friend and my secret crush, Anna, had come in.

"Hey," she said.

"Hey."

I dropped the book onto the nightstand and sat up, making room for her on the bed beside me.

I had fallen in love with Anna when she wasn't looking.

She hadn't been looking, but I had. I had watched her closely, studied her carefully, seen what no one else had, what no one else could have.

As her best friend's younger brother I had been in the utterly unique position to see her soul.

I said I had fallen in love with Anna but that's not right.

I hadn't *fallen* in love with her at all. I had grown to love her. Or rather love had grown in me for her, while observing her during a million different unguarded moments––moments in which her kindness and goodness, her fierceness and ferocity, her wit and wisdom, had been made manifest.

"Nancy told me what happened to you in Atlanta," she said. "I'm so glad nothing bad happened to you."

"Thanks."

She was wearing the green ribbon I had given her. It was a sign of solidarity with the children of Atlanta. People all across the nation were wearing them––including Robert De Niro when he had won his Best Actor Oscar for *Raging Bull* a few months back––but we were the only two people in Pottersville wearing them and it meant more to me than she would ever know.

"How're you feeling?"

I shrugged.

The truth was I was feeling everything––excited, relieved, scared, confused, disappointed, unsatisfied.

"I still can't believe you saw him," she said. "Stood up to him. Looked him in the face and . . . your dad's right. You saved someone's life."

I didn't know what to say so I didn't say anything, just looked at how beautiful she was.

"I'm just so relieved," she said. "So glad you didn't get hurt. But I'm also so proud of you. Standing up to him like that. You're . . . just . . . so . . . Do you mind if I hug you?"

I didn't. Just the opposite, in fact, but she didn't wait to hear it from me.

Suddenly, I was being hugged by the girl I most wanted to be hugged by in all the world.

I could feel the heat emanating from my skin.

She held me for a long time, her developed body pressing into mine, our cheeks touching, her hair falling onto my face.

She smelled and felt even better than all my imagining told me she would.

In a little while, when she had let go of me and life wasn't as rich, as sweet, as good as it had been a few moments before, she said, "It's hard to believe he killed nearly thirty people."

"He didn't," I said with the conviction and certainty of a child. "He didn't even kill most of 'em."

"Really?"

"Really," I said. "It'll be a while before we know. Hell, we may never know, but I'll bet you a . . . another hug . . . that he did as few as ten and at most maybe thirteen or fourteen."

"You don't have to wait that long for another hug," she said. "And you don't have to bet me for it. I'll give you another anytime you like."

"Then how about a kiss," I said.

She smiled and blushed a little herself.

"It's a bet," she said. "Now let's hug on it."

We hugged again.

"I'm so glad you're in the world, John Jordan. The world needs you. So glad."

I hugged her harder.

She had no idea of the effect of those words on me or how for the rest of my life they would ring in my ears as I recalled this moment over and over and over again.

"Wait," she said, pulling back. "Who killed all those other people?"

"I have no idea," I said, "but I intend to find out."

3

In one of the greatest ironies in criminal history, the Atlanta Child Murderer wasn't arrested, charged with, or tried for killing a single child.

Wayne Williams was indicted and tried for killing Nathaniel Cater, the twenty-seven-year-old victim pulled from the river two days after Williams had been stopped near the James Jackson bridge, and Jimmy Ray Payne, a twenty-one-year-old young man who went missing on April 22nd after leaving home en route to the Omni. He was found five days later on April 27th, his body pulled from the Chattahoochee River two hundred yards south of the I-285 bridge.

No one––not Wayne Williams, not anyone––was ever charged with the murder of any children.

Not a single one.

This bothered me more than anything else, except the fact that they were killed in the first place.

My frustration and obsession and anger and confusion continued, intensified.

So much was happening, both in my small world and in the wide world beyond it––I became a teenager, my parents split up and eventually divorced, Anna got a boyfriend and broke my heart, Mom's drinking increased, I had a spiritual awakening, Bob Marley died, the CDC reported five cases of homosexual men with weakened immune systems, Charles and Diana had a wedding in front of the whole world—but all of it, everything happening everywhere, dimmed a bit, receded into the background, overwhelmed by the foreground light of the case against Williams and the trial intending to bring him to some sort of justice.

Jury selection started on December 8, 1981. After six days, the twelve people—eight black and four white—selected and charged with delivering a verdict consisted of nine women and three men.

"He's not even being tried for a single child's death," I said to Dad.

I had just come in from basketball practice and found him watching the news coverage of the case.

I was sore from the brawl-like scrimmage I had just participated in. I was raw-bone weary from not sleeping and the mental, emotional, and psychological fatigue that resulted from obsessing over Wayne Williams and what was happening in Atlanta.

"I know, but—"

"It's not right."

I was supposed to be at home by now. Mom was expecting me for dinner, but my new routine was to have Coach drop me at Dad's after practice to talk to him about the case before walking the mile or so to Mom's.

When the coverage concluded, Dad asked me to step over to the TV and turn down the sound.

I did.

Dad's new bachelor pad had very little furniture, but he did have a brand new big television hooked up to cable, which had only recently arrived in Pottersville.

"Some of them will be admitted as evidence," he said.

"Whatta you mean?"

"Prosecutor will introduce them as pattern cases to show Williams had a pattern."

In fact, ten pattern cases were ultimately used—more than any other case before or since.

"But if they're part of the pattern and are going to be used, why not charge him with them too?"

"It's a strategy," he said. "That's all. Frank says the prosecutor's trial plan is built around what happened on the James Jackson Bridge on May 22nd because he can actually place Williams at the scene. And he's got an eyewitness who says he saw Williams holding hands with Cater earlier that night. He's using Jimmy Ray Payne because he can tie him to the same location. If he overcharges and brings in all the others, he runs the risk of them being insufficient in law to sustain a conviction. By doing it this way he can still use some of the others to prove identity, bent of mind, knowledge, intent, course of contact—things like that. He wants to get a conviction the surest way possible. And he doesn't want to overwhelm or confuse the jury. Williams only has one life to serve."

I shook my head.

His phone rang.

"That'll be your mom looking for you," he said. "Better get goin'. Need to get out of those wet clothes anyway. I'm sure she's got supper ready."

"Yes, sir."

"How're things at home?"

I shrugged.

"She drinkin'?" he asked.

"She breathin'?" I said.

"*Hey*," he said. "I know it's . . . I know it's not easy sometimes . . . but always show respect to your mother."

"Yes, sir."

"And as far as Williams goes . . . He's guilty and they're gonna get him. Don't forget that's what matters most."

"But——"

"Remember, there are no fingerprints, no eyewitnesses who ever saw Williams hurt or kill anyone. It's a circumstantial case."

The case primarily rested on transfer or trace evidence—— carpet fibers and dog hairs found on the victims, hairs and fibers allegedly from Williams's environment, his home and car—— proving contact between the victims and Williams.

"It's a thin case," I said. "They've got Williams on the bridge. They've got fibers and dog hairs. What else have they got?"

"You don't think he's the killer?"

"I think it's a thin case," I said. "And yeah, I think he's a killer. I even think he killed a few of the ones he's supposed to have."

4

The trial began on January 6, 1982.

It was presided over by Clarence Cooper, the first black judge elected to the Fulton County bench and a former assistant district attorney. The most active member of the prosecutorial team was Jack Mallard, whose nickname was Blood because of the way he went for the jugular. The defense attorney was Mary Welcome, a popular black lawyer and a former Atlanta city solicitor.

For the prosecution it was a splash in the river beneath a bridge, a suspicious station wagon above, a young man out at three in the morning with a dubious story, eyewitnesses connecting that young man with the victims, a pudgy, bespectacled, frustrated homosexual Jekyll and Hyde, carpet fibers and dog hairs, ten uncharged pattern cases.

For the defense it was the wrong man—a good, gentle, soft, weak, harmless guy—refuting witnesses, calling into question evidence, an upstate New York hospital pathologist specializing in pediatrics contradicting autopsy results, a weather service hydrologist claiming Cater's body would not have ended up where it did had it been dropped from the James Jackson

Parkway Bridge, and of course, Wayne Bertram Williams himself, confidently spouting protestations, proclaiming his innocence—a witness for the defense who may have done far more for the prosecution.

The pattern cases became the key factor for evidence to be used by the state against Williams, especially when linking similar fibers. By themselves the Cater and Payne cases were extremely weak, but by introducing evidence from each of the ten pattern cases, the prosecution was able to enter eyewitnesses and fiber connections among many of the victims.

The ten pattern cases used were Alfred Evans, Eric Middlebrooks, Charles Stephens, William Barrett, Terry Pue, John Porter, Lubie Geter, Joseph Bell, Patrick Baltazar, and Larry Rogers.

The characteristics of the pattern cases were that the victims were black males, street hustlers, from poor families, no evidence of forced abduction, from broken homes, no apparent motives for their disappearances, killed by asphyxiation by strangulation. None of them owned a car, their bodies were found near expressway ramps or major arteries and transported before or after death, they were all missing clothing when found, and they all had similar fibers found on them.

The prosecution called a successful black businessman, Eustis Blakely, and his wife because they were friends with Williams. They were asked if they knew Williams to lie and exaggerate. Blakely testified Williams had told him that he flew fighter jets at Dobbins Air Force base—something Blakely knew to be a lie because of how bad Williams's eyesight was.

Far more incriminating was the testimony of Blakely's wife. She had asked Williams after he had become a suspect if the police got enough evidence on him would he confess before he got hurt. He told her he would. She also testified that Williams told her he could knock out black street kids in a few minutes by putting his hands on their necks.

When cross-examined, the defense attorney asked if she was implying Williams had killed someone. She answered that she was, that she was sorry but she really did believe that he had.

Lugene Laster testified that he saw Jo-Jo Bell get into a Chevrolet station wagon driven by a man he identified as Williams. Robert Henry, who knew Cater, testified he saw Cater and Williams holding hands the evening of the bridge incident. A couple of youths claimed Williams made sexual advances toward them and a fifteen-year-old said Williams paid him two dollars to let him fondle his genitals.

Two other witnesses, a nightclub owner and a recreational director, discredited Williams's statements that earlier in the evening on the night of the May 22nd bridge incident he was picking up a tape recorder and playing basketball.

The defense put a number of witnesses on the stand to rebut what prosecution witnesses had said about Williams's behavior or where he was at a particular time. They even had a college student who had been recruited by Williams for a singing job testify that Williams disliked homosexuals and expected his clients to have high standards and morals, and a woman who claimed to having had what she called *normal sex* with Williams.

To refute time of death in the Nathaniel Cater case, the defense brought in its own expert who lost credibility when he testified that Cater had been in the water for at least two weeks—far less time than he had even been missing.

Others were called. No one was particularly helpful or even effective.

Finally, Williams himself took the stand.

He challenged eyewitness accounts and made it clear to the jury he was too small and weak to have quickly stopped the car on the bridge and thrown Cater over the shoulder-high guard rail into the river.

He also continually attempted to convince the jury he didn't possess the temperament to commit murder. Something he seemed more or less successful at doing until cross.

Under a lengthy, skillful, aggressive cross examination Williams snapped.

Wayne Williams was no match for Jack Mallard.

Mallard would lull Williams with lengthy, repetitive questions about seemingly small details or fine points, and then pounce. One of his associates described it as slowly pulling the hammer back and eventually letting it fall.

On the third day of cross, Mallard let the hammer drop.

As if Williams was an inadequate sparring partner, Mallard jabbed and moved, peppering him with punches, setting him up for the knockout.

Mallard used Williams's own contradictions against him and confronted him with all the lies and exaggerations and testimony and evidence and illogical and inane statements and claims he had made.

And Williams came undone.

"You want the real Wayne Williams?" he asked. "You got him right here."

Williams transformed into something the jury had heretofore not seen.

Jekyll became Hyde. The Gemini was unleashed and the defendant became a witness for the prosecution.

On Saturday, February 27, 1982, at about seven in the evening, after only eleven hours of deliberation, the jury returned its verdict.

Wayne Bertram Williams was found guilty on both counts of murder and immediately sentenced to two life sentences.

But it was ultimately unsatisfying.

I was left with far more questions than answers.

Which of the victims had Williams actually killed?

Who had killed the others?

Would anyone ever stand trial for killing the kids?

The end of the trial was just the beginning of the investigation for me.

I spent the rest of my time in high school studying the case and preparing to become a cop.

While the world was being introduced to MTV and AIDS and the personal computer, while Michael Jackson was making and releasing the biggest-selling album of all time, while Challenger was falling from the sky, I was working on the Wayne Williams case and, with my dad's help, on a fast track to becoming a certified law enforcement officer.

5

"You okay?" Merrill asked.

I didn't respond. I couldn't think of an answer that wasn't a lie.

He had found me in the bottom of an abandoned boat at the landing, sleeping it off, still clutching Mom's stolen vodka to me like a baby with a bottle.

I sat up slowly, the spinning world around me streaking by in blurs of blue and green, brown and burnt-orange, and surveyed the dusky evening.

"Thinkin' about takin' a boat ride?" he said.

"Came out here to swim," I said, holding up the bottle.

"That's not swimming. It's drowning."

I nodded. He was right and I knew it. I just didn't know what to do about it.

He was big even back then, but, like the rest of us, still hadn't fully grown into his features. Teeth and ears still slightly too big. He was wearing his basketball warmups over his uniform, the cheap fabric straining over the roping cable cords of his muscles.

"Missed you at the game today," he said. "Coulda used that jumper of yours. Lost by five."

"Not playin' anymore," I said.

"Call it what it is," he said. "Not playing anymore sound better than quitting."

"I'm quitting. Don't have the time."

"'Cause of takin' up swimmin'?"

"Yeah."

"Well, let's go tell Coach. He needs to know his best shooter sidelinin' hisself."

"I'm sure he's figured it out."

"Nah, I just left him at the gym. He perplexed as the rest of us."

"I'll tell him tomorrow at school," I said.

"Oh, you comin' to school tomorrow?"

"Believe I will."

He didn't say anything and we were both silent as the last of the sun streaking the treetops to the west finally faded out and the light in the landing changed.

After a while he said, "Tell me how I can help you."

"Would if I could," I said.

"I've been doing this a while," Dad said.

"What?"

"Law enforcement. Investigating. And I've picked up a thing or two."

I didn't say anything, just listened.

It was 1985, my junior year of high school.

It was report card day and my grades had continued their recent trend of declining, which, I assumed, was why he was in my room.

I had stopped all extracurricular activities. I had pulled back to one degree or another from any and everything but my own personal investigation into the Atlanta Child Murders.

Maps of Atlanta hung on my walls next to bad copies of crime scene, suspect, and victim photos. Stacks of witness statements, evidence reports, UNSUB profiles, and lab documents were scattered about. The small space looked far more like a squad room than a seventeen-year-old boy's bedroom.

"You're gonna drive yourself crazy if you're not careful. You've got a gift. You do. I can see it. It's rare. You're gonna make a great investigator—but only if you don't burn yourself out first."

He didn't often compliment me or anyone else. Hell, he seldom spoke. This gave all his words weight—and his compliments the impact of a punch.

"A case like this . . . " he said.

He trailed off and what for me at the time was *the* case hung there between us.

"It's . . . got . . . its own . . . I don't know . . . darkness, its own power. Maybe even presence. It's evil like you'll rarely encounter. A black hole you can lose yourself in."

I had never heard him talk like this but I knew exactly what he meant and knew why he was pressing himself outside his normal, familiar, comfortable space to do it.

"I'm worried about you," he said. "And it's not the grades. They're a symptom. Everything's a symptom. The isolation. The drinking. The sleeplessness. Symptoms of the obsession, of the frustration, of . . . how . . . close you are . . . to the void."

I nodded. Not because I agreed with his assessment but because I understood what he was saying and appreciated his concern.

I didn't know anyone except maybe Merrill knew I was drinking and not sleeping. And I knew for sure he hadn't said anything to anyone. Everything about this conversation told me my dad was a far better cop and man than my self-involved teenage self knew.

"The thing about it, son," he said, his voice gentle, entreating, "is the empathy you feel with the victims, the unquenchable thirst burning inside you for justice . . . for restoring some kind of order . . . the rage you feel at the murderer . . . the obsession with knowing, with uncovering, with finding the truth . . . They are the very things that make you perfect for this kind of work . . . but also a perfect candidate for this kind of work to crush, to chew up, and . . . and I think I can see it already starting to."

"I'm okay," I said.

"I don't think you are," he said, looking around at the glut of investigative documents and photographs that cluttered the room. "And I'm the reason you have most of this. I've encouraged you but I haven't really guided you, taught you, helped you."

"You've helped me a lot."

"Help you find a balance," he said. "Help you with how to let go."

"*Let go?*"

"The case is over, son," he said. "Williams is serving two life sentences. The murders stopped. Why can't you move on? What else is there to—"

"The murders didn't stop," I said.

"What?"

"Here," I said. "Sit down."

I swept off a pile of papers on my desk chair and he sat down.

"A lot of people believe Wayne Williams is innocent," I said, "but nobody with any credibility believes he killed all twenty-eight or -nine who made the task force list. There were two girls. There were adults, not just young black teens. Some of the victims were stabbed. Some were shot. Some asphyxiated with a ligature, others with bare hands. If Wayne Williams is the Atlanta Child Murderer and he strangled the young boys, why wasn't he tried for that? And why wasn't anyone charged with any of the other murders? If it wasn't him, an innocent man is going to die in prison for something someone else did, and the real killer remains free. Can you live with that?"

He seemed to think about it for a moment, but as it turned out he was thinking of something else entirely.

"Son, there's someone I want you to talk to, and your mom and I think it's best if you come live with me for a while."

6

When Dad had said he wanted me to talk to someone, I had assumed he meant a shrink, so I was as surprised as I was relieved when I found out it was a cop.

The cop, an L.A. detective with the same name as an Early Netherlandish painter whose work I had encountered in an art appreciation class earlier in the year, had impressed Dad during some special training on serial sex crime investigation he had attended in L.A.

The training had followed Ted Bundy's rampage in Talla-hassee at FSU's Chi Omega sorority house. Something about the viciousness of the attacks, their relative proximity to Pottersville, and the fact that the victims had been the same age as my older sister Nancy, really affected Dad, and for a while it seemed all he did was travel for training.

"Y'all share the same relentlessness and obsession," Dad had said. "He's found a way to make it work. He's one of if not the best cop you'll ever encounter. Listen to what he has to say. He won't say much, but what he does will help you."

Words of praise like those from Jack Jordan were beyond rare. They were the only ones like them I ever heard him utter.

For him to say I shared any traits at all with such a detective did more for me than anything save the conversation itself.

The conversation took place on my second night living with him.

Not only had Dad taken the trouble to set it up, but he was letting me stay up late to take the West Coast call.

I was alone in the quiet, mostly empty house when the call came.

Dispatch had requested that Dad return to his office to deal with a disturbance in the jail just minutes before—something that actually made me feel far less self-conscious about having the conversation.

The TV was off and the only sound I could hear in the small, carpeted house was that of my own reflexive respiration.

The ringing phone shattered the silence, and like so many serendipitous occurrences during this significant and seminal time for me, the call changed my life.

"John?"

"Yes, sir."

"It's Harry Bosch. No need to call me sir."

I felt an instant affinity with the detective who treated me like an adult, and the disembodied voice from the opposite side of the continent suddenly seemed far more like a brother than a stranger.

"Thank you for taking the time to call," I said. "I hear you're working a pretty big case right now."

"No problem," he said. "Sorry it couldn't be any earlier."

Faintly, in the background, beneath the voice and the static and white noise, I could hear the soft, soothing sounds of a lone alto saxophone.

There was something kind of sad and lonely about the sax that made me feel neither sad nor lonely, as if someone else feeling such things and expressing them in such ways helped abate them somehow.

I was unsure what to say next so I waited.

When he didn't say anything either, there was a moment of, at least for me, awkwardness.

The silence set an early tone for what would be a conversation with a lot of quiet in it, and I could tell that Harry Bosch, like so many of the men I admired and attempted to emulate, was restrained and self-contained.

"Jack tells me you're gonna be a cop," he said eventually. "Says you've got all the makings of a great one."

"That's not what he tells me," I said.

He didn't respond right away and I wondered if what I said had sounded disrespectful.

"I just meant . . . he's worried about me. It's why he asked you to call. I think he thinks I'm too . . . I don't know. Like obsessed or . . . something."

"Whatta you think?"

I couldn't believe he was asking me.

I thought about it for a moment.

"Not sure. Maybe. I just don't know. Maybe I am. I . . . I don't know any other way to be. I really don't. He keeps tellin' me I've got to let it go, got to be more . . . balanced or something, but I can't—not when kids have been killed, not when those who should be tryin' to solve their murders aren't, not when nobody else seems to care anymore."

I paused for a moment but continued when all I heard was the hum of the line.

"All those kids matter," I said. "All of them. They all count—not just white kids, not just rich kids, not just victims from cases that are easy to solve or that have a perp who can be prosecuted."

"Don't ever forget that," he said. "Everybody counts."

"No, sir, I won't."

Here was someone who understood, who got it.

More quiet followed. More static on the line reaching across the more than two thousand miles between us. And more music.

Harry getting it made me feel the way the music did. Less alone in the world somehow.

"Listen, John, I'm not big on handing out advice . . . I'm no expert . . . but the work matters. The victims matter. When they don't, I'd say it's time to stop."

Exactly, I thought. That's exactly it.

"The thing is . . ."

Here it comes, I thought. Here's where he agrees with Dad and undermines everything he's said so far.

"You've got to be able to do the work," he said.

That was not what I was expecting.

I thought about it.

He was right. I couldn't say the work really mattered to me if I wasn't going to do what it took to be able to keep doing it. Caring about victims, wanting everybody to count, being relentless, it wasn't enough. I had to be able to keep doing it.

The jazz saxophone stopped momentarily then started again.

"I'm not sure what else I can tell you," he said. "I'm still trying to figure it out myself."

It seemed like that was all he had to say, but he didn't end the conversation or the call, just waited.

He didn't seem to be in a hurry to hang up, and I wanted to extend the exchange if I could.

"Can I ask you . . . how you deal with the darkness?" I said.

"Probably have to ask someone else about that," he said.

I appreciated that he didn't feel the need that most adults did to have an answer for everything, but I wondered if the question bothered him.

Dad had told me he had been a tunnel rat in Vietnam so I knew he knew all about the dark. Of course that didn't mean he knew what to do about it or what to tell me to do about it.

"It's a good question. Keep asking it. I think it's different for everyone. Figuring out what works for you is part of the process. That make sense?"

I nodded before I realized he couldn't see me doing it.

"Yes, sir," I said. "It really does."

"Figure out a way to function," he said. "Not sure it has to be any harder than that."

I thought about it for a long moment, during which all he did was wait.

Something Nietzsche said about monsters shimmered at the edges of my memory. What was it? Beware of catching monsters or something similar.

"Wish I could help you more," he said.

"You've helped me far more than you'll ever know."

"You need me," he said, "you call me. And don't take too much shit from Jack, okay?"

After we hung up, I sat there and thought about all the wisdom that one conversation contained, replaying it over and over in my head.

Before I went to bed, I looked up the Nietzsche quote. Beware that, when fighting monsters, you yourself do not become a monster.

In my dream it became part of my conversation with Harry Bosch––a conversation that took place not over a telephone but over an autopsy table holding the body of Patrick "Pat Man" Rogers, in an old-fashioned operating theater in Atlanta with Wayne Williams watching from the gallery above us.

7

How can I describe what happened next?

Simply this. Something.

Something unexpected. Something inexplicable and ineffable.

Something undeniable.

Someone flipped a switch somewhere inside me. And then what exactly?––light, warmth, insight, enlightenment? Some formerly fallow ground began to burst forth with new life. Seed, water, nourishment, and a small shoot broke the surface of the soil. I woke up. Shaken from my slumber I came to consciousness.

It was not unlike falling in love.

It happened during my senior year of high school, this transformation, this moment of clarity, this line in the sand of my life, which would forever be the demarcation between before and after for me.

One day I was one way. The next another.

One moment I was walking in one direction. The next moment another.

It was extraordinary.

It changed everything.

Merrill's mom recognized it first.

Our eyes met and she saw and she smiled.

"Well now, look at the new you," she said.

I had just walked into the tiny kitchen of her small clapboard house where she was hard at work on the best fried chicken, collard greens, and cornbread anyone ever made. Ever.

She immediately stopped cooking, turned off the old gas oven, and took a seat at the narrow, wobbly, Formica top kitchen table.

"Dinner can wait," she said. "Sit down and tell Mama Monroe all about it."

Merrill had yet to come in from baseball practice. We were alone in the cramped, creaky house, the best and safest place I had yet found on the planet.

I sat down.

"Not sure I can say," I said.

"That's good," she said. "Real good."

I must have looked confused.

"Be little that had happened, you could 'splain it, baby."

I looked at her and smiled.

"That the only bit of Shakespeare Mama knows. 'Course I changed it up a little, but . . . it always stuck with me."

As usual, she had a dip of Honey Bee Sweet Snuff that poked out the skin beneath her bottom lip a bit and caused her to contort her mouth some as she spoke.

"What did?"

"'I were but little happy if I could say how much,'" she said.

"So true," I said. "Were but little changed if I could say how much. That's exactly it. Exactly right."

"Paul got knocked on his ass on the road to Damascus," she said. "Never knew what hit him. Jesus went down in the water one way, came up another. Moses came up on a burnin' bush that didn't burn up."

I nodded. "I read that when they asked Siddhartha what happened to him, he just said he woke up."

"Who?"

"The Buddha."

"Mama don't know nothin' 'bout no Buddha, baby, but she do know when the Holy Ghost done come on one of her boys."

I smiled, happy to be one of her boys.

Reaching behind her, she removed her spit cup from the counter beside the stove, spit in it, then placed it on the table in front of her. Inside the faded plastic FSU stadium cup was a couple of folded paper towels to help soak up the powered snuff and spit.

"You been touched by the hand of God," she said, wiping her mouth. "His shekinah glory is all over you, boy. Shines on your face, through your eyes. You'll never be the same again."

I wouldn't use the language she was, but I knew what she meant—and she was right about the last at least. I would never be the same again.

"I've been worried about you," she said. "Prayin' for you. Prayin' Lord Jesus help my JJ find his way."

"I've been in a bad way," I said.

She nodded. "Obsessin' over those poor black children," she said.

I thought about the darkness that entered my head and heart through the Atlanta Child Murders case, how heavy I had been, how angry and frustrated, and how much I had been drinking lately.

"Among other things, yes, ma'am."

"Frettin', worryin', weight of the whole world on your bony little shoulders, boy."

I nodded.

"Listen to me, son," she said. "God give you a good mind. You some kinda smart and got such a good heart, but let me tell you somethin'—you think your mind's your friend but it ain't. Just remember that. My mind is not my friend. It's not my boss. It's not me. It's a spirited horse needs controllin'. Understand? Don't let your mind run wild. Don't let it make you a slave."

I thought about it.

"What happened to you, happened here," she said, tapping my chest with the back of her meaty, misshapen brown hand. "Not here," she added, placing her fingertips on my forehead and giving it a good push. "Don't forget it. God's in your guts. In your heart. Not your head."

"Yes, ma'am."

She didn't say anything, just waited, spitting into her cup again as she did.

When I didn't say anything either, she said, "*Well?*"

"I had taken a bottle of vodka to the landing," I said, "but when I got there, the evening sky was so radiant, so . . . I've never seen anything quite like it. Plum-colored background, streaked with brilliant fiery flamingo feathers of pink and orange, all of which was mirrored on the glass-like surface of the water below. And there was a quality to the light, a feel to the place, a presence, a . . . it was palpable . . . a . . . I don't know . . . like a . . . holy hush I guess. It was so beautiful, so peaceful. Nothing moved. Nothing at all. I poured out the bottle . . . almost like an offering or . . . And then a small wind whirled up, troubling the surface of the waters, causing leaves to dance toward me as it came on shore. As it surrounded me––it wasn't blowing anywhere else in the entire area but right around me––I . . . I heard a voice, whispering to me from the wind."

She nodded and smiled as I trailed off, reliving for the moment the magic I had been so moved by.

After a while, I'm not sure how long, she said, "What is it, son?"

"Ma'am?"

"Somethin' changed. Somethin's troublin' you, boy?"

"Everything's changed," I said. "I feel this . . . urge to . . . help people . . . to try to share and . . . I can't be a cop now, can't just move to Atlanta after high school and work the case like I planned, can't just . . . But . . . I can't let my dad down either. He's invested so much in my becoming a . . . to follow him in . . ."

"Follow your guts, boy," she said. "Who knows? Ol' Jack Jordan may surprise you . . . or . . . you might surprise yourself at what you can do. Don't limit God. Don't think you got to be a this or that, fit here not there, all or nothin'. You just trust and obey. Trust and obey. God will make a way."

8

"Jack tells me you think the task force got it wrong," Frank said.

Frank Morgan, a middle-aged, gray-haired, Georgia Bureau of Investigations agent and Dad's friend on the Atlanta Missing and Murdered Children task force, had come to Mexico Beach for vacation and we had driven down to see him.

He was a tall, trim man with wire-framed glasses that darkened in the sun, a good, straight-talking, straight-edged guy, rigid, humorless, nerdish.

It was in the late spring of '86 just a month or so before I would graduate from high school, and though I had had a spiritual awakening of sorts and found a modicum of equilibrium, I had not been able to completely let go of my obsessive connection to the case.

"I never said y'all got it wrong," I said.

"You think Williams is innocent?"

I shrugged.

"You're not one of those who says there's no such thing as black serial killers, are you?"

"No. I'm not. I know there are, know there have been far more than what most people realize."

"But you don't think Williams is one. You think he's innocent."

"No. Not necessarily. More not proven."

"Well, that'd be on the prosecution not the task force, but it was proven to the satisfaction of the jury who heard the entire case made and the defense against it."

He was defensive but not overly so.

We were on the front porch of his small, old rented cottage across the street from the beach, in early evening.

The sun was on its way to setting. Soon it would slip behind the sea at the vanishing point of the horizon. But for now it hung in the west just above and beyond the Gulf.

Frank was grilling hamburgers, he and Dad drinking beer from the bottle.

Frank's family, a wife and a preteen boy and girl, were at the water's edge, collecting sea shells and sticking their toes in the Gulf.

"So what's your beef with the task force?" Frank asked.

"It didn't finish its job."

"Only because the killer's in prison instead of the ground."

"Whose killer? The two adults? Cater and Payne? Those are the only ones he's serving time for."

"Do you know what would've happened if he had been tried for all the murders?" he said.

"He'd've walked," I said. "Because he didn't commit all the murders, but thanks to how everything was handled there's doubt to whether he committed any."

"Oh, trust me. He did. But you're right. He didn't do all of them."

"The list—" I began.

"That damn list," he said.

"So many different victims—not just young black boys, but girls, adults—different methods of murder."

He nodded. "You're right. Don't blame me for that damn list. I didn't create it. And I kept saying the list is shit. There were victims that should've been on it that weren't and others that should've never been added in the first place."

"A serial killer has a pattern," I said. "He commits serial crimes—all part of a series that can be linked together. Serial killers have a signature. What's the pattern in this case? Which victims are part of the series? What is the killer's signature?"

"It's not that simple," he said. "Just wait 'til you work your first case, let alone a case like this. There are always things that don't make sense, that you can't answer, that will drive you crazy if you let them. Always. We're dealing with deranged human beings."

He paused and flipped the burgers with the large spatula he was holding.

"That being said," he continued, "there was a pattern. But instead of me telling you, you tell me. Let's hear what you think."

"Okay. The only pattern cases were those of the asphyxiated and dumped young black boys. That's the series."

He nodded. "Like the ones the prosecution used in the case—the pattern victims linked to Williams."

"So why was he tried for killing two adults?"

"Because they could tie him to the bridge."

"But if he killed Nathaniel Cater and threw his body off the bridge, doesn't that break the pattern? Wouldn't that mean Williams wasn't the killer of the boys?"

"You don't think killers kill outside of their pattern? Occasionally? Sometimes? Out of necessity if nothing else."

"Sure," I said. "I'm sure you're right, but doesn't it bother you that he was tried for the anomaly and not the pattern?"

"Everything about the whole goddamn thing bothers me," he said. "Everything."

"You don't think it's possible Williams isn't the killer?" I asked.

"If he's not, why'd the killings stop?"

"Did they?" I asked.

"You saying they didn't?"

"There have been other, similar killings in the area," I said. "But they could've stopped for a different reason."

"Which would be?"

"The killer moved, was killed, or incarcerated."

"It's possible," he said. "Highly, highly unlikely, but remotely possible."

"There's a man in prison right now who was a prime suspect in one of the pattern killings, who eyewitnesses say killed Clifford Jones."

"You mean Jamie Brooks?"

I nodded. "And he went to prison around the same time most of the murders stopped."

"Let's say Jamie Brooks did kill Clifford Jones," he said. "The witness was discredited, but let's say he did. He and Calvin Smith. That doesn't mean Williams didn't kill the others."

"No, *but* the green trilobal fiber that was supposed to tie Williams to the pattern cases was found on Clifford Jones. So if it was Jamie Brooks, suddenly he's tied to all the pattern cases."

Frank looked at Dad. "Smart kid," he said, pointing at me with the spatula. "Gonna make a great cop."

Dad sighed and shook his head. "He's decided to go a different direction."

"What?" Frank asked.

"What a waste, right?" Dad said. "Tell him. Now he wants to be a preacher instead."

Frank looked at me.

I shook my head.

"Not a preacher, no, but in ministry."

"Wants to save the world," Dad said.

"Not the world, no. Not save anybody . . . just . . . I . . . I just want . . . to help people."

"You've got a gift," Frank said. "And there are worse ways to help people than being a cop."

9

I was running out of time.

The fast approach of graduation loomed in the short distance like a flashing warning sign on a dark, rain-slick night, and I still didn't know what to do––or where or how.

Over the next few weeks I spent a lot of time praying and seeking and trying to figure it out, but up until the day of graduation I still had no idea.

Should I go into law enforcement or ministry?

I just didn't know. And I knew I needed to. At times I felt more strongly pulled to one than the other, but mostly they pulled at me with equal persistence and pressure.

It was time to do something, but what?

I thought about what Frank Morgan had said, how I could help a lot of people as a cop. All the while Dad kept telling me the same thing, telling me how much good I could do and what a waste it would be for me to do anything else, how not using the gifts God had given me as an investigator would be sinful somehow.

But as it turned out, it was Mama Monroe who had been most prescient on the subject.

"Don't limit God," she had said. "Don't think you got to be this or that, fit here not there, all or nothin'. You just trust and obey. God will make a way."

And the way came, like so many things back then, through my connection to and obsession with the Atlanta Child Murders.

The morning of my high school graduation, I was rereading the case files I had compiled, trying to look again with fresh eyes and a new perspective to see if a new pattern might emerge, if something might leap off the page that before had remained hidden, camouflaged among all the other words and witness statements, details and descriptions.

And as I did, it was as if, once again, I woke up, woke up this time to a new possibility that wasn't either or, all or nothing, but a way to begin to integrate the two seeming disparate callings I was sensing in my soul.

What appeared, what pounced off the page and seized me, was the possibility of simultaneously taking steps to be educated and trained in ministry while working on the case that had captured my imagination, altered my path, haunted my childhood, changed my life.

It happened as I reread and reconsidered the information I had on Curtis Walker.

Thirteen-year-old Curtis Walker was reported missing on February 19, 1981.

He was last seen, wearing a brown-and-blue shirt, blue pants, and blue sneakers, on Bankhead Highway near where he lived in Bowen Homes.

Around this time, Earl Paulk, pastor of Chapel Hill Harvester Church in Decatur, began receiving phone calls from a man claiming to be the killer.

He described himself as a twenty-eight-year-old married man and father of a small child. He said he lured the victims into his blue van by posing as a painter and offering money for part-time work, and claimed responsibility for four of the murders, saying a voice tells him to kill. "Once the voice begins controlling me," he said, "I have no control at all."

The killer claimed he had help, that someone was assisting him in each case.

Following one of the phone calls, the man had agreed to meet with Paulk at his church but never showed. Later, Paulk was told that while he waited in his office for the man, two church elders saw a blue van pull up across the street, hesitate, then drive off.

According to Paulk, two police cars were just coincidentally in the neighborhood, which led him to publicize the call in the hopes that the man would realize he had not been part of a trap.

On February 14th, Paulk issued a televised plea for the killer to turn himself in.

"I work as a church man, a pastor," Paulk said. "I will not set up a trap." He went on to quote the caller saying nobody loved him, nobody had ever loved him, not even his own mother.

The pastor said he believed the man wanted to be free, wanted to be caught. He said the man seemed frightened that the voices would come back to haunt him, that he not only felt controlled by them but was afraid of them.

On March 6th, the body of Curtis Walker was discovered floating face down, snagged on a log in the South River at Waldrop Road less than a mile from Paulk's church.

All Walker's clothes were missing except his underwear, and latent prints were found on his body. The cause of death was ruled asphyxiation by strangulation.

On March 10th, the man called Paulk again. This time the caller discussed four killings, referring to them as the first three and the last one, Curtis Walker, who he mentioned by name.

My mind, like my heart, burst into flames.

I thought of all the possibilities.

What if Pastor Paulk had been contacted by the actual killer? What if it had been a copycat, the person responsible for some if not all of the victims who shouldn't have been on the list or ones who never were?

Was he fixated on the pastor? Would he call him again? Was he a member of his congregation?

That last one stopped me.

Flipping through the files, searching for cases similar to Walker's, I dialed the church.

And that's when the next step in my path was revealed.

I was transferred to a young man named Randy Renfroe, who told me the church was starting a school of ministry in the fall.

By the time I hung up the phone, I was registered for classes at Earl Paulk Institute.

I would move to Atlanta, go to Chapel Hill Harvester Church, attend classes at EPI, studying and preparing for and engaging in ministry, while investigating the Atlanta Child Murders.

I sat there awestruck.

What just happened?

In the course of a single call everything had changed again.

A path had been revealed. A way made plain.

The wait and worry and was over, the ambiguity and indecision departed.

My adventures in ministry and murder investigation were finally about to begin.

10

"Think about what you're saying," Dad said.

"I am," I said. "I have."

"For what? All of an afternoon?"

I didn't say anything, just shook my head.

He had found me in my room packing my things, boxing books, folding clothes into a suitcase.

It had taken four boxes just to hold my case files.

When he asked why, I told him.

Back then he wore a uniform—even on Saturdays, even to his son's high school graduation.

"I just came to see if you were ready for graduation and you drop this on me?" he said.

"It can't be surprising."

"That you're moving to Atlanta? Leaving tonight? Well, it is."

Without the maps and photographs and photocopied scraps of evidence and information tacked to the wall, the room looked abandoned, barren, the white painted sheetrock walls now pocked with a million tiny holes, sad, lonely, looking like the scatter shot from a shotgun.

"You know I've wanted to move to Atlanta, to . . . work the case."

"But that's not what you're talkin' about doin'. It's nearly a year before you can get certified to be a deputy. But you're not even talkin' about that. You're talkin' about . . . what . . . Bible college. It's crazy."

"It's right. It's . . . the next step for me. I know it."

"Well, I don't."

"And?"

"What do you mean *and*?"

I was not being disrespectful in any way, but I wasn't backing down either.

Unlike my brother Jake and my sister Nancy, I had never really had any conflict with either of my parents. I had always been more or less deferential, even submissive, never defiant or disrespectful--especially to Dad.

"I'm the one who has to figure out my next step and take it."

"And you think it's uprooting your entire life, running away?"

"I'm not running away."

Was he confusing me with Nancy? She had run away. To New York. To escape. Two years before and she hadn't written or called or returned or reached out in any way. She had utterly rejected our family. Did he think I was doing the same?

"I'm just going to college," I said. "Just taking the next step in my journey. Nothing more. It's time. It's what we've been planning on. It's just college."

"It's not," he said. "It's not even a real college. It's a new upstart Bible school. It's not even accredited. It's a joke. You can't really believe it's what you're supposed to do."

"I do," I said.

His disappointment was palpable, the force of it powerful. We were in, for us, uncharted territory and it threatened to dampen my joy and excitement.

"Dad," I said, my voice peaceful and placating, "I know it

doesn't make any sense but I also know it's what I'm supposed to do."

"It's a mistake."

"I don't think so," I said, "but even if it is, it's one I've got to make."

"It's my job to keep you from making mistakes," he said.

I shook my head. "Not anymore."

"What? You're suddenly all grown up and independent because you're graduating from high school?"

"I just meant——"

"I can't let you do this," he said.

"*Let me?*"

"I won't. I can't."

"Dad, it doesn't have to be this way. Please. Don't make it something that it's not."

"I won't be a part of this," he said. "I told you I'd help with college, but not this one. I won't pay a single dime toward this . . . this impulsive error in judgment. I can't."

I nodded. "Okay."

"I'm sorry, but you'll thank me one day. Take some time to think about some real options. Like Gulf Coast or FSU. We'll talk tomorrow about those. I'll——"

"I won't be here," I said. "I'm leaving tonight."

"You can't. How will you pay for——"

"I'll figure something out," I said. "It'll work out. I believe that. It's all too irrational, illogical, unexpected, and fortuitous not to. But I'd like to at least go with your support."

"Well, I can't give you that."

A lot happened that night. It was another new beginning of sorts. I gained much from the experience, including a new level of autonomy and adulthood, but I lost something too.

I lost some innocence, a sense of home and belonging, but most of all I lost a friend.

My relationship with my dad would never be the same again.

Anna was at graduation. It was the first time I'd seen her in several months. Since Nancy had left town and she had started college we had fallen out of touch.

If anyone could keep me from leaving for Atlanta tonight it was her.

Anna was no longer a secret crush. I was in love with her. Profoundly and absolutely.

It wasn't infatuation or mere attraction, though she was the most beautiful girl in all the world to me. It was unequivocal adoration. A love only a poet could hope to understand. I loved every cell and every second of her, every moment and every molecule.

Of course, not being a poet myself, I was unable to tell her, unable to express the fire for her smoldering inside my chest.

And she had come to graduation with her new boyfriend whose sister was in my class, and I avoided her, quickly ducking out of the gymnasium at the eternal event's conclusion.

Following pomp and circumstance—or all the pomp and circumstance that could be mustered for forty-two graduates, I loaded my car and filled my tank using some of my graduation gift cash at the only convenience store in Pottersville.

After a tearful goodbye at which my mom smelled of booze and from which my dad was absent, I set out for the city too busy to hate, the birthplace of my hero and spiritual mentor Martin Luther King, Jr., who was killed the same year I was born, the home of Coca-Cola, the CDC, CNN, the Carter Center, America's baseball team, the Varsity, Stone Mountain, the Fox Theater, where Lynyrd Skynyrd's famous live version of "Free Bird" on *One More from the Road* was recorded, the place where *Gone with the Wind* had been written, and a series of murders had been committed that had affected me as profoundly as any single event in my entire life.

I drove nearly all night.

Sipping Dr. Pepper and munching on Combos, I sang until

my voice grew hoarse with Rick Springfield, John Cougar, Steve Camp, Steve Taylor, Boz Scaggs, Robert Palmer, Russ Taff, Lionel Richie, Hall and Oats, and Phil Collins.

I sang to stay awake. I sang to celebrate. I sang to forget. I sang until I couldn't picture the look of disappointment on my dad's face or the look of happiness on Anna's.

I spent some more of my grad gift money on a cheap motel room. And at nine o'clock the next morning, after only a few hours of sleep, I was walking into the exciting, integrated mega church whose pastor a killer had called, where less than a mile away the small body of Curtis Walker had been found.

11

"I hear very good things about what you're doing for the kingdom of God," Earl Paulk said. "We're so pleased you chose our school of ministry. I truly believe we've got the resources to equip our students to touch the world."

We were in his upstairs office in the back of the K Center or main sanctuary, a large building he had described as an airplane hanger, built to accommodate as many people as possible due to the growth the church had experienced over the past decade.

What would become Chapel Hill Harvester Church began in December 1960 in Saint John's Lutheran Church on Euclid Avenue, in the Little Five Points community. The thirty-nine people in attendance included founders Earl and Norma Paulk, Don and Clariece Paulk, and Harry and Myrtle Mushegan.

From the first day, Paulk was committed to opening the doors of his church to all people, regardless of racial, economic, or moral background. Not surprisingly, given his opposition to segregation, he was one of the first white pastors to open the doors of his church to black members.

The very first bulletin cover showed a picture of a white hand

and a black hand clasped together with the accompanying slogan A Church of Compassion.

The church moved to South Dekalb County in Decatur in 1972, and quickly became one of the first truly racially integrated congregations in the entire South.

The early eighties witnessed a shift in ministry and message, and explosive growth.

In addition to its unique racial unity, the church became famous for its worship style, which combined visual arts with liturgy, and its social outreach programs.

In 1982, Paulk was ordained as a bishop in the International Communion of Charismatic Churches. His public housing ministry was named one of a thousand points of light by President George H. W. Bush.

I had never been much of a churchgoer and had little use for organized religion, but I appreciated many aspects of this unique, inspiring church, especially the integration, emphasis on compassion, and the social outreach programs to the poor and disenfranchised.

It had taken me a while to get an appointment with Bishop Paulk. I had been in town a few weeks, getting settled, getting my bearings, getting a job.

"I understand you're working for us too?" he said.

I nodded.

Don Paulk, Earl's brother and co-pastor of the church, had been particularly helpful to me, welcoming, supportive, and had even found me a job on the janitorial staff of the facilities department.

"That's great," he said. "Pastor Don's very impressed with you. Says you'll soon be leading a covenant community group."

Covenant communities were the church's home meetings, small groups scattered throughout the city.

"I look forward to it."

There was a presence about Bishop Paulk, an energy

emanating from him, particularly from his mesmerizing bright blue eyes. He was trim and fit and sat upright behind his enormous desk. At sixty, his forceful bearing and youthful vitality were extraordinary.

"God's got his hand on your life," he said. "I sense a powerful calling."

"Thank you," I said. "I'm very excited to be here."

Thanks to Pastor Don waiving part of the tuition, I was already enrolled in summer classes. In addition to the classes, I had been assigned a practicum that involved, among other things, taking food and medicine into an extremely low-income apartment complex and regular visits to Grady hospital to see a man with AIDS in the last days of his short life.

And all of it—the transition from small to big town, the new job, the classes, the work of actually helping people in need—was exhilarating and exhausting.

I longed to share everything that was happening with Dad and Anna. Being unable to tinged the edges of everything with a certain ever-present, dull-ache sadness.

"Don said you plan to combine ministry and law enforcement somehow."

"I don't know how exactly or if I even can, but I feel equally called to both."

He nodded. "That's what we need. We have too many ministers limiting what they can be, spending all their time in a pulpit. I think you're right on track. Don't limit God. Just stay open to the Holy Spirit. Let me know any way we can help you."

"Pastor Don said you might be willing to talk to me about the child murders that happened a few years back."

He nodded.

"I'll never forget it," he said with a heavy sigh. "So many black parents in our congregation . . . wondering if *their* child would be next. We began a round-the-clock prayer vigil early on but became publicly involved when I received a call from

Dr. Frazier Ben Todd––he was president of the NAACP at the time.

"On February fourteenth––this was back in eighty-one––I made a television appeal to the killer or killers and ran a full-page advertisement in the *Atlanta Journal-Constitution* that said, 'If you are responsible for the crimes against our children, this television appeal is to you. Watch Saturday, February 14th, Channel 46 at 11:00 p.m.'

"I assured the killer that he could speak to me in private and I ended by saying, 'Jesus loves you and He will forgive you for what you have done.'

"The very next day, phone calls began coming in from supposed killers. On February sixteenth a mysterious caller instructed me to go to a local TV station for the six o'clock evening news broadcast. The person didn't show but later called saying, 'I didn't see you on camera.' The following Sunday afternoon, I was asked to speak to a city-wide prayer meeting held at the request of the NAACP.

"The day after that a call came in from someone calling himself 'the one Earl Paulk was trying to reach.' I rushed to the phone but when he heard my voice he hung up. He called back an hour later but refused to set a time and place to meet.

"The same voice called later and told us to look for a particular van and when it would arrive. Don and I waited in our car and saw a van matching the description drive into the parking lot across the street from our church. Another car pulled into the lot. I don't know if it was the FBI or police or what. Then two more and suddenly the van spun its wheels and disappeared, moving too fast for us to get a tag number. The two cars didn't pursue so I guess their pulling in when they did was just coincidence."

As I listened to him recount his story I realized there were differences in what I had read and thought from what he remembered, and it occurred to me that it must be that way with every report, every statement, everything I knew or thought I did.

"When he called the next time, he asked us to come to a truck stop at the edge of town. Don went with me. There were cars everywhere when we arrived. If the caller came he had apparently panicked and left.

"After that, FBI agents surrounded the church property and told us they would be monitoring our phone conversations.

"On February twenty-eighth, I made another television appeal and the caller spoke to me for the last time.

"On March sixth, the next victim was found in a creek about a mile from here.

"A few months after that, Wayne Williams was arrested and eventually convicted, but I've always believed there was more than one killer at work."

"Was there anything that made you think the caller might be a member of your congregation?"

He shrugged. "I never had a knowing one way or another but I don't think he was. He may have attended a service at some point ... but ..."

"And you were never contacted again?"

He shook his head. "Not by that person."

"Others?"

"I get calls all the time. A few others have claimed to be involved."

"Any recently?"

He nodded.

"One who called recently said he enjoyed my sermon from the previous Sunday and even quoted from it."

"Could he have seen it on TV?"

"It hadn't aired yet."

I nodded and thought about it, excitement arcing through me.

"You know who you should talk to ..." he said. "There's a lady in our congregation who runs a daycare. She's been part of STOP since the beginning. Her son was one of the victims who didn't make the list."

Ida Williams owned and operated a daycare and aftercare center called Safe Haven just down Flat Shoals Road from the church.

It was located in a converted home that had been retrofitted and zoned commercial. The large yard, now a playground, was filled with swings and sandboxes and toys, surrounded by a chain-link fence.

I pulled up, parked to one side of the circular driveway, and got out.

By the time I reached the gate, a uniformed security guard was waiting for me.

He was a rotundish, pale man with short blond hair cut in a military-style side-part, and a neatly trimmed blond mustache. His smallish light blue eyes blinked so often behind his glasses they seemed hooded.

"How can I help you?" he asked.

"I'm here to see Ida Williams," I said.

"Have an appointment?"

I shook my head.

"You'll need to make one before she can see you. She's with her kids now. Will be 'til eight. Maybe later."

"But—"

He shook his head. "Sorry. No exceptions."

"I've just—"

"I'm gonna need you to leave the premises, sir. Now."

When he raised his hands, I could see a bright orange Swatch watch stretched around his thick right wrist. It looked odd and out of place and as if at any moment the band would snap and it would slingshot off.

"Can you just tell me—"

"I won't tell you again."

I wondered what he would do instead of telling me again, but an intervening angel prevented me from finding out.

"What is it, Ralph?" she asked.

Small enough to be a schoolgirl. Shy green eyes. Straight sun-streaked blond hair. Smooth, unvarnished, suntanned skin. A simple, understated, graceful beauty I found irresistible.

I knew no one could make me forget Anna, but this alluring, vulnerable, pretty woman-child creature came as close as any to making me believe it was possible.

"No appointment," he said. "Refusing to leave."

"I'm not refusing to leave," I said to her. "I was just trying to explain that Bishop Paulk sent me over and to find out how to go about making an appointment."

"What'd you need?" she asked.

"Just to talk to Ms. Williams for a few minutes."

"Well, you can certainly do that," she said. "I'll take care of it, Ralph."

"Yes, ma'am. I'll radio and let her know you two are coming up."

Ralph opened the gate and I walked through.

"I'm Jordan Moore," she said, extending her small, cold hand.

I smiled. "Really? I'm John Jordan."

She smiled but looked a bit embarrassed, her face and neck blushing crimson.

"Sorry my hands are cold," she said. "Ninety-degree weather and my extremities are little blocks of ice."

She ushered me up the covered walkway and we fell in step beside one another.

"And sorry about Ralph," she said. "He means well. I'm sure you can tell . . . security is taken very seriously around here."

I wondered if she had used the passive voice—*is taken* instead of *we take*—because she found the measures a little extreme.

"It's sort of our speciality," she said.

"Bishop Paulk mentioned Ms. Williams had a son who was killed."

"Changes everything," she said.

We walked in silence for a few moments.

I was young and what I did next had never occurred to me to do before.

When she was looking away, I stole a quick glance at her left hand ring finger, but what I saw gave me questions not answers.

The small, thin, elegant finger held no ring, but it did bear the white, untanned mark where one had recently been.

"How long have you worked here?" I asked.

"Seems like all my life," she said. "I've lost track."

"Tell me about it."

"Daycare during the day. Aftercare in the afternoon and evening. An emphasis on a safe, positive environment. Clean. Accredited. Family owned and operated. It's not affiliated with the church but most of us go there. And most of our kids are from there."

To our right, beyond another fence, the playground was empty, the sun glinting off its shiny surfaces, a swing squeaking as it emptily back-and-forthed in the breeze.

"Where are the kids?" I said. "Figured they'd be on the playground this time of day."

"Finishing up an art project," she said. "They'll be out here" ––she looked at her watch–– "in four minutes. In fact, we can have a seat here and wait on Miss Ida to come out."

She nodded toward a plastic-mesh-covered metal bench and we sat down.

"Do you go to Chapel Hill?" she asked.

"Came to attend EPI. Just moved here a few weeks ago."

"How do you like Atlanta?"

"Haven't seen much of it yet," I said. "But I like it here. A lot. I'm from a small town in the Florida Panhandle of about a tenth of the size of the church."

"Really?" she asked in surprise. "You don't seem . . ."

"What?"

She shrugged. "I don't know."

"Yes you do. What were you going to say?"

"Small town. You don't seem that small town."

I smiled and she blushed again.

"I'm as small town as John Cougar Mellencamp."

We sat in silence a moment as I tried to work up my nerve to ask her out.

"You lived here long?" I asked.

"My whole life."

"I could use someone to see the city with," I said. "Show me around. Play tour guide. Would you like to––"

"I can't," she said. "Sorry. Let me go see what's keeping Miss Ida."

13

Ida Williams––Miss Ida to the kids in her care and the staff that adored her––was a heavy middle-aged black woman with beautiful, smooth skin, big, bright eyes, and brown lips only a shade or two lighter than the rest of her.

Her hair was up in a colorful head wrap of orange and brown and green that matched the large, loose tunic dress she was wearing.

We were seated on the same bench Jordan and I had been on. In front of us, visible through the rings in the fence, children ran and climbed and swung and jumped and talked and laughed, each of them, in one way or another, resembling the victims on the list.

And those not on the list.

Like so many others, LaMarcus Williams never made the list. As in the case with the others, I wasn't sure why. Neither was his mom.

How did she do it? How did she see them every day, day after day, these little fresh faces that looked so much like the son who would never grow old, never become any of what he might have been, never come home again?

"Nothin' in this world like losing a child," she said. "You's not much more'n a child yourself, but if you were older and had a child of your own, you still wouldn't know what I's talkin' about. I didn't. Saw all these grievin' mamas. Felt bad for 'em. Real bad. Thought 'cause I had a kid I knew what they's goin' through. Didn't have a clue."

I nodded but knew better than to say anything. There was nothing *to* say, no words in the history of all words to utter.

"They's nothin' like it, nothin' come close," she said. "But what make it even worse is not knowing, not knowing who did it and why, not knowing if his name should be on that list or not."

Across the playground, Jordan was watching a group of girls jump rope. She was one of only a handful of white faces and the only worker who was in the yard. It may have just been me imagining or wanting, but I thought I saw her looking my way occasionally, even turning red and smiling once when our eyes met.

"That's why I can't quit, can't give up," she said. "People say the man in jail, the murders stopped. Time to let go, move on."

I understood why she couldn't, why she would never be able to. At least not until—it was at that moment that I decided to dedicate myself to finding out what happened to LaMarcus Williams.

"I joined STOP even before my boy was taken from me," she said. "Been workin' 'long side Camille and Willie Mae and all the others all these years. Seen lots of people come and go."

STOP was the name used by the committee of mothers formed to stop children's murders. It began when three of the victims' mothers, Camille Bell, Willie Mae Mathis, and Venus Taylor, joined with Reverend Earl Carroll to bring attention to Atlanta, to the slaughter of the innocent, the ineffectiveness of the police, and the indifference of too many in the white power establishment.

"They's a group of us still meets every week," she said. "Every single week."

"May I come to it?" I asked. "I'd like to get involved."

She nodded. "It's open to anyone. Meet right here every Thursday night."

"I'll be here. Thank you."

"There's also a support group at the church," she said. "For anyone who's lost a child. It's a closed group, but you can come as my guest if you like."

"I would. Thank you."

She turned and looked down across Flat Shoals Road at the K Center and Chapel Hill's other facilities, her first time taking her eyes off the children.

"Not sure I'd've made it without them," she said. "The Paulks. They were all so good to me. Bishop. Don and Clariece. Still are, but I mean when it happened . . . they kept me from going crazy. Them and my daughter. I had lost my husband the year before. It was just . . . too . . ."

"Do you . . . mind . . . would you . . . be willing to tell me what happened?"

Her watchful gaze was back on the children.

"Happened right here," she said. "Wasn't a daycare then. Was our home. Saturday after Thanksgiving. November twenty-ninth."

I was here at that same time, I thought. Safely tucked away inside the Omni with my family while she was losing everything.

"He was only twelve," she said. "Just a twelve-year-old little boy."

We had been the same age, would still be had he not been cut loose from whatever it is that tethers us here.

"Out in the yard playing," she said. "The backyard. Away from the road. Back where nobody could get to him, back where I could see him. I was back and forth between the living room and kitchen, cooking supper and wrapping his Christmas presents. A Star Wars lunchbox. Guess Who game. GI Joe. Star Trek Communicators. Rubik's Cube. Train set. Michael Jackson and Kool and the Gang records. Spent too much. Didn't care. Was so happy I found them. Both rooms had big windows that looked out over the backyard. I watched him like a hawk. Always had, but once our children started bein' taken . . . I never took my eyes off of him."

But she had, hadn't she? For a moment, a split second, maybe a little longer.

She was still looking at the children before us, but I wondered what she was really seeing.

"I didn't think I had . . . I don't remember not seeing him for even a moment—least out the corner of my eye. But . . . one moment he was there, another he was gone. Just vanished. Gone. Just like that. Never saw my boy alive again."

She was crying now. Still looking straight ahead as tears streamed down her dark, round cheeks.

"I's the reason he's out there," she said. "I wanted to wrap his gifts I had just gotten the day before and get 'em up under the tree. I sent him out there. I did. I'm the reason my boy's dead."

14

EPI was too new and too small to have dormitories, so school housing was a three-story apartment in Trade Winds Apartment Complex up off Wesley Chapel Road near I-20.

My new address was 4636 Pleasant Point Drive, my home, a drug-ridden, rundown low-income complex where I shared an apartment designed for a family of four with eight testosterone-ridden late-teen men, only about half of whom were actually attending EPI. The others were single young men from the church who needed a place to live.

Many of the students complained about the living conditions at Trade Winds, the shape of the property itself, the makeup of those who called it home, but I loved it. As a young white man from a tiny town in Florida, I was an outsider and part of a small minority. I was surrounded by mostly poor African-Americans and I had never felt more at home, more at ease, never before felt more in the center of exactly where I was supposed to be, doing what I was supposed to be doing.

Of course, the truth was I had always felt more at home around Merrill and his mom and their family and friends and the black woman who had kept me as a child than I had nearly anyone else.

I had undergone a sea change long before coming to Atlanta and was now undergoing another. Not only had I gone from a small North Florida town with one traffic light to the eight-lane interstates of a crowded metropolitan area, but I had left behind my virtually solitary existence, so comfortable to my essentially introverted nature, for a crowded, close community where I was surrounded by people--lots and lots of them--nearly every waking moment of every single day.

In the mornings on my way to class, I'd stop in the little doughnut shop on Wesley Chapel for maple and strawberry iced doughnuts. In the evenings, I'd go through the drive-thru of the Dairy Queen. Both were within a block of Trade Winds and made up in convenience and cost for what they lacked in taste and variety.

This afternoon I came home without grabbing my usual chicken sandwich and fries. Hearing Ida Williams's heart-breaking account of what happened to her son left me without an appetite and with a sharp need to spend some extra time with the best friend I'd made in the city so far, my little neighbor basket-ball buddy, Martin Fisher.

Martin was the age LaMarcus had been when age ceased to be something he could be measured by, the age I had been when I had confronted Wayne Williams--something I had done just twenty short minutes from where we stood right now.

Martin was small and scrawny for his age, often sick. Chronic untreated ear infections as a small child had left him almost completely deaf and with a pretty severe speech impediment.

Martin's monotone voice was nasally and guttural and diffi-cult for most people to understand, but we had spent so much time together we had very little trouble communicating.

We both loved basketball and met each afternoon on the small asphalt court in the center of the complex.

The backboards were metal and the old, oblong goals were canted and netless.

"Yon, Yon," Martin yelled, "I . . . 'm . . . o'en."

He was dancing around under the goal with his hands up, imploring me to pass him the ball.

"Of course you're open," I said. "Nobody here but us. Move around. Post up. Get in a good position. Catch the ball. Gather. Go up strong. Ready?"

"'een 'eady."

I bounce-passed him the ball.

He tried to shoot too quickly, before he even had the ball, and lost it as he went up.

"You've got to catch it first," I said. "Catch it. Gather yourself. Go up strong."

"I 'ow," he said. "I 'ot 'is. Do it a'ain."

We did the same thing again. We got the same results.

The next time, he caught and gathered, but was too small and weak to get the ball up over the rim.

"Practice the right form," I said. "Elbow straight, arch the ball, follow through. Doesn't matter if it doesn't go in. Just shoot it the right way."

"It 'oes 'atter, Yon," he said.

I shook my head, took a dribble and then a step-back jumper from about twenty feet.

He squealed when it fell through the rim without touching anything until it hit the asphalt below.

"Get your form right now," I said. "Size and strength will come later."

I passed him the ball and he began dribbling. Unable to dribble between his legs, he lifted one and went under it to approximate the same move.

"What's for 'inner 'oonight, Yon?"

I didn't know a lot about Martin's situation, had no idea what life was like for him once the apartment door closed behind him.

He lived in the unit directly next to ours and I had seen several people come and go, but had yet to identify or meet anyone who would pass for parents.

Of the little I had been able to gather, two constants had emerged. He seemed to never be supervised and to always be hungry.

Lately, we had been taking to the kitchen to find something to feed him following our hoop exploits.

"Whatta you want?" I asked. "You can have fish sticks or I could whip up some fish sticks."

He laughed. "Yon," he said, holding out the ball.

Since I rarely cooked, I kept very little food in what was the community kitchen of the EPI dorm apartment, but after Martin identified them as his favorite, I had maintained a large bag of fish sticks in the small freezer.

"You decide buddy," I said. "It's up to you."

"'ish sticks," he shouted.

"Okay," I said. "Make ten layups on each side and we'll adjourn to the kitchen."

As he began his layup attempts, Frank Morgan pulled up in an unmarked.

I smiled. I had called his office and left a message but had not told him where I was living.

As Martin worked on his layups, I walked over to where Frank was parking.

"How'd you find me?" I asked as he got out of the car.

"Only white face in Trade Winds," he said. "Wasn't hard."

"Haven't see a lot of those in here," I said toward his car.

"Kind we send in here are far more unmarked," he said. "The hell you doin' livin' in a place like this?"

I told him.

"Your dad says y'all aren't speaking."

"I'm speaking. Just not doing exactly what he wants me to

right now. Pretty much a first. Least on anything that really mattered to him."

"We've got a spare bedroom," he said. "Welcome to it long as you like."

"Thank you. That means a lot. But this is where I'm supposed to be."

All around us the desultory sounds of poverty, of idleness, of listlessness, and waste, rose and fell, ebbed and flowed, sat still and swelled.

Grown men gathered around conversations of no consequence. They had no job, no purpose, nowhere to be. Women too-early old sitting on front door stoops, fanning themselves, watching the world spin by, spin away from them. Always away. Young men working in vain on vehicles that would never run again. Other, younger young men dealing substances to escape the disappointment and misery. Competing radios and game shows on too-loud TVs.

Ragged, rundown buildings around an asphalt parking lot dotted with a billion black stains from careless spills, discarded trash, and oil-leaking low riders, waves of shimmering heat rising up from all of them in the suffocating, will-breaking afternoon sun.

Martin continued attempting layups, his lack of success not from lack of effort or enthusiasm.

"When'd you adopt him?" Frank asked.

I laughed.

He shook his head. "Looks an awful lot like the little faces on the list."

He was right. He did. I hadn't consciously made the connection. Why hadn't I? What was my subconscious up to?

"Speaking of . . ." I said. "Why didn't LaMarcus Williams make the list?"

He smiled knowingly. "There it is. *That's* why you called."

"Yon, Yon," Martin yelled when he finally got one to go. "You 'ee 'at?"

"I did. Very nice. Keep it up. Just like that. Same way every time."

"LaMarcus Williams," Frank said. "That's the kid snatched out of his backyard on Flat Shoals. Too much was different from the others to make the list."

"There are a lot of differences between the ones that made the list."

"Told you. The list is arbitrary."

"Forget the girls and adults," I said. "Forget all but the true pattern cases of asphyxiated young boys. LaMarcus fits their profile, right? Why'd they make the list and he didn't?"

"He wasn't a poor inner city street kid. He was snatched from his backyard. He wasn't taken far. Found pretty soon after he was killed. And there were differences in the way he was killed. Can't remember what exactly, but . . ."

"Were there suspects? Was Williams looked at for it after he became the prime suspect in the other cases?"

"That I can't tell you," he said.

"Can you put me in touch with the lead detective on the case?"

He nodded. "That I can do."

15

"We ain't much," Ida Williams said. "But we are faithful."

I knew where the faithfulness came from. I knew why this small group continued to meet some four years after Wayne Williams was sentenced to serve two life sentences. They had seen what a small group of passionate people could do. If not for the three victims' mothers--Camille Bell, Willie Mae Mathis, and Venus Taylor--forming STOP and pressuring the police, politicians, and the white power structure, who knows how long it would have taken for a task force to be formed.

"Mule headed more like it," Melvin, a large black man, said.

"We surely are that," Ida agreed.

The gathering of the faithful took place in the back corner of the Safe Haven daycare center and included Ida, Melvin, a tall, thin woman named Rose Lee, a squat, muscular, fireplug of a man named Preston Mailer, and to my delight and surprise Jordan Moore.

Mailer was a retired cop. He along with everyone but me and Jordan were black.

"Wanna welcome our new member," Ida said. "This is John

Jordan. He's new to Atlanta but has been followin' the case a long time. He'll be a real asset to the group."

"Thank you for havin' me," I said. "I've been interested and invested in this case since childhood and I look forward to being involved in the work y'all are doin'."

"By way of introducin' John to our group and for us to hear from him, I thought we'd do one of our round robin brainstorm sessions tonight," Ida said.

Everybody indicated their assent.

"We learn by sharin', by aksin' questions—of each other and ourselves. Nobody got to agree with anybody on anything. Only rule is be courteous."

"That means you, Preston," Rose Lee said.

"Never been anything but," he said.

"Anything but a butt," she said.

It was said in good humor and everyone laughed.

"We're a diverse group, John," Ida said. "Some believe Wayne Williams was set up, that he's completely innocent."

Preston raised his hand.

"Some think he's guilty of all twenty-nine on the list plus some."

Rose Lee raised her hand and smiled.

"Others, like myself and Jordan, think it possible Wayne Williams did some of 'em but just as possible he didn't. We just ain't convinced either way. What we think more likely is if he did 'em, he didn't do 'em all."

I nodded.

"Why don't we start with what John thinks," Jordan said.

"Good idea," Ida said. "John?"

"I don't know," I said. "I've studied and studied the case against Wayne Williams—and I've had access to a lot of task force documents and information the general public hasn't—but I just—"

"How?" Preston Mailer asked.

"Let the young man talk, Preston," Ida said.

"How what?" I asked.

"How'd you get task force documents and information?"

Preston Mailer was a large, fleshy, light-skinned black man with thinning and receding gray hair on top of his huge head. His thick, swollen-looking skin was the color of river clay, a hint of red hue in it, his face dotted with dark freckles and moles the size and shape of the small black specks deposited in the filter of a faucet connected to an old copper pipe.

"My dad's in law enforcement," I said. "We had a friend on the task force."

"Who?"

I shook my head. "Won't tell you that."

He huffed, frowning and shaking his enormous head.

"So you've had access to this information the general public doesn't have . . ." Jordan said.

"And I still don't know. I go back and forth. Sometimes I think in spite of the weak case against Williams, he really is the killer—the main serial killer who killed with a certain pattern. Other times I think he's innocent not only of what he was charged with but the other murders as well. The fibers are compelling . . . but there are some problems with them."

"Such as?" Preston said.

"Trace evidence—hair and fibers and other substances exchanged during contact—should work both ways. Hair from Williams's dog and fibers from his carpet shouldn't just be found on the victims, but some of their hair and fibers should've been found on him—or in his home or car."

Everyone nodded, including Preston.

"There are other problems too," I said. "The fibers they found on some of the victims and tied to Williams aren't as rare as the prosecution claimed. And in at least one case, the prosecution matched fibers found on one of the victims to a car the Williams didn't own at the time."

I had everyone's attention, but most enjoyed Jordan's.

"What about there not being such a thing as a black serial killer?" Preston said.

"That's been the conventional wisdom," I said, "but it's just not true. There have been others before Williams and the more data the FBI gets, the more they see it's far more common than anyone knew."

He shook his head. "I don't buy it. Serial killers are white males, eighteen to thirty-five."

"Most are," I said. "But not all."

"What else?" Jordan said. "Keep on."

Was she reconsidering going out with me? She was certainly responding to me in a way she hadn't before.

"You started by saying the fiber evidence is compelling," Rose Lee said.

"It is," I said. "The sheer volume of it is staggering. And that it can link Williams's environment to so many of the victims."

"His environment," Ida said. "Exactly. Did anyone ever look at his dad? Could Homer Williams have committed the crimes?"

"Or Faye?" Jordan said.

"Good questions," I said. "I don't know the answers."

"But what else makes you suspect Wayne Williams?" Rose Lee asked.

"There're a lot of things. I don't put a ton of stock in them, but I don't totally discount the eyewitnesses who testified they saw Williams with some of the victims. The way in which he lies and exaggerates. His behavior in general, but after he began being followed by the police in particular—calling a press conference and the things he said, leading police to the houses of people connected to the case, failing lie detector tests, his interest in law enforcement."

"Which you and I share with him," Preston said.

I nodded. "But we were never busted for impersonating an officer."

"He was?" Jordan asked.

"He was. He also showed up at one of the crime scenes offering to take pictures for the cops."

"Really?" Preston said. "I didn't know that."

"His outbursts on the witness stand," I continued. "The way he changed so drastically. But more than anything else except the hairs and fibers is the entire bridge incident. During the weeks of river and bridge stakeouts, Williams was the only one to ever be stopped. What was he doing there? Why did he turn around and cross over the bridge again? He lied about what he had done earlier in the evening. It was three o'clock in the morning and the reason he gave for being there was bullshit. He said he had an audition the next morning with Cheryl Johnson and he had driven around trying to verify where she lived and when he couldn't, he went in search of a pay phone. No one, not the police, not the FBI, not the press, not the defense team has ever been able to find this Cheryl Johnson. This was the biggest, highest profile case since . . . maybe ever. You don't think if she existed she would've come forward by now?"

Everyone seemed to be pondering what I was saying––even Preston.

"Then there's the report that a small piece of rope and a change of clothes were found in his station wagon the night he was pulled over on the bridge," I continued. "There were also drops of blood found in the station wagon that were the same type as at least two of the victims. Witnesses say he and his dad were seen burning clothes and papers and other things that could be considered evidence in their backyard once he became a person of interest in the case. And I know a lot of people don't, but I put a lot of stock in the profile––and the fact that the two FBI profilers who worked the case, Roy Hazelwood and John Douglas, believe Williams to be guilty. All that said, I still can't be certain––which probably has more to do with the way the evidence was handled than questions about the evidence itself."

As was often the case, when I finished going through the case against Williams, I was convinced he was responsible for the killings. Unanswered questions would eventually cause doubt to creep back in, and I would never be convinced he killed everyone on the list, but in that moment I believed him to be the serial killer responsible for the serial killings within the greater list of victims.

"What about the killings that've happened since Wayne was arrested?" Preston said. "How can you explain those?"

"Same way you explain the ones that weren't part of the pattern while Wayne was out," I said. "Someone else is doing them. Probably several someone elses. To me, the serial killer—whether it's Williams or someone else—killed serially, as part of a distinct pattern in a particular way. I'd say the young black males who were asphyxiated were part of that pattern. The others, and there were and still are many, were done by others for other reasons. That means the famous list is wrong. That means that you have to exclude females and adults and the young males who were stabbed or shot. And what you have following Williams's arrest are mostly stabbings and shootings."

"You may be right," Preston said. "But if you are that means the two victims Wayne was actually convicted of killing shouldn't've even been on the list to begin with."

I nodded.

"And that my brother should've been," Jordan said.

"Your brother?" I asked in surprise.

"LaMarcus," she said.

"My boy," Ida said. "She's his sister. Me and her daddy married when the kids were still little."

I nodded.

"So why ain't he?" Ida asked. "Why ain't my son on the list?"

"I don't know," I said, "but it's the first thing I intend to find out."

16

"Wow," Jordan said. "You really breathed new life back into our little group."

We were walking down the breezeway after having locked up, the others milling around the parking lot, making sure not to leave her alone with the new member obsessed with murder.

"They're lingering," I said, nodding toward them.

"They're protective," she said.

"I get it," I said. "What they've been through, what they've seen. I'm glad they are."

"They're sweet," she said. "They've been with me through a lot over the years."

"I had no idea LaMarcus was your brother," I said. "I'm so sorry."

"No way you could've known."

The diamond in her wedding set glinted in the light of one of the overhead Fluorescent bulbs.

"I also didn't know you were married when I asked you out," I said. "Sorry. You weren't wearing your ring and . . ."

"Please don't apologize," she said. "It was the kindest, most flattering thing to happen to me in a long time. I take them off at work. They snag on everything."

"The truth is I saw the tan line and asked anyway. I shouldn't have. I'm sorry."

"That's just an excuse," she said.

"Huh? What is?"

"Work."

"I'm—"

"I don't just take my rings off because they snag," she said. "I . . . I'm . . . It's not your fault. I'm sure you were just pickin' up on . . . my . . . I've said too much already. You're too easy to talk to."

"Please," I said.

"I'm in a situation I've needed to be out of for a very long time," she said. "I just haven't been able to find a way out and . . ."

"And?"

"And I'm sure you were pickin' up on my attraction too. I've never . . . I can't remember it . . . it's never been quite so immediate or . . ."

"Come on, slowpokes," Preston called. "I'm ready to go home."

"Can I give you a ride?" I asked.

"NO," she exclaimed. "Sorry, but . . . that would be the worst thing. Thank you, but . . . I can't. And I really shouldn't talk to you again. I'm sorry. I wish things were different."

Before I could say anything else, we reached the others.

"Good meeting everyone," Ida said. "See you next week."

"So glad you joined us, John," Rose Lee said.

A black Trans Am screeched off the street and into the driveway, racing up to where we stood.

"Oh my God," Jordan said, moving away from me and over by Ida.

"It's okay, Jordan," Ida said. "You're okay, baby."

"He's supposed to be at work."

"Larry Moore," Rose Lee whispered to me, "Jordan's husband."

A smallish but muscular man in very short exercise shorts and a tank top tucked into them jumped out of the car.

His hair was feathered and blown back and he wore a large, flat gold chain around his neck, the bottom of which disappeared into his thick chest hair.

"What the hell, Jordan?" he said. "Why aren't you at home?"

"Our meeting ran a little long," Ida said. "I was just about to take her."

"Get in the car, Jordan," he said. "Now."

She actually shook.

"I . . . I thought . . . you were at work," she said. "I . . . would-n't've stayed for the meeting. I didn't know."

"My wife out to all hours of the night," he said. "What the hell? Get in the car."

He stopped when he saw me.

"Who the hell is this?"

Ida started to answer, but I stepped forward. "John Jordan," I said.

"You bowing up at me, bitch?" he said.

I didn't respond, just stood there.

"Jordan, get in the fuckin' car now. And wipe your feet."

She moved toward the car. Hesitantly. Slowly. Self-consciously.

"Come home with me, baby," Ida said.

"Stay out of it, Ida," he said. "She's coming home with her husband––where she should've been hours ago."

"She better be at work on time in the morning," Ida said. "And there better not be a mark on her."

Jordan carefully eased into the car, looking like a frightened child.

"Come on, *Mom*, you know I wouldn't do that," he said to Ida. "I never leave marks."

He then jumped into his car and sped away.

"Lord Jesus, the things that poor child done been through," Ida said.

We were walking back toward the building so she could use the phone.

"I know the scriptures say God won't put more on a body than they can bear," she said, "but I don't see how she's still gettin' up of a mornin'."

Everyone else in group had gone––including Preston. I guess he concluded I didn't have the same intentions toward Ida as I did Jordan.

"Can't help but think it's my fault," she said. "I'm the only mama she ever had, the only family for more'n six years now."

"She's lucky to have you."

"Done somethin' wrong, her with a man like that," she said.

Inside, she walked directly to the phone and punched in a number from memory.

"Sorry to bother you so late, Sergeant," she said.

She paused and listened.

"He just picked her up here at the daycare, yellin' and cussin' and showboatin' in his little vroom vroom car."

She paused again.

"Okay. Thank you. Don't know what I'd do if he hurt her again. Okay then. Goodnight."

She hung up and we locked up again.

"Okay," she said, "let's try to go get some sleep. I got to be back here in just a few short hours."

"So Jordan's okay?"

"That was Larry's brother, Vince. Said he'd take care of it. I've had to call him before. He's always handled it."

"You called him *sergeant*."

"He's not just Larry's brother, he's his commanding officer."

"He's in the military?" I asked.

"No," she said, shaking her head. "Larry's a cop."

17

I was unable to sleep that night.

All I could think about was Jordan Moore.

I saw her when I closed my eyes. I saw her when I opened them.

Was she okay? How could she be with such a shallow bully loser? Why did he have to be a cop? Why did she have to be so beautiful, so vulnerable, be in such an unbelievably bad situation?

Where was she right now? Locked in the bathroom, Larry beating down the door? Lying uneasily in the bed beside him? Unconscious? Drugged? In the hospital? Dead?

I had no way of contacting her. Didn't know her phone number, address, anything. Nothing I could really do even if I did.

I felt powerless and pathetic, a kid come to the city to uncover a killer and I couldn't even help a helpless woman in danger.

I was so damn helpless myself.

I laid down and tried to sleep but it was futile.

The phone rang a few minutes later.

I answered it in the dark, grabbing the receiver so hurriedly I dropped it, hoping it was Jordan, knowing it couldn't be.

"John?"

It was Anna.

"Hey."

"Did I wake you? I figured you'd be up."

"I am. I was. You didn't wake me."

"Are you okay?"

"Why?"

"You sound . . . I don't know. Is something wrong?"

"I'm okay. How are you? How is Chris?"

"I looked for you after graduation, but . . . I can't believe you moved to Atlanta before I could say goodbye. You Jordans don't mess around gettin' out of town, do you?"

I didn't say anything.

"Speaking of," she said, "you heard anything from Nancy?"

"Not a word."

"She probably doesn't know how to contact you."

"Probably, but she never called when she did, so . . ."

"Guess that's true."

"How'd you find me?"

"I got your number from your mom."

In the darkness of my smallish room there was only the sound of the oscillating fan and Anna's voice.

"Are you mad at me?" she asked. "Did I do something?"

"What would you have done?"

"Nothing to my knowledge."

"I better go," I said. "Thanks for calling."

She sighed.

"You haven't told me how you like Atlanta, how everything's goin', nothin'."

"We'll catch up soon," I said.

"I'm worried about you, John."

"Don't be. Really."

"Can't help it. Feel worse now than before I called."

"Good night, Anna."

"I . . . I love you, John."

After a few hours of tossing and turning, worrying and thinking the worst, I pushed my weary body out of the bed and stumbled down the stairs to the kitchen.

To my surprise, I found Aaron Iris sitting at the rickety old table eating Cap'n Crunch and reading our theology textbook, a tiny trail of milk on the table between the bowl and his mouth.

"John the Revelator," he said.

He was a pudgy, pale-faced freshman with large glasses and strawberry-blond hair, good natured if a bit grating.

"How's it goin' Aaron?"

"I'm too excited to sleep too," he said.

"About?"

"Being here. Being a part of such an amazing movement, learning Kingdom Theology, preparing to take this fresh revelation to the world."

"Oh that," I said.

"Whatta you plan to do?" he said.

"Huh?"

"In ministry. With your life. Where are you called? What are you called to do?"

I shrugged. "No idea."

"Really? I want to be on staff here one day."

"You and every other student in the school."

"You don't?"

I shook my head.

"But there's no other place like this in the whole world, no other man of God like the bishop."

I didn't say anything.

"What?"

"I didn't say anything."

"What're you thinkin'?"

"Something special is happening here," I said. "Truly. And so much of what Bishop Paulk is preaching is—"

"You don't agree with all of it?" he said. "How can you not agree with all of it? What do you have a problem with?"

"I'm just . . . Be careful, man. That's all I'm sayin'. Just be careful not to get so caught up you make idols out of places and people."

"Okay, sure, but I want to know what you disagree with."

"I agree with far more than I disagree with," I said. "I can't tell you how much I appreciate the message of compassion and social justice, community and responsibility."

"But?"

"The message and structure is too authoritarian, too para-military in a way," I said. "And too dogmatic. As much as Bishop Paulk is destroying dogmas from previous traditions, he's creating new ones. Maybe all men and movements do it. But it's dangerous."

He shook his head. "Why're you here?"

"What?"

"If you think all that. Why are you here?"

"I guess because the brochure didn't mention there wasn't room for dissent and disagreement."

When I arrived at Safe Haven the next morning, the same security guard met me at the gate with the same demeanor and disposition.

"Deja vu," I said.

"Huh?" he said, blinking behind his glasses.

"We did this same thing a few days ago."

"Did we?" he asked.

"Really?"

"You need to move your car and—"

"It's okay, Ralph," Jordan said, walking up. "He's expected."

Jordan had stopped some ten feet or so back from the gate and I rushed over to where she was standing.

"Thanks for expecting me."

"Sorry about last night," she said.

She was as radiant as the morning, her simple, unvarnished beauty gently resting on her like a light dew upon the earth. But she appeared to be weary and a bit frazzled too.

"You don't have anything to apologize for."

We starting walking back up toward the building.

Kids were already playing on the playground, their sleepy faces fresh, their drowsy movements measured, less energetic and enthusiastic as they had been when I had seen them before.

"I don't want to cause you any more trouble than you already have," I said, "but I had to make sure you were okay."

"I'm okay. I'm embarrassed, drained, a little sore, and—"

"Did he—"

"Just some shoving and shaking," she said.

"Shoving and shaking is not—"

"Can we not talk about it right now?" she said. "I'm just so happy to see you. Makes everything better. I knew . . . I knew you were the kind . . . I knew you would check on me. I knew I was right about you."

"You were right," I said. "I'm a decent human being."

"You're so much more than that. I can tell."

Our eyes locked.

"Be careful," she said, "or you'll restore my hope in the human race."

"Whoever killed LaMarcus Williams took him right here from his backyard with his mom close by," Bobby Battle said. "Wayne Williams never did anything like that. He preyed on street kids who thought *they* were hustlin' *him*."

We were standing behind the daycare center in what was once LaMarcus Williams's backyard.

It was later that afternoon, hot, humid, the sun beating down on us, the rumble of thunder rolling in the far distance.

Bobby Battle, the lead detective in the open unsolved, was walking me through the case, explaining why LaMarcus didn't make the list.

He was roughly the same age and size of Frank Morgan, but that's where the similarities ended. Where Frank wore comfortable, sensible shoes, Sears slacks, a simple cotton button down, and an out-of-date tie, Bobby was stylish and slick, expensively and smartly dressed, more a *Miami Vice* cop than an actual working detective.

"Even still, first thing I did after Williams was arrested was looked at him hard for this," he said. "And I'm not saying he didn't do it. I'm just saying it doesn't fit his pattern."

"You could't rule him out completely?" I asked.

He shook his head. "He had no alibi and check this out––he did come very close to here that same day."

"What?" I asked, my voice rising, pulse quickening.

"Says he was downtown at the Omni passing out flyers for his band."

"He was. I saw him."

"Huh?"

I told him.

"Wow. So there you go, we know where he was earlier in the day. Said when he got asked to leave there he headed down this way."

Did what I had done cause LaMarcus to lose his life?

"Says he came to pick up a piece of recording equipment from a musician who lived about a mile from here."

"Where?"

"Down off Waldrop," he said. "Not far from here."

I experienced a flutter and feeling of excitement and connection, a new feeling then, but one that would happen more and more often over the years, in ah-ha moments, in moments when the blurry Polaroid that was my mind would finish developing and come into focus, moments when a few individual puzzle pieces would be laid in place, finally revealing the whole.

"Where Curtis Walker was found three months later," I said.

"Fuck me. That's right. It was the other end but Williams

could've picked out the spot when he crossed over the bridge, filed it away for later."

I nodded.

"Goddamn," he said. "That could really be somethin'."

"Question is, did he come over this way before or after that and kill LaMarcus?"

"I just don't think so. According to the mom, she and her daughter, adopted white girl named––has your last name––Jordan, were keeping an eye on the boy while cooking a meal and wrapping Christmas presents. Swears one of 'em had an eye on him every second, but even if that's not true, it was a daring abduction."

I nodded.

It was nap time at Safe Haven. All was quiet, still, peaceful.

The area around the yard was wooded on all three sides.

"Back behind here there's a subdivision," Battle said, pointing with his radio to the trees and undergrowth lining the back of the property. "But when LaMarcus was taken they had just begun the development. Roads and sidewalks were in, a couple of houses under construction, but nobody lived back there."

"So if not Williams, a worker on one of the crews sees LaMarcus at some point," I said. "Starts fixating, fantasizing, planning, watches him from the woods, then snatches him."

"That was one theory. We checked everybody out, assuming we actually found everybody, and came up with two suspects––drywall guy named Vincent Storr and painter named Raymond J. Pelton."

"And?"

"Both alibied out. Never even found enough to bring 'em in."

"Other suspects?"

"Looked pretty hard at the dad," he said. "Well, the kid's sperm donor. That's about all he ever did for the kid. Anthony Alex Williams, Jr. Sold and installed car stereos. Was mostly a front for dealing. A lady friend said he was givin' her little

Anthony all afternoon. Always thought she was lying but never could get her to blink."

"Anyone else?"

"Neighborhood kid. Carlton Fields. Older kid. Not quite right. Not full retarded but . . . Played with the younger kids, including LaMarcus. Parents wouldn't really let us at him and I didn't have any reason to force them to, but . . . I don't know. Always thought there was somethin' there."

"You kept track of 'em over the years?"

"The suspects? Not really. Wish I had time. This ain't the only open unsolved I got, and I got more current cases than I can work effectively."

"I really appreciate you takin' the time to go over it with me."

"No problem. Frank says you're good people. You come up with anything, you bring it to me."

"I will."

"Promise?"

"Promise."

"Then let's take a look at what's really interesting about this case."

18

"So," Bobby said, "LaMarcus is playing in his backyard. His mom and sister are watching from the windows. The child murders are high profile by now, so everybody's keepin' an eye on their kids––'specially somebody like Ida Williams, who's part of STOP, right?"

I nodded.

"He's right here where we are," he said. "Fifteen feet from the window. That puts him some twenty feet or more from the wooded border on each side. And then poof . . . he's gone. Vanished into thin air."

I looked around the yard. It was still exactly as he was describing.

When I looked at the windows in the back of the house, Ida and Jordan were standing there watching us.

I gave a small wave and frowned apologetically.

They both smiled and waved.

I walked over to the window and Ida opened it.

"I'm sorry about this," I said.

"For trying to find out what happened to my boy?" she said. "Don't be."

"For stirring it up."

"It stays stirred up," Jordan said. "Always. Every single second of every single day."

"We appreciate what you're doing," Ida said.

"How long before the kids go out front to play?" I asked.

"Just a few minutes. Why?"

"Can y'all have someone watch them for a few minutes and help us with something?"

"Sure."

I turned around and took a few steps back toward Bobby.

"Do you mind if we try something?" I asked.

He looked at his watch.

"It will only take a minute."

"Sure." He nodded.

Five minutes later, I was inside the empty daycare center with Ida and Jordan.

The interior walls had been removed when the house was converted into a daycare, but Jordan was seated in approximately the same spot she had been when she was a teenager helping her mother wrap her little brother's Christmas presents. Ida was standing where she had stood.

The windows they were looking out of were exactly the same as they had been on the day LaMarcus disappeared.

Out in the yard, about fifteen feet from the window, a boy about LaMarcus's size was standing, waiting.

Both women had assured me that they were okay with this and they had chosen the best, bravest boy to stand in for LaMarcus. I was still concerned, but my need to know, to see, to get answers was overriding everything else.

"If at any time you want us to stop, just tell me," I said.

"Okay, but we're fine," Ida said. "I promise."

"Okay," I said. "Now, when I say go, Ida, I want you to walk from what was the dining room to the kitchen without looking at––without looking through the windows. Jordan, I want you to look down like you're wrapping a present. Don't look up until your mom says *now*. Ida, when you reach what was the kitchen window, I want you to pause just a moment then look up and yell *now*. Okay?"

They both nodded.

I leaned out the window and yelled, "EVERYBODY READY .. . AND . . . GO."

As soon as I yelled *go*, both women did as instructed.

From the wooded area on the right, Bobby Battle ran as fast as he could toward the little LaMarcus stand-in. When he reached him he grabbed him, hoisting him over his shoulder, and began running back to the woods.

He had only taken a few steps when Ida yelled, "NOW."

Jordan looked up. So did Ida. And Bobby with the boy dangling over his shoulder stopped in place.

"Thank you," I said.

Jordan broke down and began to sob.

I walked over to her as Bobby put down our little helper and escorted him to the playground in the front.

"I'm sorry," I said.

"No," Jordan said. "Are you kidding? It's the best thing ever. I always thought if I had just not looked down, not even for a second, LaMarcus would't've been taken."

Back outside with Bobby.

"No way somebody could run in, snatch him, and get out again before being seen," he said.

"Unless——" I began.

"There is no unless."

"Unless both women were distracted by something at the same time that lasted longer than they realize."

"Think of the split-second timing that'd have to be involved. The chances are slim to none. But add in the killer knowing they were distracted or just happening to do it at that moment . . . It's impossible."

"Unless," I said.

"I'm telling you there is no unless," he said. "Unless what?"

"The killer created the distraction."

He started to say something but stopped. After a moment he smiled. "Suppose it's possible."

"There are probably far more, but I can think of two other possibilities so far," I said.

"Yeah?"

"LaMarcus was playing closer to the woods than they realized," I said. "Both of those scenarios just mean the eyewitnesses only have to be a little off about a relatively small point."

He shook his head. "Never known an eyewitness to get anything wrong."

I laughed.

"And the other possibility?" Bobby asked.

"The killer came up along the house under the windows where Ida and Jordan couldn't see him and took LaMarcus back that same way. LaMarcus could've been even closer to the house than they realized."

"But he would've seen him approaching," Bobby said. "Why didn't he scream? Say something?"

"Because it was somebody he knew and trusted."

"Like the dad," he said.

"Or the friend," I said. "Maybe like the boy we just borrowed to re-create it, he thought it was a game."

19

"Williams always dumped his victims' bodies far from where he picked 'em up," Bobby was saying.

We had walked through the wooded area on the back side of Ida's property and were now on the paved road of Flat Shoals Estates, the subdivision behind it, slanting down a hill to an empty cul-de-sac and another wooded area beyond.

Unlike the flat sand and dark dirt Florida terrain I was accustomed to, Georgia was all red slopes and orange slants of clay hills.

"Now just remember," Bobby said, "none of these houses were here."

Each structure was built at the end of an unnecessary curved driveway on an incline rising from the road. Three slight variations and sizes of the same brick front, vinyl siding surround, cookie-cutter version of mid-level starter homes.

"Be easy to go to the wrong home in a subdivision like this," I said.

"Happens a lot," he said. "We get calls all the time from people complaining about belligerent drunks breaking into their houses."

We reached the end of the street, stepped across the cement sidewalk and through a small wooded area in the midst of which was an enormous concrete drain pipe.

"This is where the body was found," he said. "Lying here inside this culvert like he was just taking a nap. Couldn't tell anything was wrong until we rolled him over and could see the small nylon rope around his neck."

"Still had his clothes on? Had he been messed with sexually?"

"All his clothes were on but his pants and underwear were down some and sort of wadded up. Like someone had pulled them down and then didn't get 'em back up just right."

"Had he been molested?" I asked. "Raped?"

He nodded.

"How long after he went missing was it before he was found?" I asked.

"Less than three hours."

"Who found him?"

"The partial retarded kid I told you about. Carlton Fields. Claims he was kicking a soccer ball in the cul-de-sac and it rolled in here. Came in after it and saw LaMarcus. Couldn't wake him up. Went and told his parents."

"I see why you suspected him," I said.

"Do far more after today," he said.

We stood there taking it all in for a moment, neither of us saying anything.

"See what I mean about this not fitting Williams's pattern? Body dumped so close to where he was snatched. And there are other, even more compelling reasons for it not being Williams."

"You said body being dumped—he wasn't killed here?"

He smiled. "You're pretty sharp for somebody studying for the priesthood."

I wasn't sure if he was kidding or didn't know I wasn't, but decided he probably didn't care and it certainly didn't matter.

"Wanted to show you this first," he said. "'Cause it's the order we saw it in. Now I'll show you were he was killed."

"He was killed here," Bobby said.

We were back behind the daycare, in the wooded border on the right side of the property where he had run from when he came out to reenact the snatching of LaMarcus.

"So he was killed right after he was taken, not far from the spot where he was taken," I said. "Somethin' Williams never did that we know of."

"There was a small clearing inside here where he used to play," he said. "Sort of like a fort or hideout. Wasn't much. Just a little patch of clay where he'd play with Tonka trucks and matchbox cars surrounded by the bushes. Only a few feet wide."

"And Carlton?" I said. "Did he know about it? Play in it with him?"

"Probably. Never confirmed that. Did I let a kid get away with murder?"

"So why'd the killer move the body after he killed him here?" I said. "Why not just leave him here?"

"Why'd he *come back* and move him?" Bobby said. "The body laid here for a while before it was moved to the drainage ditch. So either the killer stayed here with him or left him and came back and moved him."

"You're right," I said. "Not much about this argues for it being part of the other pattern killings."

"And I haven't even gotten to the biggest reason we ruled Williams out," he said.

"Which is?"

"Remember I said we found a rope around his neck? There were some other marks too, indicating he was strangled, but . . . all of them happened post-mortem. Like the killer was trying to make it look like the others."

"So how'd he die?"

"What did I tell you it looked like he was doing when we found him in the drain pipe?"

"Sleeping."

"Cause of death was listed as undetermined for a long time," he said. "Wasn't until toxicology came back that we knew. He was put to sleep. The killer gave him something. He fell asleep. And never woke up."

20

"Should my boy have been on the list?" Ida asked.

I shook my head. "I honestly don't think so."

Tears crested her eyes and trickled down her cheeks.

We were alone in the daycare center, seated in two rocking chairs on the reading rug, Jordan and the other teachers outside watching the children play in the late-afternoon sun-dappled yard.

"Serial killers create a series, follow a particular pattern," I said. "Ritual killers observe certain rituals. If they deviate, it's out of necessity not choice."

She nodded, wiping her cheeks and eyes.

"It's possible Wayne Williams killed LaMarcus," I said. "It looks like he was in the area that day, but I don't think he did. I really don't. I think whether Wayne Williams is innocent or guilty of the pattern cases on and off the list is irrelevant to what happened to LaMarcus. Someone else killed LaMarcus, someone still out there."

Her frown and the shake of her head seemed to communicate resignation more than anything else.

"Are you . . ." I began. "Were you hoping . . . for . . ."

"Always thought if I could get 'im on the list or convince people he suppose to be . . . I might find out one day what really happened. Nobody gonna do anything now . . . not if he not one of the . . . not part of the . . ."

"I don't think anybody's investigating any of the killings," I said. "On or off the list."

"You are."

I nodded. "I am."

"But if my son wasn't killed by the Atlanta Child Murderer, doesn't that mean you not gonna investigate what happened to him?"

"Just the opposite," I said.

She looked confused.

"If you'll let me and you're willin' to help me," I said, "I'd like to just focus on finding out what happened to LaMarcus."

"*Let* you?" she said, her face brightening. "*Willin'*? Boy, don't be silly. I'd be mighty . . . Thank you. Jesus. Thank you."

"Chances are I won't be able to turn up anything the police haven't," I said. "I don't have the access, expertise, or resources they do. All I can do is look at it with new eyes. Bring a fresh perspective. I can focus on it in a way they can't--or couldn't. Not that they're doing anything on it at the moment. That's why I'm letting go of Wayne Williams and the other cases for now. LaMarcus will get all of everything I have to give. And I won't stop. Not until I find the killer or die before I do."

"Thank you," Jordan said. "I can't tell you what it means to us."

"You're welcome," I said.

By the time I had reached my car she had caught up with me.

"I hope I can help bring some closure," I said. "Seems to me you could really use something good in your life."

She looked down but I caught sight of a smile twitching at the corners of her mouth.

"What is it?" I asked.

She shook her head.

"Tell me."

"Was just a random thought."

"I want to hear it."

"I . . . I just had the thought that *you're* the something good that's come into my life. You are, aren't you?"

"If I'm not," I said with a smile, "I'll do until something good comes along."

"Are you as good as you seem?" she asked.

I thought about it for a moment. "I am what I seem. I'm not attempting to seem something other than what I am, but we're all better and worse than what we appear to be."

"I guess we are," she said.

We were centered between two sounds. On the one side, the ruckus, rowdy, joyful noises of children playing filled my left ear and her right. On the other, the whoosh and whir of traffic zipping by in both directions on Flat Shoals Road.

"Larry's not as bad as he seems," she said. "I know most people only see one side of him, but there's another, better . . ."

I didn't respond.

She looked down again, this time without the sweet smile.

"I meant that most of us are capable of more and less selfishness than we seem," I said, "that we can be more altruistic and assholey depending. Bullying, abuse, addiction, mental illness, sociopathic behavior all fall far outside of that."

"Assholey?" she said with a smile.

"I study a lot of psychology."

21

That night, after basketball and fish sticks with Martin, a little reading in a homicide investigation techniques text-book Frank Morgan had let me borrow, and catching up on a couple of chapters in my theology book, I took LaDonna Paulk out on a date.

The daughter of Don and Clariece, LaDonna was a central part of the family-run church, singing on Sundays and taking some classes with the rest of us during the week at EPI. Considered Chapel Hill royalty, she was a beautiful dark-eyed girl of nineteen or twenty with short black hair and a stable, settled maturity about her I found refreshing.

I wasn't taking her out in an attempt to get my mind off the unavailable Jordan Moore, but I could think of worse unintended consequences.

Told by the rest of the guys in the dorm that I had to take her somewhere nice, I got a recommendation from Randy Renfroe, the college's director of student affairs and the person who seemed to know more about Atlanta than anyone I had encountered, scrounged up all the money I could find, and took her to a place downtown I couldn't afford.

After she ordered, I ordered a salad and water, lying about my stomach bothering me, but could tell she wasn't buying it.

We talked for a while about Atlanta and the college and my transition, before our conversation turned to the church and religion.

"I really appreciate your approach," I said.

"My *approach*?"

"Fully committed but levelheaded," I said. "Like your dad. There's so much hysteria and bishop worship."

She smiled. "Guess it's inevitable."

I shrugged.

"You don't think so?"

"You're right. A certain amount is, but . . ."

"But what?"

"Probably shouldn't be saying this to the bishop's niece, but . . ."

"You can say anything," she said.

And I felt like I could. She was easy to talk to and, like so many people in her family and in the church, open and nonjudgmental.

"It's not exactly discouraged," I said.

She nodded.

Our food came and she immediately halved hers and insisted on sharing it with me.

"Thank you," I said.

"We didn't have to come here," she said.

"You kiddin'? I love this place."

"Close your eyes," she said.

I did.

"What's the name of the restaurant?"

Unable to come up with it I began to laugh.

After we finished our overpriced meal and were leaving, I realized how close we were to the hospital.

"Would you mind . . ." I began. "I hate to ask, but . . ."

"What?" she said. "Just say it. But just know I'm not puttin' out on the first date after only half a meal."

I laughed a long time at that, nodding appreciatively at her, catching the mischievous glint in her eye.

"Would you mind if we ran by Grady for a few minutes? Sorry, but there's someone I really need to see and I'm not sure if––"

"Of course," she said. "It's fine."

"You sure?"

"Positive."

While she graciously waited in the lobby, I went up to see Roger Lawson, a vibrant, young, talented filmmaker––at least that was what he used to be. Now he was a gaunt, weak, weary man, unable to lift his limbs without pain.

When I walked into his room, I was struck, as I always was, by the smell. It was the smell of decay, of defecation and disinfectant, of death and the process of dying.

Roger was dying of a new disease, a disease seemingly so selective it was only targeting gay men. I had been warned. I was taking my life in my hands. There was uncertainty as to how the death sentence was passed from person to person, and for all that was known I could be getting it right now just by breathing the same air as Roger.

As was often the case, he was asleep when I came into the room.

I stood there quietly for a while, a silent witness to his suffering.

He had been abandoned by his family and friends. His boyfriend and one of their best friends had already died from the same disease earlier in the year.

"John," he whispered.

"Hey," I said, stepping closer and taking his hand.

I resisted the impulse to ask how he was feeling or doing or to make smalltalk of any kind. I was here to listen, to be near, to be present.

"A . . . preacher came by . . . today," he said. "Think . . . it was . . . today."

His voice was weak and airy, and came out in small, halted, breathy bursts.

"Baptist or Pentecostal . . . I . . . think. Should've seen . . . him. Put . . . on . . . a . . . hazmat suit to come . . . in and tell . . . me . . . I was an abomination . . . and going . . . to hell."

I shook my head. "I'm so sorry. Wonder why they let him in?"

"Some of the doctors . . . and . . . nurses agree with . . . him."

"Guess religious assholes don't have a corner on the market on stupid."

His smile looked more like a grimace but his eyes showed the intent of the expression.

"You . . . really don't think I'm . . . going to hell?" he asked. "Sorry I ask you every time."

"If God's love is conditional, if she loves you less than I do and capriciously and vindictively flings people into hell, would you even want to go to heaven?"

"I . . . don't want . . . to go to . . . hell."

I realized how theoretical and unhelpful my question had been. There was nothing comforting or reassuring about it. It was too abstract, too academic, and I felt bad, felt as if I was failing him.

"You won't."

I genuinely and sincerely believed he wouldn't. But that's all it was—belief. It occurred to me that the preacher telling him he was going to hell and me telling him he wasn't weren't nearly as different as we seemed. We were men of conviction, of faith, of belief, and I found it deeply disturbing that we differed not in kind but type.

"I'm so scared," he said.

"I know. I'm sorry."

"I want my mama to love me again."

And more than anything in the world at that moment that's what I wanted too.

"I appreciate your approach," LaDonna said when we were back in the car, flying down I-20 toward Decatur.

I laughed. "Am I being mocked?"

"Only a little. Just in the *way* I said it."

I shook my head.

"I mean it though," she said.

"Okay," I said.

"No, I really do. I mean you're too earnest, too serious, and I think you hold yourself to a standard that's too . . ."

I laughed. "The whole *appreciating my approach* thing is not coming through."

"'Cause I haven't gotten to that part yet."

"If you'll recall, that was the *only* part when I said it to *you*."

"You're so . . . real," she said, ignoring me. "And . . . sincere. So compassionate . . . you seem so passionate about God, but you're one of the least religious people I've ever met. You're a . . . I was gonna say contradiction . . . but I'm not sure you are. It's just . . . you seem equally passionate about finding LaMarcus Williams's killer as you do ministering to Roger Lawson."

She's right, I thought. I am.

"Thank you," I said around the lump in my throat. "That's very . . . Thank you."

"You just might be really and truly unique, John Jordan," she said. "And how many people can you say that about."

"He who would be a man must be a nonconformist," I said.

"Or woman," she said.

"He who would be a woman is undoubtedly a nonconformist," I said.

22

When I pulled up in front of my apartment in Trade Winds, Jordan Moore was waiting for me.

"Is everything okay?" I asked.

"Yeah. I just wanted to talk to you some more."

"What about Larry?" I said. "Is it okay for you to be here?"

"He's at work. Or with one of his women. And Trade Winds is the last place in the world he'd look for me."

"Home sweet home," I said, looking around.

"You look nice," she said. "Were you on a date? Do you have a girlfriend?"

I shook my head. "No girlfriend. Just a . . . casual date."

"With who?"

I told her.

"I know I have no right to be," she said, "but I'm jealous."

Touched by what she said, disarmed by her honesty and openness, moved by her vulnerability, I took her in my arms and hugged her for a very long time.

"Wow," she said. "Didn't realize just how much I needed to be . . . I can't remember the last time I was hugged. And don't think I've ever been hugged like that."

As she spoke, I realized how much I needed it too, how much touch, warmth, contact, connection was missing from my life.

I was far from home, in a city not my own, surrounded by strangers and acquaintances.

I tried to remember the last time I had been hugged. Not the sideways, chest bump, double back tap of bros or the lean back, breast-avoiding, quick motherly kind in church, but a real, tight, intimate embrace where something like love and humanity passes between the huggers.

The last hug like that I had received and given was with Anna and it had been months before.

"Can we go somewhere and talk?" she asked.

"How about those swings over there," I said, nodding over between the tattered tennis courts and the basketball court Martin and I played on.

"Is it safe?"

"I seriously doubt it," I said.

"Okay."

We walked across the parking lot, up the small slope, through the damp grass, and sat in swings like I hadn't been in since childhood.

Facing each other, we both instinctively reached up and wrapped our hands around the chains.

"This is nice," she said.

"Luxury apartments come with a lot of perks," I said.

For a long moment we just moved back and forth a bit, enjoying the night, sounds of the unseen city all around us receding even further into the distance.

"It's not my fault he was taken, is it?" she said.

"No, it's not," I said. "And wouldn't've been even if you had been looking down and there was time for someone to run in and grab him."

"I could never figure what I had done wrong but I've lived with such . . . with so much guilt."

"It wasn't your fault."

She nodded. "Thanks to you, I know that now."

"Did anything out of the ordinary happen?" I asked. "Were you two pulled away to do anything for any length of time? Any emergencies? Anyone come to the door? Anything?"

She shook her head. "We never looked away for more than a few seconds at a time. And between the two of us maybe we didn't even do that. Mom got a phone call. I spilled my drink. We each went to the bathroom at different times, but when one of us wasn't looking––for whatever reason––the other one was. When Mom went to the bathroom I actually stopped wrapping, got up from the table, walked over to the window, and watched him from there the entire time. Even opened the window and talked to him through it."

I thought about it.

"We knew what was going on. It was in the newspapers every day, on the TV every night. That's the unbelievable part about it. I watched with all my might, really took it seriously, but no one watched him like Mom. No mother ever watched her son any closer than she did. No one. So whatever happened had to have happened when I was watching. Not her. It can't be her. Has to be me. I did something. Missed something. Have forgotten something."

"I don't think you did," I said.

She didn't respond and we were quiet a while.

"Was LaMarcus's dad involved with him? Did he ever come around?"

Her eyes narrowed. "I can only remember seeing him a couple of times. Stands out because it always involved conflict. You think he––"

"Just considering all possibilities."

"You'll have to ask Mom about him. I can't really remember much of anything about him."

I nodded.

"Tell me about LaMarcus's little fort in the bushes."

"I didn't even know it existed until he . . . until after he . . . I didn't realize it at the time, but I can see now that I was too wrapped up in my own little world. There was a lot I didn't know about LaMarcus, a lot I didn't appreciate. I was too much of a typical self-centered teenager. Something else I've felt guilty for since . . . all this time."

"Ida told me you were very good to him, like a second mom. Nothing about what she said sounded like a typical teenager."

"You're so . . ." she began. "Thank you. You're . . . you always respond with kindness. It's very rare."

"It's not all that rare," I said. "I think the company you've been keeping has caused you to forget that."

She nodded. "That's probably true."

"Can I ask you something? Can you tell me why you're with someone like Larry?"

"I . . . I'm not sure I can answer that. I'm not sure I know fully. I know it's not just one reason. Maybe this hasn't happened to you, maybe it never will, but there are times . . . Sometimes in life you wind up in a position, a place, a prison cell and you honestly have no idea how you got into it and you have no idea how to get out of it."

"Could it be . . . Is it possible . . ."

"What?" she said. "Just say it. It's okay. Just be honest."

"The way he treats you . . . the bullying, the abuse, the other women . . . You've mentioned how guilty you feel, how you blamed yourself for LaMarcus getting taken, for . . . for not knowing where his hideout was, for being what you called self-centered . . ."

"Yeah?"

"Is it possible you're punishing yourself?"

She started to say something but instead burst into tears.

She cried for a while.

I waited.

Eventually, she nodded. "I've never thought of it that way. No one's ever . . . I've just always thought I deserved any bad thing that happens. He hit me when I was pregnant the first time. I lost the baby. The second time . . . nothing he did to me ended the pregnancy, but he did enough so when the baby was born she had a lot of health issues. She was sickly all of her short life and then she died and I . . . I thought . . . you let your brother get snatched by a serial killer. No way God's gonna let you have a baby. No way. This is your fault. You did this. You deserve this. When I found out I couldn't have kids again . . . I thought . . . you deserve that too."

"But you didn't," I said. "You don't deserve bad things. You aren't being punished. You're not . . . You're punishing yourself."

"I've never seen it before, but you're . . . You wanna hear somethin' truly twisted? Part of the reason I've stayed with . . . Larry . . . part of what I kept thinkin' was . . . he lost a child too. I kept thinkin' we're the only two people on the planet who lost that child. We share somethin' no one else in the world does. And I can't really blame him when I'm the reason it happened. I'm the one being punished."

"What was her name?" I asked.

"Savannah," she said. "My little Savannah Grace. Thanks for asking."

"Yon," Martin said. "Yon."

He was crossing the parking lot in pajamas and socks, waving his small hand.

Jordan wiped her eyes.

"I can go over there to meet him if you need—"

She shook her head. "It's fine. I'm fine. Thank you. You've helped me more in the short time I've known you than anyone has in six years."

"'Ey Yon," he said when he reached us. "'Ut 'oo 'oin'."

"Just talking to my friend. This is Jordan Moore. Jordan, this is Martin Fisher."

She extended her hand and they shook and spoke.

"It's nice to meet you, Martin Fisher," she said.

"What're you doin' up?" I asked.

"Where's your mom?" Jordan asked. "Why are you up so late?"

Martin looked confused, then looked at me and told me he was hungry.

"You're in luck," I said. "I've got the best dinner rolls I've ever had, from the most expensive restaurant I've ever eaten at, right over there in my car."

He looked almost as confused as before.

"Come on," I said.

We walked over to my car and I offered each of them a roll.

"Half one with me," Jordan said.

I did.

And we stood there in silence beside the car, each eating our rolls, each seeming to enjoy them equally.

"These *are* good," Jordan said. "Where'd they come from?"

I laughed. "I have no idea."

23

"You heard from your dad?" Frank Morgan asked.

I shook my head.

"Sorry to hear that."

I nodded.

"You plan on going home anytime soon?"

I shook my head again. "Between school and work and this . . . I can't right now."

The *this* was the LaMarcus Williams case. We were at GBI headquarters to talk to the medical examiner who had worked on the case.

"You can go in now," the secretary said, smiling in a way that made me think she might find Frank attractive. Then again, she might just be a pleasant person.

Dr. Donald Douglas was an overweight, older grayish man with an overgrown gray mustache, large glasses, and a gray toupee that didn't move when the skin around and beneath it did.

"Thanks for doin' this, Don," Frank said.

"Not a problem. Not a problem at all."

"This is John Jordan, the young man I was tellin' you about."

We shook hands and all took a seat in the small, function-over-form office of hard, cold metal surfaces and wood veneer and leatherette furniture.

"This for some kind of school report or somethin'?" Douglas asked me.

Frank nodded. "It is. This young man has a bright future in law enforcement and I'm trying to encourage him, give him all the help I can get, expose him to experts such as yourself."

I smiled and nodded, trying to disguise my surprise.

"And you wanted to talk about the LaMarcus Williams case?"

"Yes, sir."

He opened a file folder on his desk and began to glance through it, his small hazel eyes blinking behind his big, thick glasses.

"All right. Very well. Fire away."

"Okay," I said. "Can we start with what actually killed him?"

"We can––and it wasn't the little rope around his neck or any of the external marks on his body. We found high levels of chloral hydrate in his system."

"Of what?"

"Chloral hydrate. It's an organic compound, a colorless solid soluble in water. It's a sedative and hypnotic that's been used as a sleep-aid for people suffering from insomnia, but it's now mainly used as an adjunct to anesthesia to help sedate people, especially children, undergoing medical and dental procedures."

So that's how he was put to sleep.

"I'm not sure how much detail you want me to go into, but . . . it's derived from chloral by the addition of one equivalent of water and was discovered through the chlorination of ethanol by Justus von Liebig in 1832. Its sedative properties weren't published until 1869. Soon its use was widespread––even recreationally."

I nodded, encouraging him to continue.

"You've heard of a Mickey, right? A Mickey Finn. It's a solution of chloral hydrate in alcohol. They call 'em knockout drops. It's potent stuff. Truth is, we don't even completely understand how it works. It's believed that a chemical produced by chloral hydrate called trichloroethanol causes a mild depressive effect on the brain. But like I said, we don't know. It's been used in date rape and both accidental and intentional death."

Since I was supposed to be a student working on a school project, I wished I had a composition book to take notes in.

"You remember Jonestown? Their Kool-Aid had chloral hydrate in it. It was in Marilyn Monroe's system at her death. It was given to Mary Todd Lincoln for her sleep problems. Nietzsche used it for years. Some say it contributed to his nervous breakdown and insanity."

Hearing the name Marilyn Monroe brought a deep, dull ache I had to the surface and transformed it into a sharp pain, making me realize just how much I missed Merrill. And not just Merrill, but his mom. And not just them but home and family and friends and familiarity and, of course and always, Anna.

"So LaMarcus was given an overdose of chloral hydrate and . . ."

He nodded. "It put him to sleep and he never woke up."

I wondered if the killer meant to use chloral hydrate to knock LaMarcus out so he could transport him easily, and accidentally gave him too much, unintentionally killing him or killing him sooner than he planned.

"It wouldn't take much," Douglas was saying. "Kid that small."

"So it could've been an accidental overdose?"

He shrugged. "Sure, I guess, but——"

Frank Morgan said, "Why give it to him if not to kill him?"

"To sedate and calm him," I said. "As part of the abduction."

He nodded, appearing to think about it.

I looked back at Douglas. "Was chloral hydrate found in any of the victims of the Atlanta Child Murders?"

"I . . . I don't know the answer to that. I don't think so, but I'm just not sure. I didn't work those."

"I'll double check," Frank said, "but I don't think so either."

"Does use of chloral hydrate indicate someone with some kind of medical background?"

He shrugged and shook his head. "No, not necessarily. It could, but just as likely not. It wouldn't be required."

"Where would the killer have gotten it?"

"Lots of possibilities, but most likely in a hospital or pharmacy."

"Which would point to a medical professional or someone with access to those places, right?"

"Maybe, but it could've just as easily have been someone with a prescription or someone who stole it from someone with a prescription."

"What kind of prescription? What would it have been prescribed for?"

"Maybe anxiety or nervousness. God knows there was enough of that going around at the time. But more than likely a sleep aid for the treatment of insomnia."

"Was he raped?" I asked.

Douglas looked at Frank. Frank nodded.

"There was trauma consistent with aggressive, violent penetration," Douglas said to me, "but the evidence indicates the assailant wore a condom. There were traces of latex and liquid lubricant but no seminal fluid was recovered in, on, or around the body. And . . . based on the fact that the skin was abraded but not bruised—there was no bruising—what was done . . . to the victim . . . occurred after death."

"A school project?" I asked.

Frank and I were standing outside GBI headquarters near his car, a boxy blue sedan that screamed *cop*—particularly when he was in it.

He smiled. "You're young and unofficial. And you look even younger than you are. He probably thought it was a junior high school project."

"So what'd you think about what he said?" I asked.

"Interesting. What you said about the killer intending to use the drug to incapacitate him for transport makes sense. Especially snatching him from his backyard."

"You'll check to see if any of the victims on the list––or off of it––were given chloral hydrate?"

He nodded.

"Were any of them raped after they were killed?"

He shook his head. "No. But I'll double check––especially those not on the list. You think it's still possible Wayne Williams killed LaMarcus?"

I shrugged. "If there's evidence of chloral hydrate being used or post-mortem rape among other victims, we'll have to consider the possibility that the Atlanta Child Murderer killed LaMarcus––whether it's Williams or someone else."

24

"This your first home-cooked meal since you been in Atlanta?" Ida asked.

"Why?" I said. "Am I eating it like it is?"

She and Jordan laughed.

The three of us were around the dinner table at Ida's. Before us, country-fried steak in white pepper gravy, mashed potatoes, turnip greens, and cornbread.

I was extremely hungry. It was extremely good. Evidently, I was eating energetically.

"Sorry, but it's so good my manners just flew right out the door."

"I like to see a hungry man eat," Ida said.

"And you haven't lost your manners," Jordan said. "You're just . . . sort of attacking the food."

"To answer your question, the Paulks have fed me several times."

Jordan's eyebrows arched above wide, questioning eyes and a cute, twisted mouth. "Oh have they? Any Paulk in particular?"

Ignoring her, I said to Ida, "Clariece is a very good cook too."

"Don't see how she do all she do," Ida said.

"Me either."

"Who?" Jordan said.

"Girl, what you goin' on about?" Ida asked.

Jordan smiled and winked at me.

I smiled back and mouthed, It was just one casual date.

Ida's small home was simple and unassuming, clean and uncluttered, warm and welcoming. Its walls and surfaces were filled with photographs of LaMarcus and what were obviously gifts from the children she had cared for over the years—Precious Moments porcelain figurines and other child-centered mementos. Joining them were LaMarcus's framed school certificates, field day ribbons, report cards, and art projects. Mixed in among them were pictures of Jordan, including a heartbreaking mother and child portrait of her holding the tiny Savannah Grace in her own small hands, but none of Larry—not even in those from her wedding day.

Underneath it all, there was an essential sadness, not unlike the one beneath everything else the two women were. It was as if both family and home were host to a foreign entity so deeply embedded it was now part of the structural DNA.

"You should've brought Martin," Jordan said. "Mom, John has the most adorable neighbor. He's—how old is he?"

"Twelve."

"He's twelve and they play basketball together and John feeds him and he just adores John."

"I'd say he not the only one," Ida said.

"Tell Mom what he said."

I shook my head. "I can't."

"It's the sweetest thing ever."

"You're embarrassin' him, child."

Jordan seemed more relaxed, less nervous, more happy, less hopeless than I had seen her before. Though in general she seemed to be improving in nearly every way over the past several weeks.

Larry was at work. He knew Jordan was having dinner with her mom. As far as I knew, he didn't know I was joining them.

Looking away from them a moment, I glanced around the room again, this time spotting something in the far corner I hadn't noticed before. Partially wrapped Christmas presents. I knew instantly they were what these two ladies were working on when LaMarcus went missing. A Star Wars lunchbox and Star Trek Communicators were visible, which meant beneath the bows and wrapping paper the other packages must have held a Guess Who game, a GI Joe, a Rubik's Cube, a train set, and records. Some of the very gifts I was given when I was his age.

"Some of the guys in the dorm are very religious in an old-school way," Jordan said. "And they were talkin' to Martin––that's his name, Martin Fisher––about Jesus, tellin' him about how much good Jesus did, how he fed the hungry and helped people and taught love. And they asked him if he knew Jesus and he said yes––John. Isn't that the sweetest thing you've ever heard?"

Ida reached over and patted my hand.

"He's so small, and kind of frail and vulnerable," Jordan was saying. "Reminds me of LaMarcus in so many ways."

Ida nodded but seemed unable to speak, her eyes misting, her lips twitching. Eventually, she said, "I'm glad he's got you, John. I'd love for you to bring him to dinner sometime."

No one said anything else for a few moments and we each found our way back to our food, eating for a while in silence.

I thought about what an odd pairing Ida and Jordan were. They were so different––from their appearance to life experience––but what they shared, loss and need and tragedy, bound them in ways that were far more profound than their deepest differences.

"Making any headway on what happened to my LaMarcus?" Ida asked at last.

I nodded. "Some. Yes, ma'am."

"He's got some questions I couldn't answer," Jordan said.

"If now's not a good time . . ." I began.

"Now is fine," Ida said. "There is no good time."

I nodded, but still didn't say anything for a moment.

"Can we start with LaMarcus's dad?" I said eventually.

"Anthony is an immature, self-centered drug addict," she said. "He's no killer. And he wouldn't kill his own son. No way. I couldn't believe that in a million years."

"Okay," I said. "But addicts don't think straight. And their minds are often altered. And they do more damage by accident than most people do on purpose."

"We both know a thing or two about that," Jordan said.

Ida nodded. "We do. And you might be right. But . . . I just . . . can't believe he could kill his own . . . son . . . no matter what kind of state he was in."

The quality of her voice was changing. A tightness and slight tremor at its edges let me know she found the discussion upsetting.

"How often did he come around?" I asked.

"Not a lot. It'd sort of go in cycles. He'd come by a few times kind of close to each other, then we wouldn't see him for months."

"How comfortable was LaMarcus with him?"

"Okay . . . not super."

"Would LaMarcus have gone with him?"

"Depends when and where, but he wouldn't go far."

He didn't go far, I thought.

"Did he ever take him anywhere—with or without your permission?"

"A few times. When I was sure he was clean and sober. He took him to the mall. Playground. Ball game."

Her hands were beginning to shake a bit and the look of distress on her face was incrementally intensifying but I pressed forward.

"Ever take him or try to take him without your permission or pre-approval?"

She nodded. "One time. Said I was ruining his son, making him soft and girly. Said it took a man to raise a man and he was gonna take him and raise him up right."

I nodded and thought about it.

"You ready for some dessert?" Jordan asked. "We have bread pudding and ice cream."

"It sounds great but I'm so full, I—"

"You can take some home with you," Ida said.

"Thank you."

"You're not leaving now, are you?" Jordan said.

I shook my head. "I've got a few more questions," I said. "About Carlton Fields and the little hideout LaMarcus had."

"Can we . . . Would you mind if we wait on them?" Ida said. "I'm not sure I can handle any more at the moment. Talkin' about Anthony's stirred up some stuff, and I can only talk or think about what happened to LaMarcus a little at a time."

"Grief's a strange thing," Jordan said. "Sneaks up on you. You're fine one moment and not the next. You can handle things that should make you fall apart, and be reduced to a puddle by the smallest, seemingly most insignificant things."

I nodded.

Ida had gone to bed. Jordan and I were standing next to each other at the sink, washing and drying the dishes, our bodies touching at the side, our hands grazing as we passed plates and pots and glasses.

"She's so strong," Jordan said. "Can handle anything and then . . . she reaches her limit and has to shut down for a while."

"Is it the same for you?" I asked.

She hesitated, starting to say something, stopping, sighing, starting again. "Honestly, I stay more shutdown most of the time.

I've had to. Or thought I did. To survive ... to keep ... functioning ... on some level."

I reached down, plunging into the soapy dishwater, and took her tiny hand in mine and just held it.

And held it.

We stayed that way for a while, neither of us doing anything else but breathing.

"We're so damaged," she said. "*I'm* so damaged."

I didn't say anything. Just listened. Just held her hand.

That's it, I thought. That's what I'm called to do––help people damaged by violent crime, salve the suffering of the living while searching for some kind of justice for the dead. As both a minister and an investigator I'd be in a unique position to do both.

"But ..." she said.

"Yeah?"

"Since you've come around ..."

She left if out there a long moment. I waited.

"I've been less shutdown ... and ... sometimes ... like now ... I'm not shutdown at all."

That night I dreamt of Jordan.

Jordan standing in the backyard, a dark, depraved figure tearing out of the woods, racing toward her, snatching her, dragging her back by her sun-streaked hair into the thicket, me stuck in the house, unable to save her.

Little LaMarcus playing in the backyard, unaware of the simian creature careening toward him. Jordan dashing toward him, reaching, grasping, just missing.

Jordan holding a swaddled Savannah, kissing her cheek, smelling her skin, singing her the sweetest song I'd ever heard. Wayne Williams slithering up behind her, snatching Savannah from her, darting away. Jordan pleading with me to do something. Me unable to do anything.

In a car. Jordan in the passenger seat beside me. Savannah in a carseat in the back between LaMarcus on one side and Martin Fisher on the other. Family trip. Happiness. Jordan's bare feet on the dashboard, sun-kissed toes. Larry plowing out of a side road in a pickup, T-boning the car, sending it spinning down a deep ravine. Falling. Screaming. Crashing. Dismemberment. Death. Despair.

25

"**D**is some kinda school project?" Anthony Williams asked.

I nodded and smiled and made a mental note to try to age myself some. "How'd you know?"

"Why else a white boy be aksin'?"

It had taken several days, but I had finally tracked down LaMarcus's dad at a huge apartment complex off Memorial Drive where he was doing day labor for a turnkey company.

He was a narrow-framed, emaciated man with very dark skin, a permanently and deeply furrowed forehead, and a wide, flat nose, below which was a black-beginning-to-gray mustache in need of trimming.

Every cell of his moist skin shined with a greasy sheen.

The apartment he was working on was hot and had the lingering stench of rotting potatoes and urine, but it was no match for the odor emanating from Anthony Williams himself.

He was patching a much marred and pockmarked sheetrock wall, the sweat pouring from him stinking of cheap booze, junk food, cigarettes, and drugs cut with something truly rancid.

The toxic body odor wafting off him stung my eyes and made

me breathe very shallowly, but when he lifted his arm to reach the spots above his head it was unbearable.

"You know you's the first person to ever talk to me about what happened to my boy."

I shook my head.

"Po-lice aksed questions, but nobody else ever even mentioned it."

I wondered if anyone in his life even knew he had a son.

"I'm sorry to hear that," I said.

"Whatcha needs to know?"

Since he thought he was helping me with a school report I had to choose my first question carefully.

"Do you think Wayne Williams was responsible for what happened to your son?"

He shook his head. "That pudgy nigger ain't killed nobody. My kid or anybody else. He's framed. Ain't no killa of any kind. They just needed a fall guy."

"They?"

"Cops, mayor, business owners. White people what run this town. Didn't care if the real killer keep killin' little black boys. Long as they got everybody thinkin' it over."

"Do you have any idea who killed LaMarcus?"

"Oh, it was the same killer killed those other youngins. Just wasn't Wayne Williams."

"Any idea who it was?"

"Don't think we'll ever know. Powers that be don't want us to."

"When was the last time you saw LaMarcus before he died?"

"It had been a while. Crazy ex old lady never let me see him much."

"Why's that?"

"She crazy. I mean really bat shit bonkers, man. But mostly 'cause I broke her heart.

She's gettin' back at me through the kid. Keepin' him from

me. Hell, punished the kid more'n me. But . . . women . . . you know?"

I nodded as if I knew.

He shook his head. "The way she treated that boy . . . like . . . he made of china or somethin'. Never let him do anythin' never let him have no fun. Made him weak and frail and . . . and then she go and marry a white man and try to make him white. No offense. Nothin' wrong with bein' white if you white but . . . notice she ain't tried to turn that white girl black."

"Did you try to stop her?" I asked. "Try to take him? Make a man out of him?"

He nodded. "Take a man to raise a man, I always say. Yeah. You get it. Yeah, I tried. Talked to him. Tried to get him to see, but he . . . she had . . . I tried to just, you know, take him with me without her knowin', but he was too far gone. Bitch had already ruined him."

"How'd you do it?" I asked. "With her watchin' him all the time the way she did, with her always smothering him . . . It'd be impossible."

"Wait 'til you're older, 'til you have kids. Nothin' you won't do for 'em, man. Nothin'."

"But how?" I said. "I don't see how it could be done."

"That's 'cause you not streetwise, young brother," he said.

"I guess so," I said. "It's just . . . I talked to her and I see what you're sayin' about how she is and the way she was over him . . . I've seen her old house, her yard . . . I just don't think it could be done. I can see why you didn't do it."

"You gots no imagination," he said. "There's nothin' to it. See the boy playin' in the back. Knock on the front door then run around to the back."

"But what if the girl goes to the door and his mama stays and keeps watchin' or his mama goes and the girl keeps watchin'?"

He shrugged.

"Duck under the windows where they can't see you," he said. "Call the boy over to you."

I nodded. "You're right," I said. "Wow. Ingenious."

He smiled.

"But what if she's got him so brainwashed he won't go?" I said. "What then? How could you save him from her like only a father can if he won't go?"

"You do anything to save your son," he said. "Give him somethin' if you have to."

"Like what?" I asked. "Something like chloral hydrate?"

"What?"

"Cough syrup."

He nodded and shrugged. "Yeah. Sure. Anything like that."

"Anything for your son," I said.

"Anything," he said, nodding even more defiantly. "Anything at all."

26

I spent nearly all my free time over the next several days searching for a couple of subcontractors. When I wasn't in class or working or studying or visiting or spending time with Martin, I was looking for Raymond Pelton and Vincent Storr.

I had very little time, no resources, and really didn't know what I was doing. And it showed. For all my efforts, such as they were, I had exactly nothing.

I had nothing and I didn't know what else to do. Except ask for help.

I called Bobby Battle at home.

It was late to be calling, nearly ten, but I wasn't sure when I'd have another chance and the truth was I didn't want to wait.

"Hello?"

A female voice that didn't sound sleepy or irritated.

"May I speak with Bobby, please?"

"May I tell him who's calling?"

"John Jordan."

"One minute."

"John?" Bobby said.

"Sorry to call so late."

"It's early around here," he said. "What's up?"

"I was calling to see . . . I'm having a hard time finding Pelton and Storr."

"Good."

"I was wondering if you could help me."

"With what?"

"Finding them."

"For what?"

He wasn't making this easy.

"So I can talk to them."

"Listen," he said. "Let me tell you something. The last thing you need to do is go anywhere near them. Understand?"

"No, I don't guess I do. I thought that was the whole idea."

"Look, talking about the case, even talking to the family, is one thing, but these are real bad men. There's no good outcome here. Best case . . . they tell you to go fuck yourself because you're a kid with no authority or jurisdiction of any kind. Worst case . . . they hurt or kill you."

"I'm not . . . I wasn't just gonna . . ."

"Tell you what, you let us handle guys like Pelton and Storr. Last thing you need to be going up against are career criminals like them. You had some good ideas at the crime scene. Morgan was right about you. You got a knack for certain aspects of detection, but theory is one thing, law enforcement is another."

I didn't say anything.

"I ain't tryin' to hurt your feelin's. I'm tryin' to save your life. You know how many cases I'm working right now? You know how many involve violent death? These people don't play. They will chew you up and spit you out. I got all these cases, but let me just tell you about one of them. This violent serial rapist mother-fucker. He attacks this young girl, about your age, Brittany Ann. He beats her into submission and tries to rape her. When he can't get it up, he rapes her with a hammer. *A hammer.* But he doesn't kill her. That's a relief, right? He tells her she can go. When she stands to leave, he throws her down on her face this time and rapes her in the ass with the same hammer. What would a civilian say or do to a man like that? I'd like to know."

After hanging up the phone with Battle, I headed straight for the bottle of vodka I had hidden in the suitcase in my closet.

No orange or pineapple or cranberry juice. Just straight vodka from the bottle and keep it comin'.

I had been dismissed, belittled, treated like . . . what I was.

I was angry and frustrated, ready to burn something down––and mostly because he was right.

Who the hell was I? What could I do?

I drank myself to a point just shy of oblivion and then I passed out on top of my made bed fully clothed.

I slept. I dreamt.

Children. Sleeping. Dead.

They all looked so peaceful, so sweet in gentle, innocent repose, but they were all sleeping Shakespeare's sleep of death.

To die, to sleep—
No more; and by a sleep, to say we end
The Heart-ache, and the thousand Natural shocks
That Flesh is heir to? 'Tis a consummation
Devoutly to be wished. To die, to sleep,
To sleep, perchance to Dream; Aye, there's the rub,
For in that sleep of death, what dreams may come.

When I woke, I called Frank Morgan.

"Good morning, sunshine," he said.

I mumbled some incoherent response.

"Up all night praying?"

"I had a thought."

"Well, hold it. I checked the pattern cases' victims on and off the list as best I could and there's no indication any were drugged with that chloral hydrate stuff and none were raped after death."

"So LaMarcus doesn't fit in the ACM pattern," I said. "We expected that. But what if he's part of a different series? That's what I dreamt last night. A series of similar victims––children all appearing to be asleep but really dead, killed by the same guy who killed and raped LaMarcus."

"That'll take a lot longer to find out and I'll need to call in some favors for help searching the files, but I'll see what I can do."

"Thanks, Frank."

We were quiet a beat, a beat in which I could feel the dull ache in my head more acutely.

"I talked to Anthony Williams," I said.

"The victim's biological father? What'd he have to say? How'd you find him?"

I told him.

"You got him to say that?"

"I was thinking, what if it started as him just trying to get his son back so he could make a man out of him? Would explain the use of the drug and him leaving him in the bushes for a while."

"You're thinkin' the overdose was an accident?"

"Maybe. But it wouldn't explain why he dragged him into his hideout in the bushes."

"I don't follow."

"I mean that particular spot. How'd he know about it?"

"Maybe the kid told him. Maybe he watched for a while before he tried to snatch him. Maybe it was the only clearing back there."

"Maybe," I said, "but what none of it explains is the rape. It's one thing to try to snatch your kid and accidentally kill him, panic and move the body, maybe even stage it to look like something other than what it was, but to rape him . . ."

"Yeah," he said. "Would seem to rule out it being an accidental overdose or the dad being the doer . . ."

"Unless," I said, "someone else came along, found him dead, and raped him."

"Two crimes," he said, his voice, rising, "two criminals. A killer and a rapist. Could be. Could very well be."

27

After my morning classes, I drove down to Willie's German Bakery in the shopping center at the corner of Flat Shoals and Wesley Chapel, grabbed a bag full of eclairs and M&M iced cookies, and drove over to Safe Haven.

The dull ache in my head felt just bad enough to be mildly annoying, but occasionally it throbbed, the pressure pounding with my heartbeat, the pain shooting down my spinal cord.

"Well, look who it is," Ralph said. "Who could've predicted this? The man with too much time on his hands."

"You sure you're not happy to see me?" I said. "I brought you an eclair."

"I wouldn't say no to an eclair," he said, "but listen to what I have to say first and see if you still wanna give it to me."

"Okay."

He stepped outside the fence and away from the gate to speak to me.

"These poor ladies have been through enough," he said. "They don't need you to keep dredging up the most horrific nightmare they ever lived through . . . giving them false hope, raising their expectations . . . all for nothin'. It's never gonna be solved. Not ever. 'Specially by the likes of you. All *you're* doin' is wasting time and doin' harm to two people I care about. And why? 'Cause you're new in town and need somethin' to do, need some attention from a sweet mama and a pretty girl? Well, the cost is too high. And I'm not gonna let you keep doin' it. Understand?"

"I understand what you're sayin'," I said. "And I genuinely appreciate your concern. I do. Ida and Jordan deserve it. They do. But I'm not doin' what you're accusin' me of. It has nothing to do with me not having enough to do or wanting attention, and I wouldn't be doin' it if I didn't think I could help figure out who did it."

"Never happen," he said.

"And you think I'm wrong to even try?"

He nodded. "Because of what it'll do to them. This ain't no game or some movie or somethin'. This is people's lives. Good people. This isn't theory or book stuff. This is the real world where people are barely makin' it and you can do damage they can't come back from. And if you're just tryin' to sleep with Jordan, stop it. This ain't the way to go about it and you don't need to anyway. She's married and too old and too good for––"

"Who is?" Jordan asked as she walked up. "Who's too old and too good for who?"

"Ma'am?" Ralph asked.

"Who is?"

"I . . . I was just . . ."

"I went by Willie's," I said, holding up the bags. "Trade you a little sugar for a little info."

She turned her attention away from Ralph and onto me, smiling in the process.

"Sounds good. Ralph, we'll talk about this later. Give you time to remember what you meant."

"Yes, ma'am."

She turned and began walking away. I followed, pausing long enough to open the bag and extend it toward Ralph.

"Eclair?" I offered.

"Seriously?"

I nodded.

He started to reach for one but stopped. "You gonna snatch the bag back when I—"

"NO," I said. "Honest offer. Don't make the lady wait. Grab one. Hell, grab two."

He did.

"What was that about?" Jordan asked.

"Just him being protective over you and your mom."

"I don't understand."

"He doesn't approve of what I'm doing. Thinks I'm stirring things up. Wasting time. Raising false hopes. And he questions my motives. Particularly where you're concerned."

She smiled. "Sorry about that. I think he's always had a bit of a crush. And he is very protective over Mom and me and the kids and everything Safe Haven. Feels like it's his job to keep us all safe—and I guess it is . . . but he goes way beyond . . ."

"What's his story?"

"Been our neighbor for as long as I can remember. Lives right over there."

She turned and pointed behind us to the small red brick house on a hill beyond the many fences of Safe Haven.

"He was so helpful when LaMarcus went missing, calming us, searching the area, dealing with the police. After we found out LaMarcus was . . . gone . . . he helped me and Mom in every way imaginable. He was a cop at one time, but has worked security at South Dekalb mall for . . . well, since I can recall. That's what he was doing when Mom decided to open Safe Haven and offered him the job. He knew how important it was to her to make the safest place possible for children and he took a pay cut to take the job."

I opened the bag of cookies and offered it to her. We each took some and ate them as we looked out across the empty playground and Ralph kept looking at us.

"Damn you, Willie," she said, shaking her fist in the air in mock outrage. "Why do these cookies have to be so good?"

I laughed and we ate some more.

"I talked to Mom," she said. "Got some more info for you. Seems like that may be the best way for her. Just let me know what you need, and I'll ask her when I know it's an okay time and let her tell me in her own way and on her schedule."

"Thank you," I said. "So you don't think I'm wasting time or stirring up things and raising false hopes?"

She shook her head. "The thing Ralph and so many others don't understand is how much it stays stirred up. If you're wasting anybody's time it's your own, but I don't think you are and I appreciate everything you're doin'. Just the fact that you're interested, that you are––that *someone* is still doin' somethin' about it . . . not just filing it away as another unsolved murder of a black boy . . . It means more than you'll ever know."

I nodded, my heart filling, my spirits being buoyed again.

"I do hope Ralph was right about one thing at least," she said.

"Oh yeah? What's that?"

"I hope your motives in regards to me are not as pure as they appear."

I smiled. "I wasn't aware they appeared pure at all, but if they do . . . just remember . . . things aren't often what they appear to be."

"Thank you for saying so," she said. "It's sweet."

We fell silent a moment, munching on the small cookies, enjoying each other's company, taking in the magnificent midmorning sun and the way the fall foliage basked beneath it.

"Mom said that LaMarcus worked very hard to keep his little hideout a secret. And he must've done a good job because I didn't know about it. But as I said, I was a self-involved teenager. Mom knew and kept an eye on him when he was in it—but he didn't know she knew about it. After the killings started, he wasn't allowed in it because she didn't want him out of her sight."

"That was something I meant to ask you before," I said. "Why didn't y'all look in there first? When he first went missing, why not look in his hideout before y'all did anything else?"

"We did. I mean we thought someone did. I was just finding out about it. The whole thing was . . . everything was pandemonium. We were all just rushing around like crazy. I thought Mom checked it. She thought I did. It was . . . It never got checked. At least not in time."

I nodded.

"Before that," she continued, "he used to play in it a good bit. The only other person she knows for sure who knew about it and played in it with him was Carlton."

"Carlton Fields, the neighbor boy who found . . . the . . . LaMarcus?"

She nodded.

"He not only knew where it was but played in it with LaMarcus?"

"Uh huh, but you can't suspect him. He's the sweetest boy in the world, a true innocent. He functions at a pretty low level, but he's guileless."

"I need to talk to him."

"Well, it won't be hard to do," she said. "His mom's back in school and is always looking for someone to keep him on Tuesday and Thursday nights."

28

After leaving Safe Haven, I went back to EPI to find a phone. Pam Palmer, the college's registrar, was just leaving for lunch and said I was welcome to the use of hers and the privacy her office afforded.

I called Bobby Battle again. This time at the station.

"Last night's conversation went so well," I said, "figured I'd call you again."

"Sorry if I was discouraging," he said, "but I'm a straight shooter and I'm just lookin' out for you. Shit we deal with is no joke."

"I know," I said, just to be saying something.

"Got a lot goin' on," he said. "What can I do for you."

"Ralph Alderman," I said.

"What about him?"

"Why'd he leave the force to become a mall cop?"

"He's a fuckup. Always was. Didn't fuck up quite bad enough to become captain but just bad enough so that he had to go."

"What'd he do?"

"Wasn't just one thing. It was a lot of shit over a long period of time. Take your pick. Some personal, some professional, some procedural, some just being a fat ass with an annoying personality."

"Did you look at him for LaMarcus Williams?"

"No. Why?"

"Not even briefly to exclude him?"

"No," he said. "Hell, he helped us. Functioned like one of the team. Why?"

"Just askin'. Tryin' to be thorough."

"Come on," he said. "What'd he do to make you suspect him?"

"Nothin'. Just—"

"Probably should've looked at him," he said. "Don't bust my balls about it. I would if the investigation was now. I've learned a thing or two since then."

"Can we look at him now?"

"*We?*"

I didn't say anything, just waited.

"I'll dig around and see what I can find out, but chances are he's got nothin' to do with it."

"But if there's even a slim chance . . ."

"I said I'd look into it. Take the win. Quit tightening the noose around my neck, and be grateful."

"I am. Thanks. What about a current cop? Larry Moore?"

"You don't think he had anything to do with it, do you? Larry's got no class and a bad temper but he's no child killer."

"No, I don't," I said. "Just asking about him. He's married to the victim's sister."

"Then more's the pity for her," he said. "Guy's a major asshole. But he's a decent enough cop. I think. He ain't gonna break a sweat bringin' in a bad guy, but he ain't crooked or anything. Far as I can tell. Okay, fun chattin' with you, but I've got to run."

After I hung up with Battle, I walked into the empty chapel and prayed and meditated for a while, then downstairs to the janitor's closet and the cleaning cart awaiting me there.

For the next few hours I vacuumed and dusted the classrooms, scrubbed and mopped the bathrooms, vodka pouring out of my pores, the pounding in my head increasing, as I thought about how and why LaMarcus Williams died and who might have done it, about Wayne Williams and if he was guilty or not, who would and would not make my list, were I to make one, about the nature of justice and the way of the world, about Jordan Moore and Ida Williams and the suffering only a mother can know, about my own mother and father and my home and—

"So why *do* the innocent suffer?"

I turned to see Jordan standing in the doorway.

"Hey. What're you doing here? Is everything okay?"

She nodded toward the chalkboard in the front of the class-room. On it was written *Why do the innocent suffer?*

The class belonged to Pastor Jim Oborne, one of the most popular and academically rigorous of the EPI instructors. It was the single remaining remnant of an inspiring and invigorating lecture and discussion about the nature of suffering.

"I had a short break so I walked down to have you tell me why the innocent suffer, why the wicked are rewarded, why the good are punished."

I laughed.

"Well, I came to see you, but I *would* like to know."

"Wouldn't we all," I said.

"Seriously," she said. "Tell me."

"I don't know," I said. "There are a lot of theories, but..."

"None you buy?"

I shrugged. "Only one," I said, "but the truth is asking *why* is mostly a waste of time. Knowing the why of suffering won't change it, won't change anything. Dealing with suffering, sitting with the suffering, alleviating suffering, when and where we can...that's far more...useful."

She nodded, narrowing her eyes, pursing her lips—agreeing but still considering it too. "Makes sense. A lot actually. But..."

What could I possibly tell this woman about suffering?

"I have to know the one thing," she said.

"What's that?"

"The one theory you buy about suffering."

"Freedom," I said. "I don't just mean human beings. I mean the entire universe. If freedom is built into everything . . . it allows for the possibility of everything--including suffering. Including the suffering of the innocent. Freedom means there's order but there's also chaos. There's love but there's also indifference. There's altruism but there's also selfishness. There's unspeakable joy but there's also unimaginable horror. I don't know. That's just another bullshit theory like all the others. Means nothin' to nobody in the face of true suffering."

"So true," she said.

"What? That I'm full of bullshit?"

"NO, I meant--"

"I know what you meant," I said.

"Spend less time wondering why we suffer and more time dealing with suffering," she said.

I nodded. "Exactly. More time helping ease the suffering of others."

"Well, you're certainly doing that, John Jordan," she said. "You're certainly doing that."

29

I finally found Vincent Storr a few days later.

He was working on remodeling an old farmhouse on Flakes Mill Road near Ellenwood, ripping out pinewood paneling and replacing it with sheetrock.

Except for the traffic on Flakes Mill, the area was quiet and had a rural feel—scattered houses on wooded lots, some of which were fenced with livestock in them.

Before I moved up here, I would never have imagined such an area in Metro Atlanta so close to downtown.

I parked on a white gravel driveway beneath an enormous oak tree that dappled the yard and part of the house with mid-morning sunlight, and walked toward a worker cutting sheetrock board on the front porch, the gravel crunching beneath my shoes as I did.

When I asked for Storr, he said, "What're you? An illegitimate child who's just tracked him down?"

"Something like that," I said.

"He's right inside," he said. "Go on in."

As I opened the door, he yelled, "VINCE. VINCE. SOMEONE HERE TO SEE YOU."

Storr was a tall, meager man with wispy, thinning black hair, deep, dark, sunken eyes, and the very heavy, very dark stubble of a five o'clock shadow at ten in the morning.

He wore white painter's pants, a loose white crew neck under-shirt, and penny loafers––all of which, and every inch of him, was covered in white sheetrock dust.

He was holding a bucket of mud in one hand and a trowel in the other, eyeing his work on a seam where two boards joined together.

The beautiful white pine board paneling was still up on one end of the room and I admired it a moment before I said anything to him.

"Why would you pull down that and replace it with sheetrock?" I asked, shaking my head.

"Only one reason," he said, looking around and lowering his voice, "niggers."

I was taken aback by his blatant racism before a total stranger and the sad assumption associated with it, but I did my best not to let it show. I needed to see and hear from the real Vincent Storr, unadorned, unguarded, unsuspecting.

"I hope you're plannin' on takin' the wood with you."

"Take wood everywhere I go, if you know what I mean," he said. "But, nah, fuckin' boss is takin' it."

"Figures," I said, shaking my head.

"What can I do you for?" he asked.

"Lookin' for a painter," I said.

"Only do sheetrock."

"Think you've worked with him before. Raymond Pelton. I really like what he did on a house over off Flat Shoals Road."

He looked at me, narrowing his eyes suspiciously and studying me. "What house?"

"One in Flat Shoals Estates. Did you work with him on one over there?"

"Sheetrock crew is long gone by the time painters come in," he said. "Don't know no painter named Pelton."

"Oh, okay," I said.

"Why would you think I would?"

"Someone told me," I said.

"Someone told you, huh? Who?"

I could tell he wasn't buying it and I felt like an idiot. I should've prepared better, should've had a contingency plan in case the first one didn't work, but as it was there was nothing I could do but try to double down on the losing hand I was backing.

"Guy doin' some work over at the church I go to. Chapel Hill."

He nodded. "Guy got a name?"

"I'm sure he does, but I didn't get it. Do you know the subdivision I'm talkin' about? It's behind where that kid got killed."

He seemed to think about it for a long moment. "Oh, yeah, the little niglet. Now I remember. I did meet a painter on that job. Had to go back and patch a wall the flooring guy fucked up and I met him. Pelton. Bet I can find him. Just leave me your name, address, and phone number and I'll have him get in touch with you."

"Thanks."

"Here," he said, handing me a pen and a scrap of paper, both covered in a fine white powder.

The worker I had encountered on the porch brought in two pieces of sheetrock, set them down against the far wall, and walked out again without saying anything.

"They never caught whoever killed that kid," I said as I wrote down my info.

I tried to make the remark seem offhand, casual, idle, but that wasn't how it sounded to me.

It was hard to imagine doing a worse job at this. I felt slow and stupid. I had so much to learn––even more than I realized.

"Thought that soft, big fro nigger with the glasses did it. What was his name? Wayne Williams––same as the little boy who he killed then fucked."

The fact that LaMarcus had been raped had never been released to the public, and only a handful of tightlipped cops and the killer knew the rape came after the murder.

Something inside me began to buzz.

"You 'bout got that?" he said, nodding toward the paper. "I gotta get back to work."

I handed him the paper.

"John Jordan," he read. "Forty-three-thirty-six Pleasant Point Drive. Decatur."

I nodded.

And then I witnessed a transformation from something that had appeared to be a man into something that more closely resembled a monster.

"Now we know where you live," he said. "Ray and I will come pay you a little visit. We usually don't like 'em as old as you but we can make an exception. Bet your little pink pucker is still nice and tight. Is, ain't it?"

How could I be so stupid?

Everything about him had changed. He didn't even look like the same person any longer. He was even giving off a different odor, the smell of something feted and feral.

I didn't say anything, just stood there staring at him, my fists clinched at my sides.

Bobby Battle had been right about these men and about me. They were animals, cold, cruel, inhumane. I was ill-equipped, in over my head, and had just made a costly rookie mistake that could get me hurt or killed––just like Battle had said.

"Come in here talkin' 'bout somebody told you I might know Ray. Either you think my setting is stuck on stupid or yours is."

"It's clearly the latter," I said.

"Admitting it is the first step. So what's your story, stupid?"

"I'm an amateur––"

"That's obvious."

"Just tryin' to figure out what happened to LaMarcus Williams."

"Why?"

I shrugged. "Need to know."

"We all have needs," he said. "Some far more dangerous than others. Some'll cause you not to fit in, not to be able to live by society's bullshit rules. Others'll get you killed."

I had nothing for that so I kept my mouth shut.

"You too young to be a cop. Already said you's a amateur. You a friend of the family or just some random motherfucker with a death wish?"

"Tell you what," I said, trying to sound far more calm and unafraid than I felt, "I'm shy when it comes to talking about myself. Why don't we wait until you and Ray visit and I'll let my friends from the force tell you all about me. And if there's anything they don't know, Frank Morgan with GBI will. Here's his card in case you want to reach out to him directly. I'll make sure he's expecting to hear from you either way."

"I screwed up," I said.

There was a pause.

I wanted to call Frank, but knew it had to be Bobby Battle.

Swallow my medicine. Straight, no sugar.

"Let me guess," he said. "You tried to make a citizen's arrest and got your ass kicked."

"Worse."

He sighed heavily, his frustration and disapproval palpable even through the phone.

"Let me have it."

I did.

"Told you, didn't I?"

"You did. I'm sorry. I should've listened. I underestimated him and was unprepared and made a mess of it."

"Yes you did."

"But—"

"Make an excuse right now and I'll walk away, hang you out to dry. Let you deal with Pelton and Storr."

"He let it slip that he knew LaMarcus was raped."

"Doesn't take much to make that leap."

"After he was murdered."

"Oh."

He was quiet a moment.

"What'd you say to get him to say that?"

"Nothin'."

"You had to say somethin'."

"I said somethin' about how the killer had never been caught and he said he thought Wayne Williams did it and went on to say his last name was the same as the little boy who he killed then fucked."

"And you're sure it was just like that? He wasn't repeatin' or respondin' to somethin' you said, not inferring what happened from somethin' you let slip?"

"Positive."

"Well, then," he said. "You still fucked up, but maybe I won't let you get killed over it."

30

"You remember LaMarcus, don't you, Carlton?" Jordan was saying.

She was holding up the last picture ever taken of her brother, one that was still on the roll of film inside Ida's camera when he was killed.

In it, he is skating at a friend's birthday party in Conyers, a large gold chain around his neck, a broad, sweet smile on his face.

Carlton nodded.

We were in the back corner of Safe Haven––me, Martin, Jordan, and Carlton––having waited until everyone else, including Ida, had gone home.

Jordan had told Carlton's mom it would be a little later than usual when she dropped him off tonight. Carlton's mom seemed grateful for the extra time.

Martin was with me because he wanted to be, had nowhere else to go, and I thought he might make Carlton feel safer. He sat at a table not too far from us, coloring with conviction.

"LaMarcus was a good boy," Carlton said. "LaMarcus was my friend."

Carlton had a big frame and a soft, fat belly emphasized by

his too-tight, tucked in T-shirt, which was shoved deep into cheap, old, ill-fitting polyester pants cinched at the waist by a wide, brown, faux leather belt.

"He was," Jordan said. "He was a very good boy and he was a very good friend."

"LaMarcus died," he said. "LaMarcus is dead. He's in heaven with the angels."

I was letting Jordan ask the questions not only because of her rapport with Carlton and her quiet, kind, gentle ways, but because of how I had handled things with Vincent Storr.

"That's right," Jordan said. "LaMarcus, your good friend, is in heaven now."

"With the angels."

"With the angels, yes."

I had to keep reminding myself that Carlton was older than I was by a few years. Everything about him but his size was small, stunted, childlike.

"Do you remember what happened to him?" Jordan asked.

"LaMarcus wouldn't wake up. He went to sleep and wouldn't wake up."

"Did you try to wake him up?"

"I did. I did try to wake him up. *Wake up, LaMarcus. Wake up. Let's play some more.* But he wouldn't wake up."

More. He had said let's play some *more.*

"Had you been playing with LaMarcus before he went to sleep?"

Carlton nodded.

"Where? When?"

"LaMarcus played with Carlton. Hide. Count. Look. Ball. Carlton loves ball. Carlton and LaMarcus love basketball."

"'Ee 'oo," Martin said softly without looking up or missing a stroke with his crayon.

I smiled and thought about how much I enjoyed playing basketball with Martin.

"What did you and LaMarcus play the day he died, the day he wouldn't wake up?"

Carlton looked confused, as if the concept of time was too much for him, as if what his mind stored wasn't locked down and ordered, but rather tossed in and jumbled.

"LaMarcus played with Carlton. Nobody else. *Get outta here you fat retard. Go on. Get.* Just LaMarcus. Sweet, good boy LaMarcus."

Jordan swallowed hard and I caught the glint of gathering moisture in her eyes.

"LaMarcus told Carlton a secret," he said.

Jordan sat up, her head turning slightly, her expression rising.

"What did he tell you?" she asked.

"It's a secret."

"You can tell me," she said. "I'm Jordan, LaMarcus's sister. Remember?"

He shook his head. "Can't tell anyone. No one. Promise me. I promise, LaMarcus."

"The thing is . . . after someone goes to sleep, after they die, you can tell their secret to their sister."

"You can?"

She nodded. "Yes. You can."

He looked over at me and then at Martin.

"We'll step outside a minute," I said. "Let you two talk."

"You color really well," I said to Martin when we got outside.

"'Ank 'oo Yon."

With nowhere to go, we just wandered around a bit beneath the covered walkway.

It was a dark night, touched at the edges by a rim of pale moonlight. A cool breeze blew leaves about, their stiff edges scraping against the concrete of the walkway and the asphalt of the parking lot.

"Is Carl'on 'onna be o'a?" (

I nodded. "He'll be fine, buddy. He's just helpin' us with something very--"

"The fuck you doin'?"

I turned to see Ralph Alderman rushing toward us.

He was out of his security uniform and looked odd, out of place in street clothes. He was wearing a navy-blue-and-white Nike jogging suit with only a wife beater and a gold chain beneath. Elephantine exercise clothes on such an enormously soft, fat man looked absurd and comical, as if he were a retired gangster.

"Waiting on Jordan," I said. "What about you? Out for a jog?"

"Where is she? What are y'all doin' here this late? Where's Miss Ida? Who is this?"

"Jordan's finishing up in the classroom. We're about to leave. Ida's at home. This is Martin Fisher, my best friend in Atlanta."

"Come on," he said. "I wanna hear it from Miss Jordan or I call the police. I'm sure they'd be happy to dispatch her husband."

We followed him to the classroom, my hand on Martin's shoulder.

"Everything's okay," I told Martin. "Nothin' to worry about."

He shrugged, seemingly not worried about anything.

When Ralph reached the door, he opened it and looked inside--and drew back as if he had seen something shocking.

I rushed around him to look inside, my heart pounding, my mind preparing for something horrible.

But everything was just as we had left it, Jordan and Carlton in the corner talking.

"Just be sure to lock up when you leave," Ralph said, quickly heading back down the walkway.

"What's wrong?" Jordan asked. "What was that about?"

She had walked over and was nearly to us.

I shook my head. "I'm not sure. He was all gung-ho to talk to you until he opened the door, and then he couldn't get out of here quickly enough."

"'Ome'in' 'ong wi' 'Arl'on," Martin said.

We looked back over to the corner where Carlton was.

He was rocking back and forth, his clenched fists up near his head shaking. "Carlton go home now. Time for Carlton to go home now. Take Carlton home."

We rushed over to him.

His pants, the chair, and the floor around him were wet where he had urinated on himself.

"It's okay," Jordan said. "It's no problem at all. I'll get you cleaned up in no time."

"No clean up. Go home. Carlton go home right now."

31

"Carlton was seriously terrified of Ralph," Jordan said.
I nodded.

Martin and I had followed her to take Carlton home, waiting in the car down the way a bit while she had walked him in and gotten him situated. Then we had come to the Dairy Queen on Wesley Chapel for ice cream and were at the tables outside—Jordan and I sitting on top of one, our feet on the bench, licking our soft serve chocolate cones, Martin atop another finishing up his art project, his pencils and crayons spread out around him. Each time he traded one pencil, pen, or crayon for another, he took a bite of his banana split.

"I wonder why?" she said.

"Maybe he saw him kill LaMarcus."

"*Ralph?*" she asked, her voice rising in shock.

"Yeah."

We were talking quietly so Martin couldn't hear us, aided by his concentration and the traffic on both Wesley Chapel and I-20.

"No," she said. "There's no way. It can't be. It's got to be something else."

"Maybe," I said. "Maybe he reminds him of someone or

maybe . . . Do he and Ralph have a history? Has anything happened at Safe Haven or––"

"No. Nothing. I don't think Carlton's ever been to Safe Haven before tonight. I just don't get it. I've never seen him like that."

"So you're saying he hasn't been around Ralph since LaMarcus was killed?"

She shrugged. "I don't know. I don't guess so. Not at Safe Haven anyway. But he would've had to have been back around the time it happened, at the funeral, visitation, in the neighborhood Carlton's family moved to. I . . . I'm just not sure. But it can't be Ralph. He's . . . he's around children every day."

"Exactly."

"But . . . to protect kids. He's there to . . . He takes his job of protecting the kids, of protecting all of us, so seriously. It can't be Ralph. He can't be . . . He wouldn't . . . He couldn't. Not Ralph."

"The more you say it, the more untrue it sounds."

"That's because the more I say it, the more I doubt it."

"Think about how hostile he's been toward us looking into what happened to LaMarcus, how threatened and defensive he's been. Maybe it isn't that he doesn't like me or has a thing for you. I've got to find out why he was fired from the force and we need to take a closer look at him."

"If he . . . if he killed LaMarcus and has been working for us all these years, pretending to care, pretending to protect . . ."

"I know."

This time when Martin put down his pencil, he took several bites of the banana and mixed the strawberry and chocolate ice cream together, his open mouth lingering over the plastic boat as he studied his work.

"Did he tell you LaMarcus's secret?" I asked.

She nodded as she finished the bite of cone she was working on, then said, "He did. Said LaMarcus told him he was going to live with his dad, that his dad was going to make a man out of him."

I thought about that, wondering when he had been told, why it stuck in his memory, and how it could fit with what had happened to LaMarcus.

Up near the street a white kid carrying an enormous boombox on his shoulder strolled by on the sidewalk in tight, black jeans tucked into black combat boots and a blue blazer customized with pins and buttons and patches. Rising out of shaved black hair, his spikey mohawk was white-blond. His ghetto-blaster was blasting a radio-recorded version of Run D.M.C.'s *Walk this Way* so distorted it was nearly unrecognizable.

"Could it be Anthony?" she asked.

I nodded.

"So not Ralph after all."

"It could be Ralph."

"But wouldn't his dad be more likely?"

"Could be both."

"*Both*?"

"Dad tries to drug him and take him away––to make a man out of him––but he gets the dose wrong and instead of calming him or putting him to sleep temporarily, kills him. He hides him in the bushes where he was just hiding before, then he flees. Ralph comes along, takes the body to the drainage pipe. Carlton sees him do it or sees him leaving after he did it and . . ."

"But why move LaMarcus to the drain pipe?" she asked.

She must not know about her brother being raped and I wasn't going to be the one to tell her. Not now. Not like this.

I shrugged. "It's just a theory."

"What're you gonna do?"

"Talk to Frank and Bobby."

She nodded.

We had both finished our cones and as our conversation came to a close, now found ourselves watching Martin as he alternated between his split and his drawing.

We sat there like that a long moment, our thighs touching, the sweet smell of her shampoo wafting over occasionally.

"I . . ." she began.

"Huh?"

"Nothin'. It was silly."

"Tell me. You can tell me. You can tell me anything. You could never be silly."

She looked at me with her sweet, kind eyes and her fresh, unadorned face, and smiled a beautiful but shy smile.

"I keep havin' this fantasy," she said.

"Oh yeah? Wonder if we're havin' the same one?"

"I know I shouldn't. Know it's silly and farfetched . . . but it's so . . . persistent. I guess it's more a picture in my head or a dream . . . I don't know."

"What is it?"

"It's us. Like this. Together. Married. Having adopted Martin. A family."

I nodded. "Sounds like a small sliver of heaven."

"So . . . you don't think . . . I'm . . . I don't know . . . you don't think it's wrong to even wish for?"

"It's lovely," I said. "And very similar to mine."

"Really?"

"Mine's the same as yours except in it Martin's in his room, in his bed sound asleep, and we're naked in ours in the way only lovers can be."

When we got back to my apartment, they were waiting
for us.

Thankfully, Martin had fallen asleep in my backseat on the
short drive over, and didn't wake up when I parked the car.

They came at us as soon as we got out, so I left Martin inside,
hoping they wouldn't see him.

We had parked beside each other, across the lot from the
apartments near the basketball court. They had appeared out of
the darkness, one on each end of the cars, trapping us between
them.

I recognized Vincent Storr so assumed the guy he was with
was Raymond Pelton.

"This him?" Ray asked.

In contrast to Vince, Ray was round and short with big,
muscular arms, thick, stubby-fingered hands, no neck, and not
much hair.

Vince nodded. "Motherfucker came to my job site."

The night was dark, the complex quiet, everyone behind their
locked doors doing what they did when they went inside.

"Who's this pretty little piece of pussy you got here?" Ray said, eyeing Jordan lasciviously, his thick tongue molesting his lower lip as he did.

"She's got nothin' to do with this," I said. "Let her go on inside."

"I don't even like girls and I'm gonna fuck this one. Show her how good it can be up the ass."

"She's got a small one on her," Vince said. "Won't be hard to pretend she's a little boy."

How stupid could I be? Not only was this my fault, but I had put Jordan right in the middle of it.

I had no weapon of any kind, no way of defending myself, let alone her. I couldn't keep screwing up like this. I had to get better at what I was doing and fast. Of course, because of this screwup, I may not get the chance to get better.

Think. Come up with something. Fast.

"I wouldn't talk that way about a cop's wife," I said. "Only thing worse than killin' a cop is doin' anything at all to one of their wives."

"You ain't no cop," Ray said.

"No, but her husband is. Like I was saying. Messin' with her is misery like you don't need."

"You're fuckin' a cop's wife but you're tellin' us not to?" Vince said.

"I haven't touched her," I said. "I know better. Like I said, she has nothin' to do with this."

Ray seemed to consider what I had said.

"All this 'cause I'm interested in information about a kid who was killed six years ago?" I said.

"Why the interest?" Ray asked.

"We're the same age. Or would be. Could've been me."

"Still could be."

"This just doesn't make sense," I said. "Why the over-response? If you didn't kill LaMarcus, I wouldn't think you'd want to draw so much attention to yourselves. And if you did, I'd think you'd want to attract even less."

"Don't try to play me, boy," Ray said.

"I'm not. I'm serious."

"I want to be left the fuck alone," Ray said. "So I wanted to know what little punk was comin' to Vince's job site asking after me and why."

I nodded.

"Vince, blade," Ray said.

So fast I wasn't even sure it had happened at first, Vince had an arm around Jordan's throat and the point of a knife at her neck.

I took a step toward her.

"Don't do it," Ray said. "If you do, she'll be dead before you get there."

I stopped.

"Here's what's going to happen," Ray said. "I'm gonna ask you a couple of questions. If you lie or I even think you are, she's gonna get her throat slit. Understand?"

I nodded.

"Show him we ain't fuckin' around, Vince."

Vince cut into the side of Jordan's neck a little and she screamed.

"That's nothin'," Ray said. "A little scratch. Imagine if he really went to work on her, slicing through her skin like thin sheetrock paper."

Beside the beat of my heart in my head, all I could hear were the not dissimilar sounds of the wind, the *whoosh* of traffic on I-20, and Jordan's panicked breaths.

Jordan's breathing was loud and labored. Blood was on her neck, the blade, and Vince's fingers.

"Satisfy my curiosity and you'll walk," Ray said. "Lie to me and I'll leave you both bleeding out on this asphalt."

I nodded. "Okay," I said, "but I was serious about her being a cop's wife."

He looked at Jordan. "What's your husband's name? Where's he work? What's his badge number?"

She told him in a trembly voice. She sounded scared but as if she was telling the truth.

As she spoke, I stole a glance at Martin. He was beginning to stir. It wouldn't be long before he was awake and climbing out of the car right into this.

Ray nodded and looked back at me. "Why are you looking into what happened to that kid?"

"It started when I was a lot younger," I said. "I met Wayne Williams, became obsessed with the case. Well, I already was, but that really sealed it for me. I've studied the Atlanta Child Murders my whole life––or what seems like it. I came to LaMarcus through them, to see if he was one of the killer's victims––*that* killer's. When I met the family and saw all they had been through . . . I just wanted . . . to help. To try to find out who killed LaMarcus and why. That's it."

He nodded.

"What's her connection?" he asked, jerking his head toward Jordan.

"She's his sister. His stepsister."

"She really married to a cop?"

I nodded.

"You really not bangin' her?"

"I'm really not."

"But you want to be?"

"I do."

"Whatta you think, Vince? He tellin' the truth?"

"Can never go wrong by cuttin', Ray," Vince said.

Ray shook his head. "I'm sorry about your brother," he said to Jordan, "but I didn't kill him––or any other kids. I swear it. And I want to be left out of it. For all sorts of reasons. Not least of which is other things I got goin' right now. Look for whoever snuffed your brother, just leave me out of it. And make sure your husband and your boyfriend here do too. If y'all do, you'll never see me again. If you don't, I swear to Christ Vince will cut your tits off and mail one to your husband and one to this boy who wants to be bangin' you. And that'll just be for starters. Nod if you understand."

She did.

"Both of you."

I nodded too.

"Nod if you're going to leave me the fuck out of all this."

We both nodded.

"Only get one chance. No bullshit. No warnings. No mercy. And we won't just kill you. We'll do things to you first, things that'll make you wish we had just killed you. Cop's wife or not. Won't matter."

Without another word or gesture, Ray turned and walked away.

Vince shoved Jordan into me, licked her blood off his blade, and followed.

33

"Are you okay?" I asked.

She nodded.

She was shaking and seemed in shock.

I was holding her, trying to hug her fear and trauma away, but needed to look at her neck.

"How's your neck?" I asked. "Let me . . ."

I pulled back a little to examine her neck but it was too dark and she didn't want to let go.

"Come on," I said. "Let's go inside and get you taken care of."

Without letting go of her, I eased over and awkwardly opened the door, woke Martin up, and helped him out of the car.

"Sorry, buddy, but you're gonna have to walk. Can't carry you tonight."

He looked up at me sleepily, nodded, then stumbled out of the car, across the lot, and up the steps with us.

It took a little doing—we moved like the infirmed and inebriated attempting a three-legged race—but eventually we were in my room, Martin on a pallet on the floor, Jordan in my bed.

She was still trembling and her small hand was pressed against her neck.

"I need to look at it," I said.

I grabbed her wrist to ease her hand back. There was something erotic about the gesture, electric, and I wondered if she felt it too, or would have had she been able to.

She seemed to come out of her shock a bit and smiled up at me. "I like that."

"Me too."

"Sorry I'm being such a wimp."

"You're not. Not at all."

Pulling her hand back, I checked her wound. It was nearly two inches but didn't seem very deep and had pretty much stopped bleeding.

"Need to clean it," I said.

I tried to think of who might have peroxide, antibiotic ointment, and a Band-Aid, and felt like an inadequate adult for not having anything but soap, shampoo, toothpaste, deodorant, and fish sticks in the apartment.

"It's fine," she said. "Really."

Martin made a noise and shifted in his sleep and we both looked over at him.

"I'm so glad he slept through it," she said.

I nodded.

"Still can't believe it happened," she said. "Just . . . right out there . . . just . . ."

"I'm sorry," I said. "I should've never gone to see Vincent, should've never put you and Martin in a situation like that. Still can't believe I screwed up so bad. It was stupid and amateurish and I'm so sorry."

She shook her head. "You saved us," she said. "You stayed calm and you talked them out of . . . what they were going to do. They came with different intentions but you convinced Ray to alter his actions. You were . . . just to be able to stay calm and deal with the situation . . . It was impressive."

"Should've never been in that situation. Think about what could've happened. I've got to get better at this. And quick."

"What're you gonna do?" she asked. "Did you believe him? About not havin' anything to do with what happened to LaMarcus and what he'd do to me if you ..."

I shrugged. "Not sure how much I believe," I said. "Don't want to put you in danger like that again ... but ..."

"They're such ... They seem really evil."

I nodded. "Not a lot of humanity there."

"Listen," she said. "I don't want you to worry about me. I don't want you stopping for me. I'll be fine. I'll be more careful. But I don't want you gettin' hurt ... or ... worse. I mean it. It won't bring LaMarcus back. It's not worth gettin' killed over."

I thought about it. Was she right? If I was going to do this, do work like this in any way, I would have to figure out what was worth dying for and what wasn't. I'd have to make peace with the possibility of an early death and then live and investigate with abandon and conviction and without fear.

"I've ... lost so ... much," she said. "It's really all I know."

I nodded, but didn't say anything.

"I'd like to know something else," she said. "I really would."

"I'd like that for you too."

"I ..." she began, but trailed off and didn't return to it.

"What?" I said. "You what?"

"I ... I feel like ... I could know something different with you. With you and Martin. Feel like I already do."

I reached down and removed a strand of hair from her face.

She looked up at me with big green eyes that were beautiful and brilliant, shy and searching. Her beauty, which was breathtaking, snuck up on you. She looked as sweet and innocent and simple and sexy as a schoolgirl who'd yet to start fixing up for boys.

"Will you hold me?" she said.

"I will," I said, "but before I do ... I ... You probably don't even need me to say this . . . so I'm sayin' it for me . . . because I need to say it and I need to hear myself say it. I'm not sayin' you want to or would . . . but . . . there are certain lines I won't cross."

"Okay . . ."

"Marriage is one of them," I said.

"I had no idea you were so opposed to marriage," she said.

"No, I meant I can't sleep with——"

"I knew what you meant," she said. "You're so sweet, John. Just precious. And I already knew . . . I could tell . . . a woman can tell things about a man."

"I just . . ."

"Two things," she said. "One, I think it's time to . . . I hope not to be married much longer . . . and two," ——she smiled a sweet, playful, seductive smile—— "just knowin', in the poetic words of Raymond Pelton, you want to *bang me*, is enough for now."

34

This was not going to be pleasant.

I was meeting Bobby Battle and Frank Morgan at the Waffle House on Evans Mill Road to discuss the case and all my mistakes.

We were in a booth in the back corner of the crowded restaurant, the two of them on one side of the table, me on the other.

"I don't have long," Battle said. "So . . ."

"Bobby, this young man's gonna close your case for you and you can't spare a few minutes."

"I'm here, aren't I? I'm just sayin' we need to get on with it."

I nodded.

"And," Battle added, "if this case could be closed it would be."

Frank smiled and winked at me.

"I need to start with my fuckup," I said.

"*Another one?*" Battle said.

"More of a continuation."

Battle blew out a frustrated sigh and shook his head.

"Relax, Bobby," Frank said, "you're gonna give yourself a heart attack. And then what would happen? Criminals would take over the entire town."

Battle took a sip of his coffee and seemed to settle down a bit.

The restaurant was loud, the clanking of plates, the clinking of cups, the constant hum and occasional outburst of conversation making it difficult to concentrate.

"Raymond Pelton and Vincent Storr paid me a little visit last night," I said.

I then went on to tell them the rest in detail.

"Told you, didn't I?" Battle said. "Goddamn it. Frank, I told him to stay away from them. And this is why. Now you got them coming where you live to threaten you."

"Means he hit a nerve," Frank said.

"Nobody ever questioned guys like them being stirred up in all kind of bad shit. Of course they're gonna come out swingin'. Doesn't mean either of them had anything to do with what happened to LaMarcus."

"There's more," I said.

"The fuck?" Battle said. "What *more* could there be?"

"They threatened the sister."

Both men looked confused.

"LaMarcus's sister?" Battle said. "Jordan Moore? A cop's wife? Why? How would she even––Was she there? She was there with you? Are you fuckin' kiddin' me? What the *fuck* is the wife of a cop doing at your apartment, John?"

"She . . . we had just come from talking to Carlton Fields. Actually, she talked to him. I just listened."

"You've got the wife of a cop mixed up in this cluster fuck."

"Long before she married an abusive asshole cop, she was LaMarcus's stepsister. She wants to find out who killed him more than anybody."

He shook his head. I had him on that.

"Doesn't explain why she was at your apartment," he said. "Does her abusive, asshole of a husband know?"

"We were goin' to talk about what Carlton said. Which you two need to hear, by the way."

"What happened?" Bobby said. "Tell me exactly what happened—what was said, what was done, all of it, every detail."

I did.

The midday sun shone brightly through the plate glass windows that served as walls, shafts of light streaking the tile floor, emphasizing random objects indiscriminately—jukebox, bubblegum ball machine, an empty chair, a napkin holder, part of a tabletop.

"Now I'm gonna have to come down hard on Pelton and Storr," Battle was saying. "Have to find something on them to send them away for a long, long time."

"That won't be hard, Bobby," Frank said. "And you know it."

"Can't have them runnin' around threatenin' to cut the tits off a cop's wife. *Fuck.* I don't have time for this shit right now."

"I'll help you," Frank said.

"I do it and you're goin' to do two things for me," Battle said to me. "Stay out of my case and away from Larry Moore's wife."

I shook my head. "I can't," I said. "I won't."

"Are you fuckin' her?"

I shook my head again. "I'm not. And I won't."

"Come on, Bobby," Frank said. "Stop all this and let's hear what he has for us on the case. He's doin' great work, helpin' us a lot. And you know it. Nothin' was happenin' on this case and nothin' was goin' to. Show him the appreciation he deserves."

Battle shook his head. "Unbelievable. Appreciation, huh?"

"What did Carlton say?" Frank asked.

I told them.

"Said it was a secret," Frank said, "that his dad was going to come get him and take him away?"

I nodded. "And that lines up with what Anthony told me, that he'd do anything he had to to make a man out of his son."

They both seemed to think about it.

"That's good," Frank said. "Isn't it, Bobby? It's real good."

"I looked long and hard at Anthony Alex Williams, Jr. back

when it happened," Battle said. "You know what really broke in his favor—I mean, apart from there being no evidence against him at all? The rape. Couldn't see him doin' all this, includin' bringin' a condom, to rape his own son. Be one thing if he lived with him or if he had any history of pedophilia, but he didn't and I just couldn't see him stagin' this whole elaborate thing to kill then rape his own son."

I nodded. "What if he didn't?"

He looked at me like I was in need of electroshock therapy. "Yeah, that's what I just said."

"What if he committed the first but not the second crime? What if he killed him—by accident—and someone else moved him and raped him? Anthony plans to come and take his son, just like he told me and LaMarcus told Carlton, but he gives him too much of the sleep aid, accidentally overdoses him. He panics. Leaves LaMarcus in the bushes. Flees. Then someone else comes along and moves the body to the drainage culvert and rapes him. That would allow for the time LaMarcus spent lying in the one position on the ground before being moved, and would mean his dad didn't rape him."

"That's good," Frank said. "Really good. That could really be it. Think about it, Bobby. That makes a lot of sense."

Battle nodded absently, his unfocussed eyes staring at nothing in the distance as his cop mind worked the theory around.

"You got anybody in mind?" Frank asked me. "For the doer. The rapist."

I nodded. "Pelton. Storr. Carlton. Ralph Alderman."

"Alderman?" Bobby said.

I told them about Carlton's reaction to Ralph.

"Could mean nothin'," Battle said.

"But it could mean somethin'," Frank said. "It really could."

"Yeah, and it could be nothin'."

"Why did Ralph leave the force?" I asked.

"GBI did the investigation," Battle said. "Ask him."

I looked at Frank.

"I'll find out," he said.

"And while he's doin' that, I'll try to make the world a safer place for people like you and a fellow cop's wife by cleaning the streets of Pelton and Storr. And while we do that, how about *you* don't do anything? Nothin' else to get somebody killed or fuck up my case. Okay? Except . . . get a pager so I can keep tabs on you. I'm serious. Get one today."

35

"What the hell is wrong with you?" the small woman yelled.

She was standing at the fence in front of Safe Haven, having just screeched up in her car and stormed up to the chain-link barrier, and was yelling over it at Jordan.

Jordan and I were sitting on the center bench on the breezeway. Besides Ralph we were the only two outside. It would be another twenty minutes or so until the kids crashed the playground.

"Oh no," Jordan said.

"Who is it?"

"Carlton's mom," she said. "Vanessa."

So short she could barely see over the fence, the tiny woman had straight black hair and a darkish complexion that made her look part Native-American.

"How could you . . ." Vanessa was saying.

Ralph was moving in her direction but from inside the fence.

"You stay the hell away from me you evil son of a—"

"Vanessa," Jordan said as we reached her. "What's going on? What is it? Why're you doing this?"

"How could you, Jordan?" she said.

"How could I what?"

"You're supposed to protect children, especially the ones like Carlton."

"Ma'am, I'm gonna have to ask you to leave," Ralph was saying.

His shaky voice betrayed his nervousness, and though it was a cool morning, his shirt was now soaked through with sweat.

"Get this fat piece of shit away from me right now," Vanessa said, "or I swear to God I'll have this place shut down by nightfall."

"Give us a minute, Ralph," Jordan said.

"But—"

"Now."

"Yes, ma'am," he said, backing away. "I'll be right over here if you—"

"Ralph," she said, "stop talking and go. Now."

He did, backing away awkwardly over to his sentry post position near the main gate.

"I can't believe you let that fat creepy bastard around my son."

"I didn't. I mean . . . not on purpose. And all he did was see him for a second from about twenty-five feet away."

"Well that was enough to upset him as bad as I've ever seen him . . . except when . . . your . . . brother died."

"My brother didn't just die. He was the victim of a violent murder."

"And you've got the man who most likely did it working for you, supposedly protecting other children. You bring him around my son. What the fuck is wrong with you?"

The conversation wasn't pleasant, but the day was. Cool, crisp air, no humidity, orange and brown burnished leaves emblazoned on the trees, and the overall good feeling of fall.

"Why is Carlton so afraid of Ralph?" I asked.

"Fat bastard terrorized the hell out of them when they were little."

I couldn't imagine Carlton ever being little, which was somewhat odd to think because his mom was an extremely petite woman, smaller even than Jordan.

"How?"

"In a thousand different ways. He bullied the bejesus out of them. Made them do things. He's creepy as hell. Never have been able to get the full story out of Carlton, but it was bad."

"I had no idea," Jordan said.

"Are you serious? How could you not know something like that? How could you have him working here? What the hell kind of haven you running here? Sure as shit ain't safe."

"Did you bully my brother?" Jordan asked Ralph.

The moment Vanessa had turned to leave, we had walked directly over to where he stood.

"What? No. Is that what that crazy bitch said?"

"Whoa," I said.

"Watch it with that, Ralph," Jordan said.

"Sorry, but . . . it's insane."

"It's not insane," I said. "You're a bully."

"I'm not. I've never . . . All I did was teach them some discipline. That's it. Neither of them had a dad around. I was the only man in their lives, the only adult to take an interest in them, in how they turned out, in what kind of men they would become."

"You never touched them?" I said.

"*What? No.* Oh God, no. See? I told you. If she said that then she's insane. I swear to God. I never. That's so sick. I would never. Not ever. Not anybody."

He was in full panic mode—red faced, raised, tight, shrill voice, wide, wild eyes.

"Did you kill LaMarcus?" Jordan asked.

"*Jordan,*" he said, his wounded voice as saddened as shocked. "Of course not. How could you even ask. I never laid a finger on him. Never. I didn't bully him or hurt him or Carlton in any way. Not ever. I swear to God. Strap me up to a polygraph right now. I'm tellin' the truth. I swear it."

Ida sat quietly thinking for a long moment, chewing her lip as she did, her brow furrowed, her eyes narrowed in concentration.

Jordan had just finished telling her what Vanessa had accused Ralph of and Ralph's response.

Kids and staff out on the playground under the watchful gaze of Ralph Alderman, the three of us were alone inside the large, empty main room of the daycare center.

The room smelled of sleep and sweat, of glue and paint, of cleaning chemicals and air freshener, every surface moist and sticky.

"Whatta you think I should do, John?" she asked. "Let him go right now? Give him a chance to respond? Try to line up a polygraph?"

I shrugged.

Before I could answer, she added, "I'd find it very hard to fire a man over an accusation. I mean, that's all we have, right? He's never given me one minute of trouble. He's overzealous some-times, but that's it."

"It'd be nice to be able to have him here so we could watch him," I said. "Dig a little deeper into his life while keeping an eye on him, but . . . the stakes are just too high."

"You think it's possible he killed my boy?"

I nodded. "It's possible he had something to do with what happened to LaMarcus––even if someone else was involved too."

"Someone else?"

"We think it's at least possible that two people were involved."

"Well find out fast," she said. "'Cause I can't fire a good employee and family friend because of an accusation."

"I will," I said, thinking that if I didn't and something happened to one of the kids in their care . . .

36

"Y ou okay?" Frank Morgan asked.

I was walking to my car when he pulled into the Safe Haven parking lot and rolled down his passenger side window.

I shrugged.

"Get in," he said.

I did.

"When's the last time you've eaten?"

"Not sure. Last night I guess. But I'm okay."

"Let's grab a burger. We'll just run through a drive-thru. Eat in the car. I'll bring you right back here in a few minutes."

"I'm not hungry," I said. "But you eat. I'll go along for the ride."

"How much money you got?" he asked.

"On me? None. But . . ."

"But," he said, "somewhere else you have plenty?"

"Well, not plenty, but . . ."

"Any?"

I nodded.

"How much? And don't lie to me."

"Gas money for the rest of the week."

"That much, huh? So you can get where you need to go—including work and working this case and Grady to help someone else, but you can't eat if you do."

"I can eat. I'm eating."

"Here's what's gonna happen," he said. "I'm gonna buy you one of these awful Cindy's burgers up here and you're gonna eat it just like it's decent. Then I'm gonna give you this crisp fifty dollar bill in my wallet and you're gonna eat the rest of this week—every day, hell, twice a day—and the only thing you're going to say is what you like on your burger. Understand?"

I had to swallow hard against the lump in my throat and blink back the tears stinging my eyes.

The relief I felt was indescribable.

"Thank you, Frank."

"*Thank you Frank* is not a condiment. Tell me what you want on your knockoff burger."

"It means more than you'll ever know."

"It's just food. It's not love."

"The hell it's not," I said. "The hell it's not."

He pulled up and we ordered. While we waited, advancing around the building one car length at a time every few minutes, he handed me the fifty out of his wallet and said, "So now that your money troubles are temporarily over, tell me what's bothering you."

"This case. When I'm not making rookie mistakes, I'm not gettin' anywhere. I suck at this. And that's not just a shame because this is what I want to do with my life, but because somebody really needs to find out who killed LaMarcus and do something about it."

He nodded. We finally got our food and we pulled back out onto the road.

"Thing is," I said, "I have too many not too few suspects. I can't exclude anyone."

"Often the case," he said. "Tell you what . . . between bites of that burger, why don't you walk me through it."

I did.

"I can see it being one perp or two," I said. "I can see it being the biological father or Pelton or Storr or Alderman or Carlton or some combination of them—one to do the killing, another the rape, but . . . I can't exclude any of them. Hell, I can't even completely rule out Wayne Williams. It's driving me crazy."

He nodded, his expression telling me he knew exactly what I meant.

"It's that way far more often than you'd think," he said. "Sometimes there's several people who could've done it and you can't pinpoint which one. Others you know exactly who did it and just can't prove it. And far too often you can never be certain about exactly what happened or who did what. Think about Wayne Williams. I'm pretty sure he's the Atlanta Child Murderer, but I'm not certain. You've looked at most of the evidence and you're not certain one way or the other. It's the job. Can you reconcile ambiguity? Can you live with not knowing? Move on."

"I don't know that I can."

"You can live with far more than you think you can," he said. "You'll learn that soon enough."

It was maybe the first time he'd treated me like anything other than a peer. I didn't like it. He was probably right. I was pretty sure he was. But that didn't mean I had to like it.

We ate in silence a few moments as he drove back down Flat Shoals toward Safe Haven.

"You know," he said, "it's at least possible that the doer is someone else entirely."

"Why I'm not gonna stop looking," I said.

"Never doubted that," he said. "Not for a minute."

37

"I would've committed suicide if it weren't for this group," a nervous, emaciated, sunbaked young woman said. "I'm not just being melodramatic. I mean it. If I didn't have you guys . . . if I didn't have this work to do . . ."

"It works if you work it," an older man with a wet, gurgley smoker's voice said. "You did the work. We just supported you."

I had come with Jordan and Ida to the support group for grieving parents held in a meeting room of the K Center at Chapel Hill.

It was facilitated by George Clarke, a tall, thin, soft-spoken African-American pastor in a navy-blue suit and burgundy clerical collar.

"Grief is a natural response to loss," Pastor George had said. "It's the emotional suffering you feel when something or someone you love is taken away. The more significant the loss, the more intense the grief will be. And there's no loss like the loss of a child. No pain like it. Nothin' compares. There's nothin' more personal or individual than the process of grieving. There's no one single way to do it. There are no steps. No rules. No particular timeframe. But there are common stages and ways of coping and dealing and healing that work far better than others. And most important . . . is having a support system. That's why we're here."

After those introductory remarks and a reminder of the group's ground rules, each member took a turn sharing.

"You get to a point where loss and pain and grief are all you know," Jordan said.

It was Jordan's turn.

She looked at me. "Someone decent and good and kind comes along, something good happens in your life, and you don't even know how to process it, but you realize if you don't, if you don't recognize the good when it comes along, if you don't receive it, then you've lost, trauma and tragedy have won, have gotten the last word. You realize that you might as well have died when your child did, because what you're doing is not living, is not life."

Several people nodded, but a few others, others probably more recently entering the grief process, still raw, weren't as sure.

"We don't want to live," she said. "We feel not just sad, not just broken from the unimaginable loss, unthinkable undoing of our very existences, we feel guilty. Guilty for being here, for being alive, guilt that is compounded and multiplied by anything with even the possibility of leading to something like joy or pleasure or even the slight lightening of the load of pain we bear."

Jordan was in her element here. She knew loss. She knew pain. She knew grief. And she spoke more eloquently about it, and with more wisdom and profundity, than in any other situation I had seen her in or on any other topic I had witnessed her address.

Next up was a youngish, buttoned-up black man with glasses and an honest to God pocket protector. "I was reading *Crime and Punishment* this week and came across this–– 'The darker the night, the brighter the stars, the deeper the grief, the closer is God.' When I first read it I really liked it. Even highlighted it and wrote it down. But the more I read it, the more I just wasn't sure. I mean . . . is it true? Doesn't really seem true except maybe for some of the time."

"God is close to a broken heart," an elderly black lady said, "an ever present help in our time of need."

"Those are just platitudes," the professorial-looking man said. "Just 'cause someone said it doesn't make it true."

"It's in the Bible," she said. "That's what makes it true."

"I'll tell you what's true," a middle-aged white man said. "Pain. Pain is truth. It's so true sometimes there seems like there's nothin' else. I just . . . I'm not sure I can keep going like this, feeling like this. I'm not sure I even want to."

"I didn't just lose a child," Ida said when it was her turn. "I lost a grandchild too. My son was the victim of violence and I still don't know who did it. There's no . . . Talk about pain. Talk about darkness and a demon that won't leave you alone. Then to see your grandchild suffer for all of her short life and then die . . . It's too much. It doesn't ever go away. Not ever. But it does become just barely bearable. Just barely. It does. Trust me. Hang on. Don't give up."

"Why?" the middle-aged white man asked. "So I can get to barely bearable? That's what I have to look forward to? That's not enough."

Sitting among the ruins, listening to the raw bone pain pour out, feeling the overwhelming oppression of loss and grief, despair and hopelessness, I realized just how little loss I had undergone, just how pain free my relatively easy existence had been thus far, and on top of every other difficult emotion I was experiencing, I also felt guilt.

"I don't see how y'all do it," I said to Ida and Jordan after the group had concluded, its members dispersed back to the despair that was the norm of their lives.

We were walking down the long, light blue-carpeted hallway of the K Center toward the door.

"To live with the . . . with what you do . . . then to . . . take in all the pain and grief of the group. It just seems . . . too much."

"Sometimes it is," Ida said.

"It really does help to share it," Jordan said. "To feel heard and understood, to get to give that back to others in a similar situation."

I wondered which I could do to help more people—ministry or investigation. How could I combine my interests, talents, and opportunities to make some small difference in the time and place and circumstance I was born into.

"Thank you again for all you're doin' for us," Ida said. "You can't know what it means, how it helps, but . . ."

I waited, unable to imagine what was coming next.

"We lived this way a long time. We gonna get by. Don't you be puttin' too much undo pressure on yourself."

I must have inadvertently expressed I wasn't following.

"We don't have any expectations," Jordan said. "We've resigned ourselves to not knowing what happened to LaMarcus and why."

"Well, I haven't," I said. "I can't. I won't."

"'For now we see through a glass, darkly,'" Ida said, quoting Saint Paul, "'but then face to face: now I know in part; but then shall I know even as also I am known.' Sometimes we just don't get to know."

"I can't accept that," I said.

She shook her head and frowned.

"You live long enough, you'll learn to."

38

Later that afternoon, Bishop Paulk's secretary, Dottie Bridges, had called the college and asked me to come to the bishop's office as soon as I had finished cleaning the classrooms.

I arrived in the dimming, dusky early evening to find Bishop Paulk and Pastor Don waiting for me.

The entire K Center was quiet, the other offices empty, the rest of the staff having gone home for the day.

As usual, both men were in suits and full clerical collars.

Having just come from work, I was in faded jeans, a gray Magic Johnson sweatshirt, and a pair of New Balance Worthy 790s with purple and yellow Laker color highlights, and I felt underdressed and out of place.

They were friendly and welcoming and asked about my classes and work at EPI and my life in general, Bishop Paulk behind his enormous desk, Pastor Don and I in the two chairs across the desk from him.

"How's your investigation going?" Don asked.

I told them.

"You must really be getting somewhere with it," he said. "Getting close to the killer."

"What makes you say that?"

"We received another call from someone claiming to be the killer," Earl Paulk said.

"Really?" I asked, my mind racing. "Wow. That's . . . Was it the same guy?"

"I can't be sure," he said. "It's been a long time. But . . . I just don't know. It could be, but he sounded different somehow."

I nodded and thought about it. "Of course it could be unrelated to anything I've done."

"Actually, he mentioned you by name," he said.

"Really?"

I just thought my mind was racing before.

Who could it be? I had talked to so many possible suspects. Was it one of them or someone I wasn't even aware of?

"What did he say?"

"That he had called me before, that he needed help, that he wanted to stop, that you were stirring it all up for him and the memories were haunting him and he couldn't take it."

I thought about who I had spoken with that would know of my connection to Chapel Hill and Bishop Paulk.

"You have any idea who it could be?" Don asked. "Got a leading suspect?"

"Not really, no."

"What would you do if you were given the chance to talk to him?" Earl asked.

I noticed he asked what would I do not what would I say, and I wondered if that was intentional.

"What would I do?"

"How would you handle it?"

I really didn't know. I had imagined various scenarios, of course, but not very seriously, not in any but the most fantastical ways.

"I'm not sure exactly."

"Would you talk to him as an investigator or as a minister?"

"I don't know. I . . . Honestly, I often find myself torn between the two, but . . ."

"Are you more interested in temporary justice or his eternal soul?"

I knew the answer immediately, but took a beat to give it because I didn't want to sound flippant. "Both," I said.

"There's got to be a place for both," Don said.

"I hope so."

"But when they're at odds," Earl said, "which will you choose?"

I didn't respond, just thought about it.

"I'm a minister," he said. "First. Last. Always. I want to help him if I can."

I nodded.

"He says he's gonna kill again if he doesn't get help."

My heart started pounding even harder.

"You interested in helping me help him?"

I said I was, but thought we might have differing ideas of what that meant exactly.

"He said he'd come see us—you, me, and Pastor Don—if and only if all three of us were here. And no one else was. No cops. No staff. No one. Only us. He said for us to be here at the church every night this week and when he was ready and convinced there were no cops, he'd come by and talk to us."

The excitement shooting through me was like a drug. I couldn't believe this was happening. This was why I was here—the earlier phone calls to Bishop Paulk the reason I was standing in his office at this moment.

"You willing to stay with us here tonight and every night this week until he shows?" Don asked.

I was nodding before he was even close to finishing the question.

I'd have to figure out a way of getting Martin fed, and I'd miss my time with Jordan, but this was something I had to do.

"And to be here as a churchman and not a lawman," Earl said.

I wasn't either. Not really. But I knew what he meant, and I nodded, though it was somewhat disingenuous. Whatever I was, whatever words fit better than churchman and lawman, I could never be either or, never be only one or the other, and I suspected he knew it.

"We're not saying you can't be who you are," Don said. "Just that you understand and respect what we're about. We're going to do our best to get him to turn himself in—"

"But we're not setting a trap for him," Earl said. "Not going to try to make an arrest ourselves and we don't want you to."

"I understand."

Sitting quietly in the enormous empty building waiting for a killer to call was creepy and unnerving.

Earlier in the evening, Norma Paulk, the bishop's wife, had brought us dinner. After eating, we had settled in to wait—sitting, standing, walking around the office.

Waiting.

For the first few hours, we had talked about the case and Kingdom Theology and the challenges I would face attempting to do both ministry and law enforcement. Later, we had each pulled a book from the shelf and read in silence. Now we just sat and waited.

I had been unable to communicate with Martin or Jordan and I wondered if they were worried.

No call came that first night.

At a little after two in the morning on the second night, the killer called back and said he wasn't coming that night either, but that he had been watching and was encouraged to see that we had not involved the cops. If that continued he'd come see us soon.

Weary and welcoming the release, we rushed out quickly toward the opportunity to get some actual sleep in our beds, and it wasn't until after the Paulks had left together that I remembered I had parked on the side of the building—something I had done for a few minutes privacy with Jordan before going in.

The night was dark and quiet, very little visible back here, no sound but that of the wind.

Beneath thick clouds that covered the moon and the stars nothing stirred, nothing contradicted my sense of utter isolation.

As I walked around the back of the enormous K Center in the blackness of the night, I kept imagining the killer jumping out of the darkness to strangle or stab or rape or brain me, and I could feel the fear starting to seize me up, mind and body.

The grass of the hilly ground was damp with dew, the soft sounds of my footfalls barely perceptible, but I thought for sure I heard others in the short distance over my right shoulder.

There's no one there. It's just your imagination, your fear. Don't look. Just keep walking.

Unable to help myself, I spun around and scanned the area as best I could.

No one was there that I could make out, but I could only see a short distance into the dark.

Turning back around, I picked up my pace, walking so fast it was nearly a run.

My footfalls were louder now.

And so were the others. Or the others I thought I heard.

I wanted to run but was unable to do anything other than was I was doing.

When I reached the edge of the building, the vast parking lot was visible—hundreds and hundreds of empty spots and there in the not too far distance a lone automobile, appearing eerie and abandoned.

As frightened as I had been back behind the K Center in the dark, I realized that I was far more vulnerable in the long lighted walk across the lot.

I pictured predator and prey on a shimmering African plain—a small gazelle separated from the herd, a sleek cheetah, the fastest land animal on the planet, designed for this, for the chase, for the kill.

Feeling far more exposed than at any other time in my entire life, I stumbled down the hill and began my trek toward my vehicle.

Not far into it, I began to jog. Not long after that, I began to run.

Glancing over my shoulder often, scanning the area all around me as best I could, I ran awkwardly, unsteadily, disjointedly, my body stiff with fear, my blood thick with adrenaline.

It wasn't until I was well into my run that I noticed the other car in the lot.

About a hundred feet away in the far rear corner, a black Oldsmobile Cutlass with darkly tinted windows had been backed into the parking spot, its nose pointing toward my car, a tiny trail of exhaust rising up and vanishing into the night air behind it.

I was too close to the car to turn around, but even if I hadn't been, the church building behind me was locked, unable to provide any sanctuary.

I ran even faster.

I could feel myself losing my balance, about to trip, to fall face first into the ungiving asphalt.

But somehow I managed to stay on my faltering feet.

As I ran, I continued to scan the entire area, but most of my focus and mental energy was trained on the Cutlass, which had yet to move.

When I finally made it to my car and was safely inside, I felt foolish, but not foolish enough not to check my backseat and speed away, my eyes darting to my rearview mirror often as I did—particularly toward the parking spot in the back of the lot where the dark car still mercifully remained.

The call came at midnight on the third night.

The loud, abrupt ring piercing the silence, startling.

Bishop Paulk's voice was dry and quiet and sounded sleepy.

My pulse kicked into overdrive, adrenaline spiking into the red, my mind reeling.

Am I really this close to the killer?

"There's no one here but us," Earl was saying into the phone. "You have my word. I even sent our security guard home for the evening . . . It's not a trap . . . I want to help you. That's all I'm interested in. I want you to know God loves you no matter what you've done . . . No, I . . . I do. I truly believe that."

I stood and began moving around a bit.

"Yes, he's here. Don too."

Bishop grew quiet, listening to what I assumed were our instructions.

"We'll do that. Just like you ask, but I don't want anyone getting hurt. We're operating in good faith. Are you doing the same?"

He waited.

"Why not meet with all three of us? Or let John and Pastor Don go home and just meet with me . . . Okay. Just don't hurt those who're trying to help you."

When the bishop hung up, he kept his hand on the receiver for a long moment, seemingly contemplating the conversation.

"Well?" Don said.

"He wants us to split up. One at each door. Wants to make sure we don't gang up on him. He'll approach one of us and if he's comfortable, whoever he chooses can lead him to the other two."

"He's just separating us so he can pick us off one at a time."

"Why? Why would he do that? He says we're to stand at three different doors but that we can keep the doors locked so we can see him approaching and know it's not an ambush."

"Something's just not right about it," Don said.

"He kills children," Earl said. "He's probably not a threat to us, but even if he is, we've got to try to stop him. God will be with us."

"What do you think, John?" Don asked.

"That you're both right. Something's definitely not right, but we can't let that stop us from trying to stop him."

"Why is he really separating us?" Don said.

"It could be what he said, but . . . I think it's far more likely that he has another motive. What if he's not really wanting help at all? What if he thinks I'm getting too close, thinks I know more than I do, and he's really just trying to get me alone."

"That makes far more sense," Don said. "Would explain why he wanted you here."

"Don and I can just go down," Earl said.

I shook my head. "I think we should do it just like he said to. There's no way I can just stay up here. If there's even a chance to talk to him, to . . . I've got to try. We can be extra careful and keep the doors locked until we see him."

Bishop Paulk stood, withdrew a key from his desk, and handed it to me. "He wants you at the front door, in the vestibule near the bookstore, me in the back, and Don on the side. Don't take any chances. Be safe. Don't open the door until he shows you he's unarmed. Let's pray before we go."

The three of us joined hands and the bishop prayed for our protection and that we might help the man God was bringing to us tonight.

I slowly walked down the dark, empty hallway of the K Center toward the front door far more afraid than I could ever remember being before.

I was inspired by Earl and Don's bravery, and I was excited about the possibility of confronting one of the killers who had haunted me for so long, but more than anything I was scared. So scared I shook with it.

The only illumination came from the blood-red glow of the illuminated Exit signs and the power indicator of the emergency backup lights.

The enormous building, which held thousands for worship services and really did resemble an airplane hanger, felt vacuous, its continuous creaks echoing through the emptiness, reminding me how very alone I was.

I moved gradually, gripping the key like a weapon, edging toward the front and my fate.

Who was waiting for me? Was it LaMarcus's killer? Pelton? Storr? Anthony Alex Williams, Jr? Ralph Alderman? Maybe it really was the killer and maybe I had no idea who he was.

Up ahead, about another two hundred feet or so, I could see just a bit less dimness, as ambient lighting from outside found its way through the glass doors and into the vestibule.

As I drew closer, inch by inch, step by step, I felt more and more dread bearing down on me, heavy, oppressive, suffocating.

When I was less than a hundred feet away, I said a prayer of my own. Please protect me. Don't let me die just as my life is getting started. Please help me catch LaMarcus's killer.

Reaching the vestibule, I reminded myself––the doors are locked. Don't get too close to them. Stand sideways. Move about. Don't be an easy target. Keep your eyes wide and unfocused. Alert on movement.

Passing by the huge staircase that led up to the balcony, I moved toward the doors a little quicker now that there was a little more light.

When I reached the doors, I checked each one to ensure they were locked. Jerking hard on each one, I confirmed that I was locked inside, that at least glass doors separated me from––

And then he was on me.

Coming up from behind, snatching me back, slinging me to the ground, pulling me back into the darkness.

On top of me now. Weight pressing down. Large hunting knife with serrated blade at my throat.

"Move a muscle and I'll slit your fuckin' throat," he hissed in a low, mean whisper.

He wore a transparent plastic mask with female features and big bright makeup––round pink dots on the cheeks, pouty red pucker at the lips, thick blue swaths beneath thick black eyebrows.

The plastic facade was made all the more frightening for its lack of expression.

Behind the feminine mask, his masculine features and five o'clock shadow looked eerie and creepy and twisted.

"See how easy it is for me to get to you," he said in a hoarse whisper. "How easily I could kill you. Right now. With just the slightest flick of my wrist, twist of my blade."

I didn't respond.

"Nod if you know I could kill you quickly, quietly, and easily right now."

I nodded, careful not to move my neck too much.

"Go back to where you came from. Quit dredging up the past. Stay away from us, stay out of shit that's got nothin' to do with you. Understand? Next time . . . there won't be a next time. You'll just be dead. So will someone you care about. For her sake stop being stupid and move along."

Suddenly, and seemingly out of nowhere, Earl Paulk, shoulder lowered, plowed into the man and knocked him off me.

When the man hit the ground, he rolled, then adroitly jumped up and began running down the opposite hallway from the one I and the bishop had come down.

He hit Don, who was coming up from that direction, knocking him to the ground.

Don got up as quickly as he could and gave chase, but came back a little while later, having been unable to catch the man.

"Y'all okay?" Don asked.

We nodded.

"You?" Earl asked.

He nodded.

"Guess we both had the idea to come check on you about the same time," Earl said.

Don smiled and nodded, then turned to me. "What did he say to you?"

"Told me how easy it would be for him to kill me and said that's exactly what he would do if I didn't go back to where I came from and leave everything here alone."

"Any idea who it was?" Earl asked.

I shook my head. "Not really. If I had to guess—and that's truly all it is, a guess—I'd say a cop named Larry Moore."

39

A few days later, Martin and I were playing basketball when
Bobby Battle sped into the apartment complex in his
unmarked car, not slowing down until he reached the parking
area nearest the courts.

Jordan, Martin, and I had fallen into a routine of sorts—
Martin and I playing basketball in the afternoon, the three of us
getting dinner of some kind, renting a movie at the video store
next to the supermarket, and hanging out when Jordan was off
and Larry was at work, then, after Martin fell asleep, Jordan and I
alone, holding each other through the late, lonely hours of
the night.

We had become something like a family. Maybe even something just like it. And Atlanta was feeling a lot like home. A lot
like it.

"Keep workin' on your jump shot, buddy," I said to Martin.
"I'll be back in a minute."

I walked over toward Battle, meeting him about halfway
between his car and the courts.

We were well into September now and the autumnal air was

cool and a bit breezy, so unlike my part of Florida this time of year.

"Thought I told you to get a pager?" Battle said.

"You did."

"Well?"

"I did."

"Where is it?" he asked.

"In my room."

"Only works if you have it on you," he said. "Keep it on you. I've been tryin' to get in touch with you for a hell of a long time."

"Okay. Sorry. I will. What's wrong?"

"Ray and Vince are in the wind."

"What?" I asked, looking around the complex before I realized what I was doing.

"We've been keepin' tabs on 'em, tryin' to catch 'em at somethin' we can come down hard on 'em for . . . and they just vanished."

I shook my head. "*Shit.*"

"I thought maybe they had you," he said. "So keep the goddamn pager on you at all times, okay?"

"Okay."

"We're lookin' for them," he said. "Hopefully we'll have 'em soon. But for now . . . lay low and keep your pager on and with you at all times."

"I will. Sorry."

"Just tryin' to look out for you. All part of the service."

"Were they under surveillance three nights ago?" I asked. "The entire night."

"Yeah. Why?"

I told him what had happened at the K Center a few nights back.

"The fuck is wrong with you, John? We had a chance to get him and you didn't even bother to tell us. Y'all could've been killed."

"I know. I just . . . I . . . Lettin' you know wasn't an option."

"You need to pick a side, John," he said. "I mean . . . goddamn. . . You can't keep . . ."

He trailed off and we were silent a moment.

"You think it was one of them?" he asked.

"Wondered if it could've been," I said.

"Maybe it was," he said. "Maybe one slipped away while the other made it seem like they were together. I'll have to check with the surveillance team. You really think it could be one of them?"

I shrugged. "At the time I thought it was Larry Moore."

"*What*? Seriously? 'Cause you're fuckin' his wife? Now ain't that a whole other cluster fuck. Son, you know how to make some shit complicated, don't you?"

"I'm not sleeping with his wife," I said. "But I notice you're not sayin' he's not capable of somethin' like that."

"What? Tryin' to scare you away from his pretty little wife? 'Cause I could see his dumb ass doin' somethin' like that. It's over the top and stupid as hell, but . . . What I *can't* see him doin' is actually killin' you. But . . . *fuck* . . . let me go see what I can find out."

He turned to head back toward his car, then stopped, spun back around. "And John, look how exposed you are out here like this," he said, sweeping his arm in a broad gesture that encompassed the basketball court. "And with the kid. What're you thinkin'? You tryin' to get him killed too?"

After tucking Martin away safely, I called Jordan to warn her about Ray and Vince, but she wasn't at Safe Haven and neither was Ida, and all the woman working knew was that they had taken some time off—Jordan all day, Ida only the evening.

I called Ida's home next. There was no answer.

I wondered if I should call Jordan at home. What if Larry answered? What if all I did was make things far worse for her than they already were?

I thought about it for a long while, eventually reaching the conclusion that with Ray and Vince unaccounted for, I had to take the chance.

I let the phone ring for a very long time but no one answered.

And then I . . . I didn't know what to do.

What could I do? I was completely powerless. I had no idea where she was or if she was okay. I had no way to contact her, to check on her, to see if Ray and Vince had her at this very moment or if she was just shopping for supplies for Safe Haven with Ida.

Think, I told myself. There's got to be something. You've got to figure out something. Come on.

Two things came to mind. I could go to Safe Haven and talk to Ralph. If anyone knew where Ida and Jordan were or were supposed to be, it would be him. Or I could call Bobby Battle.

I decided to do both.

First I called Battle.

"Jordan Moore is not at work and I can't find her," I said. "Same for Ida Williams. Is Larry on duty? Can you check on her? Find out discretely if he knows where she is? Do you think Ray and Vince could have her?"

"I'm on it," he said, and hung up.

As I was about to leave for Safe Haven to see if Ralph might be willing to part with any information he might have about the whereabouts of Jordan and Ida, my phone rang.

Roger Lawson had taken a turn for the worse and was asking to see me.

Driving far faster than I should on west I-20 toward downtown and Grady, I could only worry about Jordan, only hope she was okay, only hope Bobby Battle would make sure she was.

Actually, those weren't the only things I could do.

I could also pray. I could choose to trust. I could accept the things I couldn't change. I could change the things I could. I could find peace by acknowledging my powerlessness, serenity by letting go.

So I did—or tried to, reaching for the random blue Sparrow cassette on the backseat. As if an answer to prayer, it was Steve Camp's *One on One* and it was cued up to the beginning of "He's All You Need," which helped me find a fragile but very present peace as I sped toward downtown Atlanta.

40

"I'm scared," Roger Lawson said, his feeble voice no more than a hoarse, low, whistley whisper.

I nodded. "I know," I said. "And it's okay to be. It's natural. But you have nothin' to be afraid of."

I was standing beside his bed, holding his hand, leaning over, my face just inches from his.

"There's nothing but love waiting on you," I said.

"Are you sure?"

"I am. It's the only thing I'm sure of."

"I don't want to die, damn it," he said.

I nodded. "I know. I'm so, so sorry."

"Help me. Do something. I can't . . . this can't be it."

I thought back to my earlier prayer on I-20 and said, "God, grant us the serenity to accept the things we cannot change. The courage to change the things we can. And wisdom to know the difference."

He squeezed my hand.

"Say it with me," I said. "God . . . God, grant us the serenity to accept the things we cannot change. The courage to change the things we can. And wisdom to know the difference."

We said it several times together, until it became like a mantra, until peace entered the room, until he fell asleep. Peaceful sleep.

As he slept, I continued to hold his hand and say the prayer, repeating different forms, expanding, repeating.

"God, give us grace to accept with serenity the things that cannot be changed. Courage to change the things that should be changed. And the wisdom to distinguish the one from the other. Living one day at a time, enjoying one moment at a time, accepting hardship as a pathway to peace. Taking, as Jesus did, this sinful world as it is, not as we would have it be. Trusting that you will make all things right if we surrender to your will. So that we may be reasonably happy in this life and supremely happy with you forever in the next."

I continued praying for peace as Roger continued sleeping peacefully, continued until my mouth was dry and my hand ached, until he stopped breathing and the peace he was experiencing went way beyond sleep, beyond mortal, beyond the beyond and into what dreams may come.

Long after the nurses came, long after the tubes had been removed and the machines turned off, I was still praying the prayer of peace.

As I walked down the central corridor of the cold, sterile hospital, I felt sad and alone, helpless and hopeless.

And then I saw Ida and some of the pain and sadness abated.

In an instant I no longer felt alone, my spirits buoyed a bit before I realized what her presence her must mean.

"John," she said. "How'd you hear?"

"Hear what? What is it? Where's Jordan?"

"She's . . ."

"What happened? Is she—"

"She's . . . Come on. I'll take you to her."

She led me back down the corridor and along another to the

emergency room and the small curtained area Jordan was waiting in.

When she saw me, she burst into tears.

"Wait here with her while I go get the car," Ida said. "Had to park in Timbuktu."

I rushed over to Jordan's bed.

"Oh, John," she said. "I'm . . . I'm so . . . so glad you're here. I'm . . . I don't know what to say."

"Start with what happened."

Her arm was in a sling, her wrist in a brace. Her face was swollen, red, and puffy around her eyes, one of which was quickly turning black.

"It's just sprained, not broken. Doesn't matter now. You're here. That's all that matters."

"Who was it?" I asked. "Who did it?"

She looked confused.

"Who?"

"Larry," she said. "Who else."

"Thought it might have been Ray and Vince."

She shook her head. "No, but . . ."

"What?"

"He knows about them," she said. "I don't know how. But he claims he's gonna kill them."

"What all'd you tell him?"

"Nothin'. John, I haven't told him anything about anything. That's what I got this for. It's got to be Battle. *Brothers in blue* and all that shit."

"I'm so glad you're okay," I said. "I was so worried and––"

"Me too. You're all I've been able to think about. I can't believe you're here. How are you?"

I told her.

"Oh, John," she said. "I'm so sorry. Are you okay?"

"I am now. Now that I know you are, that I'm with you. You can never go back to him. Never."

"I'm not. I won't. I'm moving in with Mom until I can . . . until things get . . ."

I nodded.

"I'm so worried," she said. "I have such a bad feeling. Larry's crazy. He's . . . He'll do . . . He's capable of anything. And if Bobby Battle told him about Raymond and Vincent, what else has he told him?"

"It'll be okay. We'll figure it out. I promise."

"I've fallen in love with you, John. Totally and completely. Head over heels. The real deal."

"I love you," I said. "I'm so in love with you."

"I've already contacted an attorney," she said. "I'm . . . I'll be free of him at last. For good. And then . . ."

"And then," I said. "I like the sound of that."

"Speaking of sounds," she said, "I know it's way too early . . . And we'll probably never live long enough to even . . . And I'm not sayin' you would even want to . . . even way out there in the future, but . . ."

"Yeah?"

"It'll show you where my mind is. Well . . . I've thought about it. I can't help myself. I did. And . . . I just . . . I can't be Jordan Jordan."

Frank Morgan called me the next morning.

I tripped over Martin, who was asleep on the floor, on my way over to the phone.

"Did I wake you?" Morgan asked.

"No. Not at all. How's it goin'?"

"I've got meetings this morning and I wanted a chance to talk to you before I got tied up."

"I appreciate you callin'."

"Only have a few minutes, so here it is . . . Ralph Alderman was forced to leave because of inappropriate behavior—some of it involving kids. The guy's not right. If somebody had done their damn job back then, he wouldn't be working around kids now."

I thought about it.

"I don't have a lot of details. It was all handled very quietly––not a lot written down. Force gave him the chance to resign and he took it. Became a mall cop. Had some complaints there too. Eventually was pushed out. Allowed to resign. Everybody just kicked the can down the road. No complaints filed at Safe Haven so far. He's had that job a while too. So . . . maybe there was nothin' to the other stuff or he's changed."

"Or he's gotten far better at it," I said.

"Could be," he said. "Probably is. Of the three it's the most likely. Sorry I don't have more . . . but . . . it's enough . . . to warrant a second look at him."

"Yes it is."

"What kind of man keeps company with kids?" he said.

I looked over at Martin.

This kind of man, I thought, and reminded myself not to jump too quickly to conclusions where Ralph or anyone else was concerned.

"There's a few other people we can talk to about him," he said. "Get more information––kind of stuff not in the file––but it'll take some time to track 'em down."

"Thank you," I said.

"Thank *you*. Wish I had you on all my cases."

That put a small lump in my throat and I was unable to respond.

"As for the other . . ." he began.

"The other?"

"Cases similar to LaMarcus's."

"Oh."

"So far no luck. I mean, we've got a few with similarities . . . but not enough in common to . . . I don't know. If this case had a list like the Atlanta Child Murders case did and LaMarcus was the pattern case . . . I don't think any of these would make it.

We've got some killed with the same drug, the chloral hydrate stuff, but no real abductions and no rape."

"Okay," I said. "Thanks for looking."

"I've still got a few agents on it . . . so we'll see, but I think we're gettin' close to exhausting cases to examine."

"Any way I could take a look at the ones that had any similarities at all?"

"Sure."

"You sure?" I asked. "You don't mind?"

"I knew you would want to––and I know we need you to. Already made copies for you. Got a guy dropping 'em by the college later this morning."

"Thanks, Frank," I said. "Thank you so much. Before you go . . ."

"Yeah?"

"How well do you know Bobby Battle?" I asked.

"Tell me you don't suspect him."

I laughed. "I don't."

"Not all that well. But I think with him what you see is what you get. Why?"

"Would he tell Larry Moore about Jordan?"

"What about her, John?"

"About Ray and Vince and . . . He put her in the emergency room again. Told her he was going to find and kill Ray and Vince."

"He's the kind that would too. Crazy son of a bitch. I can't imagine Bobby would say anything to him, but I can't say for certain he didn't or wouldn't. I just don't know."

"How else would he know?"

"You want me to talk to Bobby?"

"I'll do it," I said.

"Tell you who you need to be talkin' to. Your dad. Have you?"

"Not yet."

"John."

"It's not for lack of effort on my part."

"Keep tryin'. You won't be sorry. I swear it."

"Thanks, Frank," I said. "I know. I know you're right. I'll do it today. I'll call him again today."

41

I was sitting at a table in an empty classroom at EPI, the case files Frank had copied for me spread out before me.

After my morning classes, I had gone upstairs and borrowed Randy Renfroe's phone and called Ida's home number to check on Jordan.

I let it ring several times, but no one ever picked up.

I began worrying about her immediately, my imagination inventing several scenarios, displaying them on the big screen of my mind in vivid detail, as I punched in the number for Safe Haven.

"Are you okay?" Randy asked.

I nodded. "Thanks."

Jordan answered the phone.

"Hey," I said. "What're you doin' there? Thought you were resting at Ida's?"

"I can't just sit there," she said. "They need my help here and it takes my mind off it."

"But you need to—"

"Larry came by."

"When? What'd he—"

"Thankfully, it was before Mom left, so she helped. We decided it was best I wasn't alone there."

"I'm glad you did. I wish I had—"

"John, be very careful. He was braggin' about what he had done and making threats about what he would do, saying he would finish takin' care of all our problems soon."

"What'd he brag about doin'?"

"Said the two faggots would never threaten his girl again. John, I'm scared."

As I looked through the files of children who went to sleep and never woke up, I thought about my conversation with Jordan and what to do about Larry.

What could I do?

The woman I loved was in real danger—hell, so was I—and what could I do about it? What could an ordinary citizen do about a cop? But I wasn't even an ordinary citizen. I was a broke college student in a new town, with no pull, no power, no connections, nothing that was of any use to Jordan or much use to anyone else.

I studied the files harder, trying to distance myself from the dread spreading outward from my core as if a poison plunged into my racing heart.

Concentrate. Focus.

I looked over Ralph's file first. Frank was right. There just wasn't much there.

Then I turned my attention to sleeping little angels.

The first few were ruled accidental overdose, which was what they appeared to be. Noctec prescribed for children with insomnia. Parents who would have to live with the fact that they had unwittingly killed their own child. In a couple of the cases, a parent had administered the drug not realizing the other parent already had. In a couple of others it was simply a case of too large a dosage. None of these involved abduction or rape. Nothing even suspicious.

Of the rest, all but two had an obvious suspect—whether convicted or even arrested or not.

That left two cases where, like LaMarcus's, there was no clear motive or suspect, where the why and the who remained unknown.

Putting aside all other files but Ralph's and these two child murder cases, I dug in, examining every detail, going back and forth between them, comparing, contrasting, questioning, challenging.

Both cases involved little black boys near LaMarcus's age when he was murdered. Both were good kids from good homes. Both were killed at home, their bodies found on or near their property.

And then I saw it.

The first boy had spent the afternoon at South Dekalb mall with his friends on the day he died. He and his friends had even had a run-in with a mall security guard, Ralph Alderman, who had given a statement to the police. The officer who took the statement was Larry Moore.

The second boy who, was killed about a year later, attended Safe Haven Daycare and Aftercare Academy. He had been particularly close to the school's resource officer, a Ralph Alderman, who had stated during his interview what a fine young man the boy had been, what a tragedy this was, and how very much he'd be missed, especially by Alderman himself.

I rushed upstairs to call Jordan.

Pam's office was empty so I helped myself to her phone.

"What is it? Are you okay?" she asked.

"Do you remember a kid who came through there named Atwood Jones?"

"Mom and I spoke at his funeral. We've done more of that over the years than I care to remember, but his was more difficult than most. Wasn't sick. Didn't have an accident. It was so sudden.

Shocking. I don't think they ever even figured out what he died of."

"They did," I said. "Same as LaMarcus."

"*What*? Really? Oh my God. Are you sure?"

"How close were he and Ralph?"

There was a long pause.

"Very. Oh, God, John. No. Please no."

"Is he there now?"

"He is."

"Okay. Just act normal. Everything's going to be okay. Keep an eye on him but be careful not to let him know you know anything."

"Okay."

"I love you."

"I love *you*."

I hung up, then lifted the receiver again and punched in Bobby Battle's number.

"I's just about to call you," he said. "Guess whose tickets got punched in an early mornin' shootout?"

"Ray and Vince?"

"Give that man a prize."

"What do I win if I guess who shot 'em?" I said.

"Wait just a minute now."

"It was Larry Moore, wasn't it?" I said. "You told him they had threatened his wife. You knew he would kill them."

"I never told him shit," he said. "Haven't spoken to the crazy bastard in a while—and then only in passing. I know maybe your head's a little messed up and you're under a lot of stress, but that's a very serious allegation you're makin'. And there's no truth in it. I swear. So do me a favor and just say thank you for callin' you with the good news."

"Thank you," I said.

We were quiet a beat while I wondered if I really believed him.

"Can you come to the college?" I said. "I've got some evidence you need to see."

"Sure, John," he said. "It's not like I'm doin' anything else."

"It's important."

"Lucky for you I was about to go to lunch," he said. "I'll stop by on my way."

"Thank you," I said. "I mean it."

"Hell," he said, "I thought you meant it before."

When I got off the phone, Pam Palmer appeared in the doorway.

"Randy, Mr. Aycock, and I need to talk to you for a minute," she said.

"Can it wait? I'm in the middle of something really important."

"We'll try to make it as brief as possible."

We walked over to Pete Aycock's office and she closed the door behind us.

Pete Aycock, a trim, suave, self-possessed middle-aged man, was the president of the school. He was a calm, plainspoken pragmatist, who often took time to talk with students, illustrating his many points with homespun stories and movie metaphors. Recently, he had used the hit movie *Top Gun* to point out to me the importance of being under authority and having a wingman.

"This is difficult," Randy said. "You're a great student and such a wonderful addition to our school and church. You're doing a good job with the facilities, and the ministry work you're doing in your covenant community is exemplary."

What the hell is so bad it requires that kind of buildup in front of the president of the college?

"You really are such an asset," Pam said. "Such an example of the kind of students we want EPI to attract."

"But?" I said. "What is it?"

"One of your fellow students said you've had a married woman in your dorm room at night."

"Oh."

"I really hope it's not true," Randy said. "Female guests are only allowed in the living room and never past midnight. But we would hope as a student at EPI and a minister in our church, you wouldn't have a married woman anywhere in the apartment."

"I understand," I said.

We were all silent a beat. Pete Aycock, who always wore a silk tie, pressed white shirt, and a conservative suit that looked tailored for him, recrossed his legs, swept away a piece of lint from his lapel with the backs of his fingers, straightened his tie, and cleared his throat.

"Is it true?" he asked.

"Is what true?"

"Are you sleeping with a married woman?" Pam said. "Having an affair? Bringing her into your room?"

"No. No. And yes. I'm not sleeping with or having an affair with anyone. But yes, a soon-to-be-divorced, technically still-married woman has been in my room. Never alone. Always with a neighbor kid, who's almost always there. Has anyone complained about him?"

Pam shook her head.

I nodded.

"Listen, John," Pete said, "just be smart. Okay? Being guileless is good, but you need to be wise too. What was it Jesus said? Be as innocent as a dove but as shrewd as a snake."

"It's best if all guests keep their visits confined to the living room," Randy said. "That's all we're saying. That's all. Follow the dorm rules. Avoid even the appearance of . . . impropriety."

42

W hen Battle arrived, I took him down to the classroom where I had the files spread out on the table.

"The fuck you doin' with these?" he said.

"Your job."

"I didn't come here to be insulted," he said, turning to leave. "I was doin' you a fuckin' favor."

"Sorry," I said. "I'm . . . I just feel . . . I'm sorry. I shouldn't've said it."

He turned back around. "You got five minutes."

It took less than four to lay out for him what I had.

"You son of a bitch," he said. "You fuckin' son of a bitch. That fits. That's . . . that really could be it."

It felt good to hear him say it.

"So, Alderman kills LaMarcus," he said. "We don't know if that's the first or if he had done it before, and since then . . . he's killed––but wouldn't there be more? Why only two?"

"Only two we found so far. I bet there are others."

"But LaMarcus's body was moved and raped. None of these others are."

"I've thought about that," I said. "Everything that's different from these other cases was done post-mortem. So either he didn't have opportunity with these once they were dead . . . or . . . LaMarcus was killed during the Atlanta Child Murders case period. So the killer tried to make it look like LaMarcus was part of that––after he was dead. Tied the rope around his neck, roughed up the body, tried to make it look like something it wasn't. Even the rape occurred after death. But what if it was staged too. What if he just put a condom on an object and inserted it to make it look like rape."

He was nodding. "Makes a certain sense."

"So we go talk to him?"

"What? No. We've got to build a case. I've got to talk to my captain. We've got to gather what we can find. See if there are other victims that we might be able to link to him. See if we can get enough for a judge to grant us a warrant. And after all that's done, see if the DA thinks we have enough for an arrest.

"Talkin' to him is the last thing we need to do right now––and the *we* I'm talkin' about is the Decatur Police Department. I appreciate what you've done. This is great shit. Really great. And it may even be the thing that breaks the case and leads to an arrest, but this is where things get very tricky. We have to follow proper procedure and protocol or the case can get tossed on a stupid technicality. This is very important. Don't fuck up a case you may very well have solved by doing anything stupid. Stay away from Alderman. Stay away from Safe Haven. Stop detecting. Understand?"

I nodded.

"I mean it."

"I know."

"Let me hear you say you will."

"I will."

"Good work, John. I mean it. Very good work."

I stood there thinking for a long while after he had gone.

I knew what he had said was true, knew it was how it had to be. What I didn't know was if I could be okay with it.

Could I sit back and do nothing? Be satisfied with the contribution I had made, occupy my mind with something else, go back to reinvestigating the Atlanta Child Murders? Or would it be so frustrating that I'd exist in a dark, angry place, thinking and drinking too much, experiencing peace and joy too little.

I'd have to figure it out, figure out what I wanted to do, who I wanted to be and become. Should I drop out of Bible college and study criminology, become a cop like Battle and Frank and my dad? Should I keep studying ministry and try to figure out a means and a milieu to bring these two disparate callings together? But what could that be?

Even if I became a cop, I'd reach a point in every case where I had to turn it over to others. The most I could hope for would be to take an investigation as far as it could go, make an arrest, look a killer in the eye, stand there and be a witness for his victim, then hand it over to others, others who make deals and plea bargains and lose cases on technicalities. Could I do that? Would that be any better than this? It would, because I could at least see a case through to its conclusion.

The classroom door jerked open and Bobby Battle walked back in.

"Guess we're not going to have to wait after all," he said. "There's a kid missin' from Safe Haven. Come on."

"Lord help me Jesus, it's happenin' again," Ida said.

She was panicking. She wasn't the only one.

We were standing on the walkway close to the entrance.

"I've got the school on lockdown," Ralph was saying to Bobby Battle. "Every child but the missing boy is inside the building and accounted for."

He was sweating profusely, wiping his brow often with his fat fingers, slinging the salty liquid off his hand onto the sidewalk.

"Here's a picture of him," Jordan said.

She passed out xeroxed copies of a young black boy who could be LaMarcus's brother.

"How long's he been missin'?" Battle asked.

Ida opened her mouth but nothing came out.

"We're not sure exactly," Jordan said. "But we can narrow it down some. The kids eat in the same place, at the same table with the same group every day, every time they eat. It's one of the ways we take count, keep tabs. We know Brandon was here at ten-fifteen for snack time. We know he was here at eleven when we did our last count before the lunch break. When we sat down at twelve-fifteen for lunch he was gone. We just don't know how long after eleven he was here."

"Okay," Battle said. "That helps. And the kid's name is Brandon?"

"Brandon Wright."

"And you've searched all the normal places?" he said. "All through the building, every room, every nook and cranny, every hiding spot on the playground and property?"

Ralph was nodding vigorously before Battle finished. "Everywhere. We wouldn't've called you if we hadn't. The boy is not on the premises."

"Who's been here?" Battle said.

Ralph handed him a sheet of paper. "I log everybody––parent, teacher, student, visitor––in and out on my log."

I glanced at it over his shoulder. There were only four names.

"This is everybody?"

He nodded.

"Who are they?"

"These two are parents. One dropped off her child late. The other picked his up for a dentist appointment. The other one was a delivery––food and kitchen supplies–– and this last one was looking the place over, trying to decide whether or not to send his kid here."

"His?"

"Recently divorced single dad."

"What'd he drive? Got a phone number, description, anything?"

Ralph's eyes grew wide as he shook his head.

"Did he sign his kid up?" Battle asked Ida. "Leave any info?"

She shook her head.

"What about the food delivery person?" he asked. "Y'all know him?"

"Her, and yes. She's been doing it for several years now."

Two Dekalb County patrol cars pulled into the driveway.

"I don't want any panicking. Everybody calm down. I want you to make sure the kids are okay, that they have no idea what is goin' on. Can you do that, while also asking if anybody knows where Brandon is or saw him leaving?"

Both Ida and Jordan nodded.

"Okay. Go do that. And do another search for him inside. We're gonna start looking around out here."

"Come on, Mom," Jordan said, and led her back to her home become daycare where this had happened before.

"I wanna head up the search," Ralph said. "I know this area better than anyone. And the kid. And this happened on my watch."

"You can help," Battle said. "Stick with me and John. But I also need you comin' up with a description and vehicle for the man who stopped by to check out the school."

The four cops from the two patrol cars joined us, and Battle explained the situation and divvied up the search assignments. "Let's find him," he said. "Alive."

As the officers headed in various directions, I said, "I want to start with LaMarcus's hideout. If he's not there, then the drainage culvert."

"Was thinkin' the same thing," Battle said.

"Oh my God," Ralph said. "Do y'all think . . . Please God no, not again."

Battle and I rushed to the backyard, Ralph following behind as best he could.

When we reached the spot where we had been reenacting LaMarcus's abduction just a few months before, we slowed just enough to keep from falling as we pressed in through the bushes and stepped inside the child's hideout become crime scene.

There was nothing there. No child. No body. No evidence. No sign anyone had been here since we were last.

Relief washed over me but only momentarily.

I took off for the drainage ditch and the culvert where

LaMarcus had been laid out, Battle beside me, Ralph falling farther and farther behind.

Rushing through the small wooded boundary at the back of the property, we jumped the fence and came out into Flat Shoals Estates.

Not waiting for Ralph, not sure if he could make it over the fence, we ran down the sidewalk, through the cul-de-sac, and into the woods beyond, no sign of Ralph as we did.

We stumbled down the slope, around the drainage area, over to the culvert, and looked inside.

It was empty.

Thank you. Thank you for that, I prayed as relief washed over me again.

"That's good," Battle said. "But what's it mean? Where can he be?"

We turned and walked back up the incline, through the woods, out the cul-de-sac, and up the sidewalk toward Safe Haven. There was still no sign of Ralph.

44

When we were in the backyard again, we walked over to the window and motioned for Jordan.

"Any sign of him?" Battle asked.

"No. We've searched the entire building again."

"How's everyone holding up?"

"The kids are fine. So are the other workers. Mom and I not so much. I can't believe this is happening to us again."

I reached up and took her hand, rubbing her fingers around her brace.

She looked down and tried to smile but when she did tears started coming.

"Do you mind callin' the two parents who picked up their kids?" I said. "Just feel them out. See if they know anything. See if maybe Brandon hitched a ride somehow."

She nodded.

"Where's Ralph?" Battle said.

"Haven't seen him lately. He's acting so . . . flakey today. I mean more so than usual. Do you think . . . He . . . He may be at his house. He was back and forth for some reason earlier."

"Shit," Battle said. "Come on."

I squeezed her fingers. "Hang in there," I said. "I love you." And then followed after him.

When we came around to the front, Frank Morgan was pulling up and Ralph was standing at his guard stand at the front gate.

"Ralph," Battle yelled. "What the hell you doin'?"

"Couldn't keep up with you two," he said. "Didn't realize it was a race."

"Did you come up with anything on the visitor for me yet?" Battle said.

"Workin' on it now."

We walked over to Frank and filled him in.

"What can I do?" he said.

"Help us with this fat fuck right here," Battle said. "Your boy here thinks he might be the doer."

He nodded nonchalantly.

"No . . . *the* doer."

"Oh."

"Tell him," he said.

I did.

"Can't believe we missed that," he said.

Battle radioed the other officers for updates. No one had turned up anything yet. He told them to expand the search in every direction, including the Flat Shoals Estates subdivision.

"Which one is fat boy's house?" Battle asked me when he was off his radio.

"Right there."

He then turned and walked back over to where Ralph stood.

"Who lives there?" he asked.

"I do."

"You?"

"Yeah. Why?"

"We need to search it. Makes it a lot easier being yours. I had no idea. Toss me your keys and we'll check it out."

"I don't understand."

"What? What don't you understand?"

"Why you need to search my house. It's locked. He can't have gotten in."

"We've got to search everywhere. You know that. You used to be on the force, didn't you?"

"Yeah."

"Then you get it."

"Sure. Yeah. Come on. I'll take you over."

Battle motioned for me and Frank, and the three of us followed Ralph over to his house.

The small red brick house smelled of starch and mothballs and mildew. Mostly of mildew.

It was dirty and in disrepair, cluttered and not cared for, but more in an inept bachelor than a serial killer way. It was what you'd expect from an unhygienic overweight slob, which didn't mean he wasn't a serial killer.

"It's a mess, boys," he said. "Maid's day off. Wasn't expectin' company. Been workin' extra hours at Safe Haven."

"It's fine," Frank said. "Looks about like my place when company drops in unexpectedly."

We split up and searched the small house, which didn't take long. While doing so, I asked to use the bathroom and let water run in the sink while I rifled through the medicine cabinet, drawers beneath the counter, and small linen closet.

I found a pharmacy.

Most pills weren't in bottles. Most of the ones that were no longer bore a label.

When I walked out, Battle was saying, "What about the basement?"

"Can only be accessed from outside," Ralph said.

"Then let's go outside and access it."

As Ralph led the way and Battle followed, Frank and I took our time.

"Anything?" Frank asked.

"Everything," I said. "Never seen so many pills in one place before."

"If this is our guy, where's the body?"

"He could be the guy and have nothin' to do with Brandon being missing," I said. "Or he could've hid him somewhere other than his home."

By the time Frank and I reached the backyard, Ralph had a key in the padlock in the hasp on the cellar doors and was jiggling it, trying to get it open.

The once white doors were covered in green mold and black mildew and needed painting. They were on the back right side of the house and stood about four feet high.

"My key's not workin'," Ralph said. "It's been a while since I've been in here but I've never not had my key work."

"Got bolt cutters?" Battle said.

"In the basement. But hell, if I can't get in, no way a little boy did. You know?"

"Does the daycare?"

He nodded.

"I'll run grab 'em," I said. "Be right back."

I ran over to Safe Haven as fast as I could.

When I opened the door, Jordan rushed over to me.

"Find him?" she asked.

I shook my head. "Not yet. Anything here?"

She shook her head.

"I need bolt cutters. Ralph said there were some here."

She nodded. "Come with me."

She led me to what used to be the house's garage. It was filled with all manner of interior and exterior tools and supplies and equipment.

I found the bolt cutters on a shelf next to a couple of padlocks still in packages and one old one that had been cut, not far from an ax, sledgehammer, and hedge clippers.

As we were about to leave, I eased the door shut, took Jordan in my arms and kissed her.

"God, I needed that," she said. "Thank you."

"More where that came from. Let's reconvene as soon as we can."

When I turned to open the door, she swatted my ass. "Such a great ass."

I rushed back over to Ralph's house with the bolt cutters and, though Ralph reached out for them, gave them to Battle.

"I'll buy you a new lock," he said to Ralph as the bolt cutters pinched one part of the metal lock bar in two.

As I removed the lock, Battle tossed the bolt cutters to the ground, and then we each grabbed one of the doors and yanked, and there on the ground was the curled-up body of Brandon Wright.

45

F rank and I ducked down into the basement as Battle tackled Ralph to the ground and cuffed him.

"He alive?" Battle yelled from behind us.

I couldn't tell yet if he was dead or just sleeping.

"IS HE ALIVE?" Battle yelled.

Frank felt for a pulse, moved his hand around to make sure, then shook his head.

I began to scoop up his small body to carry him out, but Frank stopped me. "Nothing we can do for him," he said. "It's a crime scene now. Let's slip out and preserve everything for the techs to process."

"Come on, you sick piece of shit," Battle was saying as he jerked Ralph to his feet.

"Why're you doin' this?" Ralph said. "I didn't put him in there. I'm . . . I didn't do anything."

Battle shoved him and he started stumbling back toward Safe Haven.

"We didn't make it in time," I said to Frank.

"We rarely do," he said. "We rarely ever do."

Battle then radioed the other officers, two of whom rushed over and grabbed Ralph's arms and ushered him toward their car.

"Guys, stop. Listen to me. I swear to God I didn't do it. I swear. I have no idea who did that, who put him in my basement, but it wasn't me. Are you listening? LISTEN TO ME. I DIDN'T DO IT. Please, God, you've got to believe me."

"How many have there been?" Battle asked.

"What? None."

"Was LaMarcus the first?"

"*What?* No. God, no. I didn't kill LaMarcus. I haven't killed anybody. I swear. I would never. I could never. John, tell them. John? John, please."

As we reached Safe Haven and passed by the place where Ralph stood watch every day, something across the street caught my eye.

There, across Flat Shoals Road, in the driveway of a house on a hill, Larry Moore, in street clothes, sat in his black Trans Am, the window down, his feathered hair waving in the wind. Or maybe this last was my imagination.

I walked up to Ralph. "Was Larry Moore here this morning?"

He looked confused, then nodded.

"Why isn't he on the list?"

"He didn't go inside. Was just out front for a little while. John, I didn't do it. I swear. Please believe me. Please help me. Tell Miss Ida and Miss Jordan I'm sorry. Tell them I could never hurt anybody."

As Ralph was shoved into the backseat of the patrol car by the two cops, Larry cranked up his black sports car and slowly drifted down into the traffic on Flat Shoals and disappeared.

I rushed up the walkway toward the daycare center to tell Ida and Jordan, but before I reached it the door opened and they stepped out.

"You found him?"

I nodded. "In Ralph's basement."

"Jesus, no," Ida said.

"Is he okay?" Jordan said.

I shook my head. "We were too late."

Both women began to cry, shaking as they fell into each other's arms.

"I'm so sorry," I said. "So, so sorry."

46

"Still can't believe he did it," Ida said, tears still occasionally trickling down her dark cheeks. "Ralph."

It was later in the afternoon.

All the kids were gone.

All but a few of the workers released too.

GBI's crime scene division was working the entire area—Ralph's house, the daycare, the grounds, the neighborhood.

"All this time," she said. "I just can't . . ."

We were sitting by the front windows, Ida, Jordan, and I, in the art project area, watching all the police and forensic activity outside.

We each had coffee. None of us had touched it.

"Thinking back on it now," I said, "anything stand out about Ralph? Anything come to mind that didn't seem suspicious at the time but now seems . . ."

They both seemed to think about it for a long moment.

Eventually, Ida shook her head and Jordan said, "Nothing. I still can't believe he did it."

"Did Larry come by this morning?" I asked.

"Here?" Jordan said. "No."

Ida nodded. "He did too. Saw him out back. He came to talk to you—or stalk you or whatever the . . . I told him if he didn't leave I was calling the police."

"You saw him in the back?" I asked. "Just standing in the backyard?"

She nodded. "Why?"

"Ralph said he was in the front but didn't come in. I wonder if he drove around and parked in Flat Shoals Estates and walked in through the wooded area."

"He's done that before," Jordan said.

Ida shook her head. "He needs to be in custody too."

"Did y'all know Larry when LaMarcus was killed?"

"Not really know," Jordan said. "He used to come around with his dad some."

"His dad?"

"Did our yard," Ida said. "Handyman too. Helped out a lot after I lost . . . after *we* lost Jordan's dad. That's how they met. Can't believe Larry turned out the way he has."

"Did either of you see Ralph with Brandon this morning?"

They both shook their heads.

"Were they close?"

"Not particularly, no," Ida said.

"Ralph was awkward around all the kids," Jordan said. "But he tried to interact with them. Some more than others."

"Did he spend time with LaMarcus? Do you remember him being around?"

Ida shook her head.

We all fell silent a moment.

"Safe Haven," Ida said to herself, shaking her head. "No one will ever send their child back here. It's . . . over. I've . . . lost . . . everything."

"I'm so sorry," I said.

Jordan began to cry again.

"Should've never opened it in the first place," Ida added. "Not me. Not here. It's cursed. I'm cursed. Can't take care of my own child, gonna take care of other people's."

A cop came to the door. "Detective Battle said you can go, ma'am. He'll call or come by later."

Ida nodded absently.

"And he'd like to see you, sir," he said to me.

I nodded. "Thanks."

And then he was gone.

"Ralph never had kids of his own, did he?" I asked.

Ida shook her head.

"You ready to go, Mom?" Jordan asked, reaching over and rubbing her arm.

Ida shrugged.

"I'll get the car and pull up," she said. "You've done it enough times for me."

"Can you drive with your sling?" I asked.

She nodded. "I'm fine to drive. Thanks."

She then got up, gave me a kiss, and grabbed the keys from her mom's purse.

If Ida noticed the kiss, she gave no indication.

"Did Ralph have any nephews or nieces? Ever have any kids over?"

Ida shook her head.

"I'm just wondering way back when how he got a children's sleep aid."

Ida didn't respond, just continued staring out the window.

"Stole it?" Jordan offered with a shrug. "Black market? He was a cop back then. Could've gotten it anywhere. I'll be back in a minute, Mama."

"I'll walk her down when you pull up," I said.

"Thanks."

Jordan left and Ida and I were alone in the building.

"I'm just wondering how . . . Did LaMarcus take anything to help him sleep?" I asked.

She shook her head. "That boy never had no trouble sleepin'. Head hit the pillow, he out like a light. Now his sister on the other hand . . . that's a different story."

I looked through the window and watched as Jordan walked beneath the awning toward Ida's car, and everything suddenly fell into place.

My stomach lurched and I had a hard time not throwing up.

"Jordan had trouble sleeping?" I asked, wondering if Ida could hear how different my words sounded now.

She nodded. "Child never slept. Had to take something for the little bit she did get."

"Do you remember what she took?"

"Some stuff . . . Nordic or somethin'."

"Noctec?"

"That's it," she said.

"Yes it is," I said.

I helped her up and we began making our way toward the door.

"Did you say at group the other day that LaMarcus had some health issues?"

"Poor thing," she said. "Struggled with his little system, his tummy and . . . Jordan took such good care of him, was such a good big sister to her new little black brother."

We walked out the door and started down the walkway, me finding it difficult to put one foot in front of the other.

I felt dead inside, felt as if I couldn't feel, felt distant, as if everything including my self was a great ways away, up out of the deep, dark well I had fallen into.

"And her daughter . . . Savannah . . ." I said. "Jordan said she was sickly."

"All her little life," she said.

"What did she die of?"

"SIDS. My poor, poor girl," she said, as Jordan pulled up in the car. "She's been through so much. Too much. She's the sweetest, best thing God ever created and . . . she's suffered so much."

"I need to ask you one more thing," I said. "I've been meaning to and just haven't gotten to it yet."

"What is it, son?"

"Just something I'm not clear about. When LaMarcus went missing . . . why didn't you check his hideout? I would've thought that was the first place you'd look."

"I did. Well, *I* didn't. I was on the phone to the police, but it's the first place I sent Jordan. The very first."

47

"Are you okay?" Jordan asked. "You're pale as a ghost."

I nodded.

I had just helped Ida into the passenger side of the car and felt like I was going to fall over.

"You sure? You really don't look good. All clammy and––"

"Just tired."

"Come over when you finish here. We need you. We'll take care of you too. Okay?"

I nodded and closed the door.

I could hear her saying "I love you" as the door closed.

After they were gone, I stepped over to Bobby Battle.

"You got Ralph's keys?" I asked him.

"Yeah. Why? I was just about to head back over to his house."

He tossed me a plastic evidence bag with the keys in them.

"I'll catch up with you," I said. "Wanna check something first."

On unsteady legs I walked back up to the converted house, out to the garage, and tried Ralph's cellar door key in the lock on the shelf next to where the bolt cutters had been.

It opened the lock.

Jordan had cut the lock and replaced it with another when she put Brandon's body inside Ralph's basement.

I collapsed to the cement floor and watched on the screen of my mind a very disturbed girl who made her little brother sick, who bribed him––probably with a Christmas gift she was wrapping––to hide in his hideout, who used her own sleeping medication on him, who moved the body and tried to make it look like he was a victim of the Atlanta Child Murderer––to garner even more sadness and sympathy, going as far as to stage strangulation and rape. A victim who married an abuser to get more sympathy. A deranged young woman who made her own child sick and then killed her. A murderer who went on to kill other children in her care, who mourned with their families and spoke at their funerals.

I thought about how eloquently she spoke about loss and grief to the support group, how at home she was in the center of the circle of concern and care for her, this poor, poor thing who had lost so much, who had so little left, who was so brave and strong, so good and kind.

I thought about how she had kept me away from Ida, asking to become the go-between, controlling the information, controlling everything. I wondered what secret Carlton had really told her, what else he had said that incriminated her.

Simple Larry never knew what hit him. He was her victim. Not the other way around. She had told him about Ray and Vince, not Bobby Battle.

And today she had set up Ralph, her readymade patsy, to take the fall. She had cut the lock, planted one of her victims to make another.

Pushing myself up, I went back inside the daycare and called Ida's house.

There was no answer.

Wondering where they could've gone, I called the church and

asked for Pastor George Clarke, the parental grief group facilitator.

Ten minutes later I was meeting with him in his office.

Before becoming a pastor, this tall, soft-spoken African-American gentleman was a psychologist with a large private practice in Decatur.

Without telling him any names or divulging any information I didn't have to, I set up a hypothetical scenario and asked for his assessment.

"It's MSBP," he said. "Munchausen syndrome by proxy. A behavior pattern where a caregiver exaggerates, fabricates, or actually induces health problems––physical, psychological, behavioral, or mental––in someone under their care, most often a child. Munchausen syndrome is when someone does this to him or herself. By proxy is when it is done to someone in their power."

"Can someone suffer from both?" I asked.

He nodded. "I would think so. They are very similar. The way the by proxy form of it works is an adult caregiver, most often the mother, makes a child appear sick or actually makes the child sick in order to gain the attention, affection, sympathy of others–– family, friends, doctors, nurses, strangers. Sometimes it's just fabrication and exaggeration, but others it actually involves purposely harming the child––often by poisoning, suffocation, or injection."

He paused. I nodded. He continued.

"This is one of the more misunderstood forms of child abuse and the most difficult to determine and deal with. The person suffering from this condition is a master manipulator, skilled at duplicity––the entire thing is based on deception."

48

When I left the church, I didn't return to the crime scene, but instead drove straight to Ida's.

Both Battle and Frank had paged me several times and continued to.

I didn't care.

I knew I should take what little evidence I had to them.

I didn't care.

I knew the best chance for a conviction was to get them involved now and wait for them to build a case.

I didn't care.

She had let me fall in love with her. She had used me and manipulated me and made a fool of me.

I couldn't wait to confront her. It had to be now. It had to be me looking into her eyes. Right now nothing else mattered. Nothing else in the world.

When I reached Ida's, Larry's Trans Am was in the driveway next to her car.

I didn't care.

He and Ida could hear what I had to say together.

When I reached the front door, I found it ajar, the frame and molding around it splintered and broken.

Easing it open, I entered a bad situation and was about to make it worse.

Inside, I found the three of them in the living room, Larry with a weapon pointed at Jordan's head, Ida nearby pleading with him.

"The fuck do you think you're doin'?" Larry said when he saw me.

Ignoring him, I locked eyes with Jordan. "I know," I said.

"You know what?" Larry said.

Jordan frowned and nodded, tears starting to stream down her cheeks.

"She's leaving with me," Larry said. "You can wave bye or stay there and die. Up to you."

"How many kids have you killed?"

"I ain't killed any kids, retard," he said.

"Wasn't talkin' to you."

"The fuck this nut talkin' about?" he asked Jordan.

"She killed her little brother," I said. "After makin' him sick. She did the same to your child. And other children at Safe Haven, including Brandon Wright today."

"John," Ida said. "What're you . . . Ralph's the killer."

"Ralph's the fall guy," I said. "For a very sick girl with Munchausen syndrome by proxy."

"I've heard of that," Larry said.

Ever the victim, Jordan had yet to do anything but stand there crestfallen and cry.

How could I have fallen in love with her? How was it possible to be so imperceptive? What kind of detective was I that I could be so deceived? What kind of minister was I that I could become so intimate with evil and not know it?

"John, you can't think . . ." Ida began, but stopped, and

seemed to look at Jordan as if for the first time, as if a not entirely unexpected dawning was taking place.

"It's when you make your kid sick for attention," Larry said. "You can't think that of—"

"I don't think it. I know it. And so do both of you," I said.

Neither of them said anything. Both of them seemed to consider it.

"How could you possibly think that of this poor, sweet, precious girl?" Ida said.

I told her. In detail. Everything I knew, everything I thought, everything I guessed, Larry listening intently as I did, eventually nodding as the unwitting witness to the truth.

"Think about it," I added. "There's no other way LaMarcus could've been taken from his own backyard with you watching him so closely. Had to be the other person who was supposed to be watching him, had to be a plan she came up with to make her brother an accomplice in his own murder."

Without realizing what I was doing until I had done it, I turned and looked over at the partially wrapped Christmas presents, the Star Wars lunchbox and Star Trek Communicators and other wrapped packages, gifts never given, reminders of innocents who never made it to Christmas, who would never see another Christmas again.

Ida followed my gaze, turning from me, to the presents, then to Jordan. "Baby, please tell me this isn't true. Please make it so I can't possibly believe this."

Jordan didn't say anything.

"Tell me you didn't torture and kill our little girl," Larry said. "Tell me you're not that kind of monster."

"I . . ." Jordan began. "I . . . need . . . treatment. It's . . . it's not me. It's . . . a disease. I don't want to be like . . . like . . . I don't want to have the affliction I have."

"*Affliction*?" Larry said. "No. No. No. It can't be. No. Please, God, no. Tell me you didn't do it. TELL ME."

Ida fell to the floor and began sobbing.

"Bitch, tell me you didn't kill my little girl," Larry demanded, jamming the barrel of his pistol into her forehead.

She didn't flinch. Just stood there, eyes downcast.

Eventually, she looked up at me, her eyes once again finding and focusing on mine.

"I'm so sorry, John," she said. "I really and truly fell in love with you. I so wanted us to be a family together."

"*Love?*" Larry said.

"Oh my God," Ida said. "Jordan, why did we go by John's? Jordan. What did you do to that little boy?"

Everything stopped.

"What did you do?" I said.

"I wanted . . . us . . . to . . . share . . . this."

"Jordan, no," I said. "Not Martin. Please. Not Martin too."

"You love him?" Larry said. "Look at me, you child-murdering faithless whore. Look at me."

She never looked at him. Not when he yelled for her to. Not when he thumbed back the hammer. Not when he shot her in the head before doing the same to himself.

49

Martin was lying on my bed, his small body on its side in a fetal position.

So sweet, so innocent, so peaceful.

I made my way across the quiet room.

To be, or not to be, that is the question—

Was he sleeping, lost in the sweet dreams of the underworld or . . .

I strained to hear his breathing but could not.

To sleep—

I eased down on the bed beside him, sitting on the edge, not yet willing to know what once known I would never be able to unknow.

Perchance to Dream—

"Martin," I whispered.

So still. So quiet.

Aye, there's the rub—

"Martin?"

No response.

His weight on the bed was different somehow, as if the soul is something substantial, something palpable, something measurable.

For in that sleep of death, what dreams may come—

"Martin," I said again, this time a little louder.

The increased volume revealed a shaky, unsure quality in my voice. I sounded like a child in the darkness, filled with fear and dread, asking "Who's there?"

"Martin?" I said again. "Are you asleep?"

To die, to sleep no more—

I reached for him, but stopped just shy of touching him, just shy of confirming what I had known since Ida's pitiful, *Oh my God. Jordan, why did we go by John's? Jordan. What did you do to that little boy?*

"Martin, please," I said.

If it weren't for me, if I hadn't come into his life, if I hadn't brought one of the real monsters of childhood into his little life . . .

And by a sleep, to say we end the heart-ache, and the thousand natural shocks that flesh is heir to—

Finally, I summoned everything within me and closed the small distance between where my hand hung trembling to where the face of the sweet boy who called me Yon rested.

His flesh was cold.

For in that sleep of death, what dreams may come when we have shuffled off this mortal coil—

If I hadn't come into his life, if I hadn't brought Jordan . . .

"I'm so sorry," I said. "Martin, I'm so, so sorry."

I had come to Atlanta to find and stop a child killer. Instead, I had become an accessory to one. I hadn't just looked into Nietzsche's abyss. I had dived into it. And I had pulled little Martin Fisher into it with me.

I would never get over this. Not ever. Maybe Shakespeare was wrong. Maybe it wasn't death so much as regret and guilt and grief that was the real undiscovered country from whose bourn no traveler returned.

I would not return from this.

I would spend the rest of my life trying but never quite being able to fully return from this. I would try to help others return, try to prevent others from taking the journey at all, but there was no amount of good I could do, no amount of booze I could consume, no amount of justice I could administer to ever be enough to return from this dark country I was just beginning to discover.

50

A cold numbness invaded my core and stayed there.
    I was as detached as I had ever been, experiencing everything as if from a great distance away, becoming disinterested observer rather than participant in my own life.

I wasn't just depressed. I was devastated. Ironically, I didn't drink. I was beyond depressed, beyond devastated, beyond drink.

I didn't eat much of anything, but what I did had no taste whatsoever.

Frank Morgan and Bobby Battle both reached out to me, but I couldn't face them. I couldn't face anyone.

After several days of not leaving the apartment and of barely leaving my room, I ventured outside for the first time on a rainy Thursday morning.

The moment I stepped outside my door, my eyes, against my will, moved over to the basketball court. It was empty, but I could see Martin working on his shot, hear the echo of his small, singular voice.

I blinked back the tears threatening to join the misty raindrops swirling about my face.

I knew enough to know that it was probably temporary, but at the moment I honestly couldn't imagine ever playing basketball again.

I stumbled to my car, which after sitting five days I wasn't sure would crank, and drove out toward Ellenwood to Fairview Memorial Gardens.

Driving, like all my actions, felt foreign and odd, as if I was removed a certain distance from doing it.

During the drive out the day grew darker, but the reticent rain remained the same.

Jordan's plot wasn't far from a stone statue of Saint Mark, the bearded and robed apostle holding a tablet in his left hand, below him a lion lying at his feet.

As I approached the graveside, Ralph Alderman stepped away from where he was standing beside Ida and met me as I neared, blocking my entry to the modest memorial service taking place behind him.

He poked out his chest and expanded his elephantine girth and said, "You're not welcome here."

"Yes he is," Ida said from behind him. "Let him through."

He begrudgingly stepped aside and I walked past him. Ducking down beneath her umbrella, I hugged Ida.

There were only four people present—Pastor Don, Ida, Ralph, and myself. We stood around the small headstone with the bronze plate engraved with the name of the woman, the murderess, I had fallen in love with, who some part of me was still in love with.

We were standing in a sparse garden of fake flowers, dotted occasionally by a small tree or shrub.

I was the only one without an umbrella. It wasn't raining hard. I wouldn't have cared if it had been.

Pastor Don began with a prayer.

Ida wasn't crying. No one was.

After reading a few passages of scripture and a poem, Pastor Don delivered an eloquent eulogy, prayed again, his words compassionate and comforting, then committed her soul to God and her body to the ground. Ashes to ashes. Dust to dust.

And then it was over.

Eventually, Ida and I were alone with Jordan.

In the silence between us I could hear all that couldn't be said. In the distance, the low rumble of thunder barely registered. Not far from where we stood, an American flag on a tall pole snapped smartly in the whining wind, its rigging clanging loudly.

"Got nothin' to say," she said at last.

I nodded.

"Well . . . just . . . that I won't ever get over this."

"Me either," I said.

It came out so softly, the wind taking it away so quickly, I wasn't sure she heard it. I didn't think it mattered either way.

"You loved her," she said.

"I did. Part of me still does. Probably always will."

We stood there for a few moments more, the rain and wind picking up a bit, large drops pelting my head with dull wet thumps I barely noticed. I was soon soaked through, hair dripping, clothes soggy.

"Nope," she said, "got nothin' else to say."

"Me either," I said. "Except . . . to say . . . I'm sorry."

She nodded. "Me too."

She turned to walk away. I stayed behind.

She had only taken a few steps when I turned to stop her.

"Sorry," I said, "but I need to . . . have to ask . . . Do you wish I hadn't . . . looked into . . . Would you rather I not have found out who . . . that it was her?"

She stood still for such a long moment I thought she wasn't going to answer. "Always better to know. Always. No matter the . . . cost."

She then turned and walked away and I was utterly and completely alone, the half-living among the full-dead, mourning the small, sweet, pretty monster who had done far more damage to me than if she had put me to sleep, for in this waking sleep of living death, what nightmares may come?

I have no idea how long I stood there alone, but eventually I wasn't alone any longer. Seeming to simply appear out of nowhere, Frank Morgan was suddenly standing beside me.

Like me, he had no umbrella. Like me, he was soaked through––so I knew he had been waiting a while. Like me, he said nothing.

We stood there like that, raindrops wetly thumping us, the soggy ground, and Jordan's headstone, the American flag flapping in the breeze, an unseen mourner crying for someone unknown to us close enough to be heard, neither of us uttering a sound.

We stood as stonily still and silent as Saint Mark beside us, and we stood that way for a very long time.

I don't know how long we stood there that way. I only know that during the entirety of our time together there, Frank never said a single word. There was nothing to say and he knew it. What he probably didn't know, what he couldn't possibly have known, was how much his silent presence meant to me, did for me. It was as healing as anything that had happened since I had lost everything––my surrogate wife and son, my joy, my confidence, my calling, my way entire––and I would never forget it or him or our random Thursday in the rain.

BLOOD CRIES

A JOHN JORDAN MYSTERY

COPYRIGHT

Written by Michael Lister.

This is a work of fiction. Similarities to real people, places, or events are entirely coincidental.

Books by Michael Lister

Sign up for Michael's newsletter by clicking here or go to
www.MichaelLister.com and receive a free book.

(John Jordan Novels)
Power in the Blood
Blood of the Lamb
Flesh and Blood
(Special Introduction by Margaret Coel)
The Body and the Blood
Blood Sacrifice
Rivers to Blood
Innocent Blood
(Special Introduction by Michael Connelly)
Blood Money
Blood Moon
Blood Cries
Blood Oath
Blood Work
Cold Blood

(Jimmy "Soldier" Riley Novels)
The Big Goodbye
The Big Beyond
The Big Hello
The Big Bout
The Big Blast
In a Spider's Web (short story)
The Big Book of Noir

Sign up for Michael's newsletter by clicking here or go to www.MichaelLister.com and receive a free book.

1

From the summer of '79 until the spring of '81, a serial killer stalked the African-American children of the city of Atlanta.

The Atlanta Child Murders, as they came to be known, was a two-year nightmare the city couldn't wake itself up from.

During this terrible reign of terror, twenty-eight children, adolescents, and adults were murdered.

It began on July 21, 1979, when Edward Hope Smith went missing, and ended on May 24, 1981, when the body of twenty-seven-year-old Nathaniel Cater was fished from the Chattahoochee River.

Between these two murders, some twenty-six others were committed, as many as one a week near the end.

Of course, these weren't the only murder victims in Atlanta during the time. They weren't even the only black children to be murdered. They were the only ones who made it onto the task force's ill-advised and incomplete list.

Wayne Bertram Williams, a twenty-three-year-old music promoter, was arrested on June 21, 1981.

Just a few short months before—during a family trip to

Atlanta over the last weekend of November in 1980—I had come face-to-face with Williams in the arcade of the Omni Hotel.

He was there passing out his flyers, and I had intervened when I saw him harassing one of the other kids.

I had been obsessed with him and the case ever since.

On February 27, 1982, he was convicted of the murders of Nathaniel Cater and Jimmy Payne, two of only a few adults on the list.

He was sentenced to two consecutive life sentences.

Labeled the Atlanta Child Murderer, Williams was never charged with, tried for, or convicted of killing a single child—an irony and injustice I had never been able to get over.

Following his trial, officials claimed Williams could be linked to some twenty-five of the twenty-eight names on the list through trace evidence—specifically, green trilobal carpet fibers found in Williams's bedroom and on the victims—and closed those cases.

Those same officials claimed the murders stopped.

Officials stopped counting them.

Reporters stopped reporting them.

The world stopped watching.

The list stopped.

The murders did not.

And like Abel of old, their blood cries out—tortured, mournful, inconsolable cries I couldn't help but hear, couldn't help but be haunted by.

2

I was sitting on an uncomfortable barstool in a dive on Memorial Drive, trying to find the sweet spot.

It was early in November of '86, less than a month since I had buried Jordan and Martin, and some four years after Wayne Williams was convicted.

The storefront bar was named Scarlet's and it was in the end of a tin-building strip mall with a cluttered video store, a passable pizza place, and a consignment shop with a meager amount of merchandise.

The bartender-owner was a middle-aged lesbian lush named Margaret.

She had of late become one of my closest companions and the nearest thing to a mother I had in Atlanta.

"What's your sweet spot?" I asked.

"I'm old and dried up," she said. "Got no sweet spot no more. But my niece . . ."

Always trying to set me up with her niece—for Margaret, all roads led to Susan Daniels. But she was wasting her breath. I wasn't interested in Susan or anyone else.

A thin forty-something woman with shoulder-length wavy

brown hair and big blue eyes, Margaret looked like a former tennis pro. Nothing about her looked old or dried up.

I was only interested in finding my sweet spot in, at, or near the bottom of my next glass—the one that would cause the specters of Jordan Moore and Martin Fisher to fade.

"I didn't say G-spot. I said sweet spot."

I could hear the slightest of slurs in the words tumbling out of my mouth a little too freely. But even if I hadn't, I could tell I was drunk by the way I felt my center wasn't holding.

That thought led to a line or two of unbidden verse. Turning and turning in the widening gyre . . . Things fall apart; the centre cannot hold.

"Things fall apart," I said.

"Never a truer statement uttered," she said.

"'Anarchy is loosed upon the world,'" I said. "'The blood-dimmed tide is loosed, and everywhere . . . The ceremony of innocence is drowned.'"

Meeting Jordan the first time made its way into my mind.

I'm Jordan Moore, she said, extending her small, cold hand.

I smiled. Really? I'm John Jordan.

She smiled back but looked a bit embarrassed, her face and neck blushing crimson.

"Is that biblical?" Margaret asked.

"Might as well be," I said. "Yeats."

"What?"

"Who," I said. "A Mr. William Butler Yeats."

"This about that kid?" she asked.

Little Martin Fisher trying to make a layup on the rickety basketball goal at my old apartment complex shimmered like heat lighting on the night sky that was my mind.

Though I knew she was talking about Martin Fisher, her question reminded me of the one Wayne Williams asked on the night he was stopped. This about those kids?

"Everything is," I said. "Especially Yeats."

The joint had a new jukebox but everything in it was old, and that was just fine with me.

A moaning saxophone let me know another of my selections was coming on.

It was a live version of Seger's "Turn the Page" from the Live Bullet album. When the song came on, Seger and his band had just finished Van Morrison's "I've Been Working," and he was still out of breath when he said, "This is from '72 also. About being on the road. It's called 'Turn the Page.'"

On a long and lonesome highway east of Omaha . . .

The song was about something I had been as yet unable to do —turn the page—and it perfectly captured my mood.

The isolation and loneliness of a world-weary traveler being burned up by the road.

Life is the road and it had done one hell of a number on this young journeyman, whose center was no longer holding.

What was there to do but drink and listen to good music and try not to think?

"Why were you askin' an old leathery lesbian about her sweet spot?" Margaret asked.

She had waited until the song was over.

"You know that small, fleeting spot between dulled agony and oblivion, the one you can never sustain?"

"'Cause the center doesn't hold," she said.

I nodded vigorously. "Exactly. 'Cause the center doesn't hold. I'm trying to find it and hold it."

"They say there's no treading in the bottle," she said. "Only drowning."

"To drowning," I said, lifting my glass.

"To drowning," she said, raising her glass to clink mine.

They say Margaret used not to drink the way she does now. They say it started when she lost the love of her life and business partner, Laney Mitchell.

Margaret Hart and Laney Mitchell were happy when,

inspired by the combination of their names, they started a Gone with the Wind-themed bar called what else but Scarlett's.

The joint was admittedly a bit kitschy and touristy, but it was a happy place, owned and operated by a happy couple, frequented by customers who quickly became friends.

At least that's what they say. That was all before my time.

Now that the Mitchell was gone and there was only the Margaret, the place was dim and in disrepair, the book and movie memorabilia dingy and dust-covered, and a hint of desperation hung in the air and clung to everything and everyone who entered, but frankly, Margaret didn't give a damn.

"Fuck my liver if it can't take a joke," she said, and poured herself another.

I had another myself, as time slowly ticked along and Atlanta's missing and murdered children remained missing and murdered, and frankly, no one seemed to give a damn about that either.

3

L ater when Susan, Margaret's niece and the person solely responsible for Scarlett's doors still being opened, stormed in, Margaret looked at me and said, "Uh oh, we're in trouble now."

"What're you doin'?" Susan asked.

"My job," Margaret said. "What? I can't drink with my customers? What?"

Susan huffed and shook her head. "I'm not even talkin' about how far into the bag you are. You're serving someone underage."

Susan wasn't unattractive—or wouldn't have been if she weren't so closed and rigid.

"Him?" she said, nodding toward me.

"Me?" I asked in surprise.

"He's got one of the oldest souls I've ever met," Margaret said.

"I don't think that's what the authorities check."

"He's twenty-one," Margaret said. "Says so right there on his ID."

"Hey, it's your liquor license, your livelihood—if you can call it that. I just work here. Drink yourselves into a stupid stupor and let the world burn down around you. Up to you."

"She said stupid stupor," I said.

"Tell her why we drink," Margaret said.

"Why not?" I said.

"Because the center doesn't hold," she said.

"Oh, that. Yeah," I said. "It's why the world is burning down around us too. Anarchy is loosed upon the world. The blood-dimmed tide is loosed."

"Something's dimmed," Susan said. "I'll give you that."

"I was just trying to find my sweet spot. Sorry. I didn't mean to . . . I'll sober up and . . ."

"I'll pour you some coffee," Susan said.

"Thank you," I said. "Drop a wee splash of Bailey's in it, would you?"

She sighed and dropped the cup on the counter.

"I was kidding," I said. "You're not as far gone as you think I am."

"No," she said, "I'm not."

"I said wee because Bailey's is Irish."

"When you're sober you don't explain shit like that," she said.

The tinted glass door opened and Lonnie Baker, a thin, narrow-framed thirty-something black man with large tortoise-shell glasses and a slight mustache, walked in right on time.

His arrival signified the transition from afternoon into evening.

Lonnie Baker owned the video rental store at the other end of the strip mall, and every day at five o'clock he taped the tattered piece of paper that read "Back in Five" onto the door, locked up his shop, and came down to Scarlett's.

Every day he would sit on the same barstool. Every day Margaret would pour a shot of bourbon and place it before him. Every day he would stare it down. And every day he would eventually slide it back toward her without drinking or spilling a single drop.

Lonnie Baker was a recovering alcoholic who never missed a meeting. This daily exercise of facing down his demon was part of his ritual. He had four years sobriety. What he was doing was working for him, and he wasn't about to stop working it.

Today, like every day, Margaret clanged the bell behind the bar, which was followed by a smattering of claps and cheers from the few patrons present who, permanently or momentarily, weren't close friends with Bill W.

As Lonnie stood, the front door opened again, and to my astonishment Ida Williams ambled in.

She paused for a moment to let her eyes adjust and scan the room. When she saw me, she began making her way over, but stopped when she recognized Lonnie Baker.

The two hugged and exchanged a few words, then hugged again, and Lonnie left to reopen his video store as Miss Ida made her way over to me.

I stood.

I had had only coffee since Susan arrived, but I was still a bit unsteady on my feet, and I felt embarrassed and self-conscious for Ida to see me this way.

I started to walk toward her, but figured it best if I didn't.

We embraced when she reached me, each refusing to let go for a very long moment. Like the rest of her, Miss Ida's breasts were bountiful and she held me to them as if I were her own child—and for a while there I thought I was going to be.

In addition to being a friend and a colleague in the missing and murdered children's group, Ida had been Jordan's mother and the closest thing to a mother-in-law my young self had ever had.

"How are you, son?" she asked.

"Been better," I said. "Not gonna lie."

Jordan there again, permeating my being. Small enough to be a schoolgirl. Shy green eyes. Straight sun-streaked blond hair.

Smooth, unvarnished, suntanned skin. A simple, understated, graceful beauty I found irresistible.

"What can I get you?" Margaret asked.

I shook my head. "She's not here to––"

"Jack and Coke," she said.

I looked back at Miss Ida.

"You ain't the only one what's been better, boy," she said.

I nodded and our eyes locked a moment before we both teared up and had to look away.

"Why don't y'all have a seat at the little table over there in the corner," Susan said. "I'll bring your drinks over."

We did.

"How do you know Lonnie?" I asked.

"Through his sister. She's a part of our group—or was. Her boy went missing back around the time LaMarcus did . . . back when so many were."

"What's his name? Was he on the list?"

She shook her head. "Never turned up dead or alive. Still missing. So never made that damn list. His name is Cedric. Cedric Porter."

I nodded and thought about it.

Susan brought Miss Ida's Jack and Coke, topped off my coffee, and smiled at me approvingly––whether about the coffee or talking to Miss Ida, I wasn't sure. Probably both.

Ida lifted her glass and made a toasting motion toward me without actually touching my cup. She then drank the darkish liquid the way someone who doesn't drink would––not sipping or shooting but taking a large swallow, which quickly caught up with her.

A quick intake of air, followed by a cough. Another swallow she thought would help, but didn't. Then more of the same.

"You okay?" I asked. "Want some water?"

"I'm fine. It's just been a while and they mix 'em up strong in here. I like the burn. I want it."

Susan appeared with a glass of water, set it on the table, and was gone.

"Thank you," I said, though I don't think she heard me.

"Nobody need to make a fuss over me. I'm fine."

I nodded and we were quiet a moment. "Hotel California" was playing on the jukebox. She took a sip of water—quickly, nonchalantly, as if it embarrassed her to do so.

Hollywood's not the only haunted hotel. Atlanta is. So is the world.

I thought of sitting on the swings at Trade Winds with Jordan late into the night, her wiping tears as Martin walked up. They were both so small, so frail, so vulnerable in their own way.

"'What have we, my good friend, deserv'd at the hands of fortune, that she sends us to prison hither?'" I said.

Miss Ida looked confused.

"Atlanta's a prison," I said. "Or at least a hotel that can't be checked out of. The world is one."

She shook her head. "I don't think so."

"'Why then 'tis none to you; for there is nothing either good or bad, but thinking makes it so.'"

Something Mama Monroe said joined the Hamlet and "Hotel California" mashup in my head. We all doin' time, baby. Only question is where and how.

"You still investigating the murders?" she asked.

I nodded. "When I'm not in school, at work, or . . ."

"Drinkin' yourself silly."

"Yeah."

"I want you to come back to the group," she said.

"You still meet?" I asked, my voice full of surprise.

"'Course we do. It's about all our kids. Always was. Not just mine."

"You don't blame me for . . . what happened?" I asked.

"No, child, I don't," she said. "No part of it was your fault."

More relief washed over me than I had experienced since it all happened.

"Will you come back?" she asked.

I shook my head. "I . . . don't think I can . . . Not yet. Not ever, maybe."

"We need you," she said. "From the look of it . . . you need us."

4

———

W hen I woke up I sensed someone else in the room. I rolled over to see Susan Daniels standing, staring at my Wayne Williams wall.

Instantly, his soft, eerie voice echoed through my twinging head. What's your name, boy? Just 'cause I prefer chocolate don't mean I couldn't go for some vanilla.

Dry mouth, dull ache in my head, I felt stiff and sluggish.

"It was dark when we came in last night," she said. "Didn't really see any of this. Probably wouldn't have stayed if I had."

One whole wall, the largest in the room, was covered with case files, maps, lists, witness statements, evidence reports, crime scene photographs, fiber and other forensic records—all of which was splattered with and connected by the scratch and scrawl of my scribblings.

The wall spoke of obsessive compulsive behavior to anyone listening. She had heard it right away. She'd had experience with it.

"You stayed here last night?" I said.

"My dad's a cop," she said, still studying the wall. "Lives in Tallahassee. Worked Bundy."

"Mine too."

"Yours too what?"

"Dad. Worked Bundy. He's the sheriff of Potter County."

"Probably know each other," she said. "He a drunk too?"

"More of teetotaler. You stayed here last night?"

"Mine's a drunk like you," she said. "Why I'm in Atlanta. Why nothing happened last night. I just didn't feel like driving all the way back home after I dropped your drunk ass off. And your bed looked too good and warm not to crawl into. I'd never get involved with a drunk or a . . . cop."

"I'm not a cop."

"Your wall argues otherwise."

"I'm a theology student."

She turned from the wall to face me for the first time. "I knew it."

"Knew what?"

"Knew there was something . . . Anyway . . . you don't have to have a badge to be a cop. And that's three strikes."

"What time is it? Three strikes?"

"Against you," she said. "Drunk. Cop. Jesus freak."

"Didn't even know I was at bat."

And I didn't ask to play ball.

"It's early," she said.

"I have class this morning."

"You need to hydrate and shower. So what's the deal?"

"With?"

"Why're you so obsessed with this case?" she said, jerking her head back toward the wall behind her.

"I had a confrontation with Wayne Williams when I was a kid."

"Oh yeah? Let's hear it."

"Family trip to Atlanta. Staying at the Omni. I was in the arcade playing Space Invaders when he came in with his flyers.

He approached a scrawny kid playing KISS pinball. Kid shook his head. Didn't even look at him . . ."

Look at me, little brother, he said.

The kid didn't.

Williams laid the flyer on the glass top of the pinball machine, blocking the boy's view and causing him to lose the turn.

You heard of the Jackson Five, ain't ya? You could be like little Michael.

The boy abandoned his game and walked away with his head down.

Williams followed.

I stepped away from Space Invaders and in front of him.

Said he's not interested, I said.

Whoa, little man, he said. What's your name?

I didn't respond, just held his gaze.

Anger flashed in his face when I still refused to respond.

Just 'cause I prefer chocolate don't mean I couldn't go for some vanilla, he said.

"Wow. No wonder you got obsessed with the case," Susan said, "but I thought it was solved years ago. Williams is in prison, right?"

"For killing two adults," I said. "Not any children."

"Give me a brief overview," she said. "Justify your obsession."

I did—the former, at least. I had no interest in doing the latter.

The victims, as James Baldwin wrote, were visibly black and actually poor, and here's who they were—who they are and will forever be...

5

It began in the summer of 1979, when Edward Hope Smith and Alfred Evans disappeared just four days apart. Their bodies were discovered on July 28, in a wooded area off Niskey Lake Road by a woman looking for cans.

Milton Harvey, the next victim, disappeared on September 4, while on an errand for his mother. His remains were found off Desert Road at Redwine Road on the south side by a man picking up cans.

All three victims to this point were fourteen-year-old African-American boys.

On October 21, nine-year-old Yusuf Bell became the next victim when he went to the store to buy snuff for a neighbor. A witness said she saw Yusuf getting into a blue car before he disappeared. The same witness claimed the man driving the car was Yusuf's father, John. His body was found on November 8, in the abandoned E.P. Johnson Elementary School by a former school janitor searching for a place to urinate. Yusuf was still wearing the brown cut-off shorts he was last seen wearing, though they had a piece of masking tape stuck to them. He had suffered blunt force trauma to the head, but the cause of death was strangulation.

The first female to make the list was twelve-year-old Angel Lenair, who disappeared on March 4, 1980. She had left her house in denim clothes around four that afternoon. She was last seen watching TV at a friend's house. Her body was discovered six days later in a wooded lot not far from where she lived, in the same outfit she was last seen in. A pair of white panties had been stuffed in her mouth and her wrists were bound by an electrical cord. Cause of death was ruled strangulation.

The next victim, eleven-year-old Jeffrey Mathis, disappeared on March 11, while running an errand for his mother. He was last seen at Star Service Station on Gordon wearing gray jogging pants, brown shoes, and a white and green shirt. A witness said she saw him get into a blue car with two men. His body was found in a wooded area near Campbellton Road, by FBI agents with trained dogs.

Eric Middlebrooks was the next young person to go missing and be found murdered. He was last seen at his home on May 18. He answered the phone then rushed off on his bicycle with a hammer. Supposedly, the tool was for repairing his bike and not to use as a weapon. His body was found next to his bike in a rear garage of the Hope-U-Like-It bar at 247 Flat Shoals Road. His pockets had been turned inside out and his chest and arms had stab wounds. The cause of death was blunt force trauma to the head.

On June 9, twelve-year-old Christopher Richardson went missing on his way to an area swimming pool. He was wearing blue shorts, a light blue shirt, and blue tennis shoes. His body was found in a wooded area, in different shorts than the ones he had last been seen in.

Two weeks later, on June 22, seven-year-old Latonya Wilson went missing, followed the very next day by ten-year-old Aaron Wyche.

Authorities had yet to connect the victims and there was little cooperation between agencies or across county lines.

The obvious crisis and the indifference and ineffectiveness of the police led three of the victims' mothers—Camille Bell, Willie Mae Mathis, and Venus Taylor—to join with Reverend Earl Carroll to form the Committee to Stop Children's Murders (STOP). This group along with private investigators put pressure on authorities, and soon a task force for Atlanta's missing and murdered children was created.

The next month, two more children were murdered—Anthony Carter and Earl Lee Terrell.

Then, from August through November of that year, five more murders took place—Clifford Jones, Darron Glass, Charles Stephens, Aaron Jackson, and Patrick "Pat Man" Rogers.

The first known victim of 1981 was Lubie Geter. He disappeared on January 3, and was found on February 5.

Terry Pue, a friend of Lubie Geter, also went missing in January. An anonymous caller told the police where to find Pue's body.

Two more murders took place in February—Patrick Baltazar and Curtis Walker. Three more in March—Joseph "JoJo" Bell, Timothy Hill, and Eddie "Bubba" Duncan.

Duncan was the first adult to make the list.

Twenty-year-old "Little" Larry Rogers died in April.

From this point forward all the victims were adults.

Though not found until April, Michael McIntosh went missing in March. He left his job at the Milton Avenue Foundry on March 24, and never went back. Reportedly, he was seen alive by friends and family as late as April 1. Sometime around March 25, a man who ran an import shop on Bankhead Highway said McIntosh came into his shop crying, having been badly beaten. The man gave him twelve dollars and showed him where the nearest MARTA station was.

Two other murders also took place in April—that of Larry Rogers and Jimmy Ray Payne.

The next victim, William Barrett, went missing on May 16. His body was found close to his home.

The final victim on the list was Nathaniel Cater, the twenty-seven-year-old whose body was fished out of the Chattahoochee two days after Wayne Williams was spotted near the James Jackson Parkway bridge in the middle of the night. A police team was set up on the bridge because of its proximity to the place where some of the previous victims had been found. Robert Campbell, a police recruit helping with surveillance, was beneath the bridge when he heard what he described as a big loud splash in the water and radioed the cops up top.

Williams, who had just driven across the bridge, stopped and turned and headed back across it.

He was pulled over by members of the task force in the chase car.

When asked if he knew why he'd been stopped, he responded, "This about those kids?"

"I take it you don't think he's guilty," Susan said.

"I don't think all the cases were solved," I said. "There's a difference. And it wasn't just one case. It was many. And Wayne Williams may have been responsible for some of them, but not all. The investigation and trial were so badly botched, it's hard to know. It was a very big and important case for him to be convicted the way he was for killing who he did."

"You mean two adults."

I nodded.

"You're not here for school. You're here to solve the case."

"Cases. And I'm here for both."

"Seems to me you're doing more drinking than investigating these days."

"These cases will do that to you," I said.

Images of me and Jordan and Martin playing house, being an actual family, flashed inside my head.

"What happened?"

I shook my head. "Don't want to talk about it."

Jordan rolling over to face me in the bed I had come to see as ours, her sweet, loving, longing smile, the quick glance at little Martin Fisher lying on the floor. The most happiness I had ever known.

"You don't have to," Susan said. "But it involved a woman. I'd bet my life on it. I can tell by the way you drink. So what's your theory?"

"About the case?" I said. "Sloppy police work. Lack of coordination. Inane, incomplete list. Political motivations. Overeagerness to assign guilt to one suspect. Questions about Williams's guilt. Unsolved homicides. Murderers walking free. Missing children still missing. An open wound that's not healing."

"For you or the city?"

"Both. Why is everything so either-or for you?"

She smiled, but then it faded as her gaze drifted off into the far distance to something I couldn't see.

"I babysat one of the victims," she said. "I guess he was a victim. Really don't know for sure."

"Really? Who?"

"Cedric Porter. His mom was young and . . . she wasn't . . . she wouldn't've won any Mother-of-the-Year competitions. She was one of Aunt Margaret's best customers. This was when I first moved up here. I was eighteen at the time. Too young to work in the bar. So I . . ."

I knew she was older than me, but until now I didn't know how much.

"What happened to Cedric?"

"He just . . . vanished. Here one minute. Gone the next. And he stayed gone. Drove Ada crazy. Kinda like you."

"Ada?"

"His mama. She says he's okay. That he just ran away. Had his reasons. Says he still calls her. She won't leave the house because of it. Just sits there like she's in prison waiting for his next call."

"What do you think?" I asked.

"That he's dead like all the rest."

"You think someone's really calling her or is she just imagining it—or making it up?"

She shrugged. "There have been people around when the phone rang and she sounded like she was talking to her son. She swears it's him, that she knows his voice and that he knows things only Cedric would, but . . . it's not him. It can't be."

S afe Haven wasn't safe and never had been, and now it was haunted.

I hadn't been back since the day Brandon Wright's body had been found and the place closed down.

The abandoned daycare center on Flat Shoals Road just down from Chapel Hill Harvester Church, where I occasionally attended and went to school, was in Ida Williams's converted home—the very home her son, LaMarcus, had been abducted from and murdered. And that was just one of the many very bad things that had happened here.

What was once a large front yard, and then a playground, was now a sad, tragic space where rusting, slanting swings squeaked eerily as they moved in the wind, and sandboxes surrounded by litter and tarnished toys were weed filled, splintering and splitting, spilling their sand out onto the grassless ground around them.

I parked near the handful of other cars in the circular driveway, got out, and walked in.

Haltingly making my way up the covered sidewalk, I could hear the echoes of children running, climbing, swinging, jumping, playing, talking, laughing, each and every one unaware how close a killer of children was to them.

Pausing at the bench where Jordan and I had sat together on that first morning, I reached out as if to touch it, as if to make contact with an actual, tangible object that had made contact with her, but stopped short.

This was where I first met Jordan, where we had spent so much time together, where we had fallen in love—sharing cookies from Willie's German Bakery, sneaking glances, stealing kisses.

Even more unsteadily than before, I continued walking.

Miss Ida had joined STOP before her son was taken.

She and others had continued meeting even after Wayne Williams was sentenced. They gathered to discuss the cases and what might still be done in attempt to find some sort of justice.

Eventually, the group dwindled down to just a handful of mostly old, bored people with time and not much else.

After Brandon had been killed here and Safe Haven closed, the group stopped meeting for a while.

The first time I attended the small gathering in the back corner of Safe Haven, the group included Miss Ida, a large black man named Melvin Pryor, a tall, thin woman named Rose Lee, a squat, muscular, fireplug of a man named Preston Mailer, and Miss Ida's stepdaughter Jordan Moore.

Mailer was a retired cop. Melvin was a retired mail carrier. Miss Ida and Jordan had operated Safe Haven, and I had no idea what Rose Lee did.

This time, as I passed through the dusty, disheveled daycare, where everything still lay where it was left when the place was evacuated, I could see the group had added a few new faces to replace the ones it had lost.

Safe Haven was not just the sacred place where I fell in love, but the profane place where my world fell apart.

I had truly believed I would never be back.

The three new members were introduced. The first was a shy young reporter working on a book about the case. He was a white guy in his late twenties with glasses and a touch of red in his neatly trimmed beard. The second was a skinny thirty-something African-American woman with the Free Wayne Williams Project. Odd and awkward, she seemed to lack the social skills even for a group as small and laid-back as this one. The last was by far the most interesting—a forty-something blond-haired, brown-eyed psychic with the youthful bearing and body of a teenager, a casual, unassuming kindness, and a gentle, maternal nature that made me want her to hug me.

The reporter, Mickey Davis, began by assuring everyone that everything said was off the record, that he was only here for background for his book.

"I've got somethin' to say," Melvin Pryor said. "I started not to come tonight, but I thought I owed it to the group to explain why I won't be back. I don't understand why we doin' this no more. Nobody's gonna do anything—not the cops, the FBI, the DA, nobody. Nobody cares. They've moved on. And I just don't see the use of what we're doin' here anymore. Sorry, but I don't. So . . . this will be my last meeting."

"I'm very sorry to hear that," Ida said, "but I understand. No one understands futility and frustration like we do."

"You're quitting?" Rose Lee said. "After all we done been through. How can you just . . ."

"What good we doin'?" Melvin said.

"We found out who killed Miss Ida's boy," Rose Lee said.

"We didn't. He did," Melvin said, nodding toward me.

"We helped," Rose Lee said, then looking at me, added, "Didn't we?"

I nodded.

"It's gettin' embarrassin'," Melvin said. "Bunch of old people meetin', talkin'. Not doin' shit."

"Why do you keep meeting?" Mickey Davis asked. "How long do you plan to? What do you hope to accomplish at this point?"

"'Cause somebody should," Ida said. "'Cause who else goin' to? Even if we don't do nothin' but not forget."

"So you're like a memorial group," Davis said, "a—"

Mailer cut him off. "Not just. We're tryin' to . . . by sharing information, by going over everything over and over again . . . we might just . . . uncover something new . . . make a connection that hasn't been made before."

"So you're still tryin' to solve the case?" Davis said.

"Cases," I said. "It's not just one."

Summer Grantham, the quiet psychic who had been gazing at me with concentrated intensity, nodded enthusiastically.

"So you don't think Wayne Williams is responsible for all the victims he's said to have killed?" Davis said.

"Wayne Williams," Annie Bowers, the thin black woman with the Free Wayne Williams Project said, "was a scapegoat. The city was set to explode. The leaders knew if the Klan or a white man was arrested, what Sherman did to the city would be nothing compared to the fire set off by revealing those responsible for killing our kids."

"I know some people believe that," Davis said, "but the investigation into the Klan didn't turn up anything—and it was thorough. Do you all believe that it was—"

"We don't all believe anything," Ida said. "It's an open group for the exchange of ideas and information. This is Ms. Bowers first time attending. Her views are her own. No one else's."

He nodded.

I could feel myself beginning to panic. I needed to get out now.

"I'd like to say how happy I am to have John back in the group," Ida added. "He's got a really good mind for this kind of thing, and his investigation into the case—cases—is exhaustive and ongoing. I'd like to hear from him tonight. What are you working on John?"

"Connections," I said. "I'm starting over. Going through every-thing again, anew, looking for connections—between the suspects, the witnesses, the victims—where they lived, where they were abducted, where they were found. I'm looking for patterns, coincidences, connections."

"Everything's connected," Summer Grantham observed. They were her only words during the entire meeting.

"Maybe we could all work on finding connections between now and our next meeting," Ida said. "That could be our focus. No tellin' what we might come up with."

"There's something else," I said. "Something I could really use some help with too."

"What's that?"

"I've had a blind spot—so stupid on my part. The task force's case was the Atlanta missing and murdered children case, but I've only focused on the murdered victims. What about the miss-ing? I'm about to double down on my efforts to find out who went missing and see who still is. And I could really use some help."

"I've got a list," Mailer said. "It's incomplete, but it's a place to start."

"Excellent."

"Darron Glass was never found," Melvin said. "Went missing on September 14, 1980. Still hasn't been found. Both his parents were dead. He was a ward of the state. Streetwise but immature."

"That's great, Melvin," Ida said. "What a memory you have. We really need you for this. I wish you would reconsider leaving our group."

"I'm also very interested in Cedric Porter," I said.

"His mom was a member of our group," Rose Lee said. "Stopped coming when he started calling. Now she won't leave the house for fear she'll miss his call."

"I'd like to talk to her," I said. "And—"

"We could have our next meeting at her house," Ida said. "She's offered before. Said she couldn't come to the meetin' but if we wanted to bring the meeting to her, she'd still like to participate."

"Then it's settled," Rose Lee said. "Next meeting at Ada Baker's house with a focus on connections and missing children."

7

As the others ambled out toward their cars, I hung back, lingering, until they reached the parking lot, then I sat on the bench Jordan and I had first sat on together.

I missed her so much, ached for her in ways I never had for anyone.

Memories of her and Martin and our time together swirled around me, and for a moment I could actually feel their presence here with me. The grief was overwhelming.

And then Summer Grantham suddenly appeared before me.

"You okay?" she asked.

I nodded.

"Sorry to intrude. I was just worried about you."

I stood, but didn't make a move toward my car.

"Not ready to go home, are you?"

I shook my head.

"Me either. Wanna go somewhere?"

"I know a great little bar," I said.

"I was thinking this little all-night diner I know."

I thought about it.

"I can sense how strongly you want a drink," she said. "Please come with me to the diner instead. Coffee and conversation. It'd do you so good. I promise. We could even share a waffle."

"People are expecting me," I said. "I should probably—"

"Please," she said. "Tell yourself you can always drink later."

I nodded and smiled—and told myself that very thing.

"I'll drive," she said.

She led me to a beige '68 Volkswagen Beetle like the one Ted Bundy had driven. As I got in, I glanced in the backseat for crutches, plaster casts, and crowbars.

To my surprise, the car was clean and uncluttered, though I wasn't clear on why I thought it wouldn't be.

Still relatively new to Atlanta, there was much about it I was unaware of and unfamiliar with. She drove down dark, winding roads, most of them rural, none of them seeming to lead anywhere.

There was something hypnotic about Summer, and everything associated with her and our journey had a dreamlike quality to it. There was no traffic on the back roads, only our dim headlights hewing out a small oblong cave we could drive toward but never into.

It felt as if not only the road but the earth was empty.

The windows were down, the car noisy with wind. We rode in silence, as if knowing any words uttered into the airy whirlwind swirling around us would be lost, never arriving at their intended destination.

Eventually, we came out on a side street off of a bigger busier thoroughfare and into the back parking lot of a diner that could have been designed by Edward Hopper.

The mostly empty diner, which was all jade green and cherrywood, had that hushed middle-of-the-night quiet that had a hypnotic quality all its own.

We had coffee and conversation, and, as promised, a waffle.

There were only three other patrons in the place—an old lady with a library book dozing more than reading, and a middle-aged bohemian couple whose comfortable companionship and easy conversation indicated they had been together quite a while. Of course, like me and Summer, they could have just met.

"I sense such deep sadness in you," she said.

"I could say the same about you," I said. "And I'm not a psychic."

"I'm not a psychic—whatever that is. I just get impressions. And I have the run-of-the-mill sadness most every human does, maybe a touch more, but you . . . you have a deep, dark overwhelming sadness. And it's got guilt coiled around it."

I nodded.

"It's to do with the case—at least partially, but I can't figure out how exactly. Why is someone like you so interested in the Atlanta Child Murders? What is your connection?"

"What is yours?" I asked.

"I go where I'm led," she said. "I know how that must sound, but . . . it's the only answer I have. You know what I'm talking about. I can tell you do. You're feeling your way through life, being led by . . . call it God, your guts, intuition."

I shrugged. "I guess."

"Everyone has it. Not everyone is sensitive to it—to that still, small voice. Not everyone honors it, really listens to it, trusts it, develops it."

"But what you're claiming to do is more than what your average run-of-the-mill intuition every human has."

"Not really. And I see what you did there—repeating my run-of-the-mill sadness thing. I like it. You're very empathic."

"It wasn't empathy. It was humor—a little light teasing."

"But you have to be tuned in to people to pick up on things like that. That's all I meant."

"But you claim to have a gift—something beyond what everyone else has."

"Everyone has gifts. This is mine. I don't claim anything about myself or my gift, but neither do I apologize."

"I'm not asking you to."

"You're so open in some ways, so closed in others."

"So how does it work for you, your gift? Do you see visions? Hear voices? What?"

"Hear voices? Really? Maybe I was wrong about you."

"Sorry," I said. "I'm being an . . . I need a drink."

"Maybe you need to talk about why you're hurting so much, what you're so angry about."

"I'm sure I do, but for now let's stick with how you operate in your gift."

"Ooh, I like that. Operate in your gift. That is what we do, isn't it? It's just on loan to us. We use it or we don't. We operate in it or let it lie dormant. I get impressions. Mostly images. Sometimes words. Very occasionally I'll hear something. I just pick up on stuff in the air. Sense it. Feel it. Try to respond to it. There are these pockets of energy all around us. We can walk toward them or away from them. I try to walk toward them when I can."

"Like with this case."

"Like with this case."

"So what have you picked up so far?"

"Pain. Brokenness. Disquiet and unrest. There's an unresolved quality attached to everything."

"That's all pretty vague, general stuff."

"I was just getting started, but I can only tell you what I sense. I can't make it convincing for you."

"Sorry. Please go on."

"Guilt. An enormous amount of guilt. Rage restrained. Caged. Sex. Sexual . . . acts, sexual . . . Some of it's just sex, but some of it's violent, angry, brutal, forced. Death. Sex with the dead. Children still in jeopardy, so vulnerable, so truly helpless. A sick, sick man, trying not to do it again. A truly evil man, soulless, pitiless, without remorse, without any humanity. Dangerous. Not just for kids. For you too."

She came out of the trance she had been in and looked at me, her deep, dark eyes delving into mine. "You're in danger," she said. "Your . . . drinking makes you vulnerable. Your sadness makes you vulnerable. Your . . . how closed you are right now makes you more vulnerable to . . . It keeps you from perceiving things, threats, motives—help and harm."

I nodded.

"You don't believe me, do you?" she said.

"Actually, I do."

8

The next morning I actually managed to make it to class—something all too rare these days.

Earl Paulk Institute was a ministerial college started by and connected to Chapel Hill Harvester Church—a racially integrated mega church in South Dekalb County that combined aspects of traditional liturgy with certain aspects of the Charismatic movement.

I had discovered the school and the church as a senior in high school while researching the Atlanta Child Murders. Someone claiming to be the killer had contacted Bishop Paulk and asked to meet with him. Ultimately, the meeting never happened, but that connection to the case and the opportunity to study theology and ministry had led me here.

Some of the many pastors and support staff of the eight-thousand-member church served as the professors in the college.

I had biblical Hebrew and New Testament studies with Dan Rhodes, biblical Greek with Jim Oborne, math with Lesley Ferguson, and public speaking with Don Ross.

In speech class, I sat beside LaDonna Paulk, the daughter of the founding pastors of the church, and someone I had taken out a few times.

As usual, she was dressed up—long black pencil skirt, silk stockings, and black pointed toe mules. LaDonna, like her family and most of the staff, wore her Sunday best nearly every day of the week.

Beneath the table, LaDonna had her legs crossed and had slipped the heel of her front shoe partially off and was dangling it out in front of her as we waited for class to start.

As was his custom, Don Ross, a dwarf with a flair for the dramatic and a great speech professor, said a prayer to begin class. Everyone bowed their heads, reverently, earnestly, solemnly. We were serious Bible students after all. As everyone else was praying, I slid my leg over and kicked the heel of LaDonna's dangling shoe. When the shoe hit the floor, I pulled it over to me and picked it up. Hiding it in my coat, I secretly dropped it in the trash can when I went up to give my speech.

When I finished my speech and it was LaDonna's turn to give hers, she limped to the front of the room on one heel and one stockinged tiptoe and removed her other shoe from the trash as the class looked on in bewilderment.

"I'm not even gonna try to explain," she said, then gave a great speech.

After class, LaDonna said, "You got a minute?"

"Sure."

We remained in the classroom after everyone else was gone.

"I'm worried about you," she said.

"Because of the shoe thing? That was just—"

"No," she said. "That was funny. I mean how much class you're missing, how often I smell alcohol on your breath—first thing in the morning. I mean how down you seem. You have some of the saddest eyes I've ever seen."

"Sorry," I said.

"Sorry? For what?"

I shrugged.

"I'm not getting onto you. I'm worried about you."

"I know. But I am sorry. In general. I'm sorry I'm not doing better. I'm sorry this is the best I can do at the moment."

"What can I do?" she said.

"There's always the sweet oblivion of sex," I said.

Her reaction was one of surprise but not outrage. She got the humor and the harmlessness of the statement and handled it gracefully—particularly since people didn't talk like this to her.

"That statement . . ." she said.

"Yeah?"

"Along with the shoe thing. Let's me know you're going to be okay."

"I'm glad you think so," I said. "I'm not so sure."

I met Frank Morgan for lunch at the food court in South Dekalb Mall.

We had Chick-fil-A and Orange Juliuses and talked about murder.

"Been worried about you," he said. "Was glad to get your call. Should've known it was for information on a case."

"It was for the pleasure of your company," I said. "Case info is only an added bonus."

"Right."

We ate in silence for a few moments.

Frank Morgan was a family friend. He had been involved in the original Atlanta Child Murders investigation and then on the task force. He was an honorable, decent man, a straitlaced straightedge who gave cops a good name, so square he was cool.

He had been better to me than anybody since I had been in Atlanta, and had become a kind of father figure since my relationship with my dad had become so strained.

"How are you?" he said. "Seriously."

"I've been better. Not gonna lie."

"Here's the question. Do you believe you'll be better again?"

"Not particularly, no."

He nodded slowly, and looked as if I had confirmed something for him.

"How about you?" I said. "How are you?"

He shrugged. "I'm okay. Always tired. Not enough time in the day. Too many bills. Wife wants more."

"Of?"

"Everything. Me. Money. Things. Time. Most days I'm a rat on a wheel."

"Sorry," I said.

"It's life. Whatcha gonna do? Thanks for asking."

"Sorry I haven't more."

"You kiddin'? You're the only one who ever does."

We held each other's gaze a moment, then nodded, then looked away, a little embarrassed.

We ate some more—just to be doing something.

A few students from the college came in, secured food, and sat at a table across the way. I waved.

"Think they think I'm your sugar daddy?" Frank asked.

"You did buy my lunch, but parole officer's more likely."

He nodded and smiled.

We were silent a moment, and I could tell he was working his way up to telling me something.

"What is it?" I asked.

"Not gonna be easy to hear," he said. "Need you to prepare yourself for . . . some bad news."

"I've already had the worst," I said. "Promise this will pale in comparison."

"Martin Fisher's mother," he said.

Martin Fisher, who had been like a son to me in many ways, was a speech-impaired latchkey kid who had latched on to me while were both living at Trade Winds. I had found him dead in my room less than a month ago.

"She's been pressing for charges to be brought against you," he said. "Claiming all sorts of horrible things about you."

Simultaneously, my stomach soured and tears stung my eyes.

"I've been keeping it from you," he said. "Trying to let you heal up—and because I knew nothing would come of it. I was making sure of that. But . . ."

"But what?" I said. "Charges are being filed after all?"

"No. But when she found out they weren't, she went out and found herself a lawyer. She plans to bring a civil suit against you."

"What's she gonna take? My VCR?"

"I'm working on it," he said. "But I need you to do something for me. Stay way from the mom. Keep clear of Trade Winds. Don't say or do anything about the case. And don't visit Martin's grave. Can you do that?"

I nodded.

"We'll get it straightened out. I promise. Just be smart and lay low. Let me take care of it."

"Thank you, Frank. I . . . really . . . Thank you."

"Sorry to be the one to break such bad news," he said. "Ruined your lunch, didn't I?"

"It's okay."

"You wanna just forget about Cedric Porter?" he said.

"Whatta you think?"

He smiled, and sliding the file folder beside him across the table to me said, "Cedric Porter. Didn't make the list because he never went from missing to murdered."

"But Darron Glass did," I said.

"Don't get me started on that damn list. Why Glass and not Porter? I have not a clue."

I nodded and opened the folder.

"You know in most missing kids cases—especially those who don't turn up—a family member took them. I'm not saying Cedric isn't one of Williams's that wasn't found, just that it's more likely a family member saw what a shitty mom he had and tried to give him a better life."

"'Isn't it pretty to think so?'"

"What's that? I know that one. I've read it."

"Last line of The Sun Also Rises," I said.

"Right. Hemingway. I should've gotten that one. Thing is . . . we looked at all the family. The mother . . . what's her name? Ada? And the brother, guy who has the video store . . . Lonnie. They both passed a polygraph. Had nothing to do with the kid's disappearance. The father, Cedric Porter, Sr., wasn't as cooperative. Wasn't in the picture. He and Ada never married, never lived together. I'm not sure they were ever really together for any length of time. Maybe only long enough to . . . conceive Cedric. He wouldn't agree to take a polygraph, but we looked at him pretty hard and never turned up anything."

Ada and Lonnie passing the polygraphs made me recall how Wayne Williams had failed not one but multiple.

"The mom claims he still calls her," I said.

"Really? Maybe he does. Doesn't say where he is or why he left?"

"From what I've been told just that's he's okay but can't come back."

"I think that would be best-case scenario," he said. "Maybe it's true."

"Best-case occasionally is."

"Check out Mr. Optimistic."

I smiled as I checked the date Cedric went missing and tried to recall enough to compare it to the dates of the victims on the task force list.

"The timing fits," I said. "He could've been a victim of one of the Atlanta Child Murderers."

"Murderers?"

I nodded.

"Could be," he said. "You think the mom is faking the calls? Think she's crazy or hiding something?"

"I intend to find out."

"Of course you do, and I would discourage you, but it might be just the thing you need to bring you back and take your mind off all this other shit."

"Too bad Bobby Battle's not here. He'd damn sure discourage it."

"I invited him, but . . ."

"He still blame me for the death of one of his brothers in blue?"

"Him and every other cop. Do yourself a favor and don't get pulled over."

Something inside me sank—though I thought everything was already as low as it could go.

Suddenly Frank's eyes grew wide at something he was seeing over my shoulder and he said, "Oh shit."

9

"What is it?" I asked, turning to look.

"See that guy in the white silk outfit?"

Just outside an Afrocentric men's clothing store, a large black man in white slacks, shoes, and short-sleeved shirt stood talking to a smaller white man in all black. Unlike the unadorned white guy in black, the black man in white wore a white pimp hat with a red feather in it, an enormous gold chain, and leaned a little on a red-handled wooden cane.

"Yeah?"

"That's Tyrone Jedediah Johnson."

"He looks like a Tyrone Jedediah Johnson."

"He's got like sixteen warrants for fraud and theft. I've been looking for him for a while. He's a possible witness in another case I'm working. If I can get him to testify, I'll help him out with some of his warrants."

"But not all sixteen."

He nodded. "Not all sixteen."

He unclipped his radio from his belt and handed it to me. "I can't imagine ol' Tyrone Jedediah Johnson not wanting to talk to me, but if my, ah, conversation with Mr. Johnson goes south in any way, radio for backup."

With that he was up from the table, crossing the food court, then out into the main corridor of the mall and approaching Tyrone.

As Frank approached, both men looked wary.

When he held up his ID, the white man in the black outfit bolted, but Tyrone, who didn't look capable of running, remained.

Since Frank had no interest in the white guy, my guess was it didn't matter that he took off. So I waited and watched.

Based on the body language, Tyrone Jedediah Johnson was apparently amenable to helping himself by helping Agent Morgan with his other cases.

The two men talked for a few moments, Frank making his case, Tyrone nodding and shrugging, only occasionally shaking his head.

Then from the opposite direction he had left, the small white man in black rushed up behind Frank and hit him hard with a sap to the back of the head. He did it on the run, jumping up a little at the last second and coming down with all the force of his movement and weight on the crown of Frank's head.

As Frank went down, I jumped up.

I ran toward the two men who were now standing over Frank looking down at him.

By the time I neared them, the smaller man was tugging at the bigger man's arm, trying to get him to leave with him, but the bigger man, who had pulled a gun and was pointing it down at Frank, was having none of it.

He was about to shoot Frank in the face.

All I had was a radio.

When I got close enough to the two men, I threw the radio like a baseball at the black man's head as hard as I could.

Because I was running and because I was not a baseball player, I missed.

As the big man moved to avoid the flying radio that wasn't going to hit him away, I lowered my shoulder and tackled the smaller man into him, all three of us falling to the ground a few feet away from Frank.

The smaller man began scrambling to get up right away, kicking at me as he did. But the bigger man was by far the more dangerous because he still had the small revolver in his hand.

Lunging, slipping, sliding, crawling, then gaining ground and lurching forward, I grabbed at the gun, but the best I could do was reach his wrists, which I latched onto with both hands and held on to.

He tried to break free of my grip, but I was able to hold on.

He tried to buck me off—and partially did, but I didn't let go of his wrist.

Then out of my peripheral vision I saw the smaller man pick up the bigger man's cane, pull it back like a baseball bat, and take aim at my head.

I ducked my chin down toward my chest and prepared for impact, but as the man began his swing, Frank kicked his legs and swept the man down. Once he was down, Frank raised his right leg and brought the heel of his shoe hard down on the man's face and at a minimum breaking his nose. The man dropped the cane and stopped moving.

Withdrawing his .45 from the holster on his belt, Frank slid up to where we were and jammed the barrel of the gun into Tyrone's temple.

Tyrone immediately stopped resisting and released his grip on the revolver.

"Shit, Tyrone," Frank said. "All you had to say was that you didn't want to testify."

F or a movie lover like me, Lonnie Baker's store, simply known as Lonnie's Video, was a special kind of magic.

Films at my fingertips.

Rows and rows of beautiful boxes with iconic images, each representing a VHS tape I could actually take home for the night, transforming my apartment into a movie theater, my bedroom and the small television into my own private screening room, as if I were a studio head instead of a college student.

The shop was dusty and disorganized, crowded and cluttered, but I barely noticed. It held more movies than any store I had ever been in—more than the smallish space was designed for. It held mostly VHS movies, but there were still a fair number of Betamax boxes mixed in.

Aging and faded boxes crammed onto shelves—often in the wrong category and covered in cat hair—meant that renting from Lonnie required a certain amount of patience and an openness to serendipity. But I didn't mind. I liked to browse, to lift each box from the shelf and read it thoroughly before returning it, right-side up this time, or keeping it, carrying it to the register to rent, then carrying it home, possessing it for a brief period—just long enough to be possessed by it.

When a young couple in the shop finally decided on which romantic comedy they were taking home with them and took it, presumably home, I was once again the sole customer perusing the shelves.

As I rounded the corner from Drama to Classics, I could feel Lonnie's gaze from behind the counter leave his book and come to rest on me.

"What's it gonna be tonight?" he asked.

"Can't decide," I said.

"Oh the tyranny of too many choices."

"I always get more than I can watch and have to check them out again."

"Moderation's not one of your strong suits, my young brother."

"Guess it's not."

From somewhere out of Comedy, Shaft, Lonnie's black Bombay cat, landed on the top of Classics and stared down at me. His sleek black coat was taut and shiny—even beneath the dim fluorescence of the shop.

"What do you have it narrowed down to?"

When I looked back over toward him, I saw Foxy Brown, his other black Bombay, crossing the counter in front of him, and I knew what was about to come next.

"Five, four, three, two . . ."

He sneezed loudly, pushed Foxy Brown off the counter, and blew his nose.

"Bless you," I said.

"Thanks."

"Tell me again why you have creatures you're allergic to roaming around the joint."

"Came with the store," he said. "Whatcha gonna do? So what all you gonna take home and not watch tonight?"

"Think I'll just go with Casablanca," I said.

"Again? How many times does that make?"

"A few."

"Hundred," he said. "I'm gonna get you your own copy. Hell, pretty soon you can just have that one."

"Why is that?"

"A Blockbuster is moving in across the street."

"A what?"

"Video rental superstore," he said. "It's a chain spreading across the country. You think I carry a lot of movies? I've got maybe twelve hundred. They carry over eight thousand. And tons of each one—'specially the new releases. Everything's computerized. Huge store with lots of room. No way I survive."

"Ah man. I'm so sorry to hear that."

"They claim to be all family friendly and shit. No porn. No unrated films. But they offered to buy me out and let me keep running it—until they realized I had closed down my back room. Used to have an adult section in the room right behind here," he said, pointing down the short hall that ran beside the counter. "They'll rent that shit—just through the mom and pop shops they buy and not their Blockbuster brand. But I closed that thing down probably five years ago. Ain't about to open it back up."

"How come?"

"Don't want to deal with the creeps it brings in. And closing it down is tied to my sobriety and Cedric's disappearance. The world changed for me back then. Can't go back to that."

I nodded. "What're you gonna do?"

"No idea. Stay here until I can't anymore. Then . . . I don't know."

"Anything I can do to help? We could get the word out, start a 'support your local video store' campaign before they even open."

"Thanks man, but it would only delay the inevitable. I've seen it happen to too many other stores. This scenario only ends one way."

He was resigned.

As we fell silent, I returned all the boxes to the shelves except for Casablanca, which I carried to the counter.

"Oh," he said, "a classic. Good choice. I think you might just really like this one."

He filled out the rental form, and as I signed it, he searched for the tape among the rows of brown hard plastic cases on the shelves behind him.

It was a slow, inefficient process, and watching him I felt the same hopelessness about the future of his shop as he did.

"Here you go," he said, placing the case on the countertop.

"You mentioned your nephew and I saw that you know Miss Ida," I said. "We're in a group that's trying to find out what really happened to Atlanta's missing and murdered children. We're having our next meeting at your sister's house so she can participate—and we're going to focus on Cedric and any cases similar to his. Would you mind talking to me about it?"

He thought for a long moment. "Tell you what," he said. "You go to an AA meeting with me, and I'll talk to you about it for as long as you want."

On my way back over to Scarlett's, I found little Kenny Pollard, the youngest son of Camille Pollard, the owner of the consignment shop Second Chances, playing with super hero action figures on the walkway out in front of his mom's store.

He was ten, small for his age, adorable and outgoing, and I had avoided interacting with him as much as humanly possible —not an easy feat given his extraverted little personality, the amount of time I spent in close proximity to his mom's shop, and the fact that we lived in the same apartment complex. But his older brother, Wilbur, a sullen, angry fourteen-year-old who always eyed me suspiciously, helped.

"Hey Mr. John," Kenny said, looking up at me with his big black eyes—eyes so wide, so innocent, so open, I had to look away.

"Just John," I said before I realized what I was doing.

Martin Fisher saying Yon, Yon echoed through my mind, and I had the urge to run.

"Hey Mr. Just John. How are you today?"

"I'm okay, Kenny," I said, glancing back at him as I tried to keep walking. "How are you?"

"Why ain't there a black Spiderman?" he asked. "Or Superman or Batman? Do you know? Why they all white?"

"They shouldn't be," I said, pausing a few feet away. "It's not right."

Looking down at him, I saw Jeffrey Mathis, Yusuf Bell, Edward Hope Smith, Eric Middlebrooks, Clifford Jones, Darron Glass, LaMarcus Williams, Martin Fisher, and so many other wide-eyed young black boys without their whole lives in front of them who haunted my dreams.

"Sure ain't. Do you like super heroes? I do. Wilbur don't so much. Says they no such thing. Who's your favorite?"

"Probably be Batman," I said.

"Mine too. How 'bout that."

Through the plate glass window, I could see Wilbur inside the shop, sitting in one of his mom's unsold old chairs. He appeared to be practicing his bored, disinterested look. But that couldn't be right. It didn't need any practice.

When he spotted us talking, he came to the door and told Kenny to come inside.

"Bye Mr. John," he said.

"Bye Kenny. You take care."

"You too now."

"Hey, you forgot one," I said, picking up a well-worn Aquaman.

"I know why Aquaman ain't black," Kenny said. "We can't swim so good."

I thought of Earl Terrell and Christopher Richardson, both boys last seen at or on their way to a public swimming pool, both bodies found in a wooded area some seventy-five feet off Redwine Road.

When Kenny started to return to get it, Wilbur grabbed him and pushed him inside. "I told you 'bout talkin' to strangers."

He then stepped over and snatched the figure from my outstretched hand.

"Listen to your brother, Kenny," I said. "Always be very careful. There are some really bad people in the world."

I was nursing a drink at Scarlett's when Summer Grantham walked in.

The drink special tonight was called a One-in-fourteen-hundred—the number of actresses who auditioned during the search for Scarlett.

I was not having the special.

Summer, dressed in jeans, T-shirt, and Keds, looked seventeen instead of forty-seven or whatever she actually was. She stood in the doorway until she saw me, then walked over, her long blond hair fluttering in the wake of her movement.

I must have looked surprised to see her.

"Surprised to see me?" she said.

She was wearing a faded Pink Floyd Dark Side of the Moon T-shirt that fit her girlish figure in the same way the jeans did—as if designed to do so.

"I am," I said, standing and offering to help her onto the barstool beside mine. "How'd you find me?"

She didn't take the offer of a seat.

"I'm psychic," she said. "Well, that and I asked Miss Ida. I've been trying to get in touch with you all afternoon. Are you okay?"

"Yeah, why?"

"I just felt you were in danger earlier today. Saw a man in a white suit."

"Really?"

"But you're okay?"

"I am."

"Sometimes I'm wrong, but it seemed real. I was certain--"

"You weren't wrong," I said. "But I'm okay."

"I prayed for you."

"I'm sure it helped. Can I buy you a drink? Want to join me?"

"I can't stay. Just wanted to make sure you're okay."

"Thank you. That means a lot. Sure you can't stay?"

"Take care, John. I mean be careful."

She then leaned in, kissed me on the cheek, and was gone.

Immediately, I could see Susan making her way over to me. She had been eyeing us while we spoke, and now that Summer was gone, she was determined to come over and inquire, though she tried to be subtle about it. Tried and failed.

"Who was that?" Susan asked.

She was wearing what she always wore when waitressing here, a red halter top with white lace trim meant to resemble the top of Scarlett's dress from the movie poster, and blue jean cutoffs with a Rebel flag patch on each ass cheek.

"Summer Grantham. She's part of our group."

"She's a cutie," Margaret said from behind the bar. "Got good energy."

When she wore it, Margaret's uniform was a faux tux patterned after Rhett Butler's, but she rarely wore it anymore, and didn't have it on tonight.

"Group?" Susan said.

"Missing and murdered kids."

"You should take her out, John," Margaret said. "She'd be good for you. I can tell."

"Bit old for you, isn't she?" Susan said to me, as if only tossing it out as a casual observation.

"It's not like that."

"Looked like that to me. Looked exactly like that."

Lonnie walked in and Margaret moved away to make him the drink he wouldn't.

I expected disapproval from him, but he smiled and waved.

This time instead of just staring at the drink, he picked it up.

Maybe that's why there was no disapproval. Was he about to join us in our slow, sweet self-destruction?

He then raised the glass to me and said, "Here's lookin' at you, kid."

I lifted my glass and smiled.

Without taking so much as a sip, he returned the drink to Margaret and walked out.

"What was that about?" Susan said.

I tapped the brown tape case on the bar beside me. "Casablanca."

"Again?"

"What's your nationality, John?" Margaret asked.

"I'm a drunkard."

"Makes you a citizen of the world."

We drank to that.

In all, I drank less than I had been. A good bit less. And though Susan offered to, I was able to drive myself home.

Home was Memorial Manor, an older medium-sized apartment complex a block off Memorial Drive near the I-285 exit—and, actually, just a walk through the woods from Scarlett's, though so far I had never walked it.

As usual, my apartment was empty, my roommate at work.

Stepping into the darkness, my surroundings felt strange and unfamiliar.

We hadn't been here long, and I was still getting used to the place. The bedroom was the only space in the apartment that felt in any way like mine. And it wasn't just because the living room and kitchen were communal and very sparsely furnished. It was mainly because of how little time I spent here, and how much of that time was spent in my room—which was where I walked straight to now.

Feeling my way through the darkness, I eased across the living room and down the short hallway to the closed door on the left that opened into my room.

There was nothing nice about the apartment. I couldn't afford nice. Hell, I couldn't afford this not-nice place without a room-mate. But after all that had happened, I couldn't stay at Trade Winds and EPI's makeshift dorm apartment any longer.

I had turned to Randy Renfroe, the college's dean of students and all around helpful guy. With his help, I found this inexpensive place off Memorial Drive and Rick Baxley, a roommate who worked at night. What could be better?

Memorial Drive connected the two most significant areas of Atlanta for me. On one end, the end that represented the past, were the places where a series of missing and murdered children lived, disappeared, and were dumped. The other end, the end that held a future I knew nothing of at the time, ran into the massive intrusive igneous quartz dome known as Stone Mountain, and the Stone Cold Killer I would one day encounter there.

I was lonely, felt more alone in this place, my supposed home, than any other, so I poured myself a drink and went to work on my wall.

I was tempted to dive in to Cedric Porter's file, but decided to wait to hear what his mother and uncle had to say before I looked at it any more.

I thought again about Memorial Drive and turned back to connections between the victims of the original case, searching for a geographic pattern on the other end of this seminal street.

I didn't have to search long.

There are many ways to look at victimology—and though the most common is probably the study of the psychological effects on the victims of crime and their experiences with the criminal justice system, I was far more interested in the ways in which the identities, geography, and behaviors of the victims may have led to or contributed to their victimization.

By focusing on the killer, the task force failed to perceive connections among the victims. This led to the erroneous perception of randomness in victim selection, the belief there was an opportunistic predator roaming the streets of Atlanta picking off those vulnerable souls separated from the herd. But this doesn't fit with the fact that most of the victims were described as tough, streetwise young people able to fend for themselves—something they had had a lot of practice doing.

Like most of the problems with the investigation, the lack of consideration of the victims begins and ends with the task force's inaccurate and incomplete list. The list makes no sense. Who got on it and who was left off was random and illogical. And its parameters kept changing—morphing, evolving, contorting to accommodate some victims and not others.

I began with Chet Dettlinger's map.

Chet Dettlinger was a former cop who investigated the Atlanta missing and murdered children case with a small group of private detectives. So thorough and detailed was his detecting, in fact, that he was at one point considered a suspect by the Atlanta police.

Of the many invaluable investigative actions Chet undertook, perhaps the most helpful and revealing was the map he made of the case.

In the summer of 1980, Dettlinger compiled the geographical data into three points per victim on a map—where they lived, where they went missing, and where their bodies were found.

In doing so, he discovered something astounding.

A pattern.

A geographic pattern that revealed the Atlanta Child Murders unfolded on or near twelve major streets that actually link together to form a sort of misshapen boot.

So the murders weren't random after all.

The victims lived and played and went to school in close proximity to each other, and the main road connecting it all was Memorial Drive—the other end of the road I was on right now.

After plotting the points on his map, Dettlinger decided to drive the streets to see if the lines he had drawn on paper translated into a real pattern on pavement.

He and Mike Edwards, one of the private investigators helping him, started at the eastern end of Memorial Drive where Christopher Richardson, the eighth victim, lived and disappeared. Driving west on Memorial, they passed the street where a ten-year-old boy named Darron Glass lived, victim fourteen, who is still missing to this day. In two more short blocks they passed the East Lake Meadows housing project where Alfred Evans, victim two, lived. A few more blocks west they reached Moreland Avenue. If they had turned left, they would have been able to drive straight to the place where ten-year-old Aaron Wyche, the tenth victim, died in what was said to be an accidental fall. Instead, they drove on to the next alley where fourteen-year-old Eric Middlebrooks, victim seven, was found near his bicycle.

Across the expressway was the house where Eric lived and was last seen alive.

The two men continued west, and just before they reached Atlanta Fulton County Stadium and the state capitol, they could see E.P. Johnson Elementary School where the body of nine-year-old Yusuf Bell, the fourth victim, was found.

Memorial Drive ended and they made a slight left. At the next traffic light was the block from which Yusuf disappeared. In two more blocks, they took a short detour to the dumpster where nine-year-old Anthony Carter, the eleventh victim, was found stabbed to death.

Just beyond these two places was the grocery store where Yusuf went on an errand to buy snuff for a neighbor, and beyond the store on Georgia Avenue was Cap'n Peg's, where JoJo Bell was employed and the place he left from on the day he disappeared, and where Michael McIntosh, the twenty-fourth victim, did odd jobs. It was also where Fred Wyatt, in possession of twenty-fifth victim Jimmy Ray Payne's prison ID, was arrested, and the address Wayne Williams used as his business location address on his flyers.

Within the next five blocks, Dettlinger and Edwards passed

the homes of Anthony Carter and two other victims. In another moment they were staring at a silver fireplug where Jeffrey Mathis, the sixth victim, disappeared.

Gordon Street then merged with and became Martin Luther King Drive. Approaching the intersection of Martin Luther King and Hightower Road was the first time they had to use their turn signal. They turned right, and off to their right, just one block away, was the apartment where seven-year-old LaTonya Wilson, victim nine, was kidnapped. It was also the apartment building where the twenty-eighth victim, Nathaniel Cater, one of the two adults Wayne Williams was convicted of killing, lived.

The two men then proceeded north on Hightower Road to the location where Clifford Jones, the thirteenth victim, was seen entering a laundromat and behind which his body would later be discovered.

Then after crossing US-278, they passed the Bowen Homes housing projects where a young boy named Curtis Walker, the twenty-first victim, shared an apartment with his mother and uncle.

Hightower Road broke into two streets at this point—Jackson Parkway and Hollywood Road. They chose Hollywood Road because it was closer to the points where Clifford Jones lived, disappeared, and was found dead.

Once on Hollywood Road, they passed the apartment where victim nineteen, Terry Pue, lived with his family. A short distance later was the small shopping center at Perry Boulevard and Hollywood Road, where the body of Clifford Jones was found.

Just before Hollywood Road ended at Bolton Road, they turned left and drove into the parking lot of a Starvin' Marvin store at Bolton Road and Jackson Parkway. Just six-tenths of a mile north on Jackson Parkway was the Jackson Parkway bridge where Wayne Williams would be pulled over after a loud splash was heard in the Chattahoochee River below.

Soon after Bolton Road dipped south and merged with Fairburn Road, they were passing the intersection of Nash Road where Milton Harvey, the third victim, lived, and just a block west was the parallel-running Kimberly Road, off of which was the entrance to the housing projects where fourteen-year-old Edward Hope Smith, the first victim, lived.

Soon they were at the intersection of Campbellton Road (Georgia 166) near the home of twelve-year-old and fifth victim Angel Lanier. Farther east along Georgia 166 were the Lakewood Fairgrounds and South Bend Park where convicted child molester John David Wilcoxen lived. South Bend Park was also where eleven-year-old Earl Lee Terrell, the twelfth victim, disappeared from the swimming pool.

Both Wilcoxen and Terrell, along with Jamie Brooks, would be suspects—suspects I was convinced should have been looked at much, much more closely.

They drove on for several more miles—the longest stretch without encountering a location pertinent to the murders. Finally they came to where Redwine Road merges with Fairborn Road. This took them within fifty feet of the remains of two more victims—Christopher Richardson, who was last seen headed for the swimming pool, and Earl Lee Terrell, who was last seen after being kicked out of one—lay in the woods close together near a cluster of large boulders.

Unbeknownst to them at the time, Dettlinger and Edwards had also driven by the locations where seven more victims—all alive that day—lived, would disappear from, or would be found dead. Their death map drive had also taken them within a block of the house of Wayne Williams.

13

The next afternoon, I attended an AA meeting with Lonnie Baker.

The meeting took place every day during lunch in the back of his video store, in the fifteen by eighteen room that had once housed his Adult titles.

Now a storage room, the walls were fronted by metal shelving filled with rental VCRs, video tapes, movie posters and other promotional materials, bulk kitty litter, paper towel rolls, office supplies, cleaning supplies and disinfectant, catalogs, clear plastic protective video box sleeves, and AA books and materials. Though mostly covered by shelves, the unpainted sheetrock walls were covered with movie posters. Behind the shelf directly in front of me were partially exposed promotional posters for The Boy Who Could Fly and Top Gun.

A circle comprised of ten folding metal chairs was in the center of the room, a coffee pot on a small wobbly wooden table between the first shelf and the door. Three men sat on the chairs, each with a paper cup of coffee in his hand.

I wasn't a coffee drinker, but evidently that didn't matter.

Like Lonnie, the other two men were black and looked to be

in their thirties. Unlike Lonnie, they were big men—one short and round, the other tall and thick everywhere including his hands.

"Hi, I'm Lonnie and I'm an addict. I want to welcome John Jordan with us today," Lonnie said. "Welcome John. We're glad you're here."

If the other two men were glad I was there I couldn't tell. Neither said anything.

"Roy, will you read the preamble for us?" Lonnie said.

"Hi, I'm Roy, and I'm an alcoholic," the large, thick man said in a deep, thick voice. "'Alcoholics Anonymous is a fellowship of men and women who share their experience, strength and hope with each other that they may solve their common problem and help others to recover from alcoholism. The only requirement for membership is a desire to stop drinking. There are no dues or fees for AA membership; we are self-supporting through our own contributions. AA is not allied with any sect, denomination, politics, organization or institution; does not wish to engage in any controversy, neither endorses nor opposes any causes. Our primary purpose is to stay sober and help other alcoholics to achieve sobriety.'"

I shouldn't be here, I thought. I have no desire to stop drinking. Not really.

"Thank you, Roy," Lonnie said. "Jerry, will you read how it works?"

"Hi, I'm Jerry, and I'm an alcoholic," the short, rotund man with large, gold glasses said. "'Rarely have we seen a person fail who has thoroughly followed our path. Those who do not recover are people who cannot or will not completely give themselves to this simple program, usually men and women who are constitutionally incapable of being honest with themselves. There are such unfortunates. They are not at fault; they seem to have been born that way. They are naturally incapable of grasping and developing a manner of living which demands rigorous honesty. Their chances are less than average. There are those, too, who suffer from grave emotional and mental disorders, but many of them do recover if they have the capacity to be honest. Our stories disclose in a general way what we used to be like, what happened, and what we are like now. If you have decided you want what we have and are willing to go to any length to get it—then you are ready to take certain steps. At some of these we balked. We thought we could find an easier, softer way. But we could not. With all the earnestness at our command, we beg of you to be fearless and thorough from the very start. Some of us have tried to hold on to our old ideas and the result was nil until we let go absolutely. Remember that we deal with alcohol—cunning, baffling, powerful! Without help it is too much for us. But there is One who has all power—that One is God. May you find Him now! Half measures availed us nothing. We stood at the turning point. We asked His protection and care with complete abandon. Here are the steps we took, which are suggested as a program of recovery:

"'We admitted we were powerless over alcohol—that our lives had become unmanageable. Came to believe that a Power greater than ourselves could restore us to sanity. Made a decision to turn our will and our lives over to the care of God as we understood Him. Made a searching and fearless moral inventory of ourselves. Admitted to God, to ourselves, and to another human being the exact nature of our wrongs. Were entirely ready to have God remove all these defects of character. Humbly asked Him to remove our shortcomings. Made a list of all persons we had harmed, and became willing to make amends to them all. Made direct amends to such people wherever possible, except when to do so would injure them or others. Continued to take personal inventory and when we were wrong promptly admitted it. Sought through prayer and meditation to improve our conscious contact with God as we understood Him, praying only for knowledge of His will for us and the power to carry that out. Having had a spiritual awakening as the result of these steps, we tried to carry this message to alcoholics, and to practice these principles in all our affairs.'"

"Thank you, Jerry," Lonnie said.

The readings were dry and stilted, the coffee lukewarm and bad, and I didn't want to be here—I didn't know if I was an alcoholic, but I did know I didn't want to stop drinking—yet there was something affecting about the paltry gathering, something true and transformative about the words being so badly read, and when we said the Serenity prayer I felt a faint stirring of something curative at my core.

"God grant me the serenity to accept the things I cannot change, the courage to change the things I can, and the wisdom to know the difference."

14

That night our nameless group met at Ada Baker's apartment.

To my surprise it was in the same complex as mine.

Like the victims and suspects of the Atlanta Child Murders, members of our group had far more connections, geographic and otherwise, than any of us had realized. Preston Mailer, the squat retired cop, lived in the apartment complex across the street. Melvin Pryor, the retired mail carrier, who was back despite quitting the group the last time we met, lived in a small house less than a mile away. But most surprising of all was the fact that the reporter and new member of the group, Mickey Davis, was seeing Kenny Pollard's mom Camille, my neighbor who owned the consignment shop next to Scarlett's, and had walked over from her apartment.

Our connections made a certain sense. Scarlett's became my bar because of its proximity to where I lived. Camille lived close to her shop. Ada used to walk to Scarlett's, and her missing son Cedric Porter, who we were here to meet about, used to walk to his uncle's video store.

There was nothing surprising in any of it, though I found Mickey Davis's involvement with Camille Pollard suspicious.

Everyone in our lives is connected by an unseen web of geography, interests, and relationships. So why didn't the task force search for the connections between Atlanta's missing and murdered children and the suspects surrounding them?

Ada Baker's apartment was clean and tidy, but everything in it, what little there was, was worn, faded, and frayed.

She was, like her brother Lonnie, slender and soft spoken with an essential sadness at her center.

"Sorry I got nothin' to offer y'all," she said, "but . . ."

"We didn't come here to eat or socialize," Ida said. "We're here to help if we can. We just appreciate you havin' us."

"Cedric ain't called in a while," she said. "He'a do that. Call every week for a while, then a few'a pass 'fore I hear from his again."

We were all sitting around the small living room, Melvin, Mailer, and Rose Lee on the couch, Ada in the recliner by the phone, Ida in the one opposite her, and the rest of us—me, Summer, Mickey, and Annie Bowers, the woman from the Free Wayne Williams Project—in wooden chairs pulled in from the dining table.

"Do you mind if we ask you some questions?" I said.

She shook her head. "Thought that why you here."

"Just wanted to make sure," I said.

"Rather than all us firing questions at you," Ida said, "I asked John to ask the questions."

Ada nodded.

"How certain are you that it's Cedric calling you?" I asked.

"Hundred percent. I know my boy, even with his voice changing, even with him growing into a man."

"How soon after he disappeared did the calls start?"

"Not long. Day or two. He knew I'd be worried the killer got him so he call soon as he could."

"Has he ever said why he ran away, where he went, why he calls but won't come back?"

"Say he wasn't safe no more. That he had to. He sorry but he had to. I tol' him his safety all I care about. Say he'a come home when he can."

I nodded.

"Would you mind taking us back through what happened the day he disappeared?" I asked.

Before she could respond, there was a knock at the door.

It was followed by Lonnie letting himself in carrying two brown paper bags of groceries.

"Sorry I'm late," he said. "I got soda and snacks."

"They's just asking about the day Cedric disappeared," Ada said.

He nodded, sat the groceries down on the dining table, grabbed the remaining chair, and slid it over to join us.

"Cedric wanted to watch a video," she said. "I told him he could go straight up there and straight back."

Lonnie winced a bit, but she didn't see it.

Our eyes met and he gave me a small frown and the slightest shake of his head.

How could a mother let her eleven-year-old son walk anywhere alone when a serial killer was killing boys who looked just like him?

"I knew he'd be okay," she said. "He was smart as a tack and wise to the streets. It just a short walk through them woods. Knew Miss Margaret and Miss Pollard keep an eye on him, not let anybody bother him. Knew his uncle look out for him once he got there, but he never did. He'd done it so many times before, but . . . he didn't make it this one time."

One time is all it takes.

"And nobody saw nothin'," she said.

Somebody did, I thought.

"I was worried at first. Seen some strange ones at Miss Margaret's place, but then he called and let me know he was okay."

"Were you at Scarlett's when it happened?" I asked.

"I was gonna go, went a little later, but he couldn't wait. Wanted to get his movie and get back and watch it. So I let him go on ahead. I wasn't too far behind him."

"And you never saw him?" I asked Lonnie.

He shook his head. "Never came in. It was close to closing time. I could've already been gone or in the process of locking up, but . . . I never saw him."

I opened the file Frank Morgan had given me and glanced inside.

"I was at home when the police called me," Lonnie said. "I came back to the store. We searched all over—all the businesses inside and out, all around the building, in the woods, in the apartment complex. Ada and I were both given polygraphs. Cedric's dad refused to take one."

There was one witness statement in the file. A college kid outside behind the bar said he saw Cedric running back toward the apartments, not toward the video store.

"I see there was a witness who claimed to see him," I said.

Lonnie nodded. "Ronald Nolan. Never gave a good reason for being behind the bar, but said he saw Cedric running back toward the apartments. At first, I thought he tried my door but it was locked so he went home. But if he had he would have run into Ada on her way to Scarlett's."

Unless he was lying and didn't see him, or Ada was lying and wasn't where she said she was.

"There's something suspicious about the guy—Ronald," Lonnie said. "Something not quite right. I don't trust him. And his story kept changing. Said he was on his way to his car, but that wouldn't have taken him to the back of the building. Then he said he was smoking, but he was doing that inside. Why go outside to do it? Then he said he wanted some fresh air. None of it added up."

"But it don't matter 'cause Cedric's okay," Ada said. "That's all that matters."

15

After the meeting, Summer and I walked to Scarlett's, taking the same route Cedric had.

By car, Memorial Manor was several blocks and minutes away from the little shopping center that held Scarlett's, but by foot it was maybe a two-minute walk.

Only a small wooded area separated the back of Memorial Manor from the back of the building that housed Lonnie's Video, Peachtree Pizza, Second Chances, and Scarlett's.

It was a dark night and we walked slowly along the narrow but deeply hewn path.

"What'd you think?" I asked.

"It's so sad," she said. "Just a little supervision and . . ."

"Did you pick up anything?" I asked.

"Probably no more than you," she said. "It's obvious she's lying."

"About?"

"She wasn't just a little behind him. I don't know where she was or what she was doing or why she doesn't want to say, but . . . she wasn't on this path just a little behind Cedric."

I nodded. "Anything else?"

"That's the only deception I picked up on during the entire meeting. Everything else she said and everything else everyone else said was told truthfully."

"Does that mean she is getting calls from her son?"

"Means she genuinely believes she is."

I thought about it.

"Did being there help you pick up on anything else?"

She stopped walking and nodded.

I stopped and looked down at her.

"I've gotten shock, terror, fear, and safety. I think wherever he is, he's safe but worried."

"You believe he's alive?" I asked in surprise.

"I sense that he is."

"Really?"

She nodded and started to say something, but before she could, a dark figure stepped out of the trees to our left.

"Hey man, you spare some change so I can get somethin' to eat?"

He was an old black man with bloodshot eyes and a nappy gray beard. He wore rags and smelled so bad it burned my eyes and made them water.

"Sure," I said, taking Summer by the hand and pulling her in the direction of Scarlett's.

When we were a few steps away and I could see he was by himself, I said, "I'll be back with some food in a few minutes. You like pizza?"

"'Bout all I gets 'round here."

"What kind you like?"

"Cheese. Just cheese. And God bless you, brother."

We walked faster, me pulling Summer by the hand, glancing all around us as I did.

"See how easily someone could've stepped out of the woods and snatched Cedric?" she said.

"Or his dad could've been waiting there or . . ."

"So many scenarios," she said.

After tucking Summer safely away in Scarlett's, I walked next door to Peachtree Pizza and ordered a medium cheese.

"Just cheese?" Rand Nola, the owner, asked. He glanced up at me with icy aqua eyes from the pizza he was preparing and gave me a quick smile of large, impossibly white teeth. "No sausage, bacon, pepperoni?"

"Not tonight."

He nodded as he worked, which made what he was doing look almost like dancing.

"This for Reuben Jefferson Jackson the third?"

"Who?"

"Smelly old black guy in the woods."

"Yeah."

"His is already ready," he said. "I just haven't had a break to take it to him. Figured he'd be banging on my door any minute. 'Course, he'd have to be very hungry to do so. He doesn't like coming out of those woods. If you don't mind taking it to him, you can just go through my back door, walk about fifteen feet into the woods and yell for him. He'll come running."

Later, back at Scarlett's, Summer and I sat a table in the back corner drinking and talking. I was attempting moderation with vodka cranberries. She was sipping on a dry white wine.

"You seem to be open to my gift," she said.

I didn't understand what she meant and gave her an expression that told her so.

"I've met very few people that are, and your lot usually alternate between burning me at the stake and trying to save my damned soul."

"My lot?"

"Religious. Christians. Ministers. I don't know."

"I don't either," I said.

She looked confused.

"I don't know," I said. "Don't know much of anything. Don't

know enough to be . . . Don't have many answers, don't have a corner on the market on truth. Try to remain open."

"The irony is I'm a Christian," she said. "I just have a gift. Like my grandmother did. It's a gift from God. I don't do anything to benefit from it, don't use it in any way except to help when I can, when I'm allowed to."

I started to say something, but Margaret walked up, pulled out a chair, and joined us at the table.

"Susan, who's jealous as hell, by the way, said you wanted to talk to me. Now a good time?"

"Sure. Thanks."

Tonight, for no apparent reason, she was wearing her Rhett Butler tuxedo outfit.

"What's up?" she said.

"Wanted to ask you about the night Cedric Porter went missing."

"Figured that might be it. Don't know how much I can tell you."

"Do you remember what time Ada came in?" I said.

She shook her head. "But it was late. It was sometime after ten. It was after the video store was closed—quite a while after. Pretty sure he closes at nine. Anyway, I ain't tryin' to tell tales out of school, but—and I ain't tellin' you anything I didn't tell the cop who interviewed me—but she was in a state. Upset, distraught like. You know? And high as hell. I'm not sayin' she did anything to her kid. Hell, I don't think she did. But I know for a fact she wasn't where she said she was when he went missing."

"Anybody strange or creepy hanging out here that night? Anybody leave around the time Cedric was supposed to be outside?"

"Something like this happens and you look back and begin to get suspicious of everyone. You know? The most harmless things cause you to question and suspect and . . . Something like this changes everything and everybody. All you got to do is look at Lonnie."

"Whatta you mean?"

"He was my best customer until that night. Hasn't had a drink since then. Shit like this either drives you to drink or sobers you up. Did it to everyone involved. Made most of us drink more. Anyway, there were two guys. Again, I ain't tryin' to point the finger at anyone, and I ain't saying they did anything. Just telling you what I told the cop at the time. They felt wrong. Never seen 'em before. Never saw them again. Don't know their names or anything about them. Don't know if they were together or . . . hell, I can't even remember what they looked like. But at least one of them, and I think both, left around the time Cedric was supposed to be out there. You want more than that, I'll have to dig out the notes I wrote down that night."

"Would you please?"

"Sure."

"What about the college kid who said he saw Cedric out back? What was his name? Ronald Nolan?"

"Why don't you go ask him?"

"I'd like to."

"Out that door, hang a right, one door down."

"I don't follow."

"Peachtree Pizza," she said.

"He work there?"

"Used to," she said. "Now he owns it. He changed his name a little. A religious thing I think. Now he goes by Rand Nola."

16

"He ask you for another?" Rand Nola said.

I was in Peachtree Pizza. I had come alone. Summer was still nursing her wine, waiting for me at Scarlett's.

"Huh? Oh. Reuben? No."

"He reminded you how good they are and you have to have one for yourself?"

"Yep."

"What can I get ya?"

"Medium sausage and bacon," I said.

I hadn't planned on ordering a pizza, but knew it couldn't hurt. I loved pizza and his were passible.

"It'll be my last pie of the night."

As Rand busied himself preparing my pie, I took a closer look at him. He was tall and athletic looking, with baby-fine blond hair, bright white teeth he flashed often, and aqua eyes I associated with suffering for some reason. He wore straight-legged light-colored blue jeans, leather sandals, and a pink Peachtree Pizza T-shirt.

"Okay if I talk to you while you work your magic?"

"No worries."

"I belong to a group of amateur detectives working on the disappearance of Cedric Porter, and Margaret at Scarlett's said you were the Ronald Nolan from the witness statements."

He nodded. "Changed it a couple of years back—my name. Not much, but enough. Underwent an awakening and wanted to be called something different. Wasn't trying to hide or anything."

"Didn't think you were."

"Man," he said, "that whole thing—that time, what was happening in the city, then for it to hit so close to home. Losing little Cedric like that completely rocked my world, man. I'll never get over it."

I nodded.

"It was hard enough, but then to be . . . There were people who suspected me, questioned why I was back there, didn't buy my story. It was a nightmare. To be honest, it's a big part of why I changed my name."

"I hear ya, brother," I said. "I've had a few experiences like that myself. Why don't you think they believed you?"

"Everybody suspected everybody back then anyway. It was crazy the way the city was at the time."

"Do you mind telling me what you were doing back there and what you saw?"

"Nah, man, I don't mind, but that's the thing—I've never been completely honest about why I was back there. That's the biggest reason I became a suspect."

"Okay."

"I was one hundred percent honest about what I saw, just not why I was out there."

"Why's that?"

"I couldn't be. I was with a woman—one I shouldn't've been with, or who shouldn't've been with me."

"Why can you say now?"

"Things have changed a bit. I still can't say who it was, but I am at least willing to say that's what I left out. It was hard as hell, man. Somebody who could corroborate my statement, and I could've used 'em."

"If you still can't, it leaves you in the same position," I said. "Just makes it sound like you're changing your story again."

"I know, but . . ."

"Are you still seeing the woman?"

He shook his head. "Wasn't really then. We just got together to fuck. She was in a relationship with someone else."

"Was? She isn't any longer?"

He shook his head again.

"So why can't you say who she is now?"

"Her . . . who she was with is a friend of mine."

I nodded. "So what did you see?"

"Just what my statement said. Cedric, who I knew from his uncle's store next door, running toward the woods."

"Did he have anything?"

"Have anything?"

"A video? A—"

"Nah."

"Was anyone with him or chasing him?"

"No. Not that I saw. Just saw him. He ran past, then disappeared into the woods. That's all I saw. I just thought he was running back home. Didn't think anything of it at the time. 'Course I was gettin' some of the best head I ever have. Least I was until . . ."

"Until what?"

"Until he ran by."

"Y'all stopped then?"

"Yeah."

"Why?"

He hesitated, then shook his head. "I . . . shouldn't . . . I've said too much already."

"Could you at least ask your . . . partner from back then if she would talk to me. I'd never say anything to anyone. She'd be safe. I'd protect her identity."

"I just can't. Sorry. I would actually do that if I could, but I can't. I wish I could. I really do."

When I got back to Scarlett's, Summer, Susan, and Margaret were having an animated and inebriated discussion about God.

Aunt and niece had joined Summer at our table in the back corner, oblivious to the other patrons in the bar and the exasperated expressions being directed at them.

"Here he is," Margaret said. "Now we have an expert to ask."

I laughed at that. And not only because there were no experts, but because I was someone who had a spiritual awakening, began seeking, and had only completed one quarter of study at a new and questionable Bible school.

"What is God?" Margaret asked. "I say he's a watchmaker who made this intricate timepiece and then stepped back and is watching but not participating in what is happening. Susan says . . . What is it you said again?"

"God is our father," Susan said. "He provides for us, takes care of us, disciplines us. Involved with the world, not aloof or distant or—"

"Hey, Margaret," an older man sitting on the opposite side of the bar yelled, "can I get a drink over here?"

"Get it yourself. See how hard my damn job is. Don't mix it too strong neither, Fred, or I'll know."

"Suddenly, a fuckin' self-service bar up in here. I could make my own drinks at home."

"Summer says God's a . . ." Margaret began but trailed off and took another slug of her drink.

"God is energy," Summer said. "In us, around us, in all things. We can ignore him or we can draw from him."

I nodded.

"Well?" Margaret said.

I raised my glass. "Malt does more than Milton can to justify God's ways to man."

We all drank to that.

"Seriously," Susan said. "Weigh in. What is God?"

"God is love . . . or . . . nothing else matters much."

17

I met Mickey Davis the next afternoon at Second Chances.

He was watching Camille Pollard's shop and her kids.

We sat at a secondhand dining table that had yet to sell, notes and case files spread out on the marred wooden tabletop between us.

The table was in between a small, faded recliner and a country-blue couch with a couple of prominent cigarette burns on it, in what constituted the sparse store's furniture section.

Opposite us, surrounded by a handful of sad toys and a couple of mismatched shelves of children's books, Kenny and Wilbur were lying on the floor working on their homework.

"I appreciate you meeting me here," Mickey said. "Camille's at a job interview. Gonna shut this place down if she gets it."

The afternoon sun shone through the plate glass windows in front and caused both his paleness and the red in his beard to be more pronounced.

"How long you two been seein' each other?"

"Only a few months," he said, avoiding my eye. "First black woman, older woman, and single mother I've dated, but so far so good."

He spoke softly and seemed a little embarrassed.

"How'd you meet?"

"Blind date set up by a mutual friend. Met at Scarlett's for a drink."

There was no obvious reason I should distrust the man, but I did. Probably because he was a reporter and the only member of the group profiting from the case, but whatever the reason, I wanted to get his thoughts about and reactions to various aspects and elements of the case without doing much in the way of reciprocating.

"What'd you think about what Ada said last night?" I asked.

He narrowed his smallish eyes and twisted his lips into a frown. "Felt wrong. Didn't add up, but I can't say why."

Waves of hostility emanated from Wilbur and wafted over us. I'd catch him staring at us in unadorned anger, but when I held his gaze, he looked away. Oblivious, Kenny continued coloring intensely.

"Is Cedric's case going into your book?" I ask.

"Only if we find out what happened to him and tie it to Williams or whoever the Atlanta Child Murderer is."

Hearing him say it aloud reminded me again that the Atlanta Child Murders were a series of murders surrounded by a much larger set of related and unrelated murders.

Don't forget that, I reminded myself. Don't lose sight of the saplings for the forest.

Then another thought occurred to me. Are the adult victims on the list connected to each other the way the children are? What about the female victims?

"Where'd you go?" Mickey said.

"Huh? Oh, sorry? Just thinking."

"Well?" he said.

"Well what?"

"Do you think Cedric could be with his dad?"

I shrugged. "Could be."

"Think we should take a closer look at him?" he asked.

I thought about all the various absentee fathers of all the various victims and how one witness claimed that Yusuf Bell got into a car with his father before he disappeared and was found murdered. I thought about how John Bell, Yusuf's dad, failed a polygraph.

I nodded. "I certainly do."

"I think so too. I'll tell you what else I think . . . I think we need to look at all the other similar missing kid cases from around the same time."

"Before and since too," I said. "If they continued after Williams went to prison . . . If they stopped . . ."

"You think all Williams's victims haven't been found?" he asked.

"I think it's likely that all the victims haven't been found— whether they belong to Williams or someone else, or Williams and someone else."

"I think it's Williams," he said. "And I'll tell you why. I found four other cases like Cedric's. I mean so similar they could be the same case. They even look like Cedric. All vanished. Never seen again. Never found a body or any evidence of any kind. It's a serial. I'd bet my life on it. And . . . it stopped when Wayne Williams was arrested."

I thought about it. If he was right . . . if Cedric was part of a pattern . . .

"The Atlanta Child Murderer didn't hide his victims," I said. "He dumped them. Most were found fairly quickly."

"I know. So if it's not Williams, it would be somebody else—a killer who went undetected during that time, a serial killer over-shadowed by another serial killer. But if so why'd they stop?"

I thought of Jamie Brooks.

Of all the suspects considered besides Wayne Williams, Jamie Brooks was the strongest—at least for the murder of one of the victims attributed to Williams.

Twelve-year-old Clifford Jones, in town visiting his maternal grandmother and out looking for cans, disappeared on the afternoon of August 20, 1980.

Clifford's siblings had seen him go into the laundromat in the Hollywood Plaza Shopping Center, where, according to a nineteen-year-old boy, he was raped and killed by the manager James "Jamie" Edward Brooks, and two other men.

The boy told authorities that three men fondled Clifford, that he was crying when they removed his clothes, said, "They mess with the boy's behind, chest and legs," and one of them "got him in the butt." He went on to say that the boy was hollering really loud, saying he wanted to go home, but one of the men had a yellow rope tied around Clifford's neck, which he eventually strangled him with—a detail that matches the facts. Clifford Jones was one of the few victims on the list known to have been strangled with a rope. The witness then said the men washed the body with soap and a rag, and reclothed it.

Though all the details fit, the witness's statement was disregarded because police said the nineteen-year-old boy was retarded and would say whatever he thought they wanted him to.

When Brooks was questioned, he told police that the boy came in around 4:30 p.m. asking for a job picking up trash and sweeping, and said he stayed until about 8:30 p.m.

And that was it. He wasn't questioned further—not about Clifford or any other victims on or off the list.

Jamie Brooks would eventually be sentenced on other charges in March of 1981, the same month when the last child under seventeen would disappear during the height of the murders. He was charged with aggravated assault with intent to rape and aggravated sodomy, and would serve ten months in the Fulton County Jail and be released during the Williams trial.

Perhaps most interesting of all as it relates to the list and the case against Wayne Williams is that Clifford Jones's murder was attributed to Williams following the trial—based on matching fiber evidence. Why, if the green trilobal fibers used to connect Williams to the victims and convict him for their murders are so unique, were they found on a victim that he almost certainly didn't kill?

"Maybe like Jamie Brooks he went to prison on different charges. Maybe he moved. Or died."

He started to say something, but Camille walked in.

She was a mid-thirties African-American woman with light skin and very tired eyes. Her hair had been straightened, and it, her makeup, and clothes were stylish—or would have been a few years back.

She collapsed in one of the two free chairs around the dining table and sighed heavily.

Kenny ran over and hugged her, but Wilbur didn't even look up.

After hearing about Kenny's day and speaking to Wilbur and getting a grunt in return, Kenny rejoined Wilbur and she returned her attention to us.

"Camille, this is John Jordan, the guy I was telling you about. John, this is Camille."

"Nice to meet you," I said.

"How'd it go?" Mickey asked.

She shook her head, the long side of her asymmetrical bob waving back and forth. "Too old. Too qualified. Too late. Too bad."

"You'll find something," he said. "Just a matter of time."

"What're y'all doing?"

He told her.

"Do you remember Cedric?" I asked.

The question seemed to bother her, and she glanced over her shoulder at her boys. "Don't like talkin' about it. So close to . . . He played with Wilbur. Good, sweet kid. The kind that people looked out for 'cause his mama didn't. But I don't even like talkin' about it. Scares me to think . . ."

She turned and looked at Kenny and Wilbur again.

"Did you ever see his dad around?" I asked.

She shook her head. "I really don't want to talk about it. And I'd rather y'all not work on that stuff around me and my boys."

"Okay, baby," Mickey said. "I understand. I won't do it again."

"I'm sorry," she said, looking at me. "I'm not trying to be . . . It's just upsetting. I just can't . . ."

I nodded. "I get it. It's not a problem."

"You should talk to Miss Annie Mae Dozier. We all looked after him, but she near raised him. She moved shortly after he disappeared. Broke her heart. But I don't think she went far. I've got her new address 'round here somewhere. Always send her a Christmas card."

18

"You killed a cop," Bobby Battle said.

"I didn't," I said. "He killed himself."

He was referring to Larry Moore, Ida's son-in-law, Jordan's husband, and one of his brothers in blue who killed himself a month back. It happened at Ida's house. I was there at the time.

"Ida was there," I added. "Her statement corroborated mine."

"Corroborated," he said. "That's just how criminals talk. She's covering for you."

"DA doesn't see it that way."

"Well, that's the way me and every other cop in this town see it. And don't even get me started on a dead kid being found in your room."

We were at a truck stop off I-85 north of Atlanta, because he didn't want to be seen with me.

As usual, he was dressed like a slick TV detective, but his white cotton Miami Vice suit and purple silk T-shirt looked out of place in Atlanta in November.

He held up a file folder.

"I'm doin' this as a favor for Frank. 'Cause I owe him. But I'm also doin' it because of what this is for a guy like you."

I didn't say anything and he looked disappointed.

"This is rope for a guy like you," he said, flapping the folder in the wind. "I give you enough of it and you'll hang yourself."

All around us, semi-trailers and tractors pulled in, parked, refueled, pulled out. The side lot where we were was full of them.

We were standing between our two cars even though it was a cold, damp day. It was loud and hard to hear, and I wanted to get this over with as quickly as possible.

He handed me the folder.

"Copies of the four missing kids cases Frank asked for—and one he didn't because it matches."

"Thanks," I said, opening the folder and glancing through its contents.

It was thin—a few missing persons reports, a few notes from the cops involved. Not much else.

"And before you say anything, that's all there was. I copied everything."

"I appreciate it."

"Frank is welcome."

I nodded.

"I know you didn't ask what I think, but—"

"I was just about to," I said.

"Their dads took them, not so as we could prove, but that's what happened. And I'll tell you why the fine detectives who investigated these cases didn't do anything other than what they did."

I waited but he didn't say anything. Guessing he was waiting for me to ask, I said, "Why's that?"

"Because of how shitty their mothers were. Gotta figure kids would be no worse off with their sperm donors. Hell, may even be better off."

"Do you know if any of the missing boys ever called their moms to let them know they were okay?"

He shook his head. "Never heard anything like that."

"You mind if I ask the detectives who worked the cases?"

"Hell yes, I mind. Don't even think about talking to anyone else. Not that they'd talk to you, but . . . I better not hear of you talkin' to another cop."

"You won't."

"Make sure you don't. I'll ask around about it, let you know if I hear of anything like that—so don't you. Got it?"

"Got it."

"I mean it."

"I know. I appreciate this. I'm not gonna do anything you don't want me to."

"We both know that ain't true. I don't want you doin' any of this."

19

"Do you remember any of Cedric's friends?" I asked.

I had stopped by Lonnie's to rent a movie on my way home. I was looking in Drama when it occurred to me to ask him.

He shrugged. "Not sure I knew any even back then. Why?"

"Recognize any of these names? Jamal Jackson, Quentin Washington, Jaquez Anderson, Duke Ellis, or Vaughn Smith."

I didn't have the file with me, but I had studied it in the truck stop parking lot and knew the names by heart.

He thought about it.

All five boys were between the ages of ten and fourteen when they vanished during the height of the Atlanta Child Murders. None of them were ever seen again—dead or alive. All of them had lived with a single mom with suspect parenting skills.

"A few sound sort of familiar, but . . ."

I nodded and kept looking.

In the mood for something light and romantic, I was already carrying the boxes for Sixteen Candles and The Man from Snowy River around with me.

"Were they Cedric's friends?" Lonnie said. "Could they know

something to help us find him? Can I talk to them? I'll close the shop and we can go right now."

"Just looking for connections between them and Cedric."

"Why's that?"

"They disappeared during the same time period and in the same manner he did."

"Oh. Any of them ever found?"

I frowned and shook my head.

"Found any connections between them?"

"Just started looking," I said. "Just got their names and the police reports."

"How can I help?"

Settling on the two selections I had already made, I made my way up toward the counter where Lonnie stood.

"I'll let you know," I said.

"I'll do anything," he said. "I'd give anything to get him back. I just can't fathom what happened to him. And the thought of Wayne Williams or someone like him gettin' hold of that sweet boy . . . Makes me want to drink like nothin' else ever has."

"What can you tell me about Cedric's dad?"

"Cedric Sr. ain't a bad guy. Immature. Self-centered. Didn't know nothin' about being a daddy—never had one his self."

"Could he have taken Cedric?"

He shook his head. "Wouldn't want him. Wouldn't know what to do with him. And . . . He's the first place I looked back then. He was shocked Cedric was gone. I believed him when he said he didn't have him or have any idea where he was, but I still watched him for a week or so just to make sure. Followed him everywhere he went for a while. Broke into his house and looked around when he was at work. Found nothin'. He didn't take him, doesn't have him. I wish he did."

I nodded.

"You or the group want to talk to him anyway, I can set it up or even go with you if you like."

"Thanks."

"I appreciate what y'all are doing. Cops don't care. Nobody else is looking. I'll do anything I can to help. Just let me know what that is."

I sat my two selections on the counter, and he went about finding them.

"This a little light for you, ain't it?" he said.

"Need a little light in my life," I said.

"Come to another meeting with me."

"I will. I promise. It helped."

He handed me my two movies without writing them down or having me sign anything. "On the house," he said. "Enjoy."

"Thank you, Lonnie. I appreciate that."

"Just find my boy," he said, and it occurred to me that he was the closest thing to a father Cedric ever had, and Cedric was the closest thing to a son he ever had.

20

I stopped in Scarlett's to talk to Susan.

It was the first time I had ever entered the establishment with no intention of drinking.

I sat at a table in the far corner and waited.

"What can I get you?" Susan said.

"Just a little conversation."

"No, seriously. Margaret said I had to serve you."

"Just came in to talk to you," I said.

"Really?"

"Really."

"Truly?"

"Truly."

She sat down across from me, placing her tray on the table next to the unlit candle between us.

"What happened?" she asked.

"Whatta you mean?"

"Why aren't you drinking?"

"I'm not not drinking," I said. "I'm just not drinking right now. I'm working on something."

"Cedric?"

I nodded.

It was late afternoon and Scarlett's was mostly empty. Two middle-aged men at opposite ends of the bar were staring into their drinks. Margaret, seated on a stool behind the bar, was having a moment with a drink of her own.

"That makes two of you," she said. "Cedric's death made you and Lonnie stop drinking."

My abstinence was temporary and it was because of the case, but I didn't mention it.

"Why do you say death instead of disappearance?" I asked.

She shrugged. "No reason. Nothing sinister. Just a feeling. I mean, I'm not a psychic like your girlfriend, but I get feelings too."

"How about facts?" I asked. "Got any of those or just feelings?"

"Whatta you mean?"

"You kept him. See anything? Hear anything? Anything that might help us find him?"

"Yeah, and I've been sitting on it all this time just waiting for someone to ask me in just the right way."

"Nothing that seemed fine at the time but later made you rethink it?"

"Nothing. He seemed like a good, happy kid. I didn't keep him all that much. His mom was a drunk. I don't know how bad she was to him. Think she was mostly just not there—even when she was. His uncle made sure he was taken care of. He's the one who paid me, not the mom. He's the one who made sure Cedric ate and got to school. But lots of people looked out for him."

"Like Annie Mae Dozier?"

"Her especially, but there were others."

We were quiet a moment, and I looked back over at the three lost souls at the bar.

"Do I look that sad when I'm drinking?" I asked.

"When you're drinking. When you're not."

I shook my head and forced a smile.

"What about friends his age?" I asked.

"Huh?"

"Cedric," I said. "What about friends?"

"He didn't have a lot. Played with a few kids from the apartment complex but just because they were there. Not like his mom was going to take him anywhere—no school activities, no birthday parties, nothing like that."

"Recognize any of these names?" I said. "Jamal Jackson, Quentin Washington, Jaquez Anderson, Duke Ellis, or Vaughn Smith."

"Jamal lived in the building. They played together some. Why?"

"What happened to Jamal?" I asked.

She shrugged. "He and his mom moved. Have no idea after that. Why?"

"Did you have a boyfriend during that time?"

"What does that have to do with—"

"Did you?"

"Yeah. Why?"

"Where were you the night Cedric disappeared?"

"You suspect me?" she asked, her voice equal parts anger and pain.

"No," I said, and it was only partially untrue.

"Then why ask?"

"Were you with Ronald Nolan?"

"The pizza guy?"

"Yeah."

"No."

"He said he was with a woman out back that night. Said she wasn't single, so . . ."

"You thought of me 'cause I'm such a whore?"

"No. It's a compliment. You're the prettiest, most desirable young woman I could come up with."

"Oh," she said, seeming placated for the moment. "It wasn't me," she said.

"It was an innocent question," I said. "Nothing behind it."

"Oh shit," she said, her eyes widening as if something had just occurred to her.

"What is it?"

"What if it wasn't a young woman but an older one?"

"Which?"

"The Mitchell of the Margaret and Mitchell partnership. I always suspected Laney of stepping out on Aunt Margaret. She had been with men before. Was mostly with men until she and Aunt Margaret got together. Always thought she was more bi than . . . bet she and ol' pizza boy were scratching itches they both had."

"It would explain why he couldn't reveal who it was," I said. "Why he still can't."

She nodded.

"Thank you," I said.

"Anytime."

"How did Laney die?" I asked. "I've never heard anyone say."

"That's 'cause we're forbidden from discussing it."

"By whom?"

"Whom do you think?" she said with a wry smile and a glance over at Margaret.

I waited.

She didn't add anything else.

"You gonna tell me?"

"Tragic accident," she said. "A very—"

"What's with all the whispering, you two?" Margaret said from behind the bar.

Susan popped up, grabbed her tray, and got back to work.

"I wasn't sayin' stop," Margaret said. "I just want in on it."

21

On my way home, I stopped in Peachtree Pizza to pick up the pie I had ordered from Scarlett's fifteen minutes before.

It was ready and waiting—just like Rand Nola's smile.

When the customer before me left and we were alone, I said, "Got a name for you."

"Like my native name or something?" he said with an even bigger smile.

"Laney Mitchell."

His smile faded, then vanished the way Cedric and the other boys had.

"That's why you couldn't say then or now," I said.

He nodded. "How'd you . . ."

"With a little help from Susan."

"She knows?"

"She suspected."

"She's not going to say anything to Margaret, is she? It'd just upset her for no good reason."

"She's not. No one is."

"Laney loved Margaret. I mean big time. They were like the

perfect couple. Lane just missed dick sometimes. That's all it was. Just sex."

Nothing is ever just sex, but I knew what he meant.

"So why did y'all stop when Cedric ran by?"

"We didn't. She did. Frustrated the hell out of me, man. She was good. I mean real good."

He looked away and was lost in reverie for a moment.

I waited for him to experience the sweetness of his memory.

"So why did she stop?" I said.

"She ran after him. Could tell he was upset. Knew something was wrong. She was such a decent person. Just took off after him. Left me there with my dick hanging out."

"What did she say?"

"Nothin'. Just took off."

"No," I said. "Later. Did she find him?"

"We never spoke again. I was still pouting when she died."

"How'd she die?"

"Dude, it was like so fuckin' sad. She was such a Good Samaritan. On her way home one night—from the bar I think—she stopped to help someone who was broken down. She was helpin' push the car the rest of the way onto the shoulder or something. Got hit by another car passing by. Hit-and-run, but they weren't sure if the driver even knew he had hit her. It was dark and raining. Who knows? Just heartbreakin' man. You know?"

I shook my head and thought about the obvious question.

"What is it?" he asked.

"Do you think it had anything to do with what happened to Cedric?"

"I never have thought about it," he said.

Maybe not such an obvious question after all.

"He's running—maybe for his life. She chases him. He disappears. She's killed soon thereafter."

"Fuck," he said.

"Exactly."

I had two walls now—one centered on the task force's list, Wayne Williams, and the original case, the other on Cedric and the boys who had vanished under similar circumstances. Jamal Jackson, Quentin Washington, Jaquez Anderson, Duke Ellis, and Vaughn Smith.

To this second wall I was now adding the suspicious death of Laney Mitchell. I had shared with Frank Morgan what I had discovered about Laney's actions the night of Cedric's disappearance and asked him to take a closer look at the hit-and-run report from the night she was killed.

I didn't yet know if they were one case or two, but separating out Cedric and the other still-missing victims meant I could focus on them while still searching for patterns and connections with the others.

I had made a commitment to rework the Wayne Williams case and I intended to keep it. I would continue to go back and forth between the two until I found a link between them.

So, as I ate the sausage and bacon pizza and drank Dr. Pepper, I looked for patterns and connections.

Which was what I was doing when I heard the knock at my door.

22

I started not to answer it since nearly no one knew I lived here and Rick my roommate was at work, but before I was fully conscious of what I was doing, I was opening the front door.

When I saw who it was, I was glad I did.

There in light blue jeans and a purple Prince T-shirt was Summer Grantham with a bright, sweet smile on her face. Her blond hair was down and splayed out beautifully on her purple shoulders. A single, slender braid hung on the left side near her face.

Tonight her Keds were the same purple as her tee.

"Hey," she said.

"Hey."

"Hope you don't mind. I went to Scarlett's hoping to accidentally on purpose run into you, but you weren't there."

"I wasn't?"

"You were here instead. So I came here."

"I'm glad you did. Come in."

When she stepped inside, we hugged, and when we released one another, and for the rest of the night, her perfume clung to my clothes.

"Sorry to intrude. What am I interrupting?"

"Come and see," I said, leading her back to my room. "Excuse the place. Maid's day off."

When she walked into my room, she looked around and said, "When're you gonna unpack?"

"I have."

"Oh. You spartan by choice or necessity?"

"Uh huh," I said.

She smiled.

When her eyes came to rest on the Wayne Williams wall, she grew silent, stepped over to it, and studied it for a long while.

I waited, watching her, trying to read her reactions, attempting to see the information as if for the first time.

"No wonder you're here instead of the bar," she said, then after a pause, adding as if an afterthought, "No wonder you leave here for the bar."

When she turned toward me, she touched me very tenderly on the side of my face. Our eyes locked for a moment, something kind and caring passing between us.

Then the other wall caught her eye.

"Cedric?" she asked, stepping over to it.

I nodded and turned to follow her over to it.

"So much pain in this room," she said, reaching down and taking my hand.

We gazed at the wall for a while, our fingers laced, our breathing the only sound.

"So there are six similar cases including Cedric?" she said. "Six missing boys who never came home?"

"Do you sense anything?" I asked.

She nodded, but didn't say anything, just continued studying the scant information.

After a while, she stepped even closer and touched the wall, placed her hand on each report, every piece of paper and picture, gently caressing each one.

"They're the same in some ways, but not in others. They're more dissimilar than similar, but they are connected. But not in the way we think, not the most obvious ways."

I thought about it, deciding I didn't yet know enough about the cases for anything she was saying to resonate or be refuted.

She turned back to me again.

"I want to help you," she said.

"You have," I said. "You are."

"I want to help heal you."

"Okay."

"You're so closed, so guarded, but you haven't always been."

I nodded.

She kissed me.

I kissed her back.

The kiss became passionate and we stuck with it.

"I'd like to make love to you," she said, "to love and heal you with every part of me. Would you like to make love?"

"Is that a trick question?"

"I'm old enough to be your mother. Are you sure you'd like to? I'm not . . . You don't feel pressured, do you?"

"You're not. I want to."

"Have you had sex before? You're not a virgin, are you?"

She was so direct, so grown-up about all this that I felt completely comfortable.

"I have," I said. "Not a lot. Not enough. But I have."

Between the kissing and the frank talk about sex, I was completely aroused and ready to go.

"Take off your clothes and lie back on the bed," she said.

I did.

As I did I felt a pang of guilt and pictured Jordan watching me, but did my best to let it go.

She unhurriedly undressed.

Her body was both softer and paler than I had imagined, but beautiful and unexpectedly erotic.

My bed consisted of a box spring and a mattress, no frame, no headboard, nothing else. As usual, it was unmade.

Kneeling on the floor, she leaned up on my legs, and took me in her mouth.

Her hand and mouth moved in concert to create one of the best sensations I had experienced in my eighteen years on earth, and I felt as though something not just sexual but spiritual was taking place.

It wasn't long before I was having to resist climaxing, and she must have been able to tell, because she stopped what she was doing and began kissing my body, working her way up to my mouth.

It felt as if she were kissing every inch of me, the nipples of her large, low-slung breasts grazing my skin as she did. Eventually, she reached my lips and began kissing me with her warm, wet mouth.

Leaving my mouth, she kissed her way over to my ear.

There she began whispering with the voice of God.

"You are so loved, John. So loved. You are whole. Everything you need is in you already. You are adored, John. So adored. You are precious and valued and most of all loved. So very loved. Let go of everything within you blocking the love of God from flowing in you and through you. Let love in. Let pain and darkness out. Let go. Let be. Breathe love. Be love."

She then straddled me, took me in her hand, and slid me inside her.

As we began moving slowly, rhythmically, she leaned down and I took her breasts in my hands. Cupping, caressing, loving.

I then lifted my head, my mouth finding her erect nipples, and I experienced something equal parts erotic and nurturing, and for the first time in a long time I felt connected, felt alive, felt loved.

23

I woke up from the deepest, most restful sleep I had experienced in a very long time.

The room was dark.

Beside me, still naked, Summer slept soundly, her warmth and steady breathing reassuring and buoying somehow.

I glanced at the GE clock with the green digital display on the stack of books beside my bed. It was a graduation present from a family friend and my kindergarten teacher. The Merriam-Webster's Collegiate Dictionary it sat on was a gift on the same occasion from my aunt and fourth grade teacher.

It was a little after three in the morning.

Easing out of the bed, I slipped into the bathroom, peed and washed my face.

The bedroom was cold, the bathroom colder.

Seeing my naked body in the mirror, knowing there was a naked woman I had made love to earlier in my warm bed, made me feel more mature, more like an adult, than anything in my life leading up to this moment, and I liked the way it felt.

When I opened the door to walk back into the bedroom, a shaft of light fell across the Cedric Porter wall, illuminating what

I had been about to study when Summer first knocked on my door.

Leaving the door ajar, I stepped over to the wall and began to read the information on it.

After a while, I walked over to the two bookshelves and the small table I used for a desk in the corner opposite my bed. Feeling around in the semi-dark, I located pen and paper, then returned to the wall.

Following Chet Dettlinger's lead, I made a map of the six victims on the wall. Because they had never been found, I could only mark the spots where they had lived and last been seen.

It didn't take long to perceive the pattern.

Like the Atlanta Child Murder victims of Dettlinger's map, at least five of the six on my map had a connection to Memorial Drive.

Though it was the same Memorial Drive, it might as well not have been. It was the opposite end, as different as the intercity and the suburbs. The victims on Dettlinger's map were inside the perimeter, downtown, on the mean streets of Moreland and MLK. The victims on my map were connected to the strip of Memorial outside the perimeter, between I-285 and Stone Mountain.

The different worlds of the two sets of victims were worlds apart, and didn't seem to be connected. There were plenty of connections within each group, but the two groups didn't seem to be connected to each other in any way—at least not in any way I had discovered yet.

"Bring that cute ass back to bed," Summer said.

I turned to see her looking up at me in a sleepy, sexy way that made me want to do just that.

"Just a few more minutes," I said.

"You can turn on the light."

"It's okay. Sorry I woke you."

"You found something, didn't you?" she said.

"Think so."

"Tell me."

I climbed back in bed, switched on the small lamp on the stack of books beside the clock, and showed her my map.

"This is Memorial Drive," I said, pointing to my inept sketch. "This is where we are, where Cedric lived. This is where he disappeared from. All these little houses are where the other boys lived. The stick figures are where they went missing from."

She yawned, rubbed her eyes, and studied the map. "They're all right around here," she said.

"All but one."

"One actually lived in this same apartment complex?" she said.

I nodded. "Jamal Jackson. He and Cedric played together some."

"Oh my God."

"These two, Quentin Washington and Jaquez Anderson, lived in an apartment complex on the other side of Memorial less than a block down. Duke Ellis lived in a house down off North Hairston. The only one who doesn't fit is Vaughn Smith. He lived over off Wesley Chapel."

"You think maybe he shouldn't be in this group?" she asked.

"I don't know."

"I feel like he should," she said. "I can't explain it, but . . ."

"Then he probably does," I said. "We'll keep searching until we find a connection."

"Speaking of connection," she said. "How would you like to connect again before we go back to sleep?"

24

The next morning, I attended classes with a smile on my face.

I felt more alive and alert and awake than I had in quite a while—and it showed. Several people, including LaDonna Paulk and Randy Renfroe, commented on it.

After classes and a quick lunch, I whistled my way through my janitorial work at the college, cleaning the classrooms and bathrooms with extra vigor. As I did, my thoughts alternated between my experience with Summer and what I had uncovered on the cases so far.

My limited sexual experience had not prepared me for my encounter with Summer. Prior to her there had only been two girls my age, both of whom were as inexperienced and inept as I was—and they both expected me to take the lead. With Summer, a mature, experienced woman, I was dealing with a skilled, generous lover who not only healed but taught, who not only led, but taught me how to.

The classroom door opened and I turned.

"Someone here to see you," Randy said. "A police officer. Is everything okay?"

I shrugged. "I have no idea."

I began walking toward the staircase with him.

"Where were you just then?" he asked.

"Huh?"

"You were a million miles away with the textbook definition of contentment on your face."

"Was I?"

"You were. It's good to see."

"I'm having so many incredible experiences," I said. "Learning so much. I'm so glad I came up here."

We reached the stairs and began walking up them.

"You are?" he said.

"I am."

"You haven't seemed so for a while," he said. "I thought with what happened with Safe Haven and all you were ..."

"I was. But then I ... met someone ... and had an entirely new experience of God."

"Well," he said, a big, amused smile on his face. "How about that?"

Upstairs, Randy returned to his office and I walked out the main entrance to find Bobby Battle and another detective I didn't recognize waiting on me.

Both men wore their shield on the left front side of their belt, their holstered .45 on their right. Both wore a suit, though Battle's was much more stylish than the other man's.

"John Jordan, Detective Remy Boss."

We shook hands.

"We were close by and decided to stop in and try to talk some sense into you before you do something stupid," Battle said.

"You arrived just in the nick of time," I said.

"Did I mention he's a smart-ass?" Battle said to Boss.

"Seemed an appropriate response to me," he said.

I smiled.

"So what can I tell you?" Remy said.

"You investigated the disappearances of Cedric Porter, Jamal Jackson, Quentin Washington, Jaquez Anderson, Duke Ellis, and Vaughn Smith?"

"No, just Porter, Jackson, and Anderson, but I'm familiar with all of them."

"I'd appreciate it if you'd tell me anything you recall about the cases," I said.

"Sure, and by the way, I thought Larry Moore was a wife-beating asshole. Fuck brothers in blue when a man hits a woman."

I nodded.

"Okay, the cases. Most of 'em happened during the missing and murdered kids case so we took them very seriously, conducted righteous investigations. All single moms, all street-wise, latchkey kids raising themselves, all better off with their dads or whichever family member decided to give them a real home."

"How certain are you that's what happened?" I asked.

"Fairly," he said. "I mean, between you and me, I would've liked to be more so, but as I said it was the height of the serial killings and we were stretched pretty damn thin."

He seemed to have more to say so I waited.

"You gotta remember how it was back then. In those days, you didn't find a body, you knew the kid was alive, more than likely okay somewhere, you had to move on. Our theory was that the dads saw what was happening with the murders, how similar their kids were to the kids being killed, and decided to remove them from the very situations that made them targets. We weren't about to take the kids and put them back in the most dangerous possible position they could be in."

"Did you ever see the boys with their dads?"

"We would have, but we didn't have that kind of time. It would've taken tailing the dads, staking out their pads. Best we could do was find evidence they had them."

"Such as?"

"Toys, games, clothes, their schedules altered around school, change in routine. In Jamal's case we found the outfit he was last seen in among his clothes and things at his dad's. In every case the dads told us it was stuff their kids kept there from when they visited, but Jamal's dad having the clothes he was last seen wearing proved it wasn't just that."

I thought about it. Some of what he said made sense, but there were lots of holes in it too. I knew how bad things were back then, how a dead body turning up trumped a missing kid every time, but it didn't make it right or justify sloppy, lazy, or incomplete police work.

"Only exception was Cedric's dad," he said. "He was the least helpful in our investigation, and we didn't turn up anything of Cedric's at his place, in his car, nowhere."

"Okay?" Battle said. "That enough for you? Can we go back to fighting real crime now?"

That afternoon, I drove out to Ellenwood, to Fairview Memorial Gardens, to Jordan's plot near the stone statue of Saint Mark.

It was a bright, clear day. I preferred the times it was raining when I visited.

"Last time I was here I said I wasn't coming back," I said.

Next to me, Saint Mark remained implacable, silent witness to my quandary and misery.

"I thought I meant it, but . . . I'm having such a hard time letting go—of you, of what happened. I'm angry and embarrassed and . . . I just can't . . . I haven't been able to get over it all . . . over you . . . yet. And on top of everything else . . . that really bothers me. I should've been able to let go a long time ago, to . . . I don't know."

I looked over at the bearded and robed apostle holding his tablet.

"You ever seen anything like this? You're not taking notes, are you?"

Like Jordan, he didn't respond.

"Ever experience anything like this?" I asked him. "Ever have that stone heart of yours broken?"

Still nothing.

I looked back at Jordan's headstone.

"Eventually, I will stop doing this," I said. "I'll get better. I'll heal. I'll get over you. Just not today."

25

Annie Mae Dozier was a small, gray-haired black woman with thick glasses above freckled cheeks. She wore a simple cotton sheath dress over her thin, narrow frame, and sank so far into the worn sheet-covered couch, a good portion of her wasn't visible. Like everything else in the place, the blue and white dress was old and faded and looked like something from the sixties to me.

Her apartment was even more modestly furnished than mine.

"He was such a good boy," she said, blinking behind her big glasses. "Smart. Sweet. He was my little buddy."

"He came over here a lot?" I asked.

She nodded her shrunken head. "Fair amount, that's a fact. Every time his no-good mama go down to the bar or have mens over . . . I'd hear a little tapatap on my door. He say, 'Aunt Annie, you got any of them little cookies like I likes?' I always did. I'd feed him, let him watch a video—he always had a video and his uncle gave me a VCR so he could watch 'em over here. He do that or color or both. He loved movies and loved to color. And he loved his Aunt Annie. And I loved him. He the closest thing to a grandchild I'a ever have. Only got one daughter and she ain't able to have no youngins."

"Did he ever confide in you?" I asked.

"Certainly. He get upset, this the first place he come. I talk to him. Rub his back. Directly he calm down and be back to his happy little self."

"What kinds of things upset him?" I asked.

"Ima notta gonna lie. His whole life was upsetting. Yes sir, it was."

"Was he worried about anything? Scared of anything? Anybody bothering him leading up to his disappearance?"

"He always worried 'bout somethin'. Mama like that . . . he never know she gonna hug him or hit him. Never know when he gonna eat again. No food in the house. Never know when them mens she have over gonna try to mess with him."

"Sexually, you mean?"

She frowned and nodded. "Some came just for him. No interest in that old drunk. She pass out and they mess with little Cedric. I call the police, but they ain't do nothin' 'bout it. Then on, she have a man over, Cedric stay over here. I fix him up his own little room—well a corner of my daughter's room. She was finishin' up her schoolin'. Hardly ever here. Didn't mind at all, no sir. She like Cedric. Everybody did. She done grown up and moved out now. She a pharmacist down to McDonough. So proud of that girl. Directly, I be movin' down there with her. Help out. She make good money, that's a fact."

"Did he mention anyone messing with him or anything he was worried about in the weeks leading up to his disappearance?" I asked.

It was the same question phrased in a slightly different way. She hadn't really answered it the first time.

"No, sir. No more than usual. Nothin' that stands out."

I started to say something, but her tired, old eyes opened wide and she held her bony-fingered hand up.

"Wait just a minute there now," she said. "Almost forgots about . . . Creepy bothered with him a bit more than usual 'round that time, I do believe."

"Creepy?"

"That what the kids called him," she said. "Real name was Daryl Lee Gibbons or Gibsons. Somethin' like that. Creepy fit him, yes sir it most certainly did that. He wasn't quite right in the head, eyes crossed, always staring after the kids. Big, fat, slow-movin' white boy. Always creepin' up on you. One minute he just there. In the shadows, gazing, licking his lips."

"What did he do to Cedric?"

"Nothin' far as I know, just followed him around like the rest of the kids, starin', gruntin', talkin' gibberish. But I seem to recall him bein' 'round more 'round that time. Cedric mentionin' him followin' him even more."

"Where does he live?"

"Creepy? Moved right after Cedric disappeared. Good riddance. No idea where he be at now. Just not here, thank God."

"What do you think happened to Cedric?" I asked.

She shrugged. "Somebody snatch him. Grab him up, take him away, do things to him, kill him and bury him in some woods somewhere. That what was happenin' back then. Boys just like him—no one lookin' out for 'em. Snatched. Strangled. Dumped. Gone. Forever."

"Do you remember a guy who used to live in Memorial Manor the kids called Creepy?" I asked.

I had stopped by Second Chances after leaving Annie Mae's and on my way to return my movies to Lonnie's.

"Not just the kids," Camille Pollard said. "We all called Daryl Lee Gibbons that."

She was just as stylishly dressed and looked just as tired as when Mickey had introduced me to her.

"Do you think he could've taken Cedric or the other kids?"

She shrugged. "I guess it crossed my mind, but . . . Daryl Lee just seemed too slow—mentally and physically, too simple. Seemed to me more like he wanted to be a kid, or thought he was, than wanted to hurt one. Either way, I always kept my kids away from him. They were younger, of course, but . . . The thing is . . . I've always thought the killer—or killers, if there are two—are black. And not just 'cause they'd have a better chance of going unnoticed, but because . . . You familiar with the concept of self-hatred?"

I nodded, finding it a bit difficult to take her seriously with her asymmetrical bob bobbing about.

"For some people it runs very deep. Minorities, the poor, the marginalized and disenfranchised are culturally conditioned by the majority, the power structure, to hate themselves. It's so entrenched, so deeply ingrained most don't even know they do it."

She spoke with conviction, but it sounded like something she had heard or had read—perhaps in a college class or special lecture on race and culture she had attended.

"But you can't be oppressed and tortured and told that it's your fault and you're worthless and it not have an effect on you," she continued. "You can't be poor and without possibilities when everyone else has plenty, and plenty more coming—all while they're telling you the reason you don't have more and don't do better is because you're slow and stupid and lazy and ignorant and criminal and—without it causing you to start to believe it yourself. Think about a kid in a family being told that he's less than. He grows up believing it. If he's also told that or made to feel that way by a teacher, he believes it even more. But what if everywhere you look, everything you hear, every single thread sewn into the fabric of your life, of life itself, was telling you that you and your family and your kin and kind are inferior, less than —not just a nigger, but a nigger for a reason. Women are told it. Jews are told it. So many are told it. But no one is told it like black people in America. I've always thought the killer was a self-hating black person."

I thought about it—about how this black woman who was dating a white man and had straightened her hair and dressed and spoke in a way many would describe as white, was speaking so eloquently of self-hating black people.

"But," she added, "we did mention Creepy to the police back then—both when Jamal and Cedric went missing. Don't know what they did about it. Then he vanished too. One day he was here. The next he was gone. Nobody knew where he went."

"Okay, thanks," I said.

"Let me tell you a dirty little secret," she said.

"What's that?"

As usual, her shop was empty, but she still lowered her voice.

"All the kids who got snatched back then . . . all those poor missing and murdered children . . . went missing and got murdered 'cause nobody was watching them like they should."

Blame the victim, I thought. It's what Job's so-called friends did. It's what far too many people do. Who's practicing self-hating now?

"I'm not sayin' they should've been taken or killed, just that if they were where they were supposed to be and being watched like they should've been, it wouldn't've happened."

I remember hearing Wayne Williams say something just like that.

"But Cedric's is a special case. His mom's the worst. Sorry as the day is long. So what if she had a rough childhood. So what if she been abused or mistreated or . . . whatever. It's no excuse. It's no reason to . . . be like she was with her boy. She's as self-hating as anyone I've ever seen—and not without reason. Wouldn't be at all surprised if she didn't kill her own boy."

"What can you tell me about Daryl Lee Gibbons?" I said.

Lonnie frowned, shook his head, and looked down.

I waited.

"How'd you find out?" he said.

"Find out what?"

"What I did. That's not why you're asking?"

"His name came up. Just trying to find out what I can about him."

"He didn't take Cedric," he said.

"How do you know that?"

"Because . . . I thought he did."

I waited, but he didn't say anything else.

"I don't understand," I said.

"I beat that boy bad. Real bad. Back when Cedric went missing. Creepy was the first place I went. Searched his apartment. Questioned him. I was convinced he had taken Cedric. I was out of my mind with . . . I was real messed up. Convinced Creepy had hurt and killed him and buried him in the woods between here and the apartment complex. I beat him so bad I believed he'd've told me if he had done anything to my boy."

I nodded.

"I'm ashamed of what I did, but I can't say I wouldn't do it again."

"I understand."

We were quiet a moment.

"Did he report you?" I asked.

He shook his head. "Have no idea why."

"Guilty people avoid the cops," I said.

"You think he . . . and I . . . let him go?"

I shrugged. "Not saying that. Just that it might be a possibility. Or that he was guilty of something else."

"Or that his life was such shit he just expected treatment like that," he said.

I remembered the movies in my hand and set them on the counter.

"Keep 'em. I know you ain't watched 'em yet."

"You sure?"

He nodded.

"Thanks."

"Be good to see you back at a meeting," he said.

"I will be soon," I said. "Soon as I can. It helped. I'm doin' better. I'll be back. Count on it."

"I will, then."

"I hear Daryl Lee just disappeared," I said. "Here one day. Gone the next. Do you know why or where he went?"

He shook his head. "No idea. Hope it wasn't 'cause of what I did to him or, even more so, because of something he did and I let him go, but . . . it was around that same time."

"Sorry to have to ask this," I began, then paused.

"What?"

"Your sister."

He shook his head. "Don't hold back. Finding Cedric is all that matters—and I know how she . . . what a mess she is."

"I think she's lying," I said.

"She definitely is," he said. "It just has nothing to do with Cedric's disappearance—least not that I could ever find. She's lying about where she was and when she finally made it to the bar because she was scoring some dope or turnin' a trick. Probably is indirectly why Cedric got snatched—'cause she wasn't tendin' to him—but I never found anything to say she was directly involved. And believe me I looked. And if I had, I wouldn't cover it up. She had her chance to grow up and become something, to change and be better, and she didn't. Cedric didn't get his."

"You got yours and you took it," I said. "And AA is a big part of it, isn't it?"

"The biggest. Ada is lost. Nothin' I can do about that. But Cedric . . . I was gonna make sure he made it out, made something of himself. I was gonna . . . He was gonna have a good life."

26

M ickey Davis and I were at the Varsity to see Cedric
Porter, Sr.

It was late, and the world's largest drive-in was mostly empty, its large rooms vacant, its tables in need of bussing.

We had arrived a little earlier than planned, and it would be another half hour or so until Cedric Sr. finished his shift. And though we hadn't come to eat, since we were here with a little extra time on our hands we agreed we'd be fools not to.

"What'll you have?" the large African-American woman behind the counter asked.

She wore a red shirt, white apron, a red Varsity paper hat, and the weariness of a woman needing a break from her life.

I had a cheeseburger, fries, a fried apple pie, and a Coke. Mickey had a couple of chili cheese dogs, onion rings, and a Frosted Orange.

While we waited, I read a few statistics about this unique place from a plaque on the wall. It's the world's largest single outlet for Coke. It can hold six hundred cars and eight hundred people. Every single day it serves more than two miles of hotdogs, one ton of onion rings, five thousand fried pies, and twenty-five hundred pounds of potatoes. On Georgia Tech game days some thirty thousand people come here to eat.

I thought about Rudy's little roadside diner in Pottersville and said aloud, "We're not in Kansas anymore."

"No we're not," Mickey said.

We carried our red trays of food up some stairs and into one of the empty rooms, and ate the way men do when women aren't around.

That thought made me miss Summer and long to be with her in my bed again soon.

"Guess who's got a record?" Mickey asked, his soft voice hard to hear in the empty, open space of the room.

"Who's that?"

"Creepy Gibbons. Took less than ten minutes and two calls to turn up."

I hadn't mentioned Daryl Lee to him. Camille must have.

"For what?" I asked.

"A little L and L."

He had started making a little more eye contact with me, but only a little. He still mostly had the eyes of a shy and insecure child.

Lewd and lascivious acts are any touches to the genitals, breasts, or butt of a minor—clothed or not.

"No details yet," he said. "Have no idea what he did, where, or when, but should know tomorrow."

What if he was responsible for what happened to Cedric and the others? What if that's why he moved right after? What if the murders didn't stop, just changed locations? What if he was missed somehow in the original investigation?

Eventually, Cedric Porter, Sr. joined us.

He was still wearing his red paper hat and white apron. The apron was soiled with grease and smeared with ketchup—which looked like dirt and bloodstains.

Beneath his paper hat, he was bald, his large head smooth

and gleaming. Below it, the rest of his body was big and round like his head.

"Tired and ready to go home," he said as he collapsed into the booth with us. "What this about?"

"Cedric, Jr.," I said.

"What about him?" he asked, defensive. "Whatta two white boys got to do with a missin' black boy?"

"We're tryin' to find him," I said. "Reinvestigating his case along with some other similar ones."

"Coulda save you a trip," he said. "Never had nothin' to do with that boy. Didn't take 'im. Don't have 'im. Don't know nothin' about who did."

Not quite sure what to say to that, we were all quiet a moment.

I glanced over at Mickey. He shrugged. He had yet to offer anything to the conversation. Why start now?

"Look," Cedric said. "His mama crazy. Okay? She gave that kid my name 'cause she wanted to give him a name other than her own. He wasn't my kid. I got kids. I take care of 'em. Why I work this lame-ass job. Why I'm too tired to talk about this shit. I didn't have nothin' to do with him 'cause he wasn't mine and his mama a crazy-ass bitch tryin' to run a con on me. That's it. That's all I know."

He began pushing his enormous girth up out of the booth, the table and bench creaking from the strain.

"One more question," I said.

"If it quick," he said, standing over us now.

"Do you have any idea who his actual father was?"

"No. Not really. Lots of candidates. Why?"

"Because," I said, "maybe that's who took him."

27

All day I had hoped to hear from Summer.

Since I had no way of getting in touch with her, no idea where she lived or what her number was, my only option was to wait and hope to hear from her.

I had come straight back to my apartment after leaving the Varsity, hoping she'd be here waiting for me.

She was not.

I hung around for a while, trying to do homework and work on the cases while waiting for her to call.

She did not.

After a while I gave up and walked to Scarlett's.

The dark path was spooky and seemed dangerous, and I wondered if Cedric was buried somewhere in these woods.

I heard something a few feet off the path and turned.

Through the bushes I could see a middle-aged white man leaning against a tree, his trousers down around his knees, a young black woman kneeling in front performing fellatio on him.

Were Ronald Nolan and Laney Mitchell doing something similar when little Cedric ran by? Is that the way it really happened? Why was Cedric headed back to the apartments? Had he forgotten something? Did he see something or someone who scared him? Was Nolan telling the truth?

"Make mine a double and keep 'em coming," I said to Margaret as I reached the end of the bar and the stool I thought of as mine.

"I'll join you," she said. "It's been a day."

"Wait," Susan said, walking up behind me. "You've been doin' so well."

"I'm still doin' well," I said, climbing onto the barstool.

"Then don't blow it by jumpin' down this particular rabbit hole. There's nothin' good at the bottom of it. You've got to know that better than me."

I looked at Margaret.

"I could just as easily pour you coffee," she said.

"Et tu?"

She shrugged. "Let's both have coffee tonight."

"I'll talk about the case with you," Susan said. "You can ask me anything you want. And when I get off in a little while I'll even go back to your place and watch a movie with you. Whatta you have?"

"Sixteen Candles—"

"My favorite."

"Oh sexy girlfriend," Margaret said in her best Asian accent.

"Lots of sugar," I said.

They both voiced their approval.

Margaret poured the coffee and shoved cream and sugar toward me as Susan climbed up on the stool beside me.

I had not mentioned Laney Mitchell to either of them again. As far as I knew neither of them had any idea she had run after Cedric the night he disappeared or that doing so might be connected to what happened to her. And they weren't going to hear it from me—not until I found out if there was anything to it. So I decided to pursue another line of questioning with them instead.

"What do y'all know about Creepy Daryl Lee Gibbons?" I said.

"He scared Cedric," Susan said.

"I know Lonnie beat the shit out of him tryin' to find Cedric," Margaret said. "Don't blame him. He was the most likely suspect we had. If there was even a chance he had taken Cedric, that he could still be alive, he had to try to find out . . . no matter what it took."

"What it took was twenty-three stitches and a lot of bandages and pain meds," Susan said.

"I don't think Creepy was the only one Lonnie pummeled tryin' to find out what happened," Margaret added.

"You don't remember him being around here that night, do you?" I said. "Could he be who Cedric was running from?"

"Didn't see him. Don't think he was around. Can't tell you how many times I've wondered and worried if it was someone coming in or going out of here that night that killed him."

A thought occurred to me—one I couldn't believe I hadn't had before—one I had to act on immediately.

"Can I borrow your phone?" I asked.

"Sure," Margaret said, "but be a lot quieter to use the payphone outside. Here's a quarter."

"Thanks."

It was late, but this couldn't wait. I was sure I would wake him —him and his sweet wife, but I couldn't not call him right now.

The phone booth was at the end of the lot down near the sidewalk on Memorial Drive.

I walked directly to it, stone cold sober, light but steady traffic streaking by on Memorial.

Dropping the quarter in, I dialed the number I had long since memorized.

Frank Morgan answered trying not to sound like I had just woken him up.

"I want to meet with him," I said.

"John?"

"Sorry, yeah."

"You okay?"

"I am."

"You sure?"

"I want to meet with him, Frank."

"Who?"

"You know who. Can you set it up?"

"It'll take some doin', and I'll have to be there, but yeah, if you can pass a background check, I can set it up."

"Would you?"

"I will."

"Thank you," I said. "Not sure if I've told you lately, but you've been a grace to me—one of the few since I've been here. And 'less you think that's drink talking, I haven't had one in awhile."

I started to hang up.

"Before you go," he said. "I spoke with the attorney representing Martin Fisher's mother. Told him how good you were to the kid, how bad the mom was, how you took care of him and never even saw her the entire time they were your neighbors. Told him to reconsider."

"What'd he say?"

"That if he didn't take the case someone else would. I told him we'd produce credible witnesses to refute everything the absentee mother said and that supported everything you said— including law enforcement officers."

"What'd he say to that?"

"Says that's the way it works. We produce witnesses and they produce witnesses. Wouldn't back down. I told him the only thing of value you owned was a VCR—and that it wasn't worth that much. And that's when he let it slip."

"What?"

"Since you were living in what was technically a college dorm, he thinks they can get EPI and Chapel Hill Harvester Church to settle for a sizable chunk of change."

"Oh my God," I said.

The blow was devastating—the embarrassment alone was more than I could handle, but to have the church and college on the line for something I was involved in?

"It's the way people like this think."

"I . . . I can't . . . I don't know what to say. It's too much."

"Don't get ahead of yourself. I haven't given up on this. We'll get it straightened out."

After hanging up, I was too upset to go back into Scarlett's right away.

For a while I just paced around the mostly empty parking lot.

"You okay?"

I turned to see Lonnie locking the front door of his video store.

I shrugged.

"What is it?"

I told him. Not in detail but enough to give him a sense of what I was dealing with.

"You know what to do," he said. "Don't need me to tell you. Let go of what you can't change anyway and change what you can. Breathe in peace. Breathe out worry and stress. You can do it. Say the Serenity Prayer with me."

I did.

"Again."

This time he took my hand in his as we prayed the prayer together again.

"God grant me the serenity to accept thing things I cannot change, the courage to change the things I can, and the wisdom to know the difference."

"Thank you," I said.

"You gonna be okay? I can call the guys over and we can have a meeting right now."

"I'm okay. Thanks."

"Not thinking about drinking, are you?"

I shook my head.

"Will you call me if you need anything?" he asked. "Anything at all?"

"I will. And thanks again."

28

Though Susan had offered to come back and watch a movie with me, I went home alone.

I was upset by the news Frank had given me, but was I also hoping Summer would come over at some point.

Perhaps. But that was only part of it. I wanted to work my walls, compile the information I had received so far, to look over things in the light of the new details I now had.

I intended to go straight in and get to work.

What I did instead was collapse onto my bed and fall fast asleep.

Soon I was dreaming.

Summer and I were standing in the woods between Memorial Manor and Scarlett's, talking about Cedric and the other still-missing boys when they began to rise out of the ground around us.

Digging, scratching, scooping, they clawed their way out of their shallow graves, their faces, hair, and clothes caked with dirt and mud, twigs and bugs sticking to their hair, dried blood clinging to their soiled and tattered clothes.

I was saying something when I woke up but had no idea what.

When I went back to sleep, Mickey Davis was demonstrating how easy it would be to snatch a kid. One moment we were riding in his car on I-20 toward downtown, the next he was pulling up to a street corner where a barefooted, shirtless young black boy in only cutoffs was walking home with a can of snuff.

"Get in," Mickey said.

The kid did as he was told.

"See?" he said to me.

"Yeah, see?" the kid said. "Nothing to it."

"What does it mean?" I asked.

"Nothing," they said in unison. "Nothing means nothing."

The next morning, during a discussion in my New Testament class, I was struck by how different I was from the other students, how different my experience was from theirs.

It wasn't just that their paradigm and approach to religion and the Bible was far more concrete and literal than mine, it was that this classroom, the school, the church, the practice of their faith was all consuming. I was sure they must, but it didn't seem like they had a life outside of the school and the church.

Maybe it wasn't that they didn't have one, but the way being part of the school and being a member of the church defined, dictated, and determined their lives entire.

There had been a special service at the church the night before. I was the only one not in attendance.

When I offered a dissenting opinion, a different way of seeing the same dynamic—namely God's work in the world—I was told that I just didn't get it. I would have if I had attended the service, heard the bishop's message, a message they referred to as the rest of the revelation.

"God's only work in the world is through his church," one student said. "It's only those aligned with his purpose, his set-aside and chosen people, who can come into agreement with him to bring about his kingdom on this planet."

It must have been obvious that I didn't agree.

"You disagree?" he said to me.

"I do."

When I didn't elaborate, he said, "Why?"

"Your supposition is rooted in tribalism," I said. "It's the old us-and-them formulation. I don't see it that way. I think grace flows through whoever allows it to. To label a group of people as special, as the only ones used by God isn't just imperceptive, it's dangerous. It's the same kind of thinking that says there's no truth outside of a particular sacred text, or a specific spokesperson for God. It's limiting to the point of absurdity. If there's a God, a creative, loving force that transcends being itself, she can't be limited to a single religion, book, prophet, or—"

"Pronoun, evidently," another student said.

"Exactly. It's like Paul Tillich said—'God isn't a being, but the ground of all being.'"

"Tillich also said 'the first duty of love is to listen,'" Dan Rhodes, the professor, said. "We need to make sure we're all doing that, all listening to one another."

What if Martin's mother's lawsuit causes all this to go away? What if it damages it beyond repair? What if I'm responsible for that?

It felt funny to keep calling her Martin's mother, but I had never met the woman, didn't know anything about her—including her name.

I nodded. "Sorry if I didn't listen like I should."

"I'm not saying you didn't," he said. "Just reminding us all that we need to. Let's listen to John some more. Share with us what you're feeling, what you're hearing, what you'd like to say."

"Thank you. I don't have answers, only questions. I believe the religious experience can be approached as a way of having all the answers or as a way of having none, of only having profound questioning. Back to Tillich—this will be the last time I quote him today, I promise. He said something to the effect that being religious means asking passionately the question of the meaning of our existence and being willing to receive answers, even when they hurt. For me . . . I just feel . . . like maybe our conversations and explorations are sometimes too confining, too reductive for the topics we're discussing. I'm sure it's just me, though. Thanks for letting me share that."

He nodded. "You make a good point. We believe we've been created in the image of God. We must be careful not to return the favor."

"I don't understand," another student said.

"We have to make sure we're not making God over into our image, that we're not making an idol out of ourselves—our own beliefs and preferences and limitations and superstitions."

"Which I know I'm guilty of," I said.

"We all are. First step is to recognize it. Can't deal with it until we do."

That made me think of AA and Lonnie's small, sincere group, and I committed to going later in the day.

Thinking of Lonnie led me to Cedric and gave me an idea. It would require yet another favor from Frank Morgan—something I had to be getting close to exhausting but had yet to.

Thinking of Frank in the context of this class and conversation made me think of how much good he did in the world, how much the force of God worked through him, though he would never see it that way. He was not a member of any church, wasn't religious in any way but the ways that mattered.

"Sorry again for waking you up last night," I said.

"No problem," he said.

I was in Randy Renfroe's office after class, calling Saint Frank.

"Not so sorry to keep me from asking for another favor or two, though."

He laughed.

"It's just a thought I had," I said. "Remember me tellin' you that Ada Baker claims her son Cedric calls her from time to time?"

"Yeah?"

"Could we put a trace on her phone so we can track down whoever it is doing the calling—if there is someone?"

"It's a great idea," he said. "I just don't know logistically if it's something I can get done. What's the other?"

"Trying to find a guy named Daryl Lee Gibbons."

"What's his story?" he asked.

I told him.

"Tell you what," he said. "You commit to going home for the holidays and really make an effort to patch things up with your dad, and I'll see what I can do about both. Deal?"

I thought about it for a moment. Thanksgiving was a few weeks away, and I had pretty much decided to stay up here that weekend, but . . .

"Deal," I said. "Thanks, Frank."

"Oh, I almost forgot. That hit-and-run you asked about."

"Yeah?"

"No evidence that it was anything but," he said. "In fact, cop on the scene theorized that maybe the driver didn't even know he'd done it. There were no skid marks. Looks like he never even braked."

"Which is exactly how it would look if it wasn't an accident."

When I ended my call with Frank, I walked across the hall to the chapel.

Classes completed, students gone for the day, most of the small staff at lunch, the chapel was empty, quiet, and dark, just the way I liked it.

For a while I just walked around the chapel, thinking, praying, wrestling with my mind.

I was missing Summer, agitated that I hadn't heard from her. I was anxious about the cases, the lawsuit, my conflict with my fellow students and my estrangement from my dad, and many other things I needed to let go of.

Which was what I was here for.

"God grant me the serenity to accept the things I cannot change," I said aloud into the silence of the sacred space, "the courage the change the things I can, and the wisdom to know the difference."

After a while of saying it, I began to practice it, and eventually I began to feel somewhat centered again.

29

T hat afternoon I went to the AA meeting in Lonnie's storage room.

I was sitting across from a partially visible poster of Dressed to Kill, the Brian De Palma Hitchcockian erotic thriller with Michael Caine and Angie Dickinson. The top of the poster read "Brian De Palma, the master of the macabre, invites you to a special showing of the latest fashion . . . in murder."

It peeked out from behind a shelf of cat food and cases of Coke—the latter Lonnie both sold and consumed.

As we said the Serenity Prayer and went over the Twelve Steps, I realized I had been using them to deal with Summer's disappearance from my life, the lawsuit, the case. Rather than remaining upset or so out of sorts I wasn't good for much of anything else, I had practiced accepting what I couldn't change and changed what I could.

The process and practice of AA didn't just work for alcohol addiction.

"I want to talk about something today that we can all fall victim to," Lonnie said. "Being dry drunks—something that happens when we stop drinking but don't change our mentalities, don't change our stinking thinking."

The two other men nodded as if they knew what he was talking about.

"Sobriety isn't just stopping the consumption of alcohol," he said. "It's a way of life, of being. It's a complete change in our way of thinking, behaving, living. It can only happen when we deal with our defects of character."

"Drinking is a symptom not the disease," one of the other men added.

"Exactly."

"Drinking is our way of dealing with the disease," the other man said. "The worst way."

Lonnie nodded. "We have to be so careful," he said. "We can so easily fool ourselves. We can replace drink with another obsession and think we're sober when we're not, when we haven't changed a thing."

That's when I realized all this was for my benefit. He had saved this particular discussion for when I was present.

He thought I had traded alcohol for the investigation into his nephew's disappearance and that of the Atlanta Child Murders. And he was right.

I was a dry drunk and needed to hear what he had to say, but that didn't mean I wanted or was going to.

Later that afternoon, Mickey and I located Jamal Jackson's biological father and began following him.

Our plan was to follow all the fathers to see if any of them had their sons as the cops had theorized. Of course, some of the kids would be my age by now, and could be out on their own. If they were between ten and fourteen when they were taken, they would be between fifteen and nineteen now.

We started with Jamal's father because we had to start somewhere and he was the first we found.

The first afternoon, we followed him together. From then on we alternated, changing out when we could, covering as much of the day as we could while still meeting our other obligations. Mickey had more flexible time than I did and took more shifts.

Gerry Jackson, Jamal's father, worked at night as a cook at the Waffle House on Panola Road. When he was at work, we mostly watched his house. When he wasn't, we mostly watched him, searching for any sign of Jamal.

After three days, two of which were on a weekend, we had found no sign of Jamal.

On the fourth day, we showed up at Gerry's place of work, took a booth and ordered breakfast like any other customers.

It was the middle of the night, and the place was mostly empty. When Gerry finished his final order and had a break, we asked if we could talk to him.

"Somethin' wrong with your food?" he asked.

"No, it's perfect," I said. "Very good. Please, sit down with us for just a minute."

He slowly, warily sat down, studying us as he did. "What's this about?"

"Jamal," I said.

"Y'all have him?" he said, sitting up, ready to fight.

"Nothing like that," I said. "We're looking for him."

"Whatcha mean?"

"We're part of a group looking for missing children," I said. "He's a reporter. I'm a student. We're all volunteers trying to do something the police didn't or couldn't."

"Man, don't get me started on the fuckin' cops," he said. "Didn't do shit but blame me. Convinced my ex I took Jamal from her. She still think I did. She stalk me. Sue me. Say all kind of shit about me, but I didn't take my boy. Could have if I wanted to. After all, he's my son, just as much as hers. But I didn't."

"Any idea who might have?" I asked.

As usual, Mickey wasn't saying much, just taking notes and

taking it all in. He had told me this was his preferred way to work. By letting me ask the questions, he could focus on the person we were talking to and his writing.

He shook his head. "Not really. Well, is this off the record?"

"Yes, sir," Mickey said.

"Everybody else got theories," he said. "I'll give you mine. Either Wayne Williams got him and he was either never found or misidentified . . . or . . . my crazy-ass ex did something to him and is tryin' to cover it up. She keep attacking me so nobody suspect her."

They were interesting theories. He was a smart guy—and articulate. Why was he working as a short-order cook in the middle of the night?

"Tell you one thing," he said. "Whoever was behind it—her or someone else—did a damn good job of making the cops think it was me."

"How so?"

"Planted shit of his—clothes, toys and shit—in my car, my house. Convinced the cops he had been there, that I had him or had had him. Hell, if they hadn't been stretched so thin with the murders and if Vera had been a better mother, they wouldn't've left me alone."

The door opened and a trucker with an orange vest and brown baseball cap came in.

"I've got to get back to work," he said. "I appreciate y'all looking for my boy. Y'all find him, you let me know. Food's on the house tonight. Take care now."

As he moved away, back behind the counter, back to his cooking station, I shook my head and looked at Mickey.

"What?" he said, meeting my eyes momentarily. "Your eyes are bulging out of your head. What is it?"

"What if the killer planted evidence on the dads to make the authorities think they had them to get them to stop looking?"

"Oh wow," he said. "That would be . . . wicked as fuck."

"We'll have to check with the others to confirm, and we still need to find the mothers, but if that's what it is . . ."

"It's ingenious," he said. "And it helped him get away with murder."

30

O ver the next few days, we tracked down as many of the fathers as we could—four of the six in all.

Interestingly, finding the mothers was proving far more difficult, but the fathers we found all told us the same story.

They didn't kidnap their sons and at some point someone placed something of their sons'—articles of clothing or other personal belongings—in their homes and vehicles.

Of the four dads we spoke with—Cedric's, Jamal's, Duke's, and Quentin's—all but Cedric's had the same exact experience.

"You know what this means?" Mickey said.

We were on 285 in heavy traffic, headed back toward Memorial Drive.

"What's that?"

"We're dealing with a serial killer. Wayne Williams or someone else—but that's what this is. Not fathers or other family members. Not runaways or kidnappings."

I didn't say anything, just thought about it.

"I've studied this type of killer a lot while working on my book," he said. "There's no motive—least none that we can ever understand. There are patterns. There are certain psychological signatures they leave, but . . . it's all fantasy driven for them. They're acting out some sick, horrific fantasy that involves sex and death."

I nodded.

"Scariest thing is how normal they can seem," he added. "I could be the killer, and you'd never know it."

"You don't seem that normal," I said.

He laughed.

I thought about the mask of humanity and sanity our killer might be wearing, and wondered what it might look like. Just how normal did he appear to be? How convincing was his disguise? How deeply buried was his surreal secret? Had we encountered him? Was he dead or in prison or in a psych ward somewhere? Was that why the murders stopped? Or had he just relocated? Were other people somewhere else unknowingly glancing at that mask, gazing day in and day out into an abyss that was gazing back, without even realizing that's what was happening?

"But seriously . . . we're not dealing with a human being here."

He was right, and I knew the things he was saying were true in themselves, but I questioned whether he was sensationalizing them for the sake of the story he was already crafting in his head.

"They have these extreme fantasies of sexual violence—starting in childhood or adolescence. Their isolation, compulsive behaviors, daydreaming, and increased acting out on animals and shit fuel their fantasies and eventually it all leads to murder —but not just one. A series. That's what we're dealing with here."

I nodded.

He waited a moment, then said, "You think it's the same killer?"

"Same killer as—"

"The Atlanta Child Murderer," he said. "The same one."

I shook my head. "If for no other reason than that the other killer dumped the bodies of his victims so they could be found

Blood Cries

relatively quickly and easily. In this case there are no bodies at all."

We had yet to track down Jaquez's and Vaughn's dads, and we were still having difficulty finding the moms, but we felt like we had enough to take to the police.

Lonnie let us use his storage/meeting room.

Frank Morgan, Bobby Battle, and Remy Boss, the original investigator of most of the cases, attended, and listened attentively as Mickey and I made our case.

We told them about the geographical connections between the victims, the similarity in the disappearances, and the way the killer had planted clothes and toys belonging to the victims in the dads' homes and vehicles.

When we finished, no one said anything at first.

I had expected hostility from Bobby Battle, but so far he had seemed quite sedate.

Eventually, Remy looked at Bobby and said, "Whatta you think?"

Bobby shrugged. "It was your case. You'd know better than any of us if there's even a possibility of it being true, but . . . I don't know . . . seems a little . . ."

Remy looked back at us. "I appreciate all the work you guys have done on this," he said. "And I'm not sayin' there's not something to it, but . . . the two biggest questions are the breakdowns in your pattern. Why wasn't anything planted on Cedric Porter's dad and why is Vaughn Smith so far outside of your geographical area?"

"I have no idea," I said. "And I know we've yet to speak to Vaughn's or Jaquez's dad, but . . . We could be wrong about all this, but we thought it was enough to bring to you."

"It was," Remy said. "It is. You did the right thing. We'll look into it and see if we can find the other dads, make the other connections, answer the open questions."

"You still have the problem of no bodies," Battle said. "All this time and none of them have turned up. Argues against your serial killer theory. Williams dumped his in the woods and rivers and we found them pretty quick. If he did these, why haven't we found them? If someone else did, same question. Where are the bodies?"

"Again, I have no idea," I said. "I have far more questions than anything else—just felt like they were questions worth asking, ones y'all might want to try to answer."

"And we will," Remy said. "Thanks."

And that was that.

I didn't know exactly what I was expecting, but I felt an enormous letdown as we walked out of Lonnie's meeting room and into his video store.

31

The four other men scattered quickly, each with pressing matters requiring their attention, and I was left standing there in the store that would soon be closed, looking around, but not seeing anything before me.

It wasn't until I realized Shaft and Foxy Brown, Lonnie's Bombay cats, were staring down at me from the top of the shelf I was standing in front of that I came back to the present time and place.

"You okay?" Lonnie asked.

I nodded. "Thanks for letting us use your room."

"No problem. Happy to help. How'd it go?"

I told him.

"For what it's worth, I think you're right," he said.

"Thanks."

"I'm not just sayin' that," he said. "It makes a certain sense like nothin' else ever has. If the cops drop the ball on this again . . . I'll hire someone . . . private. Not going to my grave without knowing what happened to Cedric. I can't."

I nodded. "How are you doing?"

He shrugged. "Feeling weak . . . like . . . I . . . I've been tempted to start drinkin' again."

"I'm sorry to hear that. Anything I can do to help?"

He shook his head. "Got a good sponsor. He's helpin'. I'll call him before I . . . do anything too stupid."

"Do."

"I will," he said. "Will you do something for me?"

"What's that?"

"Don't stop looking for Cedric," he said. "Don't leave it up to them."

I didn't say anything, just thought about it.

"Think about how much time they've had," he said. "And they wouldn't have anything new now if it weren't for you."

I nodded. He was right.

"Thing is, I've got nothin' left," he said. "I'll be losing my store soon. Have no idea what I'm gonna do next. But I'll spend every last cent of my savings to find Cedric. And truth is . . . I'd like to get to whoever took him before the police do—not that they ever will."

I thought about what he had done to Daryl Lee Gibbons and Cedric Porter, Sr., and knew exactly what he would do to the man who had taken his surrogate son.

When I stepped out of Lonnie's shop, I saw Frank Morgan in his car out in the parking lot not far from the phone booth I had used to call him last week.

He motioned me over.

When I reached his car, I could see that he was on his radio so I waited, watching the traffic on Memorial, the activity on the sidewalks and shops.

The wind was more biting today, and I shoved my hands in my pants pockets.

When Frank finished, he climbed out of the car and closed the door.

"How well do you know Mickey?" he asked.

"Not well at all. Why?"

"His name rang a bell, and when you said he was a reporter I remembered something about a scandal he was involved in. I called a newsman friend of mine to make sure. He used to write under the name Michael Davis. Switched to Mickey after he got fired from the Journal. You need to be careful with him."

"Okay," I said. "I have been, but why?"

"He was fired for manufacturing a story, making up quotes from sources, in some cases making up the sources themselves. If he'll do that for a newspaper story, imagine what he'll do for his book."

I nodded.

"Did anything we went over in there come only from him?" he asked.

I thought about it.

"No," I said. "Best I can recall, the only thing that has come from him during the entire course of the investigation and our group meeting is that Daryl Lee Gibbons has a record."

"Which is true. He does. Think I'm pretty close to finding him, by the way. We'll see what he's been up to and what he has to say about what happened back then."

"Great. Thanks."

"Just be careful, John. I don't trust this Michael Mickey Davis character. I don't think you should either. Think he's got a very different motive than you do, has an agenda, and it's selfish and sensational and can only hurt the investigation."

32

W hen I pulled back the curtains and looked out, I saw Summer Grantham standing there, her blond hair up in a ponytail, her eyes looking far sadder than I had seen before.

I had been alone in my room studying the cases, hoping she might come by.

I nodded toward my front door, and met her at it to let her in.

"Sorry," she said.

"For what?"

"Just showing up like this. Not calling or coming by before now. You name it, I'm sorry for it."

"Come in. Are you okay?"

We embraced for a few moments, then I led her down the hallway to my room and closed the door behind us.

"What's going on?" I asked. "Where have you been? Why did you disappear? What's wrong?"

She frowned and her eyes glistened. "Can we not talk about it right now?"

"I'd really like to," I said, "but . . . if you can't . . ."

"In a little while maybe," she said. "Okay?"

"Okay."

"How have you been?" she asked.

"Besides worried about you and wondering what the hell happened to you? Pretty fair. You?"

"Not so good. I'm sorry again."

"Could I at least get your number and address so I can contact you? You're not listed."

She shook her head. "It's under my husband's name."

"Your what?"

"I know. I'm sorry. I should've—"

"Let me walk you to the door," I said.

"Wait. Sorry. I meant ex-husband. We're not married anymore. I just never changed it over to my name."

"So you'll give me the number?" I said. "We can go there right now? We can go see your ex and he'll tell me he's in fact your ex?"

She nodded, then gave me her phone number and address though I had nothing to write them down on at the moment.

"All but the visit him part," she said. "He's in prison."

"I'm not sure I believe you, Summer," I said. "I'm not sure I believe anything you're saying—or have said to me."

She nodded, tears beginning to stream now.

"I don't blame you," she said, "but it is the truth. Everything I've ever told you is. The only thing I've done is not tell you one thing—a very big thing, but that's it."

"What's the big thing?"

"I suffer from depression," she said. "It goes along with the gift. My grandmother who also had the gift battled with the same dark demon. That's where I've been. I haven't gotten out of bed in nearly a week."

I believed her.

To the best of my ability to discern deception, I sincerely believed she was telling me the truth.

Everything in me wanted to take care of her, to hug and reassure her, to help her fight the darkness she was dealing with.

"I believe you," I said.

"You do?"

"I do. And I want to help you."

"You do?"

"I do," I said. "But I can't."

"What?"

"Are you on medication?" I asked.

She nodded.

"Are you taking it?"

She nodded again.

"Are you under a doctor's or psychiatrist's care?"

She nodded again.

"Do you have a family member or friend who can help you?"

She nodded. "My daughter. She's . . . very good at helping me deal."

"Does she know how you're doing right now?"

She nodded again. "I'm actually much better now," she said. "She knew how I was earlier in the week. She checked on me every day."

"Good," I said. "Then . . . since you have all that, I'll walk you to the door. I'm sorry. I wish I could help you—I mean, I don't even know if you wanted me to help—but I just can't. I want to. You can't imagine how much everything in me wants to. But I just did that with another woman—it's sort of my thing, I guess—and it didn't go well at all. So . . . I'm truly trying to accept the things I cannot change and change the things I can."

"That's good," she said. "That's very good."

We walked back down the hallway in silence.

When we reached the front door, we stopped.

"I didn't come here tonight looking for you to save me, John," she said. "At least the best part of me didn't. I just wanted to explain and to . . . I wanted to be close again, maybe have some of the healing that flowed through me to you, flow back through you to me, but . . . we knew what this was, what the other night was. I'm more than twice your age. My daughter is a good bit older than you. But here's the thing . . . what it was was sacred. What it was was real. What we shared, this connection, this . . . Don't lose that, don't let your aversion to drama and messiness, which I understand and appreciate, cause you to close down again and miss out on what life has for you."

I nodded.

She kissed me quickly, then turned to leave.

"Wait," I said.

She stopped.

When she turned I saw hope and desire in her eyes, and regretted calling out to her.

"Sorry," I said. "I wasn't trying to . . . I just want to walk you to your car."

I could be in bed with Summer right now.

Had I made the wrong decision? Was I being too cautious, too rigid, too—

I decided to occupy my mind with something else.

Thinking back to my conversation with Mickey earlier in the day, I turned my attention to the type of motiveless murderer we might be pursuing.

A compulsive or serial or ritual killer—I wasn't completely sure I understood the difference—is a killer who kills two or more people for psychological gratification. The murders must take place over more than a month and include a cooling off period between them. Most often the murders involve a sexual component and are carried out in a similar manner on victims who have certain commonalities—such as age, race, body type, or sex.

Serial or compulsive killers are often psychopaths or display the psychopathic traits such as sensation seeking, lacking guilt or remorse, predatory actions, impulsivity, and the need to control. In contrast with people with other major mental disorders such as schizophrenia, psychopaths can seem normal and can often be quite charming.

These type killers are often the victims of childhood abuse—emotional, physical, or sexual—often by a family member. Because of this, serial killers typically programed as children to become murderers by progressively intensifying a dark loop of dangerous, violent fantasies—elaborate mental thoughts with great preoccupation anchored in the daydreaming process. These fantasies serve to relieve anxiety, stress, tension, and fear—transforming the normal fantasies of childhood into a dangerous, compulsive form of escapism to deal with their isolation, pain, fear, abuse, neglect, and trauma.

When these dark, violent fantasies are combined with compulsive masturbation, a sexual component is added to the cognitive or mental process.

Anger, isolation, and resentment fuel fantasies, which leads to further isolation, which leads to an even greater reliance on fantasy for pleasure and relief from anxiety.

By the time a serial killer claims his first victim, he has fantasized, planned, plotted, obsessed over every minute detail of it for years. At a certain point, fantasy is no longer enough, and the killer reaches a state where he actually wants to live out his dark, violent daydreams. At this stage his victim is reduced to a mere player in the serial killer's mind movie of sex and murder.

After committing his first murder, the novice killer will obsess over his need to kill again. Having discovered the key to acting out his secret desires, some killers continue to murder in order to experience the fantasy again and again, while others grow bored and move to escalate their actions instead.

All this—all this horrific death and devastation born out of the daydreams of a weak, frightened, terrorized little child.

Could it be that a victimized child, now housed in the body of an adult, was making victims of other children?

33

I saw Summer the next day.

We were both back at Safe Haven for our next group meeting.

She seemed sad, but not overly so.

I came in a few minutes late and sat in the only seat left in the small circle, which put me directly across from her.

I nodded and gave her a small smile.

She returned it.

Over her shoulder, as if it were a month or so ago, as if he were still there, I caught a glimpse of Martin Fisher coloring at the small table—just like he had been the last night we were here together.

I blinked and he was gone, but I could still feel him, still sense his presence in the room that had held so many children over the years.

"I don't think we're doing enough for Wayne Williams," Annie Bowers, the thin, black woman from the Free Wayne Williams initiative said. "I know that everything we do is important, but . . . it seems to me that . . . well, there's only so much we can do for victims who are already deceased. But Wayne is still alive. What we do for him . . . can make a real difference."

Miss Ida cleared her throat. "Our group has no agenda," she said. "Not that one or any other. It can't. We're not here to free Wayne Williams. We're here to share information and ideas and do a little investigating where we can. If that leads to Wayne Williams being released, so be it. If it proves his guilt beyond a reasonable doubt, so be it. What we do here—not forgetting him, caring about him and his case, seeking some kind of imperfect justice, which is the only kind we get in this world—is a worthy endeavor, a noble cause. That helps me and it helps us. Sure, it won't bring him back, but does make sure he's not forgotten."

It was the most eloquent I had ever heard Miss Ida be.

"I understand what you're saying, I do," Annie said. "I'm just saying . . . we could save an innocent man."

"Lot of us don't think he is innocent," Melvin Pryor said. "Others aren't sure. We're here for the victims."

"That's what I'm saying," she said. "He is a victim of this terrible tragedy, a living victim, spending every day of his life confined for something he didn't do."

"If that's true," Preston Mailer, the ex-cop said, "then maybe the work we do will help free him. Maybe it will."

"Just be clear on why we're here," Ida said. "We don't mind that you have an agenda, but our group does not and cannot."

Annie nodded. "I understand. I don't agree, but I understand."

"John? Mickey?" Ida said. "Want to share with us what you've been doing?"

"Sure," I said. "We've talked with Cedric's father. Jamal's too. We've looked into whether the missing kids on our new list are just with their dads, like the police believe, or if something else is going on. We think something else is going on."

"Why?" Mailer asked.

I told them, with Mickey tossing in a detail or two along the way.

"So if the dads don't have them . . ." Rose Lee said.

"If they're still alive it would go a long way toward proving Wayne's innocence," Annie Bowers said.

No one responded to that.

"I had an idea," I said. "Wondered if you thought Ada Baker would go for it."

"What's that?" Ida asked.

"Tapping her phone and tracing the next call she gets from Cedric or whoever's calling her."

Ida shook her head.

"That was mentioned initially, but she said she feared for Cedric's safety, that he had to have a good reason for running and hiding and she didn't want him found until he wanted to be."

I thought about that.

"Calling her like that is such torture," Summer said. "Wonder who's doing it and why?"

They were the most words she had spoken in any of the groups.

"You don't think it's Cedric?" I asked.

She shrugged. "It's torture either way."

"We should ask her again," Mickey said. "If we can trace the call . . . we can find out what the hell is goin' on."

"I'll talk to her again," Ida said. "But don't expect much. Don't think she's likely to change her mind."

"How are you?" I asked.

Summer and I were standing beneath the covered walkway, lingering to speak to one another as the others were leaving.

"Better," she said.

"Good."

"Sorry again," she said. "For my baggage. Can't be helped. Would if it could. That Serenity Prayer thing you mentioned, I practice it too. I'm changing everything I can, everything I'm capable of."

I nodded. "Don't doubt that for a second."

Be kind. I thought of the quote most often attributed to Plato. Everyone you meet is fighting a hard battle.

"Sorry again for the hard line of the boundaries I have to set right now," I said. "I wouldn't if they weren't necessary."

"I know. Believe me, I get it."

"Hey," Miss Ida called to us. "You two feel like taking a ride?"

She was walking back toward us from the parking lot.

We began moving toward her.

"I'm goin' to talk to Ada now," she said. "Y'all want to go?"

I nodded and looked at Summer.

She shrugged. "Is it okay?"

"Sure, honey," Ida said, "I wouldn't've—oh. You meant with . . ."

"Of course," I said.

"No way," Ada said. "No way I do that to my boy. Done enough to him already."

"But it would help us find him," Ida said.

"He don't want to be found," she said. "I got to honor that. He'a come home when he ready."

"What if he can't?" I said. "What if he's being held hostage? What if they let him call as a way of controlling him, but he can't tell you what he really wants to?"

She thought about that as if it hadn't occurred to her before.

After a while, she slowly began shaking her head. "Just can't. Don't trust the po-lice to . . . Too much can go wrong."

A thought occurred to me.

"What if we hired a private firm to do it?" I said. "What if they only told you and one other person you trust? Miss Ida. Lonnie. It'd be up to you. You could then do with the information what you wanted."

"Hmm. Let me think about that one," she said.

"It's a real chance of finding him, Ada," Ida said. "It was me, I'd take it."

"What if it the wrong thing, Miss Ida? What if it harm him somehow? I'd rather him be safe without me than . . . anything happen to him 'cause I tryin' to get him back."

"I didn't sense any deception in anything she said," Summer said.

She, Ida, and I were standing out in the parking lot in front of Ada's building.

The night was cold and windy, and we wouldn't be standing here long.

"Not like I did the last time I was here," she added.

"Whatcha mean, girl?" Ida said.

"She wasn't being totally truthful about where she was between the time Cedric left the apartment and when she arrived at Scarlett's."

"Oh, yeah, that," Ida said. "Always assumed she was turning a trick or scoring some dope—probably both, the one for the other. Wouldn't mean she had anything to do with what happened to Cedric."

"Except because of neglect," Summer said.

"You probably right," Ida said, "but take it from a mother who was overprotective of her boy, you only have to turn your back for a second and . . ."

LaMarcus playing in his backyard, just a few feet away from the watchful eyes of his mother and sister. There one minute, gone the next, his body found in a large culvert in a drainage ditch later that night. He had looked like he was sleeping. That sleep of death and what dreams may come that followed it had flung his mother into a wakeful nightmare of the cruelest kind.

When I walked into the apartment, my phone was ringing.

It was Frank Morgan.

"Approval came through, he said. "Everything's set. You see him tomorrow."

Nothing else need be said. I knew who the he was. I would spend the rest of the sleepless night thinking about my second encounter with the man who obsessed my waking hours, the monster who had haunted my dreams.

34

"What're you hoping to get out of this?" Frank asked.

I shrugged. "I don't know."

What I did know was that I wasn't ready, wasn't prepared, and I didn't know how to be.

We were sitting in a hallway outside the conference room in the Admin building, waiting on Wayne Williams to arrive.

"Is there something in particular you want to ask him?" he said.

I shook my head. "Just want to look into his eyes."

"Well, now's your chance," he said. "Here he comes."

Two correctional officers escorted Wayne Williams into the building. He was neither cuffed nor shackled, and he looked to be out on a casual stroll.

We stood.

When he reached us, he extended his hand and we each shook it and spoke to him.

"Thank you for agreeing to do this, Mr. Williams," Frank said. "The GBI really appreciates it."

"No problem," he said. "Happy to help if I can."

"Right in here," one of the COs said, motioning us toward the Admin conference room.

"I'll be here if you need me," Frank said. "Just yell."

He then sat back down on the sofa, and Williams and I walked into the conference room.

I don't know exactly what I was expecting, but it wasn't this— not something as innocuous as a conference room. I had pictured either a small, empty room with two metal chairs and a metal table, Williams's cuffs and shackles chained to a hook in the concrete floor. Or a visiting booth with a plexiglass partition, each of us communicating through a telephone receiver.

A conversation in a conference room between two guys— neither of whom were cuffed or armed—was just so . . . pedestrian.

The COs remained outside with Frank. The door closed, and I was alone with Wayne Williams.

I wanted to look into his eyes, and I did. I locked onto them and didn't avert my gaze—even when I wanted to.

The eyes I looked into were hooded and blinked a lot behind large glasses.

He was smaller than I remembered, had lost some of the soft roundness in his face and pudginess around his midsection. He no longer had an afro, and his close-cropped hair appeared to be beginning to recede a bit.

Could this really be the monster who had left such a wide wake of devastation behind him, haunted my childhood, changed the course of my life?

"Do you remember me?" I asked.

He canted his head slightly and narrowed his eyes. Lifting his hand, partially pointing a finger at me as if it was coming to him. "I might . . ." he said. "You look familiar. Help me out."

"I was twelve. You were twenty-two. We met in the arcade at the Omni. You were passin' out flyers."

"Oh, yeah," he said. "I do remember. I knew you looked familiar."

He didn't recognize or remember me. He was a compulsive and accomplished liar. I knew that already.

I was now eighteen and he was twenty-eight, the six years between our first encounter and this one compressing the age difference separating us down to a point of nearly nonexistence. We were both adults now.

"Agent Morgan mentioned you're a theology student," he said.

I nodded.

"And you also have an interest in criminal investigation?"

"I do."

"You ever thought of working in a place like this?" he said. "Prison chaplain can do a lot of good."

I shook my head. "That's interesting. No, I never have."

"You should consider it," he said. "You could minister to the spiritual needs of the inmate population and reexamine the cases of those who claim to be innocent."

"You still maintain your innocence, don't you?" I said.

"I don't just maintain my innocence. I am innocent. Nobody will tell you they saw Wayne Williams kill another person, hit another person, stab another person, shoot another person, choke another person, or hurt another person in any way."

I knew that to be true. Not a single eyewitness ever came forward to say they had seen him hurt or kill anyone. There were witnesses who placed him with some of the victims, but that was it.

"Why do you think you were convicted?" I asked.

"Honestly? Let me tell you. The city of Atlanta was ready to explode. They had to have a scapegoat and he had to be black. That was me. Now look, yes, I was my own worst enemy—goin' off on the stand like that. I did a lot of stupid stuff. I was just a buzz-headed kid, but that doesn't make me a killer, does it?"

I shook my head. "No, it doesn't."

We were quiet a moment.

I tried to get a sense of the man sitting across from me. He was really difficult to read. But there was something about him, more an absence of something than a presence. I was having a hard time determining exactly what it was.

"If it wasn't you, do you have any ideas on who the murderer was?" I asked.

"Well, look, yes, I have some theories, but that's all they are. I don't have any knowledge of anything. I wasn't a witness to anything. I will say this—it wasn't just one killer. Some may've been the Klan, some parents or relatives, some some kind of sex ring—older men messin' around with some drop shot kids gettin' paid for sex acts."

"You know a lot about your case," I said. "I'm sure you've studied a lot of others like it, probably know far more than most about these kinds of things."

"Unfortunately, I guess I do."

"If there were a series of similar murders—young boys like so many of the victims in the missing and murdered children case— but no bodies were ever found, why do you think that would be?"

"How many we talking?"

"Not sure. Say six or more."

"Well, now, no body no murder," he said. "No evidence. Missing kids cases don't get much attention, but a murdered kid . . ."

I nodded. "But how could the killer keep the bodies from being discovered?"

"Think about the clown killer from Chicago," he said. "Gacy. Hid the bodies right in his house. Serves another purpose too. Keeps them close. Don't have to give them up when you're . . ."

I thought about it.

"Or he could just be buryin' them in a place no one has looked yet," he said. "Woods. Foundation at a construction site.

Graveyard. Crematorium. What if there's nothing left of them because he used acid or something like that?"

"Can you explain why you failed a polygraph?" I said.

Actually, he had failed three.

"Well, now, yes, I think . . . I believe I can. Some people . . . those tests aren't a certain science, not one hundred percent accurate. Some people can pass 'em and others fail 'em no matter what. Just one of those things."

Just one of those things.

"What about Cheryl Johnson?" I asked.

She was the woman he claimed he was supposed to meet the morning after his arrest. Said he was out looking for her address the night he was stopped on the bridge. All this time and she had never come forward. One of the biggest, most high profile cases in history and she didn't hear about it, didn't know everyone was looking for her? None of her friends or family members stepped forward and even asked if it could be her?

He gave me a half frown with a small smile peeking out behind it. "I have no answer for that. She probably just didn't want to get involved. Maybe it was a prank from the beginning. Maybe somebody was trying to set me up—and it worked."

There were so many things I wanted to ask him and we were running out of time.

What do I ask? What can I say to get him to reveal something new, something that would help with the case? Think. Come on. You don't have long.

"There were reports that you and your dad burned all kinds of items—documents, pictures, clothing, things like that—after you became a suspect. What did you burn and why?"

"It was just trash," he said. "Nothing more. Nothing sinister. I can see how it would look, but at the time . . . I just didn't think about it."

You're lying.

"How do you explain all the trace evidence connecting you to so many of the victims?" I asked.

He shrugged. "Look, I was set up. I don't know by who or what all they did, but they did enough to make it happen, right? Fake a phone call from somebody claiming to be Cheryl Johnson. Manufacture evidence. Hide evidence of other suspects. Hide evidence that contradicts the story they're weaving. I don't know. I just know Wayne Williams is innocent and no eyewitness says otherwise."

35

"Well?" Frank asked.

He had waited until we were back in his car, a GBI-issued boxy navy-blue Ford LTD, to say anything.

It was raining when we walked out of Georgia State Prison near Reidsville, a cold, hard rain that turned the late afternoon gunmetal gray and pelted us as we ran toward the vehicle.

The same hard rain was now pelting the car as we drove up I-16 toward Macon.

I shrugged.

"Not ready to talk about it?" he said.

"I'm not sure what I think," I said. "Or feel. It was very interesting—and I got to do what I wanted to do. I looked into his eyes."

"Did you see his soul?"

"I didn't."

"That's because he doesn't have one," he said.

Though on high, the wipers couldn't keep up with the water sluicing down the windshield, but traffic was light and Frank drove like he was ready to be home.

"I just feel like I . . . like it was a missed opportunity," I said.

He let out a little burst of laughter.

"'Cause you didn't get him to confess?" he said.

I smiled. "Yeah maybe. I don't know. I just . . ."

"It's all about expectation," he said. "You went in there thinkin' you were actually goin' to get him to confess or prove to you his innocence."

"I'm not so sure it was like that, but I did want to gain something, learn something new, something to justify the time and effort you put into making it happen."

"You probably got far more out of it than you know," he said. "I wouldn't be surprised if things he said didn't keep coming to you for a while. I get you––"

His pager vibrated at the same time dispatch called for him on his radio.

He radioed in and was informed that a last known address had been located for Daryl Lee Gibbons. It was on Old Conyers Road near Stockbridge. Daryl Lee and his mother were believed to be renting a basement apartment from an elderly couple.

"I'll try to swing by and pay a visit to ol' Daryl Lee tomorrow," he said.

"Or," I said, "we could swing by tonight. We'll be coming in on 75. It'd only be ten minutes or so out of our way."

"Do you know what you see when you look up the word relentless in the dictionary?" he said.

"A picture of me?"

"No, the definition of relentless. And do you know what it says after that?"

"No, what?"

"See also John Jordan."

"Is that a no?" I asked.

"No, it's not a no."

The house was a split-level ranch–style built on a hill—one story showing in the front, two in the back. It was made of beige brick and had a swimming pool behind it.

Though it was around eight in the evening when we arrived, the house was completely dark and there were no signs anyone was home.

The sweep of Frank's headlights as we pulled in to the circular drive showed a once nice home now in disrepair, a yard in need of maintenance, and a car with two flat tires that looked abandoned.

"Doesn't look like anyone's home," Frank said.

"Or that anyone lives here any longer," I said.

"It was just a last known," he said. "They could've moved on long ago. But we're here, so let's knock on the door."

We did.

Then we banged.

Eventually we heard movement inside.

And a while after that, an obese middle-aged woman with very bad teeth appeared in the darkness through the partially opened door.

Frank flashed his badge.

"Georgia Bureau of Investigation," he said. "You are?"

"Mrs. Tilda Gibbons."

"We need to speak to your son, Mrs. Gibbons."

"He ain't here."

"Then we'll speak to you," he said. "Turn on some lights and let us in."

"Lights been shut off," she said. "Come back tomorrow."

Frank pulled out a small flashlight that looked like a thick writing pen and shone it in the woman's face.

"Where are Mr. and Mrs. Ward?"

"Who?"

"The owners of this home?"

"Oh, them. They moved to Florida."

While she was still speaking, he pushed on the door and stepped inside.

I followed.

She stumbled backward, gasping and grunting as she did.

In the small spill of Frank's tiny light, I could see a once elegant, if outdated home, filled with filth and crammed with clutter.

We hadn't made it very far into the foyer when the odor hit us —a complex, layered reek of rotting food, competing fruity air-freshener flavors, dust and decay, body odor, and the unmistakable sickly sweet stench of death.

Frank drew his weapon.

36

"Why does it smell like someone died in here?" Frank asked.

"Our old cat," she said. "Crawled up in some small space and died. We can't find it. That's all. Come back tomorrow when there's light. Daryl Lee be home by then."

"Come in here and have a seat," he said, motioning her toward the den with his light.

We followed her through the foyer and stepped down into a shag-carpeted den with a fireplace, an enormous old dark wooden cabinet console television, and custom bookshelves that filled an entire wall.

"Sit," Frank said.

"I ain't no dog," Tilda Gibbons said, but plopped down onto the green vinyl sofa along the wall across from the fireplace, nearly eclipsing it as she did.

"John, I need you to go to the car and radio for backup," he said. "Explain the situation as best you can. Have them call Clayton County Sheriffs in. Oh, and tell them we need lights."

He shone his light at me and tossed me the keys, but I was unable to see them because of the light and they bounced off the side of my arm and fell to the floor. He shone the light on the floor until he found them, then I grabbed them and rushed out to make the transmission.

I was gone for maybe five minutes.

When I got back in, Frank was standing in the doorway between the den and kitchen, alternating between keeping an eye on Tilda Gibbons and sweeping the kitchen with his light.

"They're on the way," I said. "Should only be a few minutes."

"I should've had you grab my flashlight out of the trunk," he said.

"Want me to go—"

From somewhere in the house, we heard a child yell and begin to cry.

"Where's that coming from?" Frank asked.

I strained to hear.

Suddenly Tilda Gibbons erupted from the couch and screamed, "Daryl Lee, cops are here!"

She then began moving toward the hallway on the opposite end of the room from where we stood, which led to what looked to be about four closed doors.

We both began to run after her, but Frank held out his arm and said, "Stay behind me."

I did.

At the end of the hallway was a large window.

Tilda Gibbons never slowed.

Running as fast as her size would allow, she dove through the window, splintering the wood frame and shattering the panes of glass.

When we reached it and looked down, the wind blowing the bullet-like raindrops through the open hole in the house, we could see that she had fallen two stories down to a second driveway leading to a two-car garage below.

The fall had not killed her.

She lay there moaning, splayed out, unable to move, the halo of blood around her head turning pink in the thumping rain.

"Listen," Frank said. "We've got to find that kid."

We followed the sounds back down the hallway.

"Let's just try all the doors," he said.

I grabbed the knob of the door closest to me, turned it, and pushed. It was unlocked and gave a little, but something on the floor kept it from opening all the way. I shoved harder, and it gave a little more. Using my foot at the bottom, I pushed again.

Death was on the other side of the door. I could smell it.

"This one's clear," Frank said.

"Need your light," I said. "Got a bad one."

I had the door open enough to squeeze inside, and could see that a towel at the bottom was what had been impeding my progress. It was obviously there to block the smell from coming out beneath the door.

Easing in, I stood there a moment and waited for Frank to arrive with the light. He handed it to me and I scanned the room.

Beneath a ceiling fan, each blade of which was covered with hanging car deodorizers, an elderly couple, Mr. and Mrs. Ward was my guess, were dead in their bed, their bodies in an advanced state of decay.

Coughing and gagging and suppressing the vomit at the back of my throat, I shoved my way back through the door and closed it behind me.

When I was sure I wasn't going to throw up, I told Frank what I had seen.

"You okay?" he asked. "Two more doors."

"Yeah," I said, and reached for the next door.

It was locked.

Taking a couple of steps back toward the center of the hallway, I lowered my shoulder and jumped into the door.

It gave and I tumbled inside. The faint light from a distant streetlamp streamed in through the small window and illuminated the tiny room.

It was a bathroom.

There in a sunken tub, a small, naked, thin white boy of about five lay on a blanket soiled with his own urine, feces, and blood.

37

He was no longer crying, but he was alive.

"Frank," I yelled.

Reaching down, I lifted the child. I had the urge to cover his nakedness with the blanket, but it was far too foul.

"It's okay," I whispered. "I've got you. You're safe."

Frank appeared at the door.

"Oh dear God," he said.

I blinked back tears as a memory mosaic of Martin Fisher formed in my mind. I had been too late to help him, but not this little fella.

Of course, that was only partially true. In a very real sense we were too late. Way too late.

"Find him," I said. "Find him and put him down. Or give me your gun and let me do it."

A sound came from the kitchen and Frank turned toward it.

"Take the boy outside and wait for the Clayton County Sheriffs to arrive," he said. He then ran down the hallway, chasing the small beam of his light through the den and into the kitchen.

As soon as he entered the kitchen there were two quick

flashes of light, two loud explosions. Shotgun bursts. Followed by Frank falling to the floor.

I tried to set the child down on the couch, but he would not let go.

Clinging to him, I ran over to the kitchen and peaked in, using the cabinets near the door for cover.

Frank was on the floor, blood blooming out around him, his .45 still in his hand.

Crouching down, I leaned in just beyond the bottom cabinet and looked around.

There was no sign of Daryl Lee Gibbons. There was an open door on the other end leading into darkness.

With the boy still clinging to me, I leaned in, grabbed Frank's ankle, and began pulling him toward the den.

I could hear Daryl Lee Gibbons running down the stairs to the basement, so I moved in to get a better grip on Frank, grabbing his gun and checking for signs of life as I did.

Then footfalls. Running. Fast. Toward us.

Standing, turning, bringing up the gun, I could see Creepy Daryl Lee Gibbons running toward us, his shoulders lowered like he was going to tackle us.

I squeezed off a round of Frank's .45.

The boy screamed.

Then we were hit. Hard. At the legs.

Up. Airborne. Flying. Floating.

Clinging to the kid.

Banging into the window, breaking boards and glass, flying through the cold, wet, air, raindrops hitting us like scattershot.

Falling, flailing, trying to find purchase on anything.

Nothing.

Crab-crawling through the night air.

Two stories down.

Then hard, wet hit.

Sinking.

I had landed on my back on the pool cover.

Cold rain. Colder pool water.

Breath knocked out of me. Sucking air that wasn't there.

Cover collapsing onto us, sinking into the freezing dark wetness, still holding on to the small child who was no longer holding on back.

Corner of my eye, cement pad around the pool, very edge, Creepy Daryl Lee Gibbons facedown, unmoving, rain falling crimson around him.

I tried to stand, to swim, to do anything but sink, but sink was all I could do. I was wrapped in the mesh pool cover, unable to move in any meaningful way, unable to do anything but lift the child, try to hold him above the water for as long as I could.

So cold. So dark. So deep.

Sinking.

Submerged.

Engulfed.

Then . . . miraculously . . . rising.

Up out of the water.

Turning my head, I could see two Clayton County sheriff's deputies, one on each side of the pool, lifting the cover and us with it, out of the water and up into the night rain.

38

The boy, whose name was Bradley, had been abducted from the Kroger grocery market in Stockbridge a few days before.

His mom had an altercation with a fat woman matching Tilda Gibbon's description, and when she turned back around, Bradley was gone.

He was going to be okay—in one way. In many others he was not, and would not ever be.

He was taken to Henry General Hospital. His mom had been waiting for him there, and there was no doctor, nurse, or authority on heaven or earth that could make her leave his side—even if she had to scrub in for any procedures he needed.

There were two other children missing in the area, and crime scene techs were taking apart the house on Old Conyers right now, hoping they had been taken by family members instead of Creepy Gibbons and his pederast-enabling mother.

I was interviewed by a detective with the Clayton County Sheriff's Department and an agent with GBI, going over every detail of every second since we left Georgia State Prison earlier in the afternoon.

I had been allowed to dry off and change into some extra sweats they had, and though I had a blanket draped around me and the heat was on in the interview room, I still shivered.

After about two hours, Tommy Daughtry, the sheriff, walked in.

He was a tall, thick man with a bit of a belly. He wore cowboy boots and a hat, and talked with one of the thicker Southern accents I had heard in a while.

"Far as I'm concerned, you're a hero," he said. "A goddamn hero. You and Agent Morgan."

"How is he?"

Frank had been airlifted to Grady Memorial and rushed into surgery.

"No word yet," he said.

"I'd like to go see him," I said. "Least be there when he comes out of surgery. Is there anybody here who can give me a ride to my car?"

"I'll do it myself," he said. "But there's something you should know."

"What's that?"

"They took those two sick, fat fuckers there too."

"The Gibbons? They're alive?"

"Unfortunately."

We all took a moment to let that sink in.

"I don't have to worry about you finishing what you started, do I?" he said.

"I didn't start anything to finish," I said. "Both of their injuries are self-inflicted."

"Kiddy diddlers like them," the detective said, "won't last long in prison."

"You're being a bit too optimistic," the sheriff said. "I'm hoping they don't make it out of surgery."

When I was dropped off at my car, I drove directly to Trade Winds, the apartment complex I had lived in until a month or so back, the one where Jordan, Martin, and I had been a family of sorts.

Parking near the basketball court where Martin and I had spent so much time together, I got out and walked over to it in the driving rain.

I hadn't been dry long and now I was getting soaked through all over again.

I didn't care.

I stood beneath the goal where Martin had worked so hard to master the art of the layup, his smallness just too big an impediment.

In the darkness, the rain water looked like blood on the court, puddling black beneath the rain in the nearly nonexistent moonlight.

Dropping to the asphalt, I broke down and began to weep.

I wept for the world, for Martin and Jordan, for Cedric and Bradley, for all the childless mothers, for all the boys who would never grow to be men, but most of all, selfishly, I wept for me— for what I had once had and now had no longer.

Like the vanishing of everything else that had been lost, my tears disappeared into the falling rain so fast it was as if I weren't crying at all.

But I was.

I knew it.

The rain knew it.

And maybe, just maybe, somewhere in the wide, wide world, Martin and Jordan knew it too.

Later that night, back in my bedroom, I thought about the six missing boys I was looking for—not as missing orpotentially murdered, not as victims but as boys.

Holding Bradley the way I had tonight had really gotten to me, and I wanted to think of the boys I was looking for not as parts of a case, but as the vibrant, idiosyncratic little human beings they were—or had been that last time they were seen.

Cedric Porter, Jamal Jackson, Quentin Washington, Jaquez Anderson, Duke Ellis, and Vaughn Smith.

Jamal was a little jokester, always smiling, laughing, kidding around. Quentin was quiet—a large, mostly silent boy who had an inner strength that was obvious to everyone. Cedric and Vaughn loved movies, would watch them all the time if allowed. Duke adored football. He liked all sports, but adored football and could tell you every single statistic about his favorite players and teams. Jaquez, truly an Atlanta boy, loved all the Atlanta teams and followed them the way only a hometown fan can. Just ask him anything about the Hawks, the Falcons, or the Braves. He could tell you.

These were children, each one a little bundle of life and potential, each one innocent of what befell him.

Bradley was back with his mom.

Now let's see what we can do about getting the others back home with theirs.

"Sorry to call so late," Ida Williams said when I answered the phone, "but you don't sleep anyway, right?"

"Right."

"Were you asleep?"

"I wasn't," I said.

"What's wrong? You don't sound so good."

"Just tired. How are you?"

"I'm okay, son," she said. "Considering everything, I'm okay. Callin' 'cause I had a thought."

"Let's hear it."

"Mickey said y'all's havin' a hard time locating the mothers of the victims from over there."

"Yeah, I think he is."

"Before I tell you my thought, let me tell you somethin' else."

"Okay."

"Ain't no relationship in the world like that of a black mother and her son," she said.

I knew that to be true—and not just from what I had read, but what I had seen firsthand. I thought of my best friend back home, Merrill, and his mother, Mama Monroe, and the ferocious way she mothered him.

"A Southern black woman in America knows all too well what she doin' when she brings a black male child into this world, into this country, into the part of the country where we live. Our boys will always be perceived as a threat, always eyed with suspicion, always viewed as less than. Many of our boys never get to grow up."

I thought of her son LaMarcus, who had died as a child.

"If they do," she continued, "they seen as even more of a menace, even more of a threat. Live half-lives on borrowed time. Never know which day it be they don't come home. Get gunned down, arrested. This makes them extra special to us, makes us love them and care for them in a way we don't anyone else. Probably ain't all that good for 'em, but you can see why we do it— baby 'em, spoil 'em. What else can we do?"

"I understand."

I thought about something James Baldwin wrote. A black mama's instinct is to protect the black male from the devastation that threatens him the moment he declares himself a man.

Ida was saying it began long before he declared himself a man, and she was right.

But it wasn't just black mothers who did it. Homer and Faye Williams had both done it with their only child Wayne, who was more like a grandchild, they had him so late in life. And they had actually gone bankrupt indulging their doughy, daydreaming boy.

"What if y'all having a hard time findin' the mamas for the same reason you havin' a hard time findin' the boys' bodies?" she said.

At first I thought she meant because they were dead too—as if they died protecting their sons, but then I realized what she meant.

"What if because of the threat—especially at that time—they took their boys and disappeared? I wish to God I had."

It was an interesting theory, one we needed to look into—even though Ada Baker had obviously not vanished with her son. Maybe Cedric was some kind of anomaly. Maybe Ada was the exception that proves Ida's rule. Or maybe Ida was reaching for hope in an essentially hopeless circumstance.

"That's a great thought," I said. "Brilliant, actually."

"I'm gonna see 'bout helpin' Mickey track down the moms," she said. "See if I can't disprove or prove my own theory."

39

"Just because he had a white kid this time, doesn't mean he didn't abduct black kids when he lived here," Mickey said.

"True," I said, "but it does make it far less likely."

Two days had passed. Frank was still in a coma.

I was discouraged, depressed, and in need of a drink—and drink wasn't far away from where we sat at the old dining table in Second Chances.

"You don't think it could be him?" Mickey said, glancing at me briefly, then away again.

"I'm not ruling it out, but ..."

"How about this? His mom helps him snatch the kids."

I glanced over at Kenny, who was alternating between coloring and reading comics on the floor not far away.

Camille had taken Wilbur to the doctor. Mickey was babysitting Kenny and the store.

I nodded at Kenny and Mickey lowered his voice.

"Then she also helps him set up the dads and get rid of the bodies," he continued. "Two of them working together like that .. . The bodies could be buried in the woods right out back of here."

I shrugged. "It's possible, but I still think it's unlikely."

The front door opened and Miss Ida and Summer Grantham walked in.

"We came to check on you," Ida said. "Heard what happened. Why you didn't say somethin' the other night on the phone? You okay?"

"Thank you," I said, standing to hug them. "I will be once Frank Morgan wakes up."

They joined us at the table.

Today Summer was rocking an old, faded maroon Madonna T-shirt with jeans and matching Keds. She looked like she would fit in better over coloring with Kenny than sitting with the adults at the dining table.

"What you did," Summer said, "saving that poor boy the way you did . . ."

"That poor boy," Ida said.

"I'm praying for your friend," Summer said.

"Thank you."

We were all quiet a beat.

"Hey Mr. John," Kenny said, "you ever read Batman: the Dark Knight Returns by Frank Miller?"

"I haven't, Kenny," I said. "Is it good?"

"It's great. You can borrow when I'm done . . . or we can read it together."

"I'd like that, thank you."

"Speaking of superpowers," Mickey said to Summer, "use yours and tell us if Creepy Gibbons is responsible for what happened to Cedric, Jamal and the others."

She rolled her eyes. "Doesn't work that way. And it's not a superpower."

"Whatta you think?" Ida asked me.

"I think it is a superpower," I said. "She's just being modest."

"I meant about the boys and Daryl Lee."

"Not ruling anything out, but . . . predators like him usually hunt within their same race and don't usually change their MO."

"But maybe for a short while when he was here," Mickey said, "he didn't have a choice. Maybe what he did here, what they did, was opportunistic, more to do with who was here than his preference."

Something Wayne Williams said to me when I first encountered him at the Omni's arcade six years ago echoed inside me.

Just 'cause I prefer chocolate, don't mean I couldn't go for some vanilla.

Summer nodded, but I couldn't tell if it was to what I had said or Mickey.

"And one more thing," Mickey said, "and this is the biggest of all as far as I'm concerned." He paused for effect, but didn't make eye contact with any of us, which undermined it. "If it was Daryl Lee, it would explain why they stopped," he said. "They stopped here 'cause he moved. They continued somewhere else 'cause that's where he moved to."

I nodded. "You're right," I said. "That is the best argument of all."

"Somebody need to see where all else he lived," Ida said. "See how many missing children there are in those areas."

"I'll talk to Remy Boss about it," I said.

"If it turns out he took any black boys in any of the other places, it would strengthen the case for him doing it here," Summer said.

We nodded our agreement and fell silent for a moment again.

"Has Ada agreed to the tap yet?" Mickey asked Ida.

"No," she said, shaking her head, "and she ain't gonna."

"It's like she doesn't want to know," he said.

"Maybe she doesn't," Ida said, "but not for the reason you think. Once you know, you can't unknow. You can't lie to yourself anymore. No matter how hard you try or how good at it you are."

"Are girls allowed to read Batman too?" Summer asked.

Kenny and I were on the floor in the little toy area. I was

reading to him. We both looked up, but I waited for him to answer.

"Sure," he said. "Come on. You can read the girl parts."

She and I smiled at each other at the thought of girl parts.

"Is it okay?" she asked me.

"Of course," I said.

She sat down beside us, tucking her feet beneath her legs. As she did, Kenny slid toward me, then eased into my lap.

In that moment, I realized a few things. First, how closed I had been to Kenny, how completely my experience with Martin Fisher had shut me down—and not just Martin but every victim I had encountered—how much loss and pain, death and devastation I had seen. I had been in self-preservation mode—still was, and it had caused me to give far less to Kenny than I otherwise would have. I realized too just how much Kenny was looking for and in need of the attention and affection of a man, a father figure. It was that very vulnerability that most likely led to the capture of many of the victims. Finally, I felt funny with him on my lap—something I never would have before. After what I had seen in the original case and then at Daryl Lee Gibbons's house, I felt awkward having Kenny so close—not for anything having to do with him or me, but how it might appear to others in the light of all we had been dealing with.

"Ooh," Summer said. "This is good."

She slid over next to me, which made me feel better about how this looked. Before long, Kenny was in her lap, which made me feel better still.

40

"You actually sat across from Wayne Williams," Susan said.

"I did."

I was sitting across from her now—at a table in the back corner of Scarlett's drinking coffee. I found it easier not to drink anything but coffee when I didn't sit at the bar.

Remy Boss had said he would do his best to swing by to talk to me if he could. I was waiting for him and reviewing my notes on the cases—while sipping coffee and talking to Susan.

"How was it?"

"Surreal," I said.

She nodded. "I bet. Did he say anything that made you believe he was . . . innocent? Or guilty or anything?"

"I'm still processing everything he said, so . . . maybe. I'm not sure."

"Look at this," Margaret said from behind the bar. "They say we got snow coming."

She turned up the TV and we all listened.

"Metro Atlanta may see its earliest snowfall on record," a local weather man was saying.

An afternoon regular at the bar said, "Please tell us you're not going to close down, Margaret. Even if it's the storm of the century."

"It's not gonna snow," she said. "It's not, but if it does . . . whole city shuts down. You know that. At the slightest dusting of white powder. Hell, a Martha White Flour truck turned over on 285 and all the commuters stopped and hunkered down in their cars 'cause they thought the white dust was the first sign of flurries."

"Southerners, am I right?" the patron, who had lived here his entire life, said.

"We should have a snow pool," she said. "Bet on whether it's gonna snow or not."

"Yeah," the patron said. "Let's do it. Put me in for twenty for it not to. I don't think it's gonna happen. Or maybe I just don't want it to. Either way . . . Puttin' my money where my heart is."

"You believe this?" Susan said, jerking her head back toward the conversation at the bar.

I smiled. "I've never been in snow before," I said.

"Really?"

"Unless I'm blocking out some family trip from childhood."

"It's not gonna snow," she said. "But . . ."

"Yeah?"

"How long you been sober?" Susan asked.

"I've lost track," I said. "A while."

"I thought AA was all about keeping track."

"I'm not a very good member," I said. "And I'm not convinced what Lonnie and those guys do in his little room is actually AA. Why?"

"Just thought . . . if you keep it up . . . and if it does snow—two very big ifs—maybe we can hunker down during the snowstorm together. Rent a couple of movies, eat some pizza. Make out."

"Really? How much sobriety would that require?" I asked. "Just so I know."

Later in the afternoon, right on time, Lonnie came in and Margaret poured him his usual—the shot of bourbon to stare at.

Today, he stared at the drink much longer than he did other days.

Sensing something was wrong, I stood and started walking over toward him.

Instead of sliding the glass back toward Margaret, he lifted it and started to take a drink.

"Wait," I yelled and rushed over to him.

I grabbed the glass just as it reached his lips, knocking it over, it bouncing down the bar and careening off of it onto the floor behind.

"What're you doin'?" I said.

He shook his head. "I just . . ."

"Come over here with me," I said. "Come on."

I grabbed him by the arm and led him over to my table as Susan wiped down the bar and Margaret cleaned up the glass on the floor behind it.

"Can we get another coffee over here?" I said.

"Sure thing," Susan said. "Coming up."

She had it on the table in front of him by the time we sat down.

"What's going on man?" I said. "Want to go to a meeting?"

He shook his head. "Just can't take it anymore. It's too much. I've held it together so long."

I nodded. "I know you have. You've done great. You really have."

"Losing my business . . . is really gettin' to me. Got nothing else. No idea what I'm gonna do. Then stirring everything up around Cedric and those others . . . Takes me back to such a bad time. So tired of fighting."

"I know," I said. "I know you are."

"I know you think you do," he said, "but you don't. Think about how long you been doin' it. That's nothing. Hell, I been drinking longer than you been alive. Been sober longer than you've been drinking."

"I didn't mean—"

"I been so strong so long. Been holdin' it all together—for Cedric, for Ada, for my store, for . . . What's the use? Cedric ain't ever comin' back. My store's a lost cause. Ada's got her phone calls, found religion. Don't need me no more. I got nothin'. I'm done fighting. Can't do it no more."

"Drink some of your coffee and let's do a meeting, right here, right now."

"You listening, man? I don't want to do no goddamn meetin'. Don't want to say no goddamn Serenity Prayer. I want a fuckin' drink and keep 'em comin'. Got it?"

"Please," I said. "I need you. I can't do this without you."

"You don't need me, man. You're doin' just fine. Just fine."

"Because of you," I said.

"No," he said. "Not because of me. Because of you. You're doin' it. Not me."

"I couldn't've done it without you," I said. "Can't do it without you. I mean it."

"You don't mean it."

"I do. Don't believe me? Fine. You drink, I drink. You wanna drink? Fuck it, let's drink. Whatta we havin? Susan, give us two bourbons. Make 'em doubles."

She shook her head. "I won't. I can't."

"What kind of bar is this?" I said. "Margaret, come join us. Bring a bottle."

"I would, but I've got to stay behind the bar," she said. "Sorry."

"Fine, we'll move to the bar," I said. "Come on."

As I started to stand, Lonnie grabbed my arm and pulled me back down.

He didn't say anything, just held my arm with one hand and began drinking his coffee with the other.

Later, after Lonnie had gone back to work and I was still waiting for Remy Boss to drop by, Susan walked over to me.

"You weren't bluffing, were you?" she said. "You would have drank with Lonnie, wouldn't you?"

"I wasn't bluffing," I said.

"I didn't think so."

"That mean our snow date is canceled?" I asked.

She frowned. "'Fraid so."

I had almost given up on Remy by the time he finally showed up.

"Only got a minute," he said. "Can't stay."

He didn't even sit down.

"What's up?" he added when I didn't say anything.

"We were wondering if the victims here could be Daryl Lee's and if there were any black victims in the other places where he lived."

"We?"

"Our missing and murdered children group," I said.

"The investigation is just beginning," he said. "It'll be a while before we know where all he lived and if he even had any other victims. It won't be quick."

"I know, I just—"

"Look, I've tried to be patient with you, but . . . you gotta leave me alone and let me do my job. As a courtesy I'll come and talk to your little group after the investigation is complete, let y'all know anything I can."

His entire attitude had changed. It wasn't that he had been much more than indifferent or slightly patient before, but now he was actually hostile.

"Sorry," I said. "I won't bother you again."

"Lot of people blame you for what happened to Frank Morgan. I'm not one of them. Frank is the professional. You're the . . . whatever you are. Young person. He should have never gone in there, should've never taken you. Whatever happened after that is on him."

I nodded, and thought about it, remembering how I had

pressed Frank to go when he did—and to take me with him. Maybe I was to blame.

"This is serious shit," he said. "Fuck up and people get hurt or killed. Just think about that. Now I'm gonna look into these missing kids over here again—like I already told you. And I'm gonna see if there's a Daryl Lee Gibbons connection. I'm gonna do a thorough and professional investigation. I appreciate the information you've given me. Now let me use it."

41

I got in my car and I drove.

I drove angrily and aggressively.

It was dark now, traffic had thinned.

I was on 285 driving like I had somewhere to be in a hurry.

I had been at it a while, but my face still stung from embarrassment and frustration. I felt lonely and useless, isolated and guilty.

I wasn't sure how long the blue lights had been flashing before I noticed them, but I bet it had been a while.

I pulled over and put my car in park, my heart pounding, my eyes bulging.

"Where you headed in such a hurry, son?" the fifty-something gray-headed cop holding the bright light in my face asked.

"Just out for a drive," I said. "Clear my head."

"License and registration. Where do you live?"

I told him as I handed him my documents.

There wasn't much traffic on 285, but what there was streaked by in a windy whoosh then disappeared again into the dark night.

"Why do your plates say Florida?"

"I'm a student," I said. "Recently moved up here. "Permanent residence is in Florida."

He studied my license, then pointed his light back in my face. "Why's your name sound so familiar?"

I shrugged. "Not sure. But I get that a lot."

"No, I know. You're the one that . . . they found that dead kid in your apartment."

"Actually, I found him," I said.

"You got that one cop killed. What was his name? And another half-dead, fighting for his life in the hospital right now. I've pulled me over a sure enough by god menace."

I started to explain but knew there was no use.

"Just wait right here," he said, then ambled back to his car.

With Frank in the hospital and no friends on the force, I had no one to call. No friends. Only enemies. Only those who wished me ill.

As alone and isolated as I had felt before, I felt far more so now—alone, isolated, and vulnerable. Very vulnerable.

I sat there, flashing lights illuminating my car and the night around it, and waited.

And waited.

Eventually, another car, this one a dark unmarked, pulled in behind him.

This time two cops approached my vehicle—one on either side.

"Step out of the car," he said.

Stay calm. Don't give them any reason to justify use of force or anything else.

I did as I was told. Slowly. Carefully.

"Hands on the hood," he said. "Spread your legs."

I did, and he patted me down.

As he did, the other cop began searching my car.

"Larry Moore was a good cop," the guy in my car said. "Miss him. The force misses him. The city misses him."

The cop behind me put his mouth to my ear. "Think anyone would miss you?"

I shook my head.

"Hands behind your back," he said.

I did as I was told and he cuffed me.

The cop in the car popped the trunk, walked around, and began searching it.

"Hey Kyle," the cop behind me said, "how many cuffed losers resisting arrest have we had fall into oncoming traffic out here?"

"Not enough, brother. Not enough."

He grabbed my arm and turned me around to face the four lanes of 285 closest to us.

He smelled of cigarettes, fast-food, and aftershave.

"They slow down some when they see our lights," he said, "but not much. Not enough to make a difference. Hell, it'd be better for you if they sped up. Lot better to get eighty-sixed than made a vegetable."

Heart and head racing, I did my best not to let him know how much what he was doing was affecting me.

Hooking his leg around my feet, he began leaning me toward the traffic, my hair blowing in the brisk breeze the cars generated.

"Hey Kyle, could I get you to do me a favor?"

"Anything for a brother, brother."

"Kill our lights."

It took a minute but he did.

Now we were shrouded in darkness, and the speeding cars didn't slow or break until they were on top of us—many of them not even then.

"One little flick of my wrist," he said. "Wonder how many lives I'd save? How many cops?"

"Good cops," Kyle added.

A car was approaching in the lane closest to us, and I could tell he was about to toss me in front of it.

I was going to die without knowing what happened to Cedric

Porter or whether or not Wayne Williams was guilty, without knowing or learning or experiencing a million other things that really mattered, and there was nothing I could do about it.

Twenty seconds away.

He adjusted his grip.

Ten.

Repositioned his leg around mine.

Zero.

He dropped me.

I began to flail but with my hands cuffed behind me there wasn't much I could do. Nothing to grab. Nothing to grab with.

Falling.

Reaching.

Grasping.

Then he grabbed me again and pulled me back.

Tossing me back in my car, he uncuffed me, dropped a ticket for the largest amount allowed by law on top of me, and walked with Kyle to their cars without saying another word.

Turning their lights back on to make a hole in the oncoming traffic, they sped off into the dark night.

I sat there for a long time.

How had this become my life?

I had never felt so helpless, so small, so defenseless.

Eventually I had my breathing back under control. I cranked the car and turned on the lights.

Taking the next exit, I found the nearest payphone and called Harry Bosch.

I hadn't spoken to him in years, but he had said to call him whenever I needed to, and with Frank in a coma and my dad not speaking to me, I couldn't think of anyone better to call than Bosch.

Such was my trust for Bosch that even after all this time I felt comfortable to call him collect—the only option available to me at the moment.

As I dialed, pulse pounding in my throat, I searched the dark side street for patrol cars—far more afraid of them than any other nocturnal urban threats.

At my request, the operator let it ring a long time, but there was no answer.

"Is there another number you'd like me to try, sir?" she asked.

"No ma'am, thank you," I said. "I don't have anyone else to call."

I climbed back into my car and cranked it.

Breathe. Calm down. Frank's not available. Neither is Harry. That's okay. You have what you need. Find your center. Grow up. You're not a kid anymore. Here's your chance to prove it.

I pulled up the on-ramp and back onto 285.

I had never driven the entire perimeter at one time before. I was going to tonight. I was going to obey the speed limit and drive far more cautiously than I had before, but I was not going to be deterred.

I did it without getting stopped again. Sixty-four miles in a little less than an hour.

Stopping at a Circle K store when I had finished circling the city, literally driving around in a circle because I didn't know what else to do, I refueled and took off again—this time down 20 toward Grady to check on Frank.

The city was different at night. It had an ethereal quality, as if it wasn't the same place it was during the day, as if the night city and the day city weren't the same city at all.

Frank was still in a coma, still in ICU, so I did the only thing I could do—I sat alone in the empty ICU waiting room and waited.

I waited because I didn't know what else to do. What I was waiting for or how long I would wait for it wasn't something I was clear about.

After a while of just waiting, I decided there was something else I could do.

Locating the small, empty chapel, I went in and prayed. I

prayed for Frank, for his full recovery and no lasting damage at all. I prayed for Lonnie and the demon he was battling. I prayed for Summer and the different but equally difficult demon she was battling.

I prayed for a while, then went back up to ICU waiting, where eventually I fell fast asleep.

When I woke the next morning, families of very sick patients were beginning to fill the room, preparing for the first of four short visits they were granted each day.

Easing up out of my chair, I made my way into the hallway and was about to leave when I saw Frank's wife, Evelyn, and daughter walking up.

Haggard and sad, the thin, pale skin of their faces looked like parchment stretched too tightly across the bones beneath.

"John?" Evelyn said. "What're you doing here?"

"Hey, John," Becca said with a little wave. She was Frank's thirteen-year-old daughter, and seeing her made me wonder where his twelve-year-old son was.

"Just came down to be close to him, to stay with him and pray for him last night."

"You stayed all night? That means a lot. Thank you."

"Wish I could do more."

"Becca, would you go down to that coffee machine and get me a cup?" Evelyn asked, handing her daughter a dollar.

"Can I get one too?"

"Sure honey," she said, handing her another dollar. "Help yourself."

When Becca was gone, Evelyn turned back to me. "They say if he doesn't wake up in the next day or so, chances are he won't. Please pray even more, John. I don't want to lose him. I can't. I need to have the big ol' square thing around. And the kids . . . how would they ever . . ."

Fighting back tears, she patted me on the arm and pushed past me.

"Come on Becca," she called, "it's almost time for visitation."

"Thought you wanted coffee?"

"After. Let's put on our best, bright faces for daddy."

As I was leaving, I ran into Don Paulk, who was arriving.

He was here to pray with one of his parishioners prior to her surgery.

A founder of the church, along with his brother Earl and their wives, Don had been particularly good to me since I moved to Atlanta—especially at the end of the LaMarcus Williams case when everything went so badly. LaDonna, who I had class with, was his daughter.

"I was planning on coming down to the college to talk to you today," he said.

He's heard about the lawsuit.

"Your professors are concerned about how many classes you're missing," he added. "How are you, John?"

I shrugged. "I'm okay, I guess."

"Can I take you to lunch after your classes today so we can really talk?"

I hesitated a moment.

"You are planning to attend your classes today, aren't you?"

The truth was I wasn't.

"That's one of the things they wanted me to talk to you about," he said. "You can't miss any more and pass."

"Maybe I should just drop them for this quarter and start again next one," I said.

"I'd hate to see you do that," he said. "It would mess up your schedule and when you can graduate—and many people who drop out don't ever seem to start back. Tell you what, go today, then let's go to lunch together and see if we can't figure it out, okay?"

"Remember the little boy who was found dead in my room?" I said.

He nodded.

"His mother's threatening to bring a lawsuit against me," I said.

"I'm so sorry to hear that. Are you--"

"She plans to name the college and the church since the apartment was being used for a dorm."

He didn't seem surprised.

"We can talk about that today too," he said.

"But—"

"We can figure everything out, John. I promise."

42

I had every intention of attending class and going to lunch with Pastor Don.

Then Mickey called.

"Found Jaquez Anderson's dad," he said. "'Bout to go talk to him. Wanna go?"

I didn't answer right away.

"Come on," he said. "I've got a feeling we're gonna solve this thing. I really do. I've been working hard on it, but I could use your help. You know I don't like doing interviews."

"How can a reporter not like doing interviews?" I said.

"I always worked with a partner. I did the writing. He did the research and reporting and chasing down of stories. I can do it. I just don't like to."

"You pickin' me up?" I said.

"Ten minutes away."

While waiting for Mickey to arrive, I reviewed my notes on the case.

Cedric Porter, Jamal Jackson, Quentin Washington, Jaquez Anderson, Duke Ellis, and Vaughn Smith. All missing. All between the ages of ten and fourteen. All vanished during the height of the Atlanta Child Murders. All living with single mothers who were neglectful. All of them lived off this end of Memorial Drive—all but Vaughn Smith that was. He had lived up off Wesley Chapel. Cedric and Jamal had both lived here in Memorial Manor. Quentin Washington and Jaquez Anderson had lived in an apartment complex on the other side of Memorial, Duke Ellis in a house down off North Hairston.

So far every dad we had interviewed except for Cedric's had articles of his son's clothing or other items planted in his home or vehicle and had been suspected by the authorities of having taken his son.

The only parents we had yet to track down were those of Jaquez Anderson and Vaughn Smith.

I was glad Mickey had found Jaquez's dad, but believed finding Vaughn's was more important since he lived outside the pattern area.

In fact, it was one of three big questions about this case. Why does Vaughn's location break the pattern? Why does Cedric, Sr. not having items planted break the pattern? Where are the boys or their bodies?

And then it hit me.

According to Cedric, Sr., he wasn't Cedric, Jr.'s real father. Was that true? Did the killer know? Was that why he didn't have any clothing or other items planted in his home or vehicle? If so, that would explain why—and it might help us identify the killer. I'd have to look into that some more.

Major Anderson worked at the Richway store on Covington Highway.

Richway was a discount department store owned and operated by Rich's. It was known for, among other things, the colorful raised wedge skylights on the roof. Its logo was an orange sunrise with black block letters beneath it, representing the store carried everything under the sun.

We met Major on a loading dock in the back of the store during his brief morning break.

The day was cold and clear, a bright but impotent sun high in the sky.

"Whatch y'all think?" he said. "It gonna snow?"

He had big, bright eyes and a bushy beard that looked shiny in the morning light. Young, thick, and muscular, he still wore a back brace designed for lifting and I wondered if it was company policy.

"I hope so," I said.

"Not gonna happen," Mickey said.

The plum-colored smudges beneath Mickey's small eyes and his pale, drawn skin evidenced his exhaustion. Which when added to his scraggly, untrimmed reddish beard and longish, unkempt strawberry-blond hair made him look a little maniacal, and I could tell the case was getting to him far more than he had let on.

"I don't know," he said, "I'm kinda thinkin' it will."

"We shall soon see," Mickey said.

"So, y'all want to talk to me about Jaquez? I pray for that little man every day."

He held his work gloves down by his side, bringing them up occasionally when using his hands to talk, the worn-smooth fingers flapping in the breeze as he did.

"We do," I said. "Is that okay?"

"Every day," he repeated. "Without fail. I don't mind talkin' to you, but I don't know anything."

"Any idea where he might be or what might have happened to him?" I said.

He shook his head. "No idea. First thought I had was his mama got herself into some trouble and the boy paid the price, like maybe she owed somebody somethin' for some drugs and they took him just to get her to pay up, but . . . after just a few minutes with her I knew that wasn't the case. So I ain't gonna be no help."

"Did the police look at you?"

"Sure. Good and hard for a few minutes, but I didn't have nothin' to do with it, and they moved on."

"Did Jaquez ever mention a man in the area who the kids called Creepy?"

He shook his head. "That who took my boy?"

"We honestly don't know," I said. "Just trying to find out."

"I wish I knew somethin' that would help," he said. "I'd do anything to get my boy back, but . . . his moms and I wasn't together so I . . . . just don't know anything."

"Do you recall if some of Jaquez's clothes or toys were planted in your house or car during that time?"

His eyes grew wide and he stopped moving for a moment. "Those were his? Never could figure out where those came from or how they got in my place. Why were they—who put them there?"

"That's what we're trying to find out," I said.

"I don't get it. What would that . . ."

"Maybe try to make the cops think you had him," I said.

"Oh."

We were quiet a moment as he thought about it.

"How'd you even know to ask?" he said.

"It happened in some other cases of missing children," I said. "Our theory is someone planted them to put suspicion on the fathers."

"What other cases?"

I told him.

"Any of those names sound familiar?"

He nodded. "Vaughn."

"Vaughn Smith?" I said, my pulse rising.

"Yeah."

"He lived up off Wesley Chapel," I said. "How'd you know him?"

"He get taken too?" he asked.

I nodded.

"Oh my God. Was it Wayne Williams?"

"We don't think so," I said. "We really don't. How'd you know Vaughn?"

"Used to take Jaquez out for the day sometimes," he said. "Grab a burger, go for a walk, climb Stone Mountain, go to the mall, shit like that. Sometimes we'd go to a movie right there on Memorial Drive not far from where he lived with his mother. Cordelia Smith worked at the theater. Vaughn, her kid, was always with her. Single mom. No help with him. He'd hang out, watch movies all day. We got to know them. He'd sit with us sometimes."

I nodded.

He looked at the plastic watch strapped to his left wrist.

"I gotta get back to work," he said. "Let me know if you find out anything, will you?"

"We will," I said, and he rushed back inside the building.

"So," I said, "Vaughn Smith lived outside of our geographic pattern, but his mom worked right in the middle of it, and brought him to work with her—a lot from the sounds of it."

"Now the only anomaly on our list is Cedric's dad not having any clothes planted in his place or car," Mickey said.

"Maybe he did," I said.

"He told us he didn't."

"What he told us was that he wasn't Cedric's dad," I said.

"Oh shit, that's right."

We were quiet a moment, thinking about it.

"Whatta we do now?" Mickey said.

"Would still like to talk to the other mothers."

"Can't believe they're so hard to find," he said.

"Unless Ida's theory is right—is she still helping you look?"

He nodded. "It's pretty simple really," I said. "Their names have changed—or were never the same as those of their sons to begin with. They're poor so move around more. Different name in a different location—hell, that's what people trying not to be found do."

"Oh my God this is gonna make such a good story," he said. "If this doesn't wind up being connected to the original case, I've got two books—one on the Atlanta Child Murders and one on this one."

That reminded me of what Frank had said about Mickey and his motives, and made me want to get away from him.

"I'm gonna keep looking for the mothers and I've got a couple of other things to check out," he said. "Can I drop you somewhere? Don't you have class today?"

43

Regretting not going to class or lunch with Pastor Don, feeling like a self-sabotaging loser, worried about and experiencing guilt over Frank, I threw myself into my work.

Quietly, because my roommate was asleep on the other side of the thin wall, I dove into the trace evidence in the Atlanta Child Murders case like never before.

With my phone off the hook, I sat in the middle of my floor surrounded by massive amounts of data.

Most violent crimes involve physical contact between perpetrators and their victims. When this occurs, there is often an inadvertent transfer of microscopic debris—a person-to-person cross transfer. This transfer constitutes evidence and most often consists of hairs and fibers. This transfer of hairs and fibers, their discovery, collection, examination, and identification as trace evidence can be critical in linking a suspect to a victim or a crime scene.

This was certainly true of the Atlanta Child Murders case.

Textile fibers can be exchanged between two individuals, between an individual and an object, and between two objects. When fibers are matched with a specific source—a fabric from the victim, suspect, or crime scene—a value is placed on the association. This value is dependent on the type of fibers found, their color, variation of color, the quantity found, the location of fibers at the crime scene or on the victim, and the number of different fibers at the crime scene or on the victim that match the clothing of the suspect.

Whether a fiber is transferred and detected is dependent on the nature and duration of contact between the suspect and the victim or crime scene, the persistence of fibers after the transfer, and the type of fabric involved in contact.

A fiber is the smallest unit of a textile material that has a length many times greater than its diameter. Fibers can occur naturally as plant and animal fibers, but they can also be manufactured.

When two people come in contact or when contact occurs with an item from the crime scene, there's a possibility that fiber transfer will take place. The transfer is not automatic and will not always take place. Some fibers don't shed or don't shed much. A big factor in the transfer of trace evidence is the length of time between the actual physical contact and the collection of clothing items from the suspect or victim. If the victim remains immobile, very little fiber loss will occur, whereas the suspect's clothing will often lose transferred fibers quickly. The longer the passage of time between the crime and the processing of the suspect, the greater the likelihood of finding transferred fibers on the clothing of the suspect decreases.

Fibers are gathered at a crime scene with tweezers, tape, or a vacuum. Typically, they come from clothing, drapery, wigs, carpeting, furniture, and blankets. They are first determined to be natural, manufactured, or a mix of both. Natural fibers come from plants and animals. Synthetic fibers such as rayon, acetate, and polyester are made from long chains of molecules called polymers. Determining the shape and color of fibers from any of these fabrics is done by examining them beneath a microscopic.

In the Atlanta Child Murders case the only clue being found with any consistency, a clue that would only be valuable if a suspect was uncovered, was the presence of trace evidence on several of the bodies and their clothing.

The fibers were sent to the Georgia State Crime Lab for analysis, where Larry Peterson was able to isolate two distinct types—a violet-colored acetate fiber and a coarse yellow-green nylon fiber with a distinctive trilobed quality found in few carpets.

When the discovery of the fibers began to be reported in the newspaper, the killer began stripping the bodies and throwing them into the river, most likely in an attempt to wash away the trace evidence.

Once he became a suspect, Wayne Williams's home and car were searched and provided numerous fibers and human and canine hairs similar to those authorities had been collecting from the victims' bodies—beginning with a tuft of carpet fibers in the tennis shoe of Eric Middlebrooks. The floors of the home where Williams lived with his parents were covered with yellow-green carpeting, and he had a dog. When comparisons from the samples removed from the victims were compared to those of the Williamses' home, they showed good consistency.

FBI experts analyzed samples from the Williamses' rugs with special equipment and the help of DuPont, and were able to ascertain that the fibers came from a Boston-based textile company. The fiber, which is known as Wellman 181B, had been sold to numerous carpet companies, each of which used its own dye. This led to the discovery that the most likely source was the West Point Pepperell Corporation in Georgia. The company's Luxaire English Olive color matched that found in the Williamses' home.

The company had only made that type of carpet for about one year, distributing about sixteen thousand yards of it throughout the South—a very small amount adding up to about only eighty homes in Georgia or 1 in 7792 homes in Atlanta.

With the help of Chevrolet, investigators determined that there was a 1 in 3,828 chance that a victim acquired the fiber from a random contact with a car that had this carpeting installed.

Then both the odds from the home and the car were calculated—a figure that came to nearly 1 in 30,000,000.

Of course, Williams's defense team attempted to discredit the fiber evidence with the argument that a particular fiber might be in the home or vehicle of any number of people.

But when I considered the probability of a person having a particular carpet with a very unique type of fiber, the same person a particular bedspread with a particular set of light green cotton fibers blended with violet acetate fibers, and that same person also driving a 1970 Chevrolet station wagon and owning a dog who shed the type of hairs found on the victims, the evidence was overwhelming.

When I read that Larry Peterson's fiber analysis work in the case had been reviewed favorably by the world-famous microanalyst Walter McCrone—someone I was familiar with because of his work on the Shroud of Turin—I was even more convinced.

Another expert called in to consult on the fiber evidence had a connection to me, Florida, my dad, and even Susan's dad. Lynn Henson, a quiet young woman and an expert on fibers and threats who worked in the Florida State Crime lab in Tallahassee, had been called in to analyze the evidence and help provide a decisive evaluation.

Henson—whose testimony the year before figured prominently in the Florida trial of Ted Bundy that both Dad and Susan's dad, Tom Daniels, had worked on—testified in Williams's trial that synthetic fibers found on one of the victim's bodies showed no significant differences from the samples taken from Williams's home and station wagon.

Suddenly, I was homesick for Florida—for my town, my family and friends, for Anna and Merrill, and a million other things I couldn't even name.

I was overwhelmed with the urge to pack up everything, jump in the car, and head home.

Maybe I should.

I had promised Frank I'd go home next week for Thanksgiving, and though until this moment I hadn't really planned on going, what if I went home and didn't come back?

The longing for home, for any kind of comfort I could find there pulled me like never before in my entire life. But I wasn't running, wasn't hiding, wasn't going home until I had done everything I could do for both cases I was working on. I couldn't.

I couldn't leave, but what I could do was call home. I could at least do that.

But the moment I placed the receiver back on the cradle to make the call, my phone began ringing.

Snatching it up before it could wake Rick, I whispered my hello into it.

"Who the hell you been on the phone with?" Margaret asked.

"No one. What's wrong?"

"Camille's little boy Kenny," she said. "He's missing."

44

A single squad car was outside Second Chances. It was the only indication at all that anything was going on.

Margaret, Susan, Rand, and Lonnie were standing at the corner of the building near Scarlett's when I ran up.

"He never made it to his mama's shop from the bus stop," Susan said.

"Is anyone in there with her?" I asked.

"Her other boy," Lonnie said. "She ain't about to let him out of her sight."

My heart sank even more as I smelled the alcohol on Lonnie's breath.

"Is this related to Cedric and the other boys from a few years back?" Margaret asked.

"It's gotta be, doesn't it?" Lonnie said. "But . . . why wait so long in between? Why now? What does it mean for Cedric? Why would he--"

"I'm gonna go see if I can help," I said.

"Want me to go with you?" Lonnie asked.

"Are you okay to?" I asked.

His eyes locked on to mine and he nodded.

"Sure then. Thanks."

My legs felt weak as we walked the two short store fronts to her shop.

"You okay?" Lonnie asked.

I shook my head.

"Me either."

"When'd you start drinkin' again?"

"Little while back," he said. "Been hidin' it. Couldn't today."

The little bell jingled as we walked in the door, and Camille looked up, her red, impossibly tired eyes moist, her thin, light skin drawn.

"Get him the fuck out of here," she said when she saw me. "Get the fuck out of here. This is your fault. You did this. Stirring all this up again, making my little boy a mark. Get him out of here now."

"Come on," Lonnie said, grabbing me by the arm and helping me as my knees began to buckle. "Let's go. She's just upset."

He got me turned around and headed out the door.

"We're out here if you need us," he said over his shoulder.

"Find Mickey," she said. "Get Mickey here now."

"Okay," he said. "You got it. Anything else, we're right outside."

When Margaret and Susan saw Lonnie helping me, they ran to meet us.

"What's wrong?" Margaret said. "What happened?"

"Are you okay?" Susan asked.

"He'll be fine," Lonnie said. "Camille's just upset. Looking for someone to blame."

"She's blaming you?" Susan said.

"Come on," Margaret said. "Come in here and sit down."

Margaret held the door and Lonnie and Susan helped me in.

"I'm okay," I said. "I can walk. I was just . . . I'm okay. Can I use your phone?"

"Sure honey," Margaret said. "Help yourself."

I walked over on steadier legs, picked up the phone and paged Mickey.

While I waited for him to call back, Susan brought me a cup of coffee.

"Thanks."

"What's going on, John?" she said.

"I don't know."

"You've got to," she said. "You know more about all of this than everyone else put together. Why now? Why so long after Cedric and the others were taken?"

"I don't know," I said. "I wish I did."

"I bet you do," she said. "If you just let yourself think about everything. I bet you know."

"I don't."

"You have to," she said. "We've got a little boy missing and a snowstorm on the way."

Thankfully, the phone rang.

I snatched it up.

It wasn't Mickey, but a supplier looking for Margaret. I quickly got a number and told him she'd call him back later.

All around us the bar was chaos and confusion. Everyone was talking over each other in emotion-strained voices.

"There are too many interruptions here," Susan said. "Too much noise. Go back to your apartment and work on it there. I'll talk to Mickey when he calls. I'll have him call you at your place."

"I need to call Remy Boss too."

"Are you kidding? I heard the way that prick spoke to you yesterday. He's not gonna do shit. You know that."

"Bobby Battle then," I said. "Since I can't call Frank. Some detective needs to know. This can't be handled like just another missing kid case."

"So call him," she said. "From your place."

I nodded. "Okay," I said. "I'm not sure I can come up with anything, but I know I can't here. Thank you."

As I turned to leave, I saw something I had hoped never to.

With Margaret's attention at the door and our attention on the phone and each other, Lonnie had reached behind the bar, removed a bottle of bourbon, and was pouring himself drinks and knocking them back as quickly as he could.

"Lonnie, no," I said.

"Can't take it no more," he said. "It's all too much. All of it. I'll stop drinking when they find that little boy, then I'll figure out what to do with the rest of my life, but for now I'm gonna drink."

45

I didn't know what Susan expected from me, but I was pretty sure I wouldn't be able to do it.

I was an alcoholic college dropout who had gotten the best friend I had in Atlanta shot and maybe killed. I was barely an adult—some would say I wasn't yet. What could I do?

I could try.

I could go over everything again, add in everything new, including little Kenny's disappearance, and see if anything made any better sense.

Where was Mickey? Why hadn't he called back yet?

As I was pulling everything off my second wall to reexamine and repost, my phone rang.

It was Susan.

"Still no word from Mickey," she said. "Cop took Camille's statement and has just left. We've convinced Lonnie to switch over to coffee, but he was able to pour a lot down in him before we did. We're all closing early out of respect—but we would've had to anyway. Snow's coming sooner than expected. News is telling everyone to get supplies and get inside and stay there. Get back to work. I'll keep you updated and have Mickey call you the moment I hear from him."

As soon as we hung up, I called Bobby Battle.

"Figured I'd be hearin' from you," he said.

"You heard?"

"Yeah, and we're doubling up our efforts. Because of the snowstorm," he said. "Not because we believe there's a serial killer at work. There's not. Understand? There is no serial killer. Frank didn't think so either. I gotta get back to work."

The line went dead.

I hung up and returned to my wall.

Six black boys. All missing. All largely unsupervised, unparented. All with a connection to this area. Now over four years later, and after we start looking into it, another one. What does it mean? Is it even related? How can it not be? It might not be.

Absentee fathers set up for the abductions. No bodies. No evidence. Ada Baker getting calls from Cedric. No reports of any other mothers receiving calls. What does it mean? Cedric's dad not having items planted. What does it mean? Maybe Cedric's case is the anomaly, different from all the rest, the exception that proves the rule, the variation that points to the pattern. If so, what does it mean?

Why was Cedric running back toward the apartment complex? Who or what was he running from? What or who was he running to? What was his mom really doing during that time?

Did Daryl Lee Gibbons kill Cedric and or the other boys and bury them in the woods? If he did, why was Kenny taken and who had taken him?

Where were the bodies?

I stepped over to my little bookshelves in the corner and withdrew a forensic book and looked up methods of disposing of bodies, as I thought of what Wayne Williams said about how John Wayne Gacy did it.

My phone rang and I jumped.

Small voice. Crying. Distraught. Difficult to understand.

It was Frank's daughter, Becca.

"John . . . my daddy's not waking up. He won't wake up. Oh, John, I don't want my daddy to die. Please pray for him. Please help. Please don't let God take my daddy."

"I will," I said. "I will right now."

As soon as we hung up, I dropped to the floor and began to intercede for Frank. Sincerely, fervently, without self-consciousness and with no regard for dignity or decorum.

"Please heal Frank and return him to his little girl," I pleaded. "Please help me find Kenny and return him to his mom. Please."

Then something about the disposal of bodies resurfaced in my mind. What was it?

The phone rang again.

"He had no idea," Susan said. "He'll be callin' you in a minute. We're closing down here in about a half hour. You need me for anything?"

"I'll call you if I do."

"It better be in the next thirty minutes. Once I get home I won't be able to get out again. I'll be stranded. Everyone will. Whatever you do, do it fast."

"You sure there's nothing else you can tell me about Cedric's disappearance?"

"Like what?"

"Where was he running? Who to? Who from?"

"I don't know. I've told you."

"I need to go," I said. "Don't want to miss Mickey's call."

Mickey called a couple of minutes later.

"John, what the hell's goin' on, man?"

"Where are you?" I said.

"Don't be mad. I've been following up on some leads. Not far from where Daryl Lee was," he said. "I've got to get on the road to make it back before the storm hits, but I wanted to tell you a couple of things."

"Okay."

"You're not gonna like them."

"Tell me anyway and quick."

"Did you know Summer Grantham's been involved in cases like this before? She sort of specializes in missing kids. She's been a suspect in a couple of them. She's not right, man. She has what she claims is a daughter, but she's a runaway—or so they claim. I'm not so sure Grantham didn't take her. Anyway, she's not her biological daughter. Grantham's been quoted in some old newspaper articles I found as saying God put her here on earth to save at-risk kids. I think that's what she thinks she's doing, man. And get this—when Cedric and the other boys disappeared, she lived in Memorial Manor."

"Why're you down close to Stockbridge?" I said.

"On my way back from McDonough. Been tryin' to find her place. Wanted to be sure before I told you. I think she has Cedric. Maybe the others too. I don't know. But him for sure."

"What makes you think that?" I said.

"The other thing you're not gonna like," he said. "I've got a deep undercover journalist buddy of mine. He's hardcore. Nothing he won't or can't do. He specializes in deep background so he doesn't have to be concerned about whether something's legal or not. Doesn't matter. Understand?"

"Get to the point, Mickey, we're running out of time here."

"I had him bug Ada Baker's phone when she refused to let the police do it."

"You did what?"

"Yeah. The calls are real man. They're coming from a kid who sounds like he could be Cedric. The call came from McDonough —where Summer lives. No one was home. Do you think it was because she was there taking Kenny? Should I go back? Kenny, man. What a sweet fuckin' kid. I mean, fuck."

And then it hit me.

"Summer doesn't have him," I said. "But I think I know who does."

46

"The night Cedric disappeared," I said, "he came here."

"Snow already comin' down," Annie Mae Dozier said, looking past me into the night. "Won't be long 'til everything grind to a halt."

She had just opened her door to my incessant knocking, and was now watching the snow through blinking eyes and big glasses.

Snow was flurrying and falling, the world outside undergoing a sea change.

I took a step into her apartment and she had no choice but to back in.

I closed the door behind me.

"This is where he came when he was upset," I said. "This is where he was running to that night."

"Sure wouldn't be to his sorry no-good mama," she said.

"But he still calls her," I said. "After all this time, he still calls her. Why is that?"

She shrugged her bony shoulders and gave me an expression like she wouldn't care to hazard a guess.

"He calls her from McDonough," I said. "Where your

daughter the pharmacist who makes good money but can't have kids lives. Where you yourself will soon be living."

She didn't say anything.

Her small head looked shrunken atop her slumping shoulders, her eyes even more hooded behind her big glasses.

"He was upset and he came here."

"'Cause his mama was out turnin' a trick for one of the mens who'd touched little Cedric—right out in them there woods like animals. It a wonder Cedric didn't see them as he ran by."

"He's upset—maybe even more than usual, but more, less, the same, you've had enough. No more. Your daughter can take him. She can be a good mama to him, and you a good grandma."

"Nobody else linin' up to do it," she said. "Tell you that."

"You kidnapped a child," I said.

She shook her head. "No. He wanted to go. Wanted to be away from all the . . . said would it be all right if he call her sometime. But that all he want with her, just to let her know he okay."

"You stayed behind to make sure no one suspected you, but you needn't have bothered. Cops didn't do much lookin' at all."

"I gots to sit down," she said.

She eased her way over to the sofa and bent a little ways but seemed to be stuck. I stepped over and helped her down.

She was even thinner and bonier than I realized, and couldn't have weighed more than ninety pounds.

"Much 'bliged," she said.

I sat down across from her.

"Why'd you stay so long?"

"I stay with them lots. Not here much. Just enough. Her old place was small. Wasn't sure I wanted to move. I got to see him plenty. Still get to be here close to my friends, my gentlemen callers."

I smiled. I wanted to do more. Merely smiling showed enormous restraint.

"Did y'all take all the boys or just Cedric?"

"What all boys?" she said.

"Did Laney Mitchell come over here that night?"

"Who?"

"Laney Mitchell, co-owner of Scarlett's, the little bar on the other side of—"

"Oh, her. No. Why?"

"She ran after Cedric when she saw him running back here."

"Nobody but him. I looked all around. Made sure he wasn't followed."

"Why're you being so forthcoming?" I asked. "Not that I don't appreciate it, but I am surprised."

"Your questions were different," she said. "And the stuff those other womens was sayin' you said about . . . all that other . . . Knew it just a matter of time 'til you be comin' back."

I waited but she didn't say anything else.

"And?"

"And what? Oh. You can't prove anything, can't prove I did anything."

I was puzzled.

"Mickey Davis, a reporter who's helping me, is in McDonough right now waiting for me to call with your daughter's address. You can give it to me and he can go get Cedric, or I can call the police and they can go."

"Go where?" she said.

"I just told you."

"And I tol' you we seen you comin', boy. They long gone—gone and you nor nobody else ain't never gonna find 'em."

"She ran with him?" I said. "Mind giving me the address so Mickey can check it out?"

"Help yo-self," she said, and gave me the address.

"May I borrow your phone?"

"Be my guest, but you shouldn't have that poor boy traipsing around down there on a fool's errand when it about to snow."

"Shit, John, I thought I was coming down here to find Cedric and Kenny and the others, and instead I got nothin' and now I'm stranded down here. I need to be with Camille, need to be helpin' find Kenny and I'm . . . fuckin' stuck down here."

"No one's there?"

"No."

"Is it an empty house?"

"No, it's a fully furnished home. Got pictures of Ms. Dozier and a woman I'm guessing is her daughter, but no boys. And there's a note addressed to you on the table."

"You're kidding."

"Can't make shit like this up."

"Do you mind reading it?"

"Got shit else to do, do I?"

He opened the letter and began to read.

"Dear Mr. Jordan. If you're reading this it means Mom was right. She's a wily old goat. I'll give her that. We have vanished and will be extremely difficult if not impossible to find. But I'm asking you not to look. Not to report us to the authorities and not to look yourself. I'm asking this not for me or my mother, but for Cedric. He's been through so much. Abuse like you can't imagine. He's just now beginning to trust and heal and begin to see what he might be able to be. Don't take that away from him. Please. Think of the pitiful little child, consider the young man he's becoming. Please pray about it and do the right thing."

That was it. A completely unexpected thing.

"So," Mickey said, "she only has Cedric. Where is Kenny? Who has Kenny?"

"I don't know."

"I'm stranded way the fuck down here," he said. "You've got to find him. Please."

We ended the call and I looked at Annie Mae Dozier again, this time with a new and greater appreciation.

"That was impressive," I said.

"We been protectin' that boy for some time now. Learned a thing or two 'bout it."

"They've gone without you," I said.

She shrugged her bony shoulders again, and this time scrunched her face up in a way that seemed to multiply the dark freckles on her face.

"Too old and slow to run."

"You're giving him up—him and your daughter," I said.

"'Greater love hath no man known than to lay down his life for another,'" she said.

I had always thought of that Bible verse in terms of dying for someone, but she was right. Laying down her life—what was left of it anyway—was exactly what she was doing, and it was astounding.

"And you didn't take the other boys?" I said. "Don't know what happened to them?"

"Know nothin' 'bout no other boys."

"Last question," I said, "and I'll leave you alone. What was Cedric running from? What was he so upset about?"

"Didn't say. Never has said. I got no idea. Maybe he did see his moms out in the woods rutting like an animal. I just know it was bad. Final straw for him and us."

47

I walked back to my apartment in the falling snow, humbled, perhaps even a little humiliated.

The night air was thin and cold and easy to breathe, the swirling white snow magical somehow.

Was Kenny, lifeless or otherwise, out in it?

Where was he? Who had him?

It was all that mattered right now, and I couldn't figure it out.

When I entered my apartment I found a note from Rick saying he had gone to spend his snow day at his girlfriend's place.

In my room, I ripped everything off my second wall, scattered it on the floor, and sat in the middle of it.

Rather than focusing narrowly, I intentionally kept my mind broad and open, flittering randomly from thing to thing like a butterfly drunk on spring.

This time, don't just think about the cases. Think about everything you've encountered since stepping into this little community.

As I continued to think, continued to feel the pressure of the clock pounding its time in my head, my mind sped up.

My butterfly became a bee and I buzzed around from item to

item trying to mentally cross-pollinate seemingly disparate bits of information to see what they might produce.

Nothing came of it.

It was all too much.

Kenny was going to die and I couldn't stop it.

He's dead already. So's Frank.

I could feel myself beginning to panic, and I wanted a drink in the worst kind of way.

Stop. Stop it. Breathe. Work yourself up into a frenzy, and you won't be any good to Kenny or anyone else.

I'm no good now.

I took a deep breath and then another and another.

"God grant me the serenity to accept the things I cannot change, the courage to change the—"

My mind hit on something, some connection, then it was gone—too quick for me to grasp.

What was it?

It was no good. I couldn't get it back.

Get out of your head, back into the moment. Start over.

"God grant me the serenity to accept the things I cannot change, the courage to change the things I can, and the wisdom to know the difference."

You can't change the circumstances. Stop trying. You can't control the world. Let go.

"God grant me the serenity to accept the things I cannot change, the courage to change the things I can, and the wisdom to know the difference."

What can you do? You can breathe. You can think. You can do what you can. Nothing more. Nothing else. And it's enough.

"God grant me the serenity to accept the things I cannot change, the courage to change the things I can, and the wisdom to know the difference."

Cedric was the anomaly. He was different. Why?

Think about everything. Take it all in. Let go of preconceived notions of what things mean. See them for only what they are. Remove contexts. Remove juxtapositions.

I thought again about where the bodies could be, then back to what Wayne Williams had said about John Wayne Gacy.

And then I had it.

I didn't like it, but I had it. Or thought I did.

I rushed outside.

Raised in Florida, I didn't have a winter wardrobe, and what I had on now—a button-down over a T-shirt—was inadequate in the extreme. I didn't care.

I ran toward the woods. Just like Cedric had.

Blanketed in white, the silent city was serene.

I thought about how I just used the Serenity Prayer to calm myself, as a kind of self-talk that would help me deal with the bad patterns in my thinking. I had done the same thing at the hospital while experiencing the guilt over Frank.

The wooded area separating Memorial Manor from the shops on Memorial Drive looked like an isolated mountain forest, each limb and leaf snow-dusted and picturesque.

Continuing past the woods, I ran up behind the shops and around the corner of Scarlett's to the front.

Eerie. Abandoned. Everything closed. No traffic on Memorial.

It was as if I were the sole survivor of a cold, harsh apocalyptic nuclear winter.

The pinkish-orange lighted letters of Peachtree Pizza's sign shone brightly in the hazy night. I thought about the guy who now called himself Rand Nola and what he said he saw the night Cedric vanished.

Had the other little boys been among his customers? Did they collect cans, scrape up their money to buy a pie together? Did they come here for pizza while their mothers drank at Scarlett's the way Cedric's had? Had Vaughn Smith's busy working mom stopped here for pizza on her way home? She probably let him rent a video too—something Lonnie would have a record of.

I had to get in to check. But how?

I walked over and pulled on the door, trying to figure some way to break in without breaking the glass and letting snow in.

The door rattled but didn't give.

"Whatta you doin'?" Rand Nola asked.

He had just come out of his pizza place and was locking the door.

Think fast.

"You saw how Lonnie was drinking earlier," I said.

"Yeah?"

"Wanted to feed his cats," I said. "Maybe even take 'em home with me in case it gets too cold. What're you still doin' here?"

"Same thing," he said.

"Really?"

"Not literally," he said. "When it snows or gets real cold I let Reuben Jefferson Jackson sleep in the back room."

"He's in there now?" I asked. "Not in back, not in the woods?"

"Yeah. I was just checking on him. I live within walkin' distance. I've got a key to Lonnie's shop for emergencies. I can let you in."

"That would be great," I said. "But I hate for you to wait. Can I borrow the key and give it back to you tomorrow?"

"I know what you're doin'," he said.

"You do?"

"You're gonna pick out some movies to ride out the storm with," he said. "I did the same thing earlier. Sure man. No worries."

"Thanks."

"I just hope Lonnie won't be off the wagon for long."

"Me too."

He removed the key from his ring, asked me to make sure it was the right one, then crossed the street and disappeared into the darkness on the other side.

48

The shop was warm and dim. The only illumination came from a single nightlight behind the counter.

From some unseen place in the semidarkness, Shaft and Foxy Brown purred contentedly.

Quickly making my way over to the counter, I grabbed the small metal index card box, moved closer to the nightlight, and began flipping through the cards with the membership information on them.

It didn't take long.

All the victims and their moms were members.

Another confirmation. How many do you need before you get truly bold?

I think that was it.

I returned the box to its spot beneath the counter and started to walk out when a still-drunk Lonnie pressed the barrel of a revolver to the back of my head and cocked the trigger.

"Son a bitch think you gonna loot me . . . not during this or any other storm."

"Lonnie," I said. "It's me."

"John? John, what're you doin' here?" he said, stumbling across the words and pulling back the gun.

"Came to check on your cats," I said. "Thought you were passed out somewhere sleeping it off."

"You're not here to rob me?"

"I'm not," I said. "I may take a movie, but I'll bring it back. And I'll pay for it."

"You don't have to pay me anything for it, buddy, no sirree."

"Thanks man."

"What were you doin' in my membership box?"

"Huh?"

"What were you doin' in my membership box?"

I drew a blank.

"Ah, oh . . . seein' if you had an address for Margaret's niece Susan," I said.

"Shouldn't you be lookin' for little Kenny Pollard instead of tryin' to dip your wick?"

"You're right," I said. "I should."

"'Less that's what you're really doing here," he said, suddenly sober. "How'd you know?"

"Know what?"

"Playtime's over, John. Tell me what you know. It's just us. The whole city's shut down. And I've got a gun. How'd you figure it out."

"Sobriety," I said.

"Sobriety?"

"Yeah. I've used the principles of AA and the Serenity Prayer a few times recently to help with things other than alcohol."

"Yeah?"

"Made me realize someone could use them to quit something other than drinking—like compulsive killing, say. I remembered your sobriety happened around the time Cedric disappeared—which was the time the killings stopped. What happened to Cedric sobered you up, changed you. It was your moment of clarity that led to sobriety. You were able to stay sober, to stop killing by using AA."

"Was until you started stirring all this shit up again. Compulsive is right. I'm not a bad man. I'm not some kind of monster. I'm a man—a man like every other man, with two wolves inside him. You've heard the old Cherokee legend of the wolves, haven't you?"

Everybody has, I thought, but if it keeps you talking, if it gives me time to figure out what to do . . .

"One evening an old Cherokee man told his grandson about the war that wages inside all souls. The battle is between two wolves, he told him. One wolf is anger, envy, jealousy, sorrow, regret, greed, arrogance, self-pity, guilt, resentment, inferiority, lies, false pride, superiority, ego, even evil. The other is goodness, joy, peace, love, hope, serenity, humility, kindness, benevolence, empathy, generosity, truth, compassion, faith, even God."

He paused but I only nodded encouragingly.

"The boy thought about it for a while, then asked, What determines which wolf wins? The old man simply replied, The one you feed. I've been feeding the good wolf since Cedric disappeared. I have a compulsion, but I've been controlling it with the Twelve Steps."

"Tonight I remembered you drinking this afternoon and how that coincided with Kenny's disappearance. At first I had thought the killer might have gone to prison for another crime or moved and was committing the murders somewhere else, then it occurred to me you might be using AA in the way I was."

"Don't ever let anyone tell you AA doesn't work," he said. "It works." He then added with a demented smile, "If you work it. Or until you stop working it. Think about what I did. I stopped. I used AA to stop killing. Has anyone else ever done that? Ever? And I couldn't tell anybody. I knew something that could change the world, but had to keep it to myself."

"I kept asking who or where Cedric was running to," I said. "But when I turned it around and asked who or what he could be running from, I had to go back to where he was going in the first place. Here. To you. He was running from what he saw you doing."

"Guess he was, but I never saw him. Didn't know he had even come in. Thought I had the door locked. And maybe I did. He sometimes snuck in the back. When I realized he had been here, that this was the last place he had been before he vanished . . . it brought me up short."

I nodded.

"What it is you think he saw?" he asked.

"You raping or killing the final victim, Jaquez Anderson," I said. "My guess is your little meeting room back there wasn't just an adult room, but your playroom where you raped and killed and what? Recorded? Did you make videos of the boys? Did you rent them?"

"I never raped anyone," he said. "I'm a . . . I have a compulsion to kill, sure enough, but I never forced myself on anyone. I paid them boys to let me touch and film 'em, and to touch and do sex stuff to me, but I never forced 'em."

"That's a distinction without a difference," I said. "The very kind of stinking thinking AA deals with."

"And it did. Right up until you forced your way into my life and kicked the shit out of my serenity. Don't you get it? I stopped. I used the program to stop myself. I worked the shit out of it and was able to stop—until you had to dredge it all back up."

"Always someone else's fault," I said. "Big part of that same mentality."

"You act like you know somethin', for some punk kid who just started the program."

"I don't know anything," I said. "Except where Cedric is."

I knew that really meant something to him.

"Do you? You do, don't you? You son of a bitch."

"How'd you lure Kenny?" I asked. "Comics?"

"And coloring books. Easiest thing in the world. Find a boy

without a father. Thing he wants most in the world is some mature masculine attention. Where is Cedric?"

"Where is Kenny?"

"Where are any of the boys?" he said.

"In your walls," I said.

"How the hell did you—"

"That was something else that coincided with your sobriety and Cedric's disappearance. Your remodeling of your back room."

"Been tryin' to figure out what to do with them when I shut the place down," he said. "Couldn't come up with anything that didn't involve me gettin' caught."

"And why keep cats around when you're allergic to them?" I said. "Because you use the kitty litter on the bodies. It has a desiccant and odor-absorbing agent—and you can buy it in bulk without looking suspicious. But it would be suspicious if you didn't have cats. So you have Shaft and Foxy Brown and sneeze your way through every day and have bags and bags of kitty litter in your storage-meeting-burial chamber room. Wayne Williams reminded me that John Wayne Gacy hid his victims in the walls and floors of his house. Is Kenny already in there? Is that what you've been doing?"

"I'll tell you what I been doin', boy," he said. "I've been battlin' with demons you couldn't begin to understand, to keep from so much as touching that boy. Two wolves wagin' war inside me the likes of which you couldn't imagine. That's it. Worse thing I did to him so far is drug his Kool-Aid so he fell asleep before he got to finish his first comic. That's it."

"Let that be it," I said.

He laughed. "And what? Turn myself in? I've already done more than what any prison could do. I rehabilitated myself. I used the only program known to work for addiction and I stopped my addiction. Whatta they gonna do for me? Cage me? What's that gonna do? No, sir. I don't think so. Think instead I'll set you up for what's about to befall Kenny."

"By planting some of his clothes and comics in my apartment or car?"

"That was a nice touch," he said, "but an unnecessary one. Cops didn't care. Especially when they's havin' a new body every week. Missin' ain't murder. Missin' don't make it into the paper. Missin' don't come with no political pressure. Biggest mistake Wayne ever made was dumping them bodies."

"Let me see Kenny," I said.

"Let me see your brain," he said, holding up the gun a little higher. "It's pretty impressive. I want to see it."

"Did you kill Laney Mitchell?"

"Laney Mitchell? Now I'm a hit-and-run killer too?"

"Thought she might have seen something or found out something and had to be silenced."

He shook his head. "Sure it was just some drunk. Like you and me. Didn't mean no harm. Didn't stop him from doin' plenty, though, did it? Okay. Time to die."

"Wait. I know you want to know what happened to Cedric," I said. "I know you want to see him. Let me see Kenny. Let me take Kenny home and you can go see Cedric."

"No way he's alive," he said.

"He's very much alive," I said. "I swear it. I'm telling the truth. Put it to the test."

That reminded me of Lonnie passing a polygraph in relation to Cedric's disappearance. Of course he did. He had nothing to do with it. Had he been asked about the other boys, that would've yielded a very different result.

"How?"

"You can ask who helped take him," I said. "She's close by."

"She?"

A jingle at the door then—someone opening it, triggering the bell—Lonnie's attention momentarily diverted. Me lunging, grabbing, falling.

We hit the ground, the gun between us, both of us vying for control over where the barrel was pointed.

Then Susan there. Spraying him with mace. Him releasing his grip, pawing at his eyes. Me grabbing the gun. Jumping up. Pulling her back out from behind the counter.

"Check the back room," I said to her.

As she did, I pointed the revolver at Lonnie and blocked his exit from behind the counter. Not that he was trying to exit. He was still rolling around on the floor writhing in pain, spitting, crying, coughing, choking.

"It's empty," she said.

"Are you sure?"

Light from the room spilled out into the hallway.

"Positive."

"Check the bathroom."

She did.

"He's here," she yelled. "He's alive. Seems okay. Just sleeping I think. John, he's alive. He's okay."

49

"What're you doing here?" I asked Susan.

"I felt bad for all the pressure I had put on you. I was going to come to your apartment to surprise you and see if I could help."

We were waiting for the police to arrive.

Lonnie was still lying on the floor, but now he was crying, appearing to literally be wallowing. His self-pity was as pathetic as it was predictable.

"I had just finished cleaning and locking up," she said. "Already had my mace out. Saw Rand crossing Memorial and you come in here. Decided to take a look. I was feeling paranoid."

"Glad you were. Best surprise in a long time. Thank you."

"Did you really find Cedric?" Lonnie asked between snobs and sniffles.

"He didn't kill Cedric too?" Susan said.

"Just the others."

"Where are the bodies?"

"In the walls of the back room," I said.

"Oh my God. Right in there? Where you sent me to look for Kenny?"

"I didn't send you into the walls."

"Still."

"Did you really find him? Is he okay?" Lonnie said.

I nodded. "I think so."

"Where is he? Who took him?"

"I haven't decided whether or not I'm telling anyone," I said, "but I'm certainly not telling you."

With an inhuman growl, he lunged at me.

Unable to shoot him, I hesitated just long enough for him to be on me, tackling me to the ground, the gun falling out of my hand and skittering across the floor, disappearing beneath a video shelf.

Susan screamed.

Lonnie began beating me about the face, neck, and shoulders, his tears and snot falling down on me as he did.

Susan went for the gun, running past us, momentarily drawing Lonnie's attention.

I bucked him up off me and kicked him hard with both feet.

He went sailing back toward the back room, flailing as he did, and crashed into the large bookcases holding the thousands of video tapes in their hard plastic cases.

The shelves fell over, Lonnie following behind on his back, and knocked a hole in the sheetrock wall behind them, a hole out of which dropped a small, ashen, mummified hand along with a rain of white sheetrock dust, paper particles, and kitty litter.

Eventually, the cops came, Bobby Battle and Remy Boss among them.

"Looks like we owe you an apology," Remy said as Lonnie was being taken away.

"And that's the extent of it right there," Bobby said. "So enjoy it. And don't be a dick about it."

A crime scene tech had already begun to open the walls behind the shelves and movie posters in the back room.

We had moved to the front of the store to be as far away from it as possible. I had no desire to see any more of the mummified murder of innocence I would never be able to unsee. The hand and all my imaginings were enough, were too much. Susan seemed to feel the same way.

"I have one favor to ask," I said.

"You and your goddamn favors," Bobby said.

"It's just because I'm young and have no authority and can't do them for myself. If I could, I'd never ask for anything. Believe that."

"I'll be glad when Frank is better and can get back to doin' them for you himself. He woke up a few minutes ago, by the way. He's gonna be okay."

Tears stung my eyes. "Thank God."

"What's the favor?"

"Let me and Susan take Kenny back to his mom."

"Seems the least we can do," Remy said.

"Which is what we try to do when we can," Bobby said. "He'll have to be taken to the hospital and checked out right after, but you can take him to the mom first."

"Thanks."

Camille Pollard burst into tears the moment she opened her door and saw us.

Her hair wasn't fixed. Her casual, comfortable clothes were worn and faded, and the light skin of her face held no makeup. It was the first time I had ever seen her not fixed up, not stylish, not made up, and she looked more youthful and more attractive than she ever had previously.

"Is he . . ."

"Just sleeping," I said.

Lights from the cop car that had brought us over flashed on the door and walls and still-falling snow.

I added, "They're going to take him to the hospital to check him out, but he's gonna be fine. An ambulance will be here in a minute."

I handed him to her.

As soon as I did, Wilbur pushed past her and hugged me.

I bent down and hugged him back.

"Where was he?" Camille said. "Who had him?"

I told her.

"Oh my God. Are you sure? Right next door all this time. Is he the . . . Did he kill the others?"

I nodded.

From the building across the way I could see Annie Mae Dozier open her door and look out at us.

"I actually was beginning to think it might be Mickey," she said. "Thought he might be doing this for his damn story. Where is he?"

"McDonough. He's fine. Was looking for Cedric. Now he's just waiting until the storm passes and the roads open again."

An ambulance pulled up.

"Come on," she said to Wilbur. "Let's get your brother to the hospital."

50

Over the next several days, I spent a lot of time prayerfully pondering what I should do about Cedric. Turn over what I knew to the authorities in an attempt to find him and bring him home, or leave him where he was?

I didn't feel adequate to the task of deciding the fate of this little boy who had been through so much. I wasn't adult enough, mature enough, wise enough.

Who was I to say what was right or best for this child?

And yet . . .

Fate had made the decision mine to make, and Mickey had agreed to go along with whatever I decided.

Was he better off where he was or back with his mother?

I didn't want to decide, but more than that I didn't want to abdicate the responsibility I had been given.

In one sense, Annie Mae Dozier and her daughter were criminals—kidnappers who had stolen a child. In another, they were two caring women who had acted heroically in an attempt to save an abused and neglected child. Who knows, maybe the actions they took ensured that another isolated and traumatized child wouldn't turn to dark fantasies that would lead to much darker actions.

I realized I didn't have enough information to make the best decision possible, which let me know what I needed to do.

I went back to Annie Mae Dozier's.

"Figure I see you again," she said through her open door. "Heard you caught the killer. Tol' you that family was no good for Cedric."

I nodded.

"Why you here?"

"Trying to decide what to do," I said.

"'Bout?"

"Cedric."

"Leave the boy be."

"I'm inclined to," I said. "And I think you should be with them too."

Tears filled the old eyes behind the big glasses, and she stopped blinking.

Suddenly, this ancient, freckled, narrow, emaciated, parchment-covered thing before me was younger, more vibrant, and bent over no more.

"Y'all can be together," I said. "No running. No looking over your shoulder. All I want to do is talk with Cedric and your daughter. That's it. I have to make sure he's good before I can let it go. If you agree and he is doing well, no one will ever know and I'll be out of it forever. If you don't, I'll be forced to go to the authorities and . . . your daughter can be found. It wouldn't even be that difficult. You know it's true."

She nodded. "I do. Know somethin' else true too. That boy couldn't be any better or any happier. You'll see."

And I did.

And that was that. And like Kenny, a positive result was achieved for Cedric—something far too infrequent in what had become my work.

Susan and I started dating a little later. She had saved my life after all. It seemed the thing to do.

I still missed Jordan and I still felt conflicted about it.

I still missed Martin and I felt no conflict about that.

I stopped going to the missing and murdered children group. I never saw most of the members again, including Summer, who seemed more like a specter than anything else. Miss Ida and I stayed in touch. We had shared too much not to. Most often we'd meet at Jordan's grave.

I never found any evidence that Laney Mitchell's death was anything but a tragic, senseless, preventable accident. Maybe Lonnie was right. Maybe it was just a sad, sorry drunk like us.

Mickey continued calling and coming around while he was working on his book, but not much after that.

Frank got out of the hospital and made a full recovery. He continued to be the person in Atlanta I could count on most.

Two people who never got out of the hospital were Daryl Lee Gibbons and his mother—his mother because she died after a little less than a week inside and Daryl Lee because, when he was eventually able, he was sent straight from the medical hospital to a psychiatric one.

In the end, Martin's mother dropped her lawsuit for the most unexpected reason imaginable. Bobby Battle told her if she didn't he was going to arrest her for killing her own son and a hundred other charges besides, and that he could make them stick. She must have believed him. I never heard anything out of her again.

I found a new AA group and continued going. I stopped drinking.

I got back in school—the first day back after the snowstorm in fact, and dug in to theology and my studies in a way I hadn't before.

And the reason I was able to do all this was because I was able to make a certain imperfect peace with the Atlanta Child Murders.

There were things I would never know and I was learning to live with that.

Were the victims connected? Yes. Many of them were intimately connected. Were there geographical and social relationships between victims and suspects? There were. Many.

Was there a child sex ring and more than one killer? I believe so.

I suspected John David Wilcoxen, Jamie Brooks, and others of all manner of evil—including murder of one kind or another—but because of the nature of such cases and the mistakes made by the various law enforcement agencies involved, there is much we will never know or be able to prove.

I believe that poor, at-risk, vulnerable street kids—the type of kids Wayne Williams called drop shots—were crushed by those streets and the predators lurking on them. I believe some kids sold their bodies and certain sexual services for money and attention and affection. I believe others were just available prey, children whose ancestry and geography sealed an impossibly cruel fate for them.

When people learn of my fascination with and investigation into the cases, they always ask me the same questions. Is Wayne Williams guilty? Did he do it?

It has taken a while, but I finally have an answer.

I believe Wayne Bertram Williams is the Atlanta Child Murderer. I still have many questions, but I am convinced by the evidence against him. There's simply too much of it, particularly trace evidence—the combination of fibers and human and dog hairs too unique, the probabilities against it being him too low—for it not to be Williams.

Wayne Williams also failed a polygraph three times.

But it's not just all of that. It's that he had such a ridiculous story about why he was on the James Jackson Parkway bridge the night he was stopped, or that the person he claimed to be looking for never came forward, or that he burned evidence, or that he had so many connections to so many of the key places, people, and victims, or that eyewitnesses claimed to have seen him with some of the victims, or that the relatively rare trilobal green carpet fibers from his bedroom as well as nearly twenty other fibers and hairs from his home and vehicle were found on so many of the victims, or that he used Cap'n Peg's as the address on his flyers, or that his flyers turned up in so many of the areas where the victims lived and were taken. It was Williams himself.

I don't believe Williams. I don't buy his explanations and find his protestations incredible.

That said, I don't believe he's responsible for killing everyone on the task force's list. I don't think it very likely he killed Clifford Jones, for example—or the two female victims, Angel Lenair and LaTonya Wilson. Or some of the others. And the blood of each and every one still cries out—for justice, for acknowledgment, for truth.

I believe Wayne Williams is a practiced and habitual liar. In short, I believe him to be a compulsive, sociopathic serial killer.

Partly because of the way the investigation was conducted, partly because of the nature of such cases, there are truths and facts about the cases we'll never know. Crimes will remain unsolved. Guilty people will remain free—or at least free from answering for these particular crimes.

Am I okay with that?

Do I have a choice?

ALSO BY THE AUTHOR

Sign up for Michael's newsletter by clicking here or go to
www.MichaelLister.com and receive a free book.

Join Michael's Readers' Group and receive 4 FREE Books!

(Remington James Novels)
Double Exposure
(includes intro by Michael Connelly)
Separation Anxiety
Blood Shot

(John Jordan Novels)
Power in the Blood
Blood of the Lamb
Flesh and Blood
(Special Introduction by Margaret Coel)
The Body and the Blood
Double Exposure
Blood Sacrifice
Rivers to Blood
Burnt Offerings
Innocent Blood
(Special Introduction by Michael Connelly)
Separation Anxiety
Blood Money Blood Moon
Thunder Beach
Blood Cries
A Certain Retribution
Blood Oath
Blood Work
Cold Blood
Blood Betrayal
Blood Shot
Blood Ties
Blood Stone
Blood Trail

(Jimmy "Soldier" Riley Novels)
The Big Goodbye
The Big Beyond
The Big Hello
The Big Bout
The Big Blast
In a Spider's Web (short story)
The Big Book of Noir

(Merrick McKnight / Reggie Summers Novels)
Thunder Beach
A Certain Retribution
Blood Oath
Blood Shot

(Sam Michaels / Daniel Davis Novels)
Burnt Offerings

Blood Oath
Cold Blood
Blood Shot

(Love Stories)
Carrie's Gift

(Short Story Collections)
North Florida Noir
Florida Heat Wave
Delta Blues
Another Quiet Night in Desperation

(The Meaning Series)

Meaning Every Moment
The Meaning of Life in Movies

Sign up for Michael's newsletter by clicking here or go to www.MichaelLister.com and receive a free book.

www.ingramcontent.com/pod-product-compliance
Lightning Source LLC
Chambersburg PA
CBHW022016050726
47499CB00004BA/1009